AL-TOUNSI

AL-TOUNSI

A NOVEL

ANTON PIATIGORSKY

Cover design by Elmarie Jara/ABA Design.
Interior design by Betsy Kulak/ABA Design.

Printed in the United States of America.

20 19 18 17 16   5 4 3 2 1

ISBN 978-1-63425-609-4

Discounts are available for books ordered in bulk. Special consideration is given to state bars, CLE programs, and other bar-related organizations. Inquire at Book Publishing, ABA Publishing, American Bar Association, 321 N. Clark Street, Chicago, Illinois 60654-7598.

www.ShopABA.org

"Who, then, in law, is my neighbor?"
—Lord Atkin, *Donoghue v. Stevenson*

PART 1

CERTIORARI

THE CAT

The ancient buzzer sounded in Justice Rodney Sykes's chamber. Although afternoon conference would begin in ten minutes, he was still not fully prepared. He slipped his bony fingers beneath his half-moon glasses and pressed the soft flesh around his eyes, but the kneading did little to dispel the ache in his temples, and nothing to alleviate his overwhelming fatigue. He hadn't been able to work effectively all morning.

The problem wasn't his environment. His chambers were impeccable and quiet, arranged to his exact specifications. His secretaries had angled his venetian blinds downward, blocking the view and allowing for dimness, not darkness. They had closed his door and—he presumed—hung his *Do Not Disturb* sign on the knob. They had neatly stacked his cert petitions—the most urgent pieces of business for this Friday—in a high pile on his otherwise empty desk.

Justice Sykes had been disquieted by images flashing through his mind. He was distracted, of all the ridiculous things, by thoughts of his sick cat.

He stood, tightened his tie, and skimmed the final dozen cert briefs. He snatched his suit jacket off the chair and headed for the door. After forcing a smile for his two secretaries in the front room of his chambers, Rodney stepped into the marbled corridor, where he almost collided with Chief Justice Eberly.

"Whoa there, sorry!" Charles Eberly patted Rodney on the back.

"No, no. I'm at fault."

Rodney rubbed his heavy eyes as the two strode in tandem toward the Conference Room. Tall, bald and plagued by athletic injuries, Justice Eberly limped slightly. He had a constant pain in his left knee.

"Something the matter, Rodney? You seem a tad—I don't know."

"I'm perfectly fine, Charles, thank you."

"All right, then. We missed you up in the Dining Room."

The best thing about Charles Eberly, an old, conservative jurist with a gravelly voice, dry sense of humor and unpretentious directness—all products of his isolated childhood in the red desert of rural Utah—was that he would never ask too many intrusive personal questions. The two justices walked down the marbled hallway, the red-and-gold carpeting muting the sound of their steps.

Justices Sarah Kolmann and Talos Katsakis were already in the Conference Room. The colleagues greeted each other with sharp nods. Justice Kolmann, her eyes magnified by large glasses, smiled politely at Charles, but grinned at Rodney with genuine affection.

"Do you have plans for the weekend, Sarah?" Rodney asked her.

"I certainly do. My daughter is coming down from Boston with my grandson. Already seven years old!"

"My, my, how quickly they grow."

Sarah Kolmann steered their conversation to Massenet's *Manon*, currently in production at the Kennedy Center—and what did Rodney think of it?, and could the best of Massenet ever compare to worst of Verdi?—when Justices Quinn and Rosen entered the Conference Room together, Killian Quinn in the midst of some operatic performance of his own. He spread his arms wide, his face glowing red with excitement.

"Aaaaaamerica," he cried, "are you ready to rrrrrrrrumble?"

Gideon Rosen shook his head. It was rather impossible to tell if he was annoyed or amused by his outrageous colleague's antics. Perhaps a bit of both. Justice Kolmann chuckled and covered her big grin with a veiny hand.

"My youngest is into all this wrestling business." Killian's voice was always higher and thinner than what Rodney expected to come out of such a large man. "I mean, my Lord, these steroid types with all their screaming and neon tights."

"Now, that's fine, Killian." Justice Rosen's Chicagoan accent switched his O into an A. "I won't complain about it as long as you don't pile drive *me*."

"How about a flying clothesline?"

"Pile-drive?" Justice Kolmann smiled, unrestrained.

"That's when one of the big guys drops the other on his head," explained Justice Rosen.

"Come on, Gideon, I'm not going to pile-drive you!" Killian, laughing, waddled his corpulent body from side to side with some urgency, as if his feet might fall asleep. "We're tag team, *tag* team! In spite of our jurisprudential differences. We work together for the greater good. We need a couple of those Mexican masks—you know. We could keep them in the closet along with our robes!"

Justice Joanna Bryce, the newest member of the Court, snuck into the Conference Room under the cover of the chatter. She stood beside Justices Eberly and Katsakis, hands clasped before her, her turtleneck pulled up to her chin. She was frowning sternly, watching Killian laugh and pump the air with his meaty fist. When his mouth parted and his gold fillings flashed, Bryce curled her lip in disgust.

Rodney turned away before Joanna noticed him staring. This was the all-too-typical arrogance of Justice Bryce, a woman who believed herself correct in all circumstances, who assumed that because she found Killian's colorful antics distasteful they should be condemned or dismissed. Rodney understood her longing for tradition, as he too preferred more restrained comportment, but never in a million years would he dream of being so bold as to stand in condemnation. How could Rodney or Joanna or anyone else dictate the moods and manners of their colleagues? The Court comprised nine equals. He was neither Justice Quinn's father nor his boss.

Justice Bernhard Davidson pushed open the Conference Room door and hobbled through the threshold. He was supporting some of his weight with his cane, while his other arm rested in the patient hand of his escort, Justice Elyse Van Cleve. Justice Davidson wore a tweed jacket with elbow patches and a small bowtie. His clean white hair was parted to the side, combed smooth against his scalp, oiled with pomade. Justice Van Cleve wore pearls and a navy suit, her brilliant gray hair a marked contrast to the dark fabric. Although Van Cleve was in her mid-70s, her tall, athletic body looked like a paragon of strength when juxtaposed to aged Davidson, who was so stooped that he only come up to Van Cleve's shoulder. She helped the old man sit in his chair at the head of the rectangular table, opposite the Chief Justice—the position reserved for the senior most member of the Court.

"Thank you, Elyse." Bernhard Davidson patted her hand and rested his cane against the table.

"All here." Chief Justice Eberly nodded at Justice Bryce. "Joanna, please, the door."

Eight jurists gathered around Davidson's chair and shook each other's hands, one by one. As Rodney's palm met the firm grip of each colleague, he felt the odd and unnamable distress of his morning fade away. How thankful he was that Chief Justice Melvin Fuller had long ago initiated this ritual of the 36 separate handshakes, that subsequent justices had continued this 19th-century practice into the present era. Indeed, it unified their nine disparate minds into one single team, and encouraged them to forget their small domestic trials. Court rituals were such a comfort, such a balm.

Rodney took his assigned seat on the far side of the table, facing the door and the inlaid bookcases stocked with matching tan bindings: the complete and ever-expanding *US Reports*. Chief Justice Eberly studied the 12 certiorari petitions he had placed on the discussion list, as well as the six additional cases penciled in by other justices. "May we vote to deny cert to the cases which didn't make our list?"

The justices murmured their agreement—and so ended the prospects for dozens of cases to reach the United States Supreme Court.

The Chief announced the remaining cases one by one, offering his concise summaries of their histories and legal questions. This usual routine, with the justices voting in sequence either to grant or deny the petitions, was disrupted only once in the first seven cases, when Sarah Kolmann shook her head in disagreement of a denied petition.

"Something to say, Sarah?" Charles retreated into the dour tone he reserved for tangential conversations with potential to bog down their smooth progress.

"No. I disagree, but obviously I've been overruled."

They arrived at case 06-1172, *Majid Al-Tounsi, et al., Petitioners, v. Mark L. Shaw, et al., Respondents.* Charles Eberly summarized the case quickly and announced that they would vote in the usual fashion, from senior justice to junior, beginning with himself. "I vote to deny." He tapped the discussion list, not making eye contact with any of his colleagues. "Bernhard?"

"Also deny."

Gideon Rosen slapped his palms against the hard wood of the conference table, jolting everyone. He leaned forward, mouth agape, and glared in fury at Justice Davidson. "What in God's name did you just say, Bernhard?"

"Gideon!" scolded the Chief. "We are *voting* on this case."

Gideon pressed his palm against his eyes and shook his head. "I cannot believe what I have just heard." He crossed his arms and shot another fiery glance at Bernhard.

Charles proceeded, ignoring Justice Rosen. "That's two votes for denial. Killian?"

Justice Quinn seemed to be having a hard time containing his pleasure. Smirking, raising his bushy eyebrows and rubbing his wide hands along his big belly, he managed to eke out the word *deny* without actually laughing.

"Elyse?"

"I vote to grant."

"Talos?"

"Deny."

"Goddamn it." Gideon rubbed his brow as if he were in pain. Indeed, the cert petition for this sensational case would almost certainly be denied.

"Rodney?"

"I also vote to deny."

Rodney marked a check beside *Al-Tounsi* on his discuss list, as he always did after voting. He did not find this to be a difficult case. When he read the complete cert petition in chambers, he thought, contrary to his clerk's memorandum, that the main question *Al-Tounsi* asked—whether or not the foreign citizen enemy combatants imprisoned in the U.S. Naval Base in Subic Bay, Philippines, had a constitutional right to the writ of habeas corpus—was premature. The Military Commissions Act of 2006 had not only stripped their cases of federal court jurisdiction, but it had also established alternate procedures for processing the detainees. It did not matter that there was a reversal from the district court ruling, or a 2–1 circuit court split. Nor did it matter that the media adored the story of those high-profile detainees, with articles appearing in the papers almost daily, and TV pundits chattering incessantly about them on talk shows. The Military Commissions Act was the *law*, passed by Congress, signed by President Shaw. Furthermore, it was a *new* law, meaning that its procedures had yet to be put into full effect. It had only been a year since it had passed. The government was correct that the Court should only take a case like *Al-Tounsi* after those new procedures had been fully implemented, when it would be possible to assess with some neutrality their constitutionality. Until that future date, ruling on *Al-Tounsi* was presumptuous and political, and, moreover, it did not fit within the framework of Justice Sykes's steady principle: to defer to the other branches of government whenever possible.

The remaining three justices voted as expected: Rosen and Kolmann to grant, Bryce to deny. As if to underscore the case's import, Chief Justice Eberly removed his glasses as he announced their verdict. "The certiorari petition for case number 06-1172, *Al-Tounsi v. Shaw*, is hereby denied by a vote of 3–6. Next on the list we have—"

"No!" Justice Rosen pursed his lips and blinked rapidly. "This *can't* be. I have something else to say."

"One comment, Gideon. Please keep it brief."

Justice Rosen paused, tapping his fingers on the desk as he prepared his best argument. "We need to consider this. Do we really want to tell Congress and the President that we won't even review their decision when they suspend habeas corpus?"

"Christ, Gideon, it's not suspended. Stop, already, with the dramatics. The MCA has installed a clear remedy in its place."

"No, Killian, we have to at least review the case in order to see if there is an adequate remedy."

"It's too early!"

"A constitutional question regarding Article I can never be too early."

"All right." The Chief Justice held up his hands. "Enough."

"I find it hard to believe that we'd actively shirk—"

"Gideon, Gideon, *please*." Justice Davidson's shaky voice rolled out from the far end of the table. His trembling fingers fiddled with his tight bowtie. "Let's just hold on a moment here. You know I personally dislike the Military Commissions Act as much as you do. But we have an obligation to at least give these new procedures the benefit of the doubt until we have reason to question them. It's too early. Killian's quite right."

As the others nodded, and Eberly moved on, Gideon studied Justice Davidson with a sly squint. Rodney understood his suspicion. It seemed to Rodney there was something disingenuous about Davidson's denial of *Al-Tounsi*. It lacked consistency with the senior jurist's well-known liberal principles. Those detainees in the Subic Bay Naval Base had exhausted all options but for this final appeal to the U.S. Supreme Court. They had been imprisoned indefinitely, without charge, protected only by the MCA's new procedures, which most liberal federal judges considered highly dubious. From Justice Davidson's perspective, those prisoners were powerless, left without a voice. So what was he up to? Davidson was the fourth vote. All he had to do was say *yes* to granting certiorari and the Court would be forced to hear *Al-Tounsi*. He didn't have to explain himself, or even convince another colleague.

As Charles Eberly summarized the next case on their list, a peculiar and insistent question entered Rodney's mind: What if his cat were the petitioner in *Al-Tounsi*, fighting for a writ of habeas corpus?

Rodney had awoken that morning to find Stone, his gray tabby with a notched ear, lying prostrate by his bed, panting like a dog. His eyes were glassy. His swollen tongue protruded from his mouth and bubbles oozed onto the floor. His limp head was settled into a pool of frothy white vomit. It was a gory tableau, and it had shocked Rodney. All morning, no matter how hard Rodney had tried, or how much work he had needed to do, he simply could not erase that image from his mind. And here he was now, thinking about habeas corpus as it pertained to his cat.

Like a detainee in Subic Bay, Stone too was powerless. The cat had lived for years trapped in the Justice's two-bedroom apartment, his movements curtailed, his closest contact with any natural element being his perch on the high-backed sofa beside the rarely opened window, and even then he was barred from the outside world by a thick mesh screen. He had no means of escape, no recourse to any court.

Of course, the absurdities of Rodney's comparison were obvious. Cats were not persons in any law, nor could they be active participants in legal proceedings. Even the term *prisoner* was ridiculous. Cats were creatures of a different consciousness, to be owned and used, subjected to human needs, and at best afforded minimal protections by, in this instance, a combination of District statute and the federal Animal Welfare Act. As well it should be.

Granting cats a constitutional right to habeas corpus was pure folly.

"Rodney. Your vote?"

The Chief Justice was glaring at him. Rodney glanced at his notes for the next case on their list. "Deny."

He closed his eyes. There, again, was Stone, a rude interruption to his concentration, a defiant apparition, now lying in a cage in the dingy back room of Dr. Vry's Animal Care, with its barred windows and stacked cardboard boxes, heaving for breath, unable to move his head, his fur wet and matted.

Rodney opened his eyes. A framed painting of Chief Justice John Marshall was mounted to the wall above the ebony fireplace behind Charles Eberly. For 16 years Rodney had been comforted by that expressionless, bust portrait of the Court's greatest justice, and he had long imagined that Marshall's steely image watched over the justices in the Conference Room, demanding their best behavior. Marshall was a model for almost all of them, their north star. But today the portrait's fierce eyes burrowed holes into Rodney. Would John Marshall have denied certiorari for the petitioners of *Al-Tounsi*? Would John Marshall have tolerated any formal, legalist arguments in this case of imprisoned detainees? Rodney turned away from the painting. Best to keep things in perspective. Although Chief Justice Marshall was an exemplary leader of the Court for 35 years, he was also a committed slave owner. That was certainly a more serious moral lapse than denying the appeals of a few indefinitely imprisoned enemy combatants. The real John Marshall, Rodney decided, as he crossed his arms, would have only stared intently at Rodney while trying to ascertain his price in the local slave market.

When Rodney arrived at his chambers after conference, his secretary handed him a message from Kim Vry, requesting that he please call her office at his earliest convenience. He closed the door and dialed her number.

"I'm sorry, Justice Sykes, I don't think Stone's going to make it."

Rodney paused, unsure of how to respond. "Please, you may call me Rodney."

"He's got a very advanced and untreatable cancer. We can wait it out a few days and he'll die on his own, or we can have him put down."

It seemed the veterinarian was awaiting his instructions.

"I would like to see him once more. To say a proper good-bye." Justice Sykes listened to himself in astonishment. A proper good-bye? He had never cared much for that cat.

They made plans to meet in an hour, and Rodney hung up the phone. His hands trembled in his lap; his face felt hot. Perhaps Stone's illness was, somehow, inexplicably, caused by his own neglect. Would the vet accuse him of mistreatment when he arrived?

Preposterous. Yet he had also wondered that morning, idling on the Connecticut Avenue sidewalk, after dropping off his gravely ill cat, if the receptionist in Animal Care had judged him for the poor state of Stone's health. "I simply don't know what happened to him," he told the receptionist, as if he were trying to convince her of his innocence, with his hand stuck into Stone's plastic carrier, his palm resting on his cat's heaving belly. "He was perfectly well last night." She offered him an opaque smile. Surely there was no way she could have arrived at a verdict against him from the information he had provided. Moreover, why should he care if the receptionist or Dr. Vry judged him? He was not a thinned-skinned creature.

Still his blood rushed inside him.

Rodney had never been an affectionate owner. Any overt, loving attention had seemed unnecessary for an independent cat. Some might say, then, that Rodney was distant, cold. Of course, he had not engaged in any *actual* criminal neglect or mistreatment.

He held his breath, slowed his heart purposefully. He needed to be more reasonable, more rational about this. First things first. His daughter, Cassandra, out in San Francisco, would want to know about Stone's sudden illness, as she had had such passion for animals in her childhood: bake sales and door-to-door fund-raising for the World Wildlife Federation; dressing up Pumpkin, their semi-compliant terrier, in T-shirts, cloaks and bonnets; submitting her plush raccoons and koalas to elaborate veterinary games. Cassandra used to trundle through their old house in the Oakland hills with her stuffed menagerie piled into that miniature stroller, along with her favorite Black Astronaut Barbie.

Rodney removed his glasses and laid them on his big mahogany desk, the same desk once used by Chief Justice Charles Evans Hughes. He could just pick up the phone and call her, even though this was not his usual time: first Sunday of the month, right after dinner. He could call Cassandra, couldn't he?

The colonial mantle clock scolded him with its uniform *tk tk tk*.

He dialed Samuel instead. As the phone rang, Rodney felt his muscles, old and withered, hanging from his bones, as if chunks of flesh might fall from his limbs, as if his skin could peel off in flakes like brown leaves blowing off an ancient tree. He was in the autumn of his life, quickly approaching winter. Rodney's son answered.

"Are you in the building this afternoon, Samuel? Down in the press room?"

"No, I'm in D.C. Superior all week, covering this crazy school takeover referendum business. Why, is there news? Did you guys do the *Al-Tounsi* cert this afternoon?"

"You know I can't talk about that."

"Just whether you voted or not. I don't need the details or verdict. The paper's pushing for anything on Subic Bay, anything at all."

"Samuel, no." Rodney cleared his throat.

"You okay, Dad?"

"Everything is fine. I have a cold. Listen, I need to visit the vet's office this afternoon. Your mother's cat, Stone, has to be put to sleep. I thought you might accompany me, and then we could have dinner at my place following."

"God, Dad. Sorry to hear it."

"We could share a Greek salad and chicken Parmesan from Giordino's. And I have a rather dazzling bottle of Macchiole Messorio to accompany, if we have time to decant it properly."

"Stone's the gray one, right? Hey, what ever happened to the other one, Felix?"

"He died before your mother." Rodney shuffled the papers his secretaries had put on his desk when he was in conference. "It must have been over two years ago."

Rebecca, the Justice's late wife, smiled at Rodney from the photograph on his desk, her bountiful warmth a provocation, a sharp irritant. Cassandra had come to resemble her mother more and more, although she was more aloof as an adult than Rebecca had been. She had a harder expression, tighter lips. Cassandra's curly hair could be gelled and worn shoulder length, thanks to her mother's Ashkenazi genes. Cassandra's brow was often furrowed and her protruding chin raised, as if to repel intrusive questioning. It was disconcerting to Rodney how Cassandra liked to wear those sheer scarfs tied so snugly around her neck—so that she looked somehow both austere and sexual.

"I can't do dinner," said Samuel. "I've got a deadline on this story and there's no way in hell I'm making it as it is. How about our usual Sunday? When is that, next week? Giordino's, of course."

"Not a problem. But perhaps you can do me a favor. Will you call Cassandra and tell her?"

Samuel hesitated. "Honestly, Dad, I'm not going to speak to her for a while. We're on different schedules. Why don't you leave her a message?"

"Yes, of course."

"I'm really sorry about the cat."

The silence in Rodney's chambers deepened as he got off the phone. Why had it seemed so imperative to those around him—his secretaries, clerks, colleagues—that he publicly express his grief over Rebecca's death that previous September? Rodney did not want to disappoint them, so he had placed this photograph on his desk, but in truth he had never taken any comfort from Rebecca's image.

He stood and paced behind his desk. Nine days until his next dinner at Giordino's with Samuel—third Sunday of each month. Usually the span of time between their meetings was perfect, but today those remaining nine days felt like an epoch. There must be some way to encourage his son into dinner tonight. In Samuel's reporting for *The Washington Post*, more and more he was covering the thorny legal issues around the Subic Bay prisoners, and he was eager for news on the *Al-Tounsi* petition. Why not offer him a few choice details from the justices' private conference—or no, merely suggest that those details might be forthcoming were Samuel to eat dinner with his father? Samuel could use that secret information to write a short article for the *Post*'s Sunday edition, a good four days before the justices' cert decision would be released to the public.

Rodney collapsed in his chair, pulled himself to his desk, and centered his jittery palms on his blotter to steady them. That thought was well beneath him. Unethical in the extreme. Such behavior would be worthy of impeachment. Did he want to be the first justice to suffer that fate since Samuel Chase in 1805?

There was a knock on his door. Rodney stiffened his back, told his guest to please come in.

Cindy Chin, one of four clerks he had for the term, holding a draft memo out before her as if it were a shield, entered Rodney's office and meekly asked if the Justice wouldn't mind clarifying an incongruity she had discovered between two historical opinions, one of which she was relying on as a precedent for *Bakerson*. "I've, uh, asked Gautam and Alex about it." She tucked a lock of straight hair behind her ear and approached the Justice's desk. "They both agree that the '97 ruling, which was your opinion, is in conflict with the, uh, one from '53. But in the later one there's no explicit mention of overruling Frankfurter. I was just, well . . . I don't know why that would be."

This clerk was a familiar specimen. She reminded Rodney of himself in his mid-20s: studious, disciplined and rigorous, but perhaps not as imaginative as her peers, Gautam, Alex and Leanne. Most justices on the Court did not like hiring clerks like Cindy Chin, preferring the brilliant and rogue Harvard thinkers who

chatted freely about their opinions, who longed to blaze new legal
ground—no matter how unsubstantiated—and who boldly stated
their intentions to follow their bosses onto the federal bench. But
why would Rodney want a clerk who pushed the boundaries of
the law without fully understanding it first? The biases of his
colleagues had made him long all the more for the Cindy Chins
of this world, these intellectually modest clerks who memorized
rather than innovated, who deftly handled the assignments that
teachers and judges had given them, and who reached the top of
their elite law schools through pure, grinding effort rather than
through the miracle of brilliance. Good daughters and good sons.
These young people who badly wanted to excel in the eyes of their
seniors. Cindy Chin must have loved the law for the same reason
Rodney did: because it was an inherently good and just system,
providing the necessary borders and limitations on human behavior, the scaffolding for a sturdy society. And because it created
and respected responsible citizens.

Rodney watched her stammer and blush. He had never been
able to put his clerks at ease, not once in his 16 terms on the Court.
It was the fault of his antiquated manner, his perfect grammar, his
demand that everyone—outside a few select friends, colleagues,
and family members—call him Justice Sykes. His insistence on
addressing these young adults in their late twenties as "Ms. Chin"
or "Mr. Tyler" had established relationships governed by behav-
ioral codes that this generation had outgrown. Regular meetings
with formal procedures. Traditional dress, speech, action, neither
subverted nor lightened. Of course that made them tense. None of
these clerks—especially this present batch, born circa 1980—could
have possibly recalled social codes and mores that were already
passé when Rodney was their age. Cindy Chin was very pretty with
her long face and bright green glasses. Her youth declared itself in
every feature: the thickness of her dark hair, the smoothness of the
skin around her eyes. He was incapable of putting this girl at ease.
He had never befriended any clerk, past or present.

Cindy stood before her boss's desk with her high forehead
and dark eyes, waiting for his answer. Rodney's chin quivered,

his muscles tightened and he started to tremble. He pinched the bridge of his broad nose and stared up into the light and, unable to stanch the rising tears, broke into snuffling sobs. His whole body shook.

"Oh my God." Cindy dropped her memo on his desk. "Justice Sykes?"

Rodney closed his eyes and held up his palm. Hot streams flowed down his cheeks.

"Do you want me to leave?"

"No, please." Rodney inhaled, calmed his sobs, and steadied his voice. "Forgive me, Ms. Chin." He wiped away his tears. "My veterinarian has just informed me that my cat needs to be put down this afternoon."

"Oh no!" Cindy's nostrils flared, her eyes and mouth expanding in shock, *real* shock.

"I am sincerely sorry to subject you to this silliness. That's a fine question you've asked, and if you leave me with a copy of your memo I'll address it thoroughly over the weekend."

Cindy ignored the memo and any quandary it might have posed, and instead pressed Rodney for more information: How long had his cat been sick? What were the symptoms? Had Rodney been expecting this?

"You don't need to waste your time with my pet. It's not a priority."

"I would just freak out entirely." Cindy had abandoned any attempt to sound professional. "I have two cats and I can't even imagine."

She pulled an armchair in front of his desk, seemingly unembarrassed by her concern for his pet or by the breakdown of formality. Although the Justice wanted to stop her inquiry on the spot, to tell her it was ridiculous, that there was a great deal of work to be completed, and that, contrary to his reaction, he had never before cared about his cat, he found himself giving Cindy a full description of Stone's condition and the events of that morning. He was surprised by his own loquaciousness, and by his desire to sit with her at all. He was soothed and relieved by Cindy's exuberant attention and high emotion. He enjoyed discussing the details of Stone's symptoms with this intelligent young woman.

When Rodney told her of his intention to visit the vet's office to watch Stone die, Cindy looked horrified. "You can't go alone. And then just drive home? That's too awful. Let me come with you."

Rodney smiled at her, but shook his head. "Absolutely not necessary, Ms. Chin. I will be fine, I promise you."

"I'd feel better, Justice Sykes, if you didn't go alone."

He bit his lip. Didn't Hugo Black play tennis with his clerks? Didn't Taft invite the young men of his employ over for Thanksgiving turkey? And doesn't Elyse Van Cleve carve pumpkins with hers on Halloween? And Killian Quinn, by God—he probably wrestles his clerks to the ground on their first day in chambers. Clerks who received personal treatment were quick to protect their bosses: they brought them groceries when they were old; they spoke of their justices as profound mentors, and respected them as paragons of righteousness. This young woman said she was available, she seemed to really care, and sincerely wanted to accompany him to the vet.

"Are you absolutely certain you don't have other commitments?"

Cindy assured him that she was free. She would be thrilled to go with him. Before Rodney could reason himself out of it, he had packed his briefcase and donned his overcoat, waited as Cindy gathered her things, and found himself walking down the hallway toward the elevator, intending to leave in this young woman's car—a first in his 16 years on the Supreme Court.

Rodney slipped into the passenger seat of Cindy's aging Hyundai, pushing aside the plastic wrappings of nori snacks and Lara bars, noticing two cigarette butts in the ashtray—certainly this young woman's sole vice—and feeling like a fool. Cindy apologized for the mess. She sheepishly closed the ashtray and drove up 2nd Avenue toward Massachusetts. The passenger seat was pushed too far forward, so the dashboard pressed against his knees, a strange sensation, as Rodney stood only five and a half feet, and never felt cramped in cars. He struggled to find the right lever to push the seat back. He was sweating profusely. Rodney cleared his throat, smiling at the windshield, saying nothing. Cindy reached for the radio dial, but stopped before turning it on. She returned her hand to the wheel.

The embassies along Massachusetts Avenue blurred together; Rodney couldn't distinguish Togo's flag from Ukraine's. While rounding onto Connecticut, Cindy broke the excruciating silence to discuss the charms of Dupont Circle, the quality of the neighborhood's local bookshop, the proliferation of its coffee houses, the exorbitance of its rent. Rodney agreed with her observations.

She found a parking space on Connecticut Avenue near the city's border with Chevy Chase, a half-block from the vet's office. Rodney was relieved to climb out of the passenger seat and stand on the sidewalk as Cindy locked the car. He held the door to the vet's office and bowed his head as she passed through. The chime from the alarm system gave him pause in the threshold. He had come here to witness his cat's death. The cat that had caused him to cry, inexplicably, embarrassingly. Surely he would not do that again.

The receptionist ushered Rodney and Cindy into the clinical room, where Dr. Vry stood in pale yellow scrubs beside her assistant, who was finishing up a procedure on a lethargic black lab. As Dr. Vry approached to shake Rodney's hand, Justice Sykes suddenly remembered that he had asked this veterinarian to call him *Rodney*. Could he take back that request?

"Hello, Justice Sykes."

Rodney sighed in relief as the vet glanced curiously at Cindy. "I'd like to introduce Ms. Chin, my clerk. She has been kind enough to accompany me to your office today."

"Cindy." The two women exchanged handshakes.

The vet's assistant carried Stone, who more resembled a ragged stole than a living creature, and laid him on the cool stainless steel table, where he sprawled and panted, unable to lift his head. Dr. Vry rubbed the cat's back.

"He's in bad shape, as you see. He's having difficulty breathing."

The veterinarian looked to Rodney, an invitation to say the final goodbye he had requested. Cindy and Dr. Vry parted to give him space at the table. He would have to perform the gesture for them, but without making too much of it. He stroked Stone's soft fur, watching the animal's gut rise and fall with each labored breath.

"He's a good cat, and I shall miss him."

Rodney turned to Dr. Vry and nodded his approval for the lethal injection. The veterinarian found a good point of injection near Stone's neck and deftly stuck the needle into him. The cat didn't flinch or make a sound.

Rodney's hand rested on Stone's increasingly quiet body, right beside Dr. Vry's. Cindy Chin cried without restraint, whispering *poor, poor thing*. A minor clutch of sadness tightened Rodney's chest, but it wasn't genuine. It was nothing, really, but the appropriation of excess grief emanating from Cindy.

He cupped his hands before him and lowered his head. He had stood like this at Rebecca's funeral ten months earlier in Memorial Park, graveside, amidst the roses and azaleas in the heat of late May. There, too, he had been surrounded by sobbing loved ones who carried him along in their collective grief. Rebecca, dear Rebecca. Her death still seemed abstract, incomprehensible—the young and independent woman he had met and courted at Stanford Law all those years ago, whom he had married in her parents' well-groomed backyard in Brentwood, with whom he had raised two intelligent and confident children, and who had shown such strength and self-sufficiency even during their hardest years. Had she really disappeared from this world, gone for all time, because of nothing more than a slick spring rain, a swerving Honda, and the panicked driver of an 18-wheeler? Even when shoveling dirt into her grave, as dictated by her family's Jewish tradition, he did not break down.

The remoteness of his grief that day was, in a sense, the perfect crystallization of his *problem*, as Rebecca had liked to call it. "Goddamn it, Rodney, I might as well talk to Stone." She had scolded him like that only weeks before her death. He hadn't responded adequately to some worry she had expressed. The sting of that. What was she so upset about? Some fight with her sister or a friend? He had mumbled *mmm* to her cruel comment and retreated into his tiny office, closing the door behind him.

A *problem*. Her words, not his. His cool stoicism, although it had indeed caused difficulties in their later years, was also what had attracted Rebecca to him in the first place. For all the so-called damage his phlegmatic disposition had caused his wife, hadn't it also boosted her strength and happiness, especially when Rebecca was a fiery young woman in the early 1970s? Of course. She had taken great pleasure in marrying such a steady man—kind, intelligent and calm—who had had absolutely no reservations about her independence and abilities and right to do whatever she wanted, and who had expected, and even demanded through his unyielding detachment, that she take full responsibility for her own emotional well-being. In the balance of their relationship, his benevolent distance must have been more of a comfort than an irritant. It had signaled his intrinsic trust. It had gelled with her second-wave feminist aspirations, offered her hope, bolstered her confidence, and encouraged her self-realization. Surely Rebecca would have understood why Rodney hadn't cried at her funeral; she would have understood why he was not capable of crying over a dying cat while standing in the vet's office with Cindy Chin.

And yet he had cried earlier in chambers. Over nothing. Sobbed. What of that?

Stone's breathing abruptly halted. Dr. Vry removed the syringe and pulled away from the table. After an interminable moment of silence, she suggested that Rodney and Cindy step outside so she could take care of the cat's body.

In the waiting room, Cindy wiped her nose, smiled at her boss, and scoured his face, no doubt for some sign of the emotion that she had witnessed earlier, that bizarre hiccup in chambers—so distant now, altogether inaccessible. Imagine: torrential tears, for a pet, of all things! Rodney tucked his hands together before him, as he did when meeting foreign dignitaries or the High Justices of other nations' courts, and bowed his head slightly.

"Ms. Chin, I cannot thank you enough for your company this afternoon. You've helped me immensely through a difficult experience. But you do not have to sacrifice your entire evening for me."

"I don't mind. Really."

"I live only a few blocks away."

Cindy nodded somberly. "If I were you, Justice Sykes, I'd be careful about going home right now to an empty apartment. That's when the loss will hit you hardest."

Rodney couldn't help but smile at the innocence of this young woman shuffling on the linoleum.

He should say something generous, less cold. His usual formality suddenly felt like a comic exaggeration. With Cassandra he often behaved with this same dignity. No matter how much he planned for lightness and ease, formal grammar and measured sentences always emerged from his lips. But that restraint was due to Cassandra's seething anger and obvious unhappiness, which had gotten so much worse this past year. Cassandra made him nervous. Cindy did not.

"I can see you want to be alone." Cindy took her car keys out of her purse.

Rodney laid his hand on his clerk's shoulder. "On the contrary, I'd be delighted to treat you to dinner. You've been so kind. I know an excellent Italian place on Wisconsin."

Cindy shook her head. "I don't want to go to a restaurant like it's a celebration. Why don't I come and make you dinner? It'll keep you from spending too long in your apartment alone. I mean, without Stone."

"Oh, I couldn't possibly—"

"I'd prefer it, Justice Sykes. I'm an insanely good cook and it relaxes me. Please, let me do this for you."

Rodney grinned; he was unable to hide it. But he was allowed to enjoy her quite extraordinary consideration, wasn't he? A blurring of professional and personal boundaries did not have to be a travesty, just so long as he was careful and avoided all discussion of his earlier breakdown.

The clerk, who was proving quite adept at reading his physical clues, patted her squirming boss on the arm as if he were a friend, and as if the culture of formality that he had so strictly enforced had once again been rendered irrelevant by one small show of his emotion. It was really a wonder how young people these days, even serious ones like Cindy Chin, were so readily casual with their superiors.

"Great! It's all settled then."

Cindy offered to buy groceries while he returned home. Rodney forced $60 into her hands, despite her repeated claims that the money was unnecessary, and parted ways with his chipper clerk. He paid the vet's exorbitant bill and patiently acknowledged Dr. Vry's sincere condolences. As Rodney ambled south on Connecticut toward his apartment building, he was surprised by his own happiness. The sky was bright and cloudless, the air warm and fresh, two storefronts displayed freshly cut dogwood blossoms. Soon he would have a lovely dinner with Cindy Chin, not taken in from Giordino's, but freshly prepared in his own kitchen, and they would discuss their recent cases and her term on the Court, and it would all be a delightful departure from routine.

He whistled a favorite Verdi aria while striding past the doorman, riding the elevator to the fourth floor, and marching down the hallway to his apartment. But when Rodney opened his front door, he halted his humming, and paused in the threshold. Acrid, ammoniacal air pervaded his airways, as if a rank cheesecloth had been pressed against his face. Had the stench been this terrible in the morning? Rodney flipped on the lights and immediately proceeded into the unused guest bathroom off the foyer, where he had stashed Stone's litter, and which he had avoided rather religiously for several weeks. He covered his mouth with his hand, but the air still burnt his lungs.

The speckled gray plastic litter box was so full that even from the doorway he could see excrement stacked in rolling mounds like a collection of blackened, volcanic rocks. A thin coating of light blue gravel was spread over the tiles. Additional mounds of excrement laid in the room's corner by the toilet, and tucked by the vanity's base. Pressing his nostrils shut, Rodney investigated the bathtub. More still, dispersed across the tub's smooth porcelain.

He left the bathroom, and closed the door behind him. Maureen, his cleaning lady, had moved to Atlanta in January, but before leaving she had pressed in his hand the phone number of her cousin LaVonne, who had cleaned bathrooms at the Department of Agriculture for 15 years. She had noticed that he was a busy man, and would he like her to call LaVonne? Rodney insisted on calling himself, but then he hadn't done it. He had decided that adding cleaning duties to his routine would focus his attention on practical tasks and bolster his strength, as he had been feeling rather low all winter, quite low, and indeed had more time on his hands than he had ever thought possible for a Supreme Court Justice, and he had few pressing social engagements. Now he realized he had let certain responsibilities slip.

Rodney retrieved the mop and detergent, the broom and dustpan, and the dishwashing gloves from the kitchen pantry. Stone's swampy water dish and filthy food bowl, encrusted and highly bacterial, taunted him on the floor. He had fed his cat yesterday, hadn't he? Certainly feeding was part of his morning routine, opening the cans of chunky paste at 7:55 a.m, between his second cup of black coffee and his retreat to the walk-in closet, where he chose his shirt, tie and jacket, and executed a sturdy Windsor. But in recent days he had loitered at his kitchen counter, staring into his coffee, only rousing when the time was well advanced, and then he rushed to gather his papers and dress before his Town Car arrived to drive him to work. It was possible he had forgotten to feed Stone from time to time. There were those mornings when Rodney had awoken to mews and scratches on the side of his bed. He must admit facts: there was a distinct pattern of neglect.

And it wasn't just the cat. He had not called Cassandra the last three appointed Sundays: January, February, and March. Today was Friday, March 30. If he failed to call her again this weekend, that would be four.

Rodney swept the foyer bathroom, gathered the litter and feces, emptied the nauseating mess into a double-ply garbage bag.

He tied it tightly and whisked it out into the hallway disposal. He mopped the tiled floor briskly, while running the shower on hot to steam the room and clean the tub. He wiped the porcelain down with disinfectant when all else was done. At the kitchen sink, Rodney grit his teeth and scrubbed Stone's bowls with vigor, until they shone like polished silver. He worked the vacuum across the rugs, although the ubiquitous cat hair was too sticky to remove entirely. In his own *en suite* bathroom, major tasks completed, he checked the knotting of his tie and the wrinkles on his shirt, deeming himself presentable, and then stood an extra moment to regard his image in the mirror, emptied of all expression: a distinguished, stoic gentleman, with a large round head that was too big for his small body, which gave him the odd appearance of an overgrown child. Gray-haired, broad-nosed, with pronounced smile lines and wide-set eyes. This was how he would look in a mug shot.

His clerk rang the bell to his apartment. Cindy entered his foyer, blushing and looking altogether out of place. She glanced around at his Italian sculpture, tapestry and art: the urns and orbs and painting of nudes with winged cherubs the Justice favored. And then the oil paintings that Rebecca had chosen, which he still found too blurry. He had done a decent job of cleaning his home in limited time. The place was tidy and smelled strongly of lemon verbena. Certainly no sign of any crimes against his cat. Cindy asked her boss for directions to his kitchen and Rodney pointed the way, interpreting her request as a sign of deference rather than an actual inquiry—the kitchen was right in front of her.

"Please, let me take your bags," he said.

She gave the Justice a bag stuffed with vegetables, meat and jarred sauces, and followed him into the small kitchen. She seemed to relax somewhat as they started to unload the groceries.

"Make yourself at home." Rodney knew, of course, that it would be impossible for Cindy to be truly comfortable here. "If you can't find any pots or utensils, I'll be happy to assist you."

The logically organized kitchen was stocked with quality cookware and a full array of spices, none of which Rodney had

touched since Rebecca's death. Cindy found her bearings easily and
was soon chopping, sizzling and boiling, scraping together small
mounds of ginger and hot pepper and dried tangerine peel. Rodney
perched on a stool at the counter, watching her work, wanting to
speak but unable to think of anything to say. Cooking seemed to
soothe her. She moved around the small space with confidence.

She was preparing an elaborate, four-dish Chinese feast. "All
my grandmother's recipes." Cindy stirred the contents of a pan
with one hand and adjusted the heat with the other. "From back
in Taiwan. Except for this garlic shrimp, which I've updated a
bit."

A beef noodle soup boiled on a back burner, wafting scallion,
soy sauce, anise. Pungent steam rose from an amaranth and mushroom stir-fry, and still more steam plumed from the pork dumplings that Cindy had pinched together with remarkable dexterity.
Rodney loved Chinese food, but he had never had an authentic
meal cooked in his own home. What wine did one pair with this
feast? It was near the end of a stressful day, and he would welcome at least a single glass of a good red, a nightly indulgence he
did not wish to forgo. Might he decant that bottle of Macchiole
Messorio 2001 he had promised Samuel? Probably he shouldn't:
the smoke and depth of a great Tuscan Merlot would overwhelm
the soy sauce, scallion and sesame oil. But was it even appropriate to open wine and light candles tonight, as if he were trying to
seduce this young woman?

Rodney asked Cindy about her family. The clerk spoke freely
of her trips to Taipei, of her grandfather's early death and her
grandmother's circumspect life in that crowded city, of her parents' emigration to Chicago and her mundane, all-American
childhood on the North Shore. She was the hard-working second
child of upwardly mobile, middle-class parents, an engineer and
a nurse. Although proud of their daughter for sailing through a
prestigious law school (NYU), her parents were somewhat baffled
by Cindy's post-graduate choice to clerk for a Supreme Court Justice, a job with shockingly nominal pay. Why not take one of the
high-paying corporate jobs that had already been offered?

"I guess it's kind of a typical culture shock, seeing as they've worked so hard to get me here, coming from nothing themselves. They just can't imagine why I wouldn't want to make tons of money right away. Plus, they're suspicious about government—that's something else. They don't fully get how the legal system can be fair in this country, how working for the highest court might actually be a valuable and prestigious thing. They get it in theory, I think—I mean, they're not idiots about this country—but their hearts don't fully believe it."

While she was speaking, Rodney decided it would be best to offer Cindy an unspecified drink. Let her decide on beer, wine or whatever.

"And what about you?" Cindy pulled her perfect dumplings off the stove and gave the mushroom-vegetables a final stir. "I mean, I know the basics, of course, but not much more. Your mother must have been thrilled to see you appointed to the Court."

"Well, no." Rodney finished setting Rebecca's family's flatware on the dining room table. "My mother passed away before I was appointed to the D.C. Circuit, so she never had an inkling that I would be anything other than a trial lawyer. I, of course, did not foresee this twist to my career."

"She was in Oakland, right? And you had two brothers growing up?"

"Quite right. I'm sure you know our story."

Under normal circumstances, Rodney would have deflected the probing question and changed the subject, but with Cindy now filling platters to take into the dining room table, he found his defenses disabled. He was surprised to hear himself say: "My older brother's life has been a great tragedy. I'm only fortunate that Marshall did not manage to drag me down with him."

Cindy set the platters on the table, sat down across from her boss and surveyed her steaming work. She sighed with satisfaction.

"Extraordinary."

"Let's dig in."

"But would you like a drink? Wine, perhaps? Or beer?"

"No, I'm fine. Just hungry."

"You must have something. I insist."

Cindy raised her brow and shrugged. "Well, I guess if you insist, a little white wine would be okay."

Not his first choice, but a white was better than nothing. Rodney hurried into the kitchen and returned with a bottle of Riesling. He poured two full glasses as Cindy served the soup.

"You have heard of my older brother, Marshall, and I'm sure you recall the trouble he caused me during my confirmation hearing. Those fierce questions about the Black Panther events I attended, and the article I wrote for the Berkeley student paper, and that rather awkward exchange about zebras with Senator Wexler. To be perfectly frank, I was surprised and relieved that the good senator had enough self-restraint to speak only of zebras changing their stripes and not 'coons changing their coats.'"

Cindy guffawed and raised a hand to cover her parted lips.

"What I am certain you don't know, however, is that my brother petitioned me directly two years after my confirmation. Marshall filed a pro se petition for habeas, on the grounds that he had received ineffective assistance of counsel during his trial and after. I don't have to tell you, Cindy, of all people, about the strict procedural barriers to such a petition. Of course, we were under no obligation to consider the dubious merits of his case. Still, I felt his petition put me in an awkward position. Technically, yes, we retained the right to review his imprisonment. I passed the request on to Justice Van Cleve, who relieved us of the burden and handled it appropriately."

Rodney rubbed a fingertip around the rim of his wine glass. The alcohol had warmed his chest. He was tired and relaxed, eager to talk about himself for what felt like the first time in his life.

"Do you ever visit him in prison?"

"I have, but it's been many years. Eight or nine, perhaps more. I used to go more frequently. He's in California, you see, at San Quentin. It's quite difficult for both of us. Not just logistically."

Rodney sipped his wine. Yes, it was as if the sweet Riesling had been vinted to pair with this spicy Taiwanese meal. He took a second sip, and then a third. Cindy, across the table, had pulled her hair back. Her cheeks were slightly flushed; her expression was open, non-judgmental, and kind.

"During my confirmation, I didn't tell Senator Wexler or the American people the primary reason why I attended those Black Panther events back in 1969, or why I wrote that misguided opinion piece for *The Daily Californian* praising a political organization I had deep misgivings about even then. My brother Timothy, with whom I was very close, had been killed in Vietnam only weeks earlier. His death shook me to my core. It had been my unstated role in the family to protect Timothy, to provide some order to his life, some stability. I loved him dearly, and liked him moreover, and for the entire, grueling year that he was in Vietnam I wrote him constantly, and wished every moment I could go over there and shield him from harm, as I had always tried to do in Oakland. During our childhood, our father was not present. Our mother worked two jobs, and when she was with us, she was a disciplinarian, a police officer, strict and cold and rather severe. She wasn't a source of affection, comfort or happiness."

Rodney stared at the ceiling trim instead of at his attentive young guest. His chest tightened with crushing sadness, a distinct ache, a feeling he recalled quite clearly from his childhood dinner table—those silent meals with his brothers and mother, always loaded with an unidentifiable shame.

"You see, my older brother Marshall was an angry young man, cruel and rebellious from the start. I never really understood his anger. He was a dropout and a drug addict, and quite self-important as well—*poor me*, you understand, and all that—and he soon fell in loosely with the Panthers, although I'm sure they smelled a million miles off that he was a bad seed, and in the movement only for the drugs and sex. He had the political conscience of a rock, which is why, I'm sure, Marshall never rose above the party's most basic membership. At any rate, when Timothy died, I was more alone than ever, so I decided I would make an attempt to bridge the gap with Marshall. I began to call him with some frequency and even smoked cannabis with him on one occasion—an absurd sight, let me tell you, me in my coat and

tie, inhaling a joint passed around some dingy basement decorated with African masks and leopard skins by pseudo-soldiers
in black berets—and then I attended those awkward Panther
events, including that infamous rally for Huey Newton which
later caused me so much trouble in my hearings, and I wrote not
unfavorably about the Panthers in that opinion piece at Berkeley,
hoping my words would impress my older brother, and perhaps
make him like me a little bit more. Which didn't work, of course.
My frustrating reparations with Marshall ended abruptly one
night when he crashed in my student dorm in the fall of 1969
and then left in the morning with the wristwatch my uncle had
given me when I matriculated at Berkeley, a valuable timepiece,
sentimental as well, and one that Marshall, no doubt, quickly
converted into cocaine or heroin or whatever. We had a tense
encounter. A full denial on Marshall's part, and his pointed use
of the term *house nigger.* And I, of course, realized right then and
there that no amount of effort on my behalf would ever transform
Marshall into Timothy, and that nothing I could do would ever
bring Timothy back, and that I should really turn my full attention toward my studies and forget about Marshall altogether."

Rodney paused. Such a torrent of words. He sipped his wine
and devoured three dumplings, but only after carefully divid-
ing them into small bites with his knife and fork. He dabbed
his mouth with a napkin, and offered a trite comment about the
meal being stupendous. When at last he mustered the courage
to glance up at Cindy, her open face, so young and pretty, once
again astounded him. He took another sip of wine and held the
glass suspended at his lips. He had forgotten precisely what he
had been saying.

"As you can see, I'm not in the habit of talking about such
matters."

"Uh huh." Cindy's wide eyes were fixed on him. He must have
seemed to her like an utterly transformed man.

"I hope my candor is not unwelcome."

"No, no. It's fascinating."

"Did you know, Ms. Chin, that my daughter, Cassandra, is—like you—presently clerking for a federal judge?"

"Really? Which judge?

"Emmanuel Arroyo, on the Ninth Circuit."

"I hear he's tough on clerks."

"She works long hours for him, certainly."

More than works, Rodney could have said if he had so dared. Cassandra's affair with Judge Arroyo—if it were true, if Morris Bayfield was to be believed—must have begun under similar circumstances as this. A casual dinner after work, perhaps a drink in some San Francisco wine bar. A sympathetic conversation on the topic of Judge Arroyo's recent divorce. Probably Cassandra had consumed too much Zinfandel and let it be known with a gesture, a laugh, a touch of her hand, that she was interested in him. But did she consider who that man was? What it would mean to her father if she slept with him?

Morris claimed that Cassandra's and Judge Arroyo's affair was mere conjecture, a rumor from the Browning Federal Courthouse, but Rodney's friend would never lie or mislead him, and would never report such troubling news if he doubted it himself. Either way, it was not a matter of Rodney's concern. That was precisely what he had told Morris, after thanking him and assuring him that he harbored no ill will toward the messenger. Cassandra was an adult, a grown woman, and Rodney believed wholeheartedly that people must independently make their ways through the fog of this world guided by their own codes of behavior and moral compasses. They must take the call to freedom seriously and respect the varied results, even when they find them uneven or shocking. And he had to admit that he did not know the inner workings of Cassandra's relationship with her husband, Denny—the limits of their commitment, any perverse licenses allowed or strict penalties incurred in their marital agreement.

Cindy Chin shifted in her seat. Perhaps it would be best for Rodney to wrap things up, draw some wise conclusions for his clerk.

"I think what my life shows, especially in regards to that unfortunate opinion piece in *The Daily Californian*, is that one must always be careful, exceedingly diligent, not to let one's personal viewpoints or present traumas affect the rigor of one's behavior, especially when one is charged with the solemn responsibility of upholding the law."

Cindy shrugged and stirred the amaranth and mushroom mix on her plate. "I don't know. Seems you've got no choice sometimes other than to let those things come out. You can't do everything right all the time."

Rodney leaned his elbows on the table. "Just use a little bit of common sense." His voice was deeper now, weary with fatigue. "That's all I mean. I was not as diligent as I might have been."

"Oh, God, Justice Sykes. You were supposed to be completely mature at twenty years old, or whatever you were, right after your brother died? To know better than to try again with your only other brother? Really?"

Rodney nodded solemnly. "You know, the most absurd aspect of that whole ordeal with my brother occurred a couple of months after Justice Van Cleve had respectfully denied his habeas petition. Marshall sent to my chambers a long letter, strident and fierce, on stationery issued by the San Quentin penitentiary, which proceeded to 'educate me' on the proper functioning of habeas corpus in criminal proceedings. He lectured me, in the mean and condescending tone that I knew all too well, on the history of the Great Writ."

"You're kidding!"

"Not at all. It was insufferable. I can still hear him *spitting* those words. How habeas corpus has been used by federal courts to review state convictions since Reconstruction, and how due process and the Fourteenth Amendment incorporated the Bill of Rights. He repeated that magnificent Oliver Wendell Holmes quote—I'm sure you recall the one, how the writ cuts through all forms to the very tissue of the structure—and footnoted his entire miserable, rambling document with absurd references to *Ex Parte Bollman*, and liberally quoted Brennan from *Fay v. Noia*, and sprinkled the whole thing with bits of Title 28 section 2241, as if the U.S Code was the Koran he worshipped in his cell."

Rodney gritted his teeth.

"Forgive me for going on at such length—it still makes my blood boil. I am a Justice of the United States Supreme Court, only the second African-American to ever hold that title, and yet my felony-convicted brother wants to lecture *me* on the functioning of law? My criminal sibling, who has never had any respect for anything, who drove my mother to an early grave, and who will spend the rest of his life in prison because some convenience store cashier dared to swing her baseball bat at his thick head, and got herself shot dead, instead of just letting that drug addict slink out of her damn store with a week's worth of her pay?

"My brother thought it gravely unjust that I—personally—denied his appeal. Unjust because brotherhood is a bond that supposedly exceeds law. That was the real reasoning behind his inept legal rant. He said he was not asking me for freedom, but merely for additional access to the courts. He wanted me to cut through the procedural tape, to grant him one more chance to prove his point. But I don't believe for one second that Marshall deserved a writ of habeas corpus on legal grounds. It does not matter that I sympathized with his suffering, and still long for his happiness."

Rodney sighed and finished his glass of wine. "And what do you think of that, Ms. Chin? Was I right? Was I just?"

Cindy squeezed her lips together, suppressing a giggle. She shielded her mouth with her hand. Indeed it was strange and out of character for Rodney to ask her those questions about his personal behavior. No wonder she wanted to laugh.

"My opinion is that you did the right thing, of course," Cindy said. "You can't respond to a personal appeal from a family member, and you had to pass that request onto Justice Van Cleve. But there's a bigger question, too, whether his appeal had any merit on its own and deserved habeas. Now, obviously I don't know the exact details of your brother's case, or if there was some terrible procedural mistake in his trial, but I highly doubt it from what you're saying. I know you would have been alert to a problem if there was a real one—that's just the way you are. So, of course you did the right thing, Justice Sykes. You're always fair. You're always just."

"No, not always."

Rodney crossed his arms against his chest. He stopped himself from confessing that he hadn't been fair to Stone. Cindy didn't have to know about that. Why did he feel the urge to treat this young woman like a confessional priest?

"Oh, the ties that bind us all. The ties we are born into and inherit and carry along with us. They are overwhelmingly stringent. But I will say, Ms. Chin, in spite of Marshall's offense, in spite of *everything* he has done to himself and to others and to me, I cannot disown him. He remains my only living kin."

"Of course."

"I should visit my incarcerated brother more often. That is a fact. I should look in on Timothy's grave more often, as well. His final resting place lies just over the Potomac at Arlington. I don't make either journey nearly often enough. I've ignored them, selfishly, and that is never the right choice."

Cindy looked like she wanted to say something kind, but couldn't think of any good excuse for him.

"It's sad, really. My two brothers in their respective prisons. I know they are both stuck, and I often feel responsible for their fates. Perhaps I am responsible in some manner. Perhaps they judge me."

"Well, Timothy doesn't judge anyone anymore."

Rodney smiled. "No, you're right. Not Timothy."

An ambulance roared down Connecticut, the pitch of its siren rising and falling as it passed. An emergency. How remote that seemed—the suffering or death of the patient speeding by in that ambulance.

"You know, this morning, when I found Stone lying sick on my floor, I spoke directly to him, using his name, as if my cat were a person. And I did it again, in the vet's office. Twice I said his name, out loud, in a single day. I can't recall ever doing that before, speaking directly to a cat."

Cindy cocked her head. "You never talked to your cats?"

"Well, of course I said things to him. But I spoke with certain formalities, I should say."

She laughed. "That doesn't exactly surprise me, Justice Sykes."

"Forgive me. I've had a bit too much to drink."

He put down his glass. Finished. Done. He would allow himself no more mistakes. Rodney steered the conversation toward a safer subject: Cindy's eye-opening year at the Court, her grueling schedule, what she thought of her work. They loosely discussed several cases on the docket, and then Rodney brought the conversation around to the incongruity that Cindy had discovered that morning in preparation for *Bakerson*, those two opposing rulings—his own from 1997 and Frankfurter's from 1953—the question that had brought Cindy into his private chambers. He pushed back from the table and crossed his legs. How relieving it was to revert to their standard roles, the justice and his clerk, albeit in his dining room. Their intimate conversation had changed something, though. There was more humor between them, a more relaxed tone. When they had finished their meal, Rodney successfully fought off Cindy's offer to wash his dishes. She hovered by the front door, coat in hand, purse dangling off her elbow. Softened by wine, scrambled by circumstance, Rodney touched his clerk on her shoulder and pulled her close for an embrace, but was careful to hug her with enough force and formality to guarantee it would be understood as a paternal gesture.

"Ms. Chin, I appreciate this more than you can imagine."

"It's okay!" Cindy patted him on the back, grinning widely. Her full smile exposed her upper gums. "I'm really glad I could help. I'm thrilled. And I am just so *so* sorry about your cat."

She backed out of his apartment, waving awkwardly, like a nervous child. Once she had turned toward the elevator, he closed the door. Alone in his foyer, Rodney imagined Stone as a corpse. Were cats at Dr. Vry's incinerated, or carted away and buried? Either way, he would sleep alone in his apartment, without wife, child or pet, for the first time in 34 years. The fading alcohol in Rodney's system made his temples pound and gave rise to faint nausea. Sadness slackened his muscles, and a slow stream of self-accusations flowed through his mind. Why had he not visited Timothy's grave? He could have taken the Metro across the Potomac River on any warm spring day and laid some flowers before his white tombstone. It would have been nothing more than a two-hour excursion. And Marshall in prison? It was so easy to drive up into Marin County over the summer. Pleasant, even. Why hadn't he cleaned the cat litter, or scrubbed the bowl, or made sure the poor thing in its last weeks of life was properly fed? Perhaps such unhygienic conditions had contributed to Stone's illness. And why hadn't he allowed Stone outside his apartment at least once in his life? It was not right to deny an animal an experience of the natural world.

He had been forthcoming and honest with Cindy Chin tonight. Remarkable. Or perhaps it was remarkable that Rodney had never spoken so freely about Marshall or Timothy with either of his children, or with Rebecca, for that matter. Not once in his life, and now it was too late.

He could call Cassandra. It had been three full months. Shameful, shameful. Would Cassandra have sought solace from an older man's bed, from Emmanuel Arroyo's bed, if Rodney had communicated with her as openly as he had with Cindy Chin? But he couldn't call his daughter now. He was drunk and dizzy: the Italian Court rug on his foyer floor seemed to gradually tip to his left, realign itself in a sharp blink, and begin tipping again. And Cassandra was so wildly angry, so reckless and venomous in what she said and how she said it, lashing out at Rodney since Rebecca's death, as if he himself had driven the truck that had killed her mother! And when she wasn't expressly furious, then she was remote. Did other daughters call their fathers by their first names, as Cassandra did? He could never be forthcoming with Cassandra. Because she *did* judge him; she was not at all positively predisposed. And yet when Rodney closed his eyes, he saw Cassandra, laughing at some joke, his beloved little girl, and he heard himself asking all the eager questions he longed to pose, questions that had never before occurred to him to ask her, but now seemed imperative: *Why are you furious at me? And what do you know about your mother? I know she felt distant from me by the end, but did she ever complain directly, or say that I had failed her? Was I really so terrible a husband? So awful a father? Did I impede or limit you? Did I ignore any of your needs? What can I do about it now? Will you ever forgive me? Tell me, Cassandra, please: Was I just?*

2

WHAT WOULD BRANDEIS DO?

Whenever Senator Lionel Mahoney dropped by Gideon Rosen's chambers, Justice Rosen got chatty and twitchy. Today he squirmed in his stiff wingback chair, longing to stride around the room as he described the opinion he was drafting, how it would forever change the standing of third-party lawsuits filed against telecommunication conglomerates. No matter that he thought *Deniston v. Globalsmart* was an unimportant case, a bland consensus, and that his opinion was poorly written. Gideon felt an urge to twist and magnify it; he wanted to heighten its significance to impress his old friend.

Senator Mahoney slouched on Gideon's low black sofa, his shoes resting on monographs from National Gallery exhibitions stacked on the coffee table. The senator's shock of white hair matched in color and brightness the sea foam and taut sails on the racing yachts in the painting behind him. The wrinkles on the senator's face were deep and grooved, and though his once-firm cheeks had slackened into saddlebags, aging had only slightly diminished his movie-star good looks. It was easy to imagine Mahoney's spry hazel eyes, speckled green like opals, settling lasciviously on a young woman, erasing the tired face around them. But so what? So Lionel was

good looking—why should that irritate Gideon? Justice Rosen
had no need to womanize, no need for superficial conquests, and
there was nothing about Mahoney's professional life to envy. The
senator's serial philandering with statuesque models and actresses
had been exposed by an intrepid *New York Times* reporter in the
mid-1980s, which prevented him from cake-walking his way into
the Democratic nomination and the White House. Lionel was just
another casualty in a long list of frustrated presidential candidates,
taken down by greed or lust. What was so enviable about that?

"*Al-Tounsi* might be moribund," the Senator said, as he
crunched an almond from a nearby bowl, "but that's not dead."

"We voted and it's buried."

"Ah, but you don't know what I know."

The Justice tucked his hands beneath his thighs and balled
them into fists, like an overexcited kid trying to contain his enthu-
siasm. Even the slimmest chance that *Al-Tounsi* could be revived
made Gideon want to grab the senator by his lapels and shake
the pertinent information out of him. But Lionel, taking his time
now, popped a second almond into his mouth and crushed it with
his back molars.

"Good nuts." The senator held up another. "Though I can't
say they hold a candle to bacon." Mahoney ran his tongue around
his teeth and inspected his tie for wayward bits. "Got a Health
and Education Committee meeting coming up at ten, and the only
nuts I want on me are my very own precious."

Gideon suppressed his desire to scream.

"See, that's the thing about electoral politics. Were I to show
up on the hill with my tie all dirty, it would have political consequences. Newspaper articles. Snide comments."

"I'll bet."

"I have got to say, Justice, that's what I envy most about your job.
Lifelong tenure. It's like diplomatic immunity." Mahoney panned
his gaze back and forth across the room, as if he needed time to
take in its splendor. "I cannot believe the laid-back atmosphere of
your chambers here. This kind of ease is not possible in Dirksen.
I've got interruptions from here to tomorrow—staff lawyers, advis-

ers, interns. Fucking constituents phoning me every ten minutes to voice their petty complaints about cuts to some neighborhood pig roast. And you would not believe the non-stop train of lobbyists." Mahoney chuckled. "Solitude, *real* solitude, here in Washington? I don't think there's a room in this city matching yours."

"Lionel, what have you heard about *Al-Tounsi?*"

Mahoney displayed his victorious smile, full of white teeth. "You know that *Saghir* case down in D.C. Circuit? Seems last week the government called to testify the rear admiral in charge over at Subic Bay. Guy by the name of Ryan Bonairre."

"I know. I read his testimony."

"Yeah, well, so did this army lawyer named Michael Inge—a lieutenant colonel in the reserve, who served on one of Subic's Combatant Status Review Tribunals for two long years. Seems after reading Bonairre's bullshit testimony in *Saghir*, Colonel Inge got enraged by all the lies. He contacted one of the pro bonos representing *Al-Tounsi* over at Cardom Green and confessed his contrary opinion of the CSRTs. He said they assign detainees Enemy Combatant status like clockwork, indiscriminate, and they're total shams. Apparently this Inge guy complained about all this to Bonairre himself down at Subic, but, as you can imagine, the rear admiral disagreed with him rather vehemently on that point. So Colonel Inge made a sworn declaration against the CSRTs and Bonairre's testimony yesterday afternoon in Cardom Green's D.C. office."

"He'll get prosecuted."

"No chance." The senator smiled at Gideon's political naïvety.

"Absolutely he will. Defense Department memos stipulate all former CSRT members must stay one hundred percent confidential about every aspect of the procedure."

"That's just their horseshit scare tactic. They won't follow through. Can you imagine the publicity of a prosecution? Please. Besides, Colonel Inge is willing to take that risk. My contact at Cardom says their lawyers are presently dotting their I's and crossing their T's and getting ready to include Inge's damning declaration in an upcoming reply brief for this Court. They're going to push you guys to rehear *Al-Tounsi.*"

"When?"

"Probably end of the month."

Gideon couldn't help but laugh. He even slapped his thigh.

"I thought you'd like that." Senator Mahoney released a little sigh of satisfaction. He stood, stretched his back and mumbled something about sailing on the Chesapeake over the weekend, about how the weather was plain perfect this time of year—just plain perfect—and then started saying that Gideon and Victoria really needed to get themselves out to the eastern shore at least once that summer, that there would be a whole bushel of very trayf, Old Bay–spiced Maryland blue crabs steaming in Lionel's kitchen, waiting to have their shells malleted open and their meat and guts devoured by the esteemed Associate Justice and his delightful wife. Gideon agreed. Spiced crabs sounded great. He and Victoria would love to visit Lionel on the shore and sail the bay in his 22-footer.

Gideon accompanied the senator to the door. "Can't say I don't feed you the good gossip, can you, Gid?" With his elbow, Lionel mischievously nudged the Justice in the ribs.

Gideon shrugged, thinking yes, actually, it was great gossip, though he didn't want to admit it. His long friendship with the senior senator from Illinois, dating back to high school, too often felt like the relationship between a legal guardian and a young child. Lionel's rapacious ego was like a kid's; he always wanted more and more attention. Right now he wanted Gideon to say something along the lines of *I'd be screwed without you, Lionel.*

"Ah, come on, Justice!" Mahoney tried to pinch a bit of fat on Gideon's waist. "You're happier with me than that."

"Don't pinch me," warned Gideon.

Mahoney laughed, and let him go. "You haven't got any meat on your damn bones to pinch."

"And you've got too much."

The senator wrapped his arm around Gideon's shoulder, as only a childhood friend could. "Now admit I gave you some pretty good information. It's precious stuff. Admit I delivered!"

"It's a fine delivery, yes. Reminds me of the old Lane Tech game. Another one of your perfect passes."

Mahoney threw back his head and laughed. He released the Justice, patted him once on his shoulder. "Exactly! Lane Tech! I was pretty good back in the day, wasn't I? Not too bad a quarterback, all in all."

"You were all right."

"You know, we ought to get the old Nic Senn junior varsity team back together one of these days, don't you think? A little scrimmage? A little reunion?"

"Too many bad knees between us. Some of us are not so fit for running."

"Nah, we'd do great. I could still pull off a pass action, fall back, find you out on the deep post. *Bang*, drop the ball right on your fingertips. As long as you're steady and not weaving all over the goddamn field every which way. What do you say, Gid?"

"My football days are behind me."

"Too bad." Mahoney straightened his trousers, opened the door and slipped out of chambers.

"Great to see you, Lionel."

"You're welcome for the news!" Mahoney spoke over his shoulder, just loudly enough for Gideon's secretaries to hear. The Justice nodded and closed his door after him.

Gideon lingered before the framed and signed photograph of smiling Louis Brandeis positioned on the bookshelf next to his pictures of Victoria and the twins. He had been given that portrait by one of the famed Justice's grandchildren in an honorary degree ceremony at Brandeis University and had long ago placed it on a prominent shelf, so Brandeis could offer his encouraging winks and smiles whenever Gideon needed them. Justice Rosen studied Brandeis's thin and mousy—but happy and vibrant—face.

"Hot damn, Louis. I think *Al-Tounsi* is going to be the one."

Gideon drafted *Deniston* for the rest of that morning, albeit ineffectively. His words blurred together, his phrases were difficult to decipher, and when he focused long enough to string together sentences, his opinion's small-minded reasoning and painfully dry language embarrassed him. It was a clunky piece of work. Worse: uninspired. The Justice stared at his humming monitor and felt his will to write waning. His lean torso slouched in the high-backed chair. He couldn't even muster the strength to sit up straight. *Deniston* would never amount to more than a procedural footnote in civil law.

There was nothing he could do about it. It was impossible in this day and age to write a revolutionary opinion. The vast majority of cases that came before him were, like *Deniston*, obscure questions of law in need of clarification, mundane disputes on technical issues that had to be resolved by the trained monkeys on the federal appellate bench in order for the day-to-day functioning of U.S. governance to proceed without blockage. *Do the Florida Bar rules that prohibit direct mail solicitation of accident victims violate the free speech of personal injury attorneys? Are communications between a client and his or her lawyer protected under the attorney–client confidentiality doctrine, beyond the Fifth Amendment's protections against self-incrimination, even after the client's death?* How could he establish expansive new guidelines for individual rights or propose innovative readings of existing law when these were the actual day-to-day problems confronting a modern Supreme Court justice? There was no room in his day for the stirring stuff of *Brown v. Board of Education* or *Griswold v. Connecticut*.

There were only five or six cases a year that held even marginal significance for the larger story of what it meant to be an American in the 21st century, and then obstacles stood in the way of transforming those special cases into any kind of meaningful contribution. Wasn't he wise to reduce the scope of his rulings to their narrowest readings whenever possible? Didn't that mean he ought to opt out of big and bold decisions on procedural grounds most of the time—as he was doing here, in *Deniston*—and also diminish the implications of broader rulings on merits in other cases? Good jurisprudence meant curbing radical results. Moreover, he needed four other votes to win any case. He had to be reasonable to get those votes. He had to be prudent.

Hell, Gideon *wanted* to be prudent: it was an essential quality of being a great justice.

The bottom line, though, was that in all his years of prudence Gideon had authored a string of opinions just like *Deniston*: meticulous, technical, boring, and insignificant.

Justice Rosen locked his sinewy hands behind his chair, leaned back and stretched his shoulders. Metal sprinkler pipes twisted across the yellowing plaster of his ceiling, with institutional red glass bulb sprinkler heads protruding from it like snakes' tiny tongues. In truth, this quasi-sacred "chamber" of his was nothing more than a dressed up federal office. Desk, bookshelf, pictures. Dented metal filing cabinets, boxy telephones. A banal government building in Washington, D.C., decked out with fancy marble surfaces and brass features—lipstick on a pig. And Gideon Rosen wasn't anything, really, but an overintellectualized version of the government bureaucrat.

He switched off his computer and flicked on the electric kettle beside his printer. A cup of tea might help him. Too often hopelessness and despair followed Mahoney's visits, a product of their shared history and sadomasochistic adolescent relationship: all those JV football games, Saturday night outings with Lionel sweet-talking the convenience-store merchants of North Chicago into selling them six-packs, and their so-called double-dates, arranged by Lionel as contests of virility that Gideon could never win. Lionel used to enjoy setting up Gideon with the homelier friend of whichever striking cheerleader he was pursuing at the time. On the night Gideon kissed and fondled Cynthia Gamlich's breasts in the back row of Senn's darkened stadium bleachers—and believed himself the greatest teenage lover to ever have lived—Mr. Future Illinois Senator one-upped him yet again by screwing the incomparable Amy Alben with characteristic gusto down on the 50-yard line. Oh, life was just high school repeated ad nauseam, even if you made it to the upper echelons of the U.S. government. Gideon was so gangly and shy and Jewish-looking back then, while Mahoney looked like some sun-bronzed, Christian surfer god peeled off of a California billboard.

The Justice sipped his Earl Grey on the sofa. One person's
success should have nothing to do with another's failure, especially when the goal is creating good law, or adjudicating wisely.
Mahoney's many accomplishments as a lion of the Senate did not
mean that Gideon was rendered insignificant as a Supreme Court
justice.

Especially with *Al-Tounsi* rising. That case was a rare opportunity, a possible milestone in legal history, with the potential to
set precedent for all future law on presidential power and habeas
corpus. It was the kind of case he longed to write, and exactly the
one he had known would rise to the Court at the beginning of the
War on Terror, from the instant those airplanes struck the twin
towers, crumpling them to the ground. He had been patient as the
nation massively increased domestic and international security,
bolstered spying agencies, deployed troops to Afghanistan and
waged a dubious war against Iraq. He knew this endgame would
someday come even as *Bayat* and *Hajri* and the other preliminary
cases worked their way through federal courts. On that September day, when the Justice watched American identity fracturing
before his eyes, right there on TV, a couple hundred miles up I-95,
his prescient mind whirled, and although Gideon had been wise
enough to resist telling his friends and colleagues about his spot-
on prediction, he also had the good sense to declare to Victoria
at the dinner table that night that a case testing the constitutional
right to habeas corpus would someday be the primary battlefield
for the nation's upcoming, ideological war. So she could vouch for
him under oath if it came down to it. Or maybe she could just let
his prediction slip to a future biographer.

But even with the bombshell of Colonel Inge's declaration, that
beautiful case would only be his to write if everything played out
perfectly: Davidson switching his vote, the Court granting cert
next term, the liberal side winning, and then Gideon securing the
assignment to draft the majority opinion. And even if everything
fell into line, how would he marshal the facts and statutes and
constitutional language to expand the right of habeas corpus to

non-citizens? Was that even what he wanted to do? What did he actually want to say about *Al-Tounsi*, even if only in the dicta, that was so damn important?

Maybe the answers would be more apparent if he considered the larger trends of U.S. history rather than the minutiae of this particular case. He had given a speech last October at the University of Chicago Law School to an auditorium packed full of students, professors, lay people and journalists, with C-SPAN cameras in the back, which addressed those trends in relation to *Bayat* and *Hajri,* the two earlier Subic Bay habeas cases. Gideon returned to his computer, unearthed that speech from his files and searched its introductory section, which he had structured as a refresher course on habeas corpus—when and where the concept had originated, how it had been used throughout history, and what it meant today.

The writ of habeas corpus has been recognized as a basic human right for hundreds of years. It is utilized in rare instances when someone is jailed without clear prerequisites, and a judge wants to determine whether or not that person has been imprisoned rightfully or wrongfully. The writ orders the jailor to bring the living body of the prisoner before the bench—habeas corpus: "you shall have the body"—so the judge can ask him or her key questions. Are we sure this person deserves to undergo legal proceedings of any kind whatsoever? Are we certain this imprisonment isn't a wanton abuse of power by the executive? Issuing the writ doesn't often result in the prisoner's freedom; it merely guarantees that no gross injustice has slipped by unnoticed.

The right to habeas was so well ensconced in the western legal tradition by 1787, when the U.S. Constitution was written, that it was included in the main body of that text: Article I, Section 9, clause 2, known as the Suspension Clause: "The privilege of the Writ of Habeas Corpus shall not be infringed, unless when in Cases of Rebellion or Invasion the public Safety may require it." Whereas all our other personal rights, such as freedom of press, speech and religion, or the right to keep and bear arms, had to wait for the amended Bill of Rights to find their expression, this one did not. Habeas corpus was, and remains, the sole individual right enumerated in the main body of the Constitution.

The framers gave The Great Writ, as it is commonly called, this position of importance because the young nation had recently experienced a long and brutish revolutionary war. They understood that gross abuses of individual freedom were sometimes necessary in extreme war, but they also wanted to ensure that the right to habeas corpus would remain sacred. The Suspension Clause makes both of those declarations simultaneously. It draws a line in the sand between sacred time, when peace reigns, and profane time, when there is invasion, rebellion, or guerilla warfare—and suggests that different rules exist in those two situations. Marking that division was an essential act of the Constitution.

Yes, that was it: the Shaw administration was presently trying to clip the wings of the Suspension Clause, and that, ultimately, was an attempt at redrawing the boundary between war and peace. *We are living in a time of perpetual war*—that was what the Shaw administration had declared through its recent legislation and actions in Subic Bay. *Our War on Terror is a new kind of war. It might take us to Afghanistan and Iraq, where we wage conventional battles, but ultimately it is a war without a fixed army or nation as our enemy, and because of this, it can have no end or final victory. There will no longer be a firm line between war and peace. The profane rules that govern society in times of war will now be our new "normal"; peace, with all its sacredness, is now our exception.* Thus habeas corpus would no longer be an assumed right in the Constitution. The larger trend in U.S. history was clear. *Al-Tounsi* was poised to be the battle that either reinstated or redefined, once and for all, the line between war and peace.

Gideon placed his half-empty mug on a tile coaster. He was excited now, slightly caffeinated, sitting up straight, tapping his feet on his Persian rug. He felt alive and ready for battle. There was no use grinding out *Deniston* this morning. Better save that opinion for a clearer head, a lesser week. Securing the future of *Al-Tounsi* would be his real work today.

When Gideon's secretary announced Victoria's arrival at noon, for a second he was unsure who that was. Only when she repeated his wife's name did the Justice remember that Victoria had asked to visit him for lunch. As he tossed on his desk the printed and bound copy of *Hajri v. Garfield*, Victoria strode into his chambers, wearing her dark pant suit and pastel blue blouse, as if this were a professional meeting. Her shoulder-length silver hair was clipped back in a barrette, and she clutched a brown Whole Foods shopping bag. As she unpacked the take out containers on his coffee table, Gideon wondered when was the last time she had come to chambers. Over a decade, at least. Probably not since his first term.

"I won't stay more than twenty minutes." Victoria wasn't looking at him, but surely she knew him well enough to feel his surprise at her presence from across the room.

"It's fine, Vic. No problem."

She moved his books and papers onto the floor, and on the cleared coffee table laid out containers and folded napkins, straightened the plastic cutlery, opened their respective bottles of iced tea. He watched her lovingly, half-surprised that his fastidious wife with her strong sense of New England propriety hadn't stashed a tiny bouquet and vase in that bag along with the food.

"Shall we eat?"

Gideon joined her in the armchair across the couch. He flipped open his biodegradable salad container. It looked perfect, and he told her so. Beets, kale, artichoke hearts on a bed of greens.

"What are Max and Jacob up to today?" Gideon sliced a beet in half.

"Working, I think. They wolfed down breakfast before I left, and went right back up to their room. They were discussing their screenplay. We have two very diligent sons."

"With good work ethics, like their mother."

"Ha. More like their father."

Gideon unearthed a tree of raw broccoli and popped it in his mouth. The strangeness of Victoria's presence in his chambers magnified for him. She was sitting tight-lipped on his couch, parceling small bites onto her fork. The Supreme Court Building was far from her office in Arlington, making this lunch visit a real effort and inconvenience.

"What are you doing here, Vic?"

His wife gave him a measured glance. There was a question buried in that glance: *how frustrating is my visit?*

"I don't mean that as an accusation. I'm happy to see you here."

"It's just unprecedented, I guess." Victoria laid her fork beside her salad, never one to eat while speaking. "I wanted to talk to you without distraction, because I doubt you're going to like what I have to say."

Gideon put down his fork. Victoria's face had adopted a familiar cold austerity, impossible to read. She retreated into this stoicism whenever they fought or had any serious disagreement, shielding herself from the tumult of violent emotions, his or her own.

"I'm retiring," she said. "At the end of this year. I've given it lots of thought and my decision's final."

Gideon's cheeks slackened and his jaw hung, as it did on that hot afternoon on Oak Street Beach, years ago, when she told him she was carrying twins.

"You've told Angie?"

"Not yet."

So maybe it wasn't final. Nothing was final until she told her co-director. So maybe Victoria had come here because she wanted Gideon to convince her otherwise.

"You're rather young to retire."

"Not *that* young."

"You enjoy your work. I mean, I'm surprised."

"Finding something rewarding is not the same thing as enjoying it."

"But still. You're done? What about all those fraudulent and malfeasant doctors in the Commonwealth of Virginia who will now escape prosecution? Tragic, isn't it?"

She didn't laugh or smile. "There are plenty of good young prosecutors on the rise, and the bad doctors will get theirs, believe me."

A stunned, baffled grin pulled Gideon's face tight.

"I'm done. I have had a great career, and a positive effect on my small world. I see that—the difference in the medical establishment between now and when I started—but I'm ready for a new phase."

"But are you sure?"

"Yes, I'm sure. That's what I'm saying."

So much for his plan to convince her otherwise. Gideon slapped his palms on the armrests and feigned some pleasure. "That's wonderful news, then."

Victoria's trim fingernails picked at the cardboard fiber of her take-out container. "Although that's not really what I came here to say. The thing is, Gideon, I don't want to be stuck in Washington for ten months of the year. Rock Creek Park has only got so many pileated woodpeckers and great horned owls—I practically know them by name. I've got my bird log ready, and off the top of my head I can think of several hundred species scattered around the world I want to see before I die. That's without even trying. And I don't particularly desire flying off to Indonesia or South America by myself."

"Well, there's summer in a couple of weeks. And we can go anywhere we want this year, any of those places. We can go see the King penguins in the South Georgian Islands. I'm sure we can still arrange it."

"Gideon, in 36 years of marriage I haven't asked you for all that much. Not once have I expected you to put in fewer hours here or back on the circuit, or even asked you to come home for dinner when the boys were little. That was all part of our unspoken deal, I know. You work hard, and I have always admired it."

"So do you! You're no slouch!"

"I'm not talking about me. I'm talking about a shift. I look at Bernhard and Sarah and Elyse, and the others around here, and see what it would mean for us as a couple if you held onto this seat for another decade. There's no golden retirement for ancient justices and their families. When Bernhard finally does leave, he won't have time to travel or relax, he will just wither away. He's in his nineties, for Christ's sake. He's already too old for a meaningful retirement. I don't want us to be like that. I don't want us to kick around Washington until I'm hobbling on a cane or getting pushed down the sidewalk in a wheelchair, waiting for our time together." Victoria took a deep breath, and held it. Gideon tightened his chest against what was surely coming. "I want you to step down. I don't mean immediately. You don't have to write a letter to the President this afternoon or anything, but I would like you to start planning your exit strategy."

Gideon's cheeks heated. "You realize if we let Mark Shaw nominate my replacement it will be the end of responsible law in this country for, oh, I don't know, a generation at least, and probably longer?"

"Gideon, please. I mean, at your next opportunity. President Shaw will be out in 18 months, and—"

"You honestly think in this climate a Democrat will be—"

"I'm saying when you have the *chance*. All right? And yes, I do imagine that it will be sooner than you think. Two years, end of the 2008–09 term, I suspect there will be a Democratic president, and then I would like for you to go. Okay? You will have had 15 excellent years on the Court at that point, and—"

"Fifteen years is nothing. Fifteen years is just warming up."

"I want some time with you. I want a bit of your attention. You can write memoirs, or books and articles on law, all kinds of things, but just not this grueling schedule that keeps us in this boring city all year and you in these chambers all night. I didn't have any time with you at the beginning of our marriage or in the middle, and I don't want to miss the end."

Gideon crossed his arms tightly against his chest. His tongue felt huge in his mouth, sweat pooled under his arms and dripped down his sides, and he blinked uncontrollably. "Victoria." Her name came out like a moan.

"Can you promise me that you will at least think about it?"

The dark-green folds of his lemon-juice coated Romaine now looked to Gideon like unappetizing tree leaves.

"I don't ask this lightly."

He looked away. Victoria had never asked anything of him, had always accepted him as he was. She wasn't manipulating him. She had never pushed him to give her more attention, hadn't even confronted him directly about Ellen back in '85, or threatened him with divorce, or punished him in any meaningful way. There were those weeks of steely silence and monosyllabic exchanges after his confession, but that was all unavoidable, given how his stupid affair must have surprised and pained her. There had been nothing cruel or destructive about her behavior back then. In her cloistered ruminations, Victoria must have written the whole thing off as a common midlife crisis—and that's really what it had been. She had let the whole mess slide, and that had been unspeakably kind of her. And she was right about his workaholic tendencies: living his life in these chambers, and his previous offices, alone, all waking hours, never at home. She had never objected to his obsession. She had never demanded that he compromise.

"I don't think you owe me anything." Victoria, as usual, had somehow read his mind. "I'm just telling you what I want so there won't be any mystery about it."

"I understand."

Victoria nodded, and pressed her thin lips together. "I hope you don't think that's unfair."

"You have never been unfair."

"I don't want you to resent me."

"I don't resent you. I think you're right about everything. And I promise I will consider your request seriously. It's just—retirement would be a dramatic change for me."

"Of course." Color seeped back into Victoria's cheeks. She picked up her fork and dug into her salad. Gideon sat back, and regarded the Gerald Sargent Foster painting of yachts on the wall behind the sofa. *Racing*, while not quite a masterpiece, had been the perfect painting for his chambers since his first term, when he borrowed it indefinitely from the Smithsonian American Art Museum. Six severely pitched yachts ripped through a choppy sea, their sails twisted and taut, harnessing the prevailing winds in an attempt to eke out a small victory. The painting always reminded him of life on this Court. But if that race on the water was a metaphor for his career, how would it extend to his life in two years' time? Was he supposed to slacken his sails, straighten his hull, watch the others zip away into the horizon? Bob along the waves and go fishing, for fuck's sake? The curator at the Smithsonian, an obsequious bald man, twitched his ears with delight when he realized that this Sargent Foster painting was en route to decorating an associate justice's chambers in the Supreme Court Building—delighted and honored to be lending it to *him*. The magnitude of Gideon's new position had struck him just then, when confronted with that man's twitching ears—the scope of the opportunity he had been given, the chance to do important work, to make a difference in U.S. history.

Victoria put down her fork. "Another thing. I'd like you to come home for dinner tonight and sit at the table with the boys. They're only in town for a week, then back to California for God knows how long, and you have barely seen them. I know it's June, and the busy season around here, and you're swamped, but still. It's so fleeting. It would warm my heart if you could put aside your work for a night, so we can be all together, like other families. Do whatever the boys want. Do you think that's possible?"

"Of course it's possible. What time?"

"Six, six thirty."

"Absolutely, I'll be there." Gideon reached out and touched Victoria's knee.

After Victoria had packed away their take-out containers, wiped down the coffee table and left him alone, Gideon sprawled on the sofa with his shoes off and his feet raised on a pillow, sweating and queasy, his heart palpitating. His stomach felt distended, though he had hardly eaten his lunch. Two years left on the Court wasn't anywhere near enough. His accomplishments so far had been petty at best, marginal work reminiscent of forgotten justices like Bushrod Washington and Morrison Waite, not the giants like William Brennan and Louis Brandeis. God, how he wanted to be like them!

He hadn't felt envy this severely since the weak-kneed misery of his 24th year, sitting alone in the library of Harvard's Langdell Hall on that frigid afternoon, his pale face stinging as if slapped, his eyes pulling up from the large volume of *US Reports* resting on the oak table, opened to Brandeis's monumental concurrence in *Whitney v. California*. Out the window, ashen snow spiraled skyward in an updraft. His breath was short and his body tingled, as if he had just gotten zapped in the solar plexus with a taser. That dreadful day in his third year of law school, when Gideon realized the depth and breadth of Justice Brandeis's legal revolution—certainly the most important development of law in the 20th century—awakened him to just how much brilliance it would take, along with how many grueling years of effort, to make any significant contribution to American jurisprudence. A toxic and suicidal monologue looped through Gideon's brain in the weeks following his discovery, a rush of self-doubt, pathological comparisons of himself to his peers, terror at the prospect of graduating Harvard Law with anything less than *summa cum laude*. Possessing all the genius in the world would not necessarily translate into a single Brandeis-worthy achievement; it would only guarantee his career as a preening, stuffy, know-it-all lawyer, a fate that had no value, one that disgusted him, frankly. Gideon worked diligently for the rest of that term, reading everything Brandeis had written, both as a revolutionary lawyer and as a towering Supreme Court justice—briefs, law review articles, opinions and dissents, even the casual but mellifluent letters that Louis had scribbled to his brother Alfred back in Kentucky. Brandeis had bellowed his radical ideas into the wind like a Biblical prophet, a lone and unheard voice in a conservative, *laissez-faire* nation: the re-definition of free speech and the First Amendment to protect dissonant beliefs; the inauguration of sociological research in legal briefs via *Muller v. Oregon*; a new conception of privacy, or rather the right to be let alone, as protected by the Constitution, first outlined in his prescient article for the *Harvard Law Review* back in 1890. But all that detailed knowledge of Louis Brandeis's work only increased Gideon's despair. Whenever he concocted a potential new reading of some settled clause or statute, he was quickly able to trace the roots of his idea to a footnote or line of reasoning originating with Brandeis. He was plagued for months, all through that hellish Cambridge winter, stuck in that ratty old Salvation Army armchair in his drafty apartment smelling of burnt bacon, until his angst peaked on a single day in March, when his hand went numb, triggering a humiliating, false-alarm, myocardial infarction trip to the Cambridge emergency room: clutching his chest while dialing 911, his Gray Street neighbors teetering out their windows as he moaned in the stretcher, that ridiculous oxygen mask pressed against his face, the roaring ambulance, and of course the physician's condescending smile while reporting to him the results of his flawless EKG.

Gideon sat up, slipped on his shoes. He had come so far since law school, had achieved so much, and he still had at least two full terms on this Court. Two years was not long, no, not relative to the glacial pace of legal progress, but it was time enough to force the hearing of *Al-Tounsi,* and to transform that ruling into a majestic statement like *Whitney v. California* or *Olmstead v. United States.* One case, fortuitously timed and magnificently written, could be posited as the go-to precedent for an entire area of law. He needed a memorable crown if he was going to even consider ending his uninspired career.

Justice Davidson's ancient chambers had occupied the same trio of rooms on the first floor of the Supreme Court building since the mid-1970s, a short walk from Justice Rosen's along perpendicular corridors. Now Gideon stood before Lorraine, a secretary almost as old as Davidson himself, and asked if he might briefly bother the senior Justice to discuss an important matter. Lorraine stammered, unsure of how to respond. She fiddled with glasses that resembled a flattened butterfly, a pair she had worn for as long as Gideon could remember, probably from well before his arrival at the Court, and then picked up the phone and buzzed her boss. Davidson readily agreed to see Gideon, in spite of their unspoken code of meeting all together in conference or the Dining Room to avoid the appearance of factionalism. But that was to be expected of the old man. Bernhard was nice to everyone; he honored all entreaties that came before him. He hobbled over to the doorway to meet Gideon at the threshold. The Justices exchanged a few pleasantries before closing the door and moving to Davidson's seating area. No couch, here. Just a couple of plush chairs and a coffee table facing the fireplace.

Gideon hadn't visited Bernhard's chambers since their friendly meet-and-greet during Justice Rosen's first term on the Court. A photograph of Bernhard's wife and their three middle-aged kids hung beside an honorary doctorate from the University of Pittsburgh. On the counter behind Bernhard's desk, there was a signed football sealed away in a plexiglas case and, next to it, a photograph of a much younger Bernhard Davidson posing with a large, grinning man in a pinstriped suit. Gideon pointed to it.

"Why do I have the feeling that your football there has been touched by more than just one Pittsburgh Steeler?"

Bernhard, who was fiddling with his loose bowtie, laughed and nodded. "I'm proud to say that it was one of the three used in Superbowl Thirteen. In Miami, Florida, January 1979."

"Won, I take it, by the Steelers?"

"Would I have it here if they had lost? Of course they won! 35 to 31, over the Dallas Cowboys. Sheer bliss, I tell ya. I was at the game. Even got to meet the whole team the day before they played. Hence that picture of me and MVP Terry Bradshaw, you see, up there. They promised me one of the game balls if they won, and signed it even, all of them—Coach Noll and Bradshaw, Franco Harris and Lynn Swann, Lambert and Joe Greene and—"

"Oh Lord, Bernhard, please tell me you're not going to name the entire roster of the 1979 Pittsburgh Steelers."

Davidson laughed. "Well, you see, those were the days when people actually knew my name." The old jurist fixed his watery eyes on nothing in particular, the long-gone apex of his fame. "I had just recently been appointed to the Court. New kid on the block, cat's pajamas, and all that. Dan Rooney, the Steelers' owner, son of the great Art Rooney, reading in the papers of my affection for the hometown team, offered me prime seats. And then the network showed me on TV during the game. VIP treatment, it was. And I gotta tell you, Gideon, I've met my fair share of presidents and senators and royalty since then, but there are few human beings on earth who can still set my ancient heart jumping like Mr. Terry Bradshaw."

It was hard not to like Bernhard. Gideon had never heard him utter a rude or self-important comment, and the long paper trail of Davidson's storied career, which Gideon had read almost in its entirety, was filled with empathetic rulings and an overwhelming sympathy for victims—even, in one memorable obiter dictum from a minor criminal case, to the opponents of his beloved Steelers. Although his prose style had never graduated past the flatly pragmatic, his jurisprudence sparkled with passion and creativity. Davidson had given countless supportive speeches to unions, civil rights groups and lawyers on the cusp of radicalism, and his legendary tales about his colorful father, Gary, a Pennsylvania steelworker and union organizer, which he lovingly recounted at lunches in the private Dining Room, always made Gideon smile.

"But I suspect you're not here to talk about the rise and fall and subsequent resurrection of my Steelers. What's going on?"

Gideon offered his colleague a brief rundown of what he had learned that morning from Senator Mahoney: the existence of the Michael Inge declaration and the soon-to-be-filed petitioners' reply brief asking the Court to reconsider its denial of *Al-Tounsi*.

As he spoke, Gideon recalled a decisive sentence that Davidson had written in his opinion on the Court's denial of that case: *The exhaustion of available remedies must occur as a precondition for the Court to accept jurisdiction, but of course that does not require the exhaustion of inadequate remedies.* Gideon finished his little speech by repeating those words, putting special emphasis on *inadequate*. Davidson listened with a scowl, his fist pressed against his soft chin and jowls.

"Well, that's not good news."

"Of course, we'll have to read the Inge declaration before deciding anything, but I thought it might change your opinion on cert."

"It certainly does take the wind out of my sails." Davidson rubbed a hand through what was left of his thin, gray hair.

"So I'm thinking we can probably raise another vote in conference by the end of the month. And we should change our minds, in my opinion. Grant this thing an argument for next term."

"You know we haven't changed our opinion on a cert denial in over sixty years, Gideon. The Court just doesn't do that."

"I know we don't. But we haven't gotten hit with a declaration like this in sixty years either. I'm thrilled."

"Oh, you shouldn't be thrilled." Bernhard frowned and again fiddled with his bowtie. "The last thing either of us should want is to hear *Al-Tounsi*."

Gideon regarded his old colleague carefully as he shook his head and stared at the rusted grate inside the fireplace. "What do you know that I don't?"

Bernhard sighed. "I don't like playing games, Gideon. All this horse trading and gossip behind the others' backs—but yes, there are some occasions when the smart thing to do is poke around a bit and see if you can't suss out which way the chips will fall if it comes down to a vote. So here it is. My little secret, as it were. One of my clerks confessed a few months ago that she talked to one of Katsakis's about *Al-Tounsi*. Talos, apparently, has gotten very worked up about the Military Commissions Act and its severe limitations on constitutional habeas."

"Wait a second—Talos didn't think the case ripe six weeks ago, but once we grant it cert, he'll go with us. I mean, that's guaranteed. He joined us on *Hajri*."

"I'm not talking about ripeness, Gideon. Talos held his nose and went with us on *Hajri* because my jurisdictional loophole let him off the hook on the big questions. That's the only reason.

There was no rebuking Congress there. He didn't have to tell them that they had blatantly disobeyed the Constitution when they passed the Detainee Treatment Act. But this is different. Even granting this thing cert, with the MCA explicitly denying us that right, why, that would be a huge slap both to the President *and* Congress, which Talos does not want to do. It would make them all look very, very bad. And I tell you, he doesn't want it."

"The man has principles on habeas. He joined us on *Bayat*."

"*Bayat* was nothing compared to this. You know that. *Bayat* was ultimately a jurisdictional case that avoided all the big issues. It was statutory bullshit, excuse my Russian. I mean, come on, Gideon, this is the Constitution we're now messing with. You think Talos is willing to say that both Congress and the President flouted one of the most basic provisions of the Constitution when they passed the MCA, and that they're basically just a bunch of vicious crooks elected by a bloodthirsty mob? Talos Katsakis? A man who would throw all precedent under the bus if it could only—please God—make his saintly, rose-colored United States of America look better? You really think that?"

"Yes, if he believes it, which I think he does."

"Well, you're wrong, then. He won't do it. It's too severe and damaging. And I don't think he believes the Constitution extends that far, either."

"Come on, Bernhard. His *Hajri* concurrence? All that high principle and sweeping rhetoric? Talos acting like some goddamn Superman?"

"I don't want to debate this, Gideon. He won't go with us. His clerk made that very clear to mine. We wouldn't have his vote if we heard *Al-Tounsi*."

Gideon rolled his head back and groaned. "Well, so what, then? We don't have Santa Claus's vote either, doesn't mean we shouldn't grant this thing cert."

Bernhard laughed. "Gideon, please, *think*. Who do we have? The usual suspects: Kolmann, Van Cleve, you and me. Do the math. The MCA's strict on its prohibition of habeas—we're talking about an absolute for the Subic detainees; there's no more fancy footwork for me to do here, no more loopholes or minutiae to exploit. Katsakis was our only swing on this. So there you have it. If we hear this case, Gideon, we lose it. It's not *Bayat* and it's not *Hajri*. There are no more hedges to hide behind. We don't have the votes. And if we lose this case, God forbid, there will be a very nasty precedent on the books prohibiting habeas for enemy combatants in Subic Bay or anywhere else, clear as day. I mean, Killian would probably end up writing that opinion, and who knows how it would be abused by subsequent executives. It would be *very* hard to overturn. No, I promise you, the best thing we can do here is try our best to put off making any decision about this contentious thing until we have got a more favorable Court. Believe me, it pains me to deny cert when I think of those men stuck in Subic Bay—some of whom, I'm sure, shouldn't be there. I know they would be freed in due course if they could just get their proper habeas. But I really do think it's better in the long run, better for *justice*, if we can just sit back and show a little patience here. We'll have another chance at this, and pretty soon, I think. But not with this case. Not now. We need patience, Gideon."

So there it was. Davidson's logic was cynical as hell and unseemly—justices, after all, were not supposed to consider politics in their decisions; they were supposed to interpret active legal disputes in a neutral fashion—but it was pragmatic and realistic, the product of a rational mind with a long and nuanced view on history. At least it was comforting to know that Davidson's resistance hadn't stemmed from the abandonment of his heroic progressivism. Moreover, come to think of it, the senior Justice was right. They *would* lose the case if they heard it. Almost certainly. But goddamn it, Gideon thought, as he sat back in his chair and nibbled on the outside of his finger with the same intensity that his poodle chewed on pigs' ears, it wasn't his responsibility to cast other justices' votes, only his own. If the right side didn't win *Al-Tounsi*, he could still write a scathing dissent that would be championed by legal scholars and human rights watchers all over the world.

"Look, Bernhard, you can't take responsibility for Talos or Killian or anyone else on this Court. Only yourself and your vote. And neither can you take responsibility for a country of idiots electing a fool like Mark Shaw president. *Al-Tounsi*'s the crucial question of whether the Constitution protects habeas for these detained people, and it begs our ruling. Now, we might end up offering a dissent instead of an opinion, but we still have the responsibility to say something on this issue. You know that's right."

Davidson nodded, but looked rather sad at the prospect of adopting Justice Rosen's idealism. He smiled faintly at Gideon, grabbed his cane and scooted forward, as if he were about to stand. He was certainly indicating that he didn't want to talk about this forever, that he was uncomfortable with it, and only wanted to make one final point.

"You're right in theory. But this is the real world. If I were you, Gideon, I would be looking right now for a way to minimize the importance of that Colonel's declaration, not maximizing it. I don't know what's going to happen here, and I suppose your revelation of this Colonel Inge thing might damn well make it impossible for me to vote against cert a second time—I mean, it might not leave me any good pretense that I can twist my logic around—but I have got to tell you, I'm going to be pulling out every trick in the book to look for a way *out*, not a way *in*. I remain convinced. We'll lose *Al-Tounsi* if we hear it, and that would be very bad news indeed for the United States."

When Gideon and Victoria Rosen moved to Washington, they bought their small brick house on Porter Street in Cleveland Park mostly because of its proximity to Maret, the school they had chosen for their twins, but also because the house itself was situated atop a small, wooded hill rising to the north, which meant it offered surprising privacy near the bustle of Connecticut Avenue. The neighborhood was leafy and green and lush in that mid-Atlantic way, vines on the trees and semi-tropical flowers in bloom. In the height of the humid summers, crickets stridulated all afternoon, fattened by copious greenery and strengthened by the strong sun, a daily reminder that Washington's roots dipped well beneath the Mason-Dixon line. The Rosens' kitchen and breakfast room featured a big glass-paned door that opened out into a back yard of two tall pin oaks on their side of the fence and an enormous poplar on the Quebec Street property behind them. The Justice loved his home.

Now, at six o'clock on a mid-June evening, not even close to twilight, Gideon occupied his favorite seat at the breakfast table, tapping his fingers, studying the giant poplar on his neighbor's property. Trees that large didn't grow in the Chicago area; every day he was astounded by its magnificence. Open take-out containers were spread across the table, food he had purchased from Banjara, the Indian restaurant near the Cleveland Park Metro station, on his brisk walk home. Victoria was fetching glasses and water from the kitchen.

"Max! Jacob!" She moved to the stairs, pitcher and glasses in hand. "Dinner." The floorboards above them creaked with the boys' movements. Victoria returned to the table and sat across from Gideon, tucking a lock of hair behind her ear, and registering his impatience. "Thanks for doing this."

He forced a smile for his wife.

Goldie, their aging poodle, stood from her bed on her creaky knees and wagged her tail to greet Max and Jacob as they skipped down the stairs in mid-conversation. Gideon's sons were two good looking, sandy-haired, half-Jewish boys, Jacob noticeably buff from the gym, Max gangly and tall. Although both were grown men now, they were unshaven and disheveled like college kids, wearing sweatpants and threadbare T-shirts. Gideon recognized Max's shirt. He used to wear it frequently during his high school days. It featured a black-line portrait of a bearded man with bushy eyebrow and bedraggled hair, a blazing heart fixed to the center of his chest and a shimmering corona emanating behind him, as if his head blocked the sun in a perfect eclipse. One of his loosely outstretched arms invoked Jesus's serenity, but the other rested on a Mitchell BFC 65mm film camera. His placid, almond-shaped eyes gazed heavenward in full acceptance of his suffering. Beneath the drawing, block letters inquired: *What Would Kubrick Do?* The joke had appealed to Max when he was an irreverent, 16-year-old would-be auteur, but now that he was in the process of realizing his dream, having just graduated with an MFA from USC's School of Cinematic Arts, he must have relegated it to sleepwear for these visits to his childhood home. They pulled up chairs on either side of the table, facing each other.

"What are you two talking about?" Victoria handed Max the water.

"Tornados," said Jacob. "And whether or not one of them tearing through town at precisely the moment when act two transitions into act three is too ex machina for our screenplay."

"Ah."

"I say *yes*, Max says *no*."

"'Cause we're hamming it up and playing with style." Max handed the water pitcher to his brother. "It'll all work with a bit of self-consciousness."

"Max, as usual, gives too much credence to self-consciousness."

"No, I don't. It's Coen brothers territory."

Victoria scooped a small helping of palak paneer onto her plate and glanced back and forth at her boys, amused. Max and Jacob gobbled down equal-sized portions of butter chicken and aloo gobi—twins with the same taste in food, as much else— while Victoria picked at her creamed spinach. With a mound of vindaloo on his plate, Gideon took a bite, and thought about the image on his son's T-shirt.

Max had worshipped Stanley Kubrick as a teenager, and probably continued to do so. While in high school, the boy regularly heaped glowing praise on the camera angles used in *2001* or *The Shining,* or expressed his grave disappointment with *Eyes Wide Shut.* All Kubrick, all the time. He used to speak with an ironic coolness, like so many in his generation, which Gideon had found baffling and infantile. But the more subtle manifestations of Max's Kubrick mania, including the way his son had walked back and forth across the kitchen while pontificating about his idol, had always reminded Gideon of his father, Seymour Rosen. Max even looked like Seymour, with his skinny body, bobbing gait and early balding. It was eerie to watch Max in action, like his father reincarnated.

Max happily spooned Indian food onto his plate, and then shoveled it into his mouth. Such ease and lightness, after a full day writing a screenplay with his brother up in their old bedroom, a couple of overgrown kids, seemingly in full confidence of their creative abilities, their future successes. Gideon's throat tightened. His sons were pursuing careers in cinema. They had translated that sensation of awe—sitting in a darkened movie theatre as a child—into their professional choices. God, the thrill of the movies! When Gideon was ten years old, he used to bike with Abigail on hot Saturday afternoons down to those packed art deco theatres like the Music Box and the Portage for a matinee of a western, film noir or gritty war story. What could beat that? The rapture of a thousand excited kids surrounding him in plush seats, entire north Chicago neighborhoods, all of whom, like Gideon, had happily spent their full week's allowances on the price of a ticket, a bag of popcorn and a small sack of gumdrops. And that burning, gnawing desire to be Gary Cooper in *High Noon*, to embody Sheriff Will Kane in a town of cowards, forced out of his pacifism by a gang of cold-blooded murderers. And Gideon's concomitant desire to have Gary Cooper's off-screen status, so that all the kids in Lake View, Uptown and Albany Park would point at him awestruck as he strolled by their stoops—Gideon Rosen, movie star. All the neighborhood kids would identify with his on- and off-screen exploits; they would envy his life and his talents. How many hours had he passed alone in his backyard with various tree-branch firearms, or running through West Ridge's streets, acting out scenes from his favorite movies? Of course, he had long ago made the more mature choice to enter law. But now here were his twins, refusing to abandon their youthful dreams. Their boldness and confidence seemed to dig deeper, and to stretch well beyond what he had ever experienced. Gideon, feeling old, slumped at the dinner table and swallowed hard as his sons ate.

Max glanced up from his plate, fork in hand, and caught his father studying him. "What?" He widened his eyes like a teenager busted for sneaking home too late.

"Did you know I wanted to be an actor when I was young?"

"Oh, brother." Victoria groaned as she reached across the table for the pitcher of water. The boys chuckled.

"Now, don't worry, I'm not going to start regaling you with my war stories."

"An actor?" Max looked genuinely surprised.

"Absolutely. I wanted to be in the movies and on stage. I was very serious about it."

"Actors have awful lives. And you're not exactly slumming it these days, Dad. I can say with confidence you made the right choice." Jacob was posturing an authority that he must have acquired along with his cinematic skills at USC.

"Well, thanks for your approval."

"I'm just saying."

"I could've been decent. I showed early talent. In eleventh grade, I was in my high school production of *Awake and Sing!*, and then in my senior year *School for Scandal*. I was Sir Benjamin Backbite. Apparently, I was pretty good. That's what I was told."

Victoria and the boys studied him skeptically.

"I kid you not."

"Who told you that? Your *mommy*?"

"Actually, *yes*, my mother, your grandmother." Gideon remembered Estelle Rosen sitting in the center of the third row of each performance, how she had cooed and beamed and praised him to the moon backstage afterwards. "She, among others."

And he *could* have succeeded as an actor. He had inched along that path; he was well on his way. He was not a wooden wannabe with an inflated sense of his own gifts. He had had the skills to succeed but had chosen another endeavor. Max must have sensed a darkening shift in his father's mood, because he grinned and raised his palms to signal capitulation.

"Don't look so angry, Dad. I'm sure you had talent."

"I think he wants us to give him a part."

Victoria and Max laughed.

"I'm not angry. I just thought you might want to know that little fact about your father." Gideon took another bite of his chicken vindaloo.

"We're not giving you any preferential treatment, Dad. If you want to get cast in one of our movies, study your sides, get in line, and audition with the others."

After they had finished dinner and washed the dishes, they gathered in the living room to watch a film the twins had recommended. "I love this movie," pronounced Jacob, as he slipped the DVD into their old machine, turned off the lights and retreated to the armchair. Max, Gideon and Victoria settled on the adjacent couch. Gideon tapped his feet on the fluffy rug while the opening credits ran. He was much too antsy to enjoy a movie, with the precedents and logical twists of *Deniston v. Globalsmart* churning in his mind, along with short dissents on other cases, and a new pile of cert petitions that needed review, and a mountain of related habeas opinions to read for *Al-Tounsi*. But the boys had been talking a lot about this one, and he had promised Victoria he would do what they wanted like "a normal family."

The Lives of Others followed a prominent playwright in East Germany and the Stasi officer assigned to spy on him. Right from the start, Gideon found the story absorbing. The boys, who were sometimes prone to showing off their cinematic knowledge, limited their running commentary to a few choice insights, keen and wise. As he watched and listened to them, Gideon warmed with admiration for his sons. They were right to like this film, right to recommend it to him, and correct in their analysis of how it worked. Max and Jacob were going to be successful filmmakers. Maybe they would turn out like the Coen brothers, just as they planned. Gideon shifted on the couch. Perhaps in 50 years a couple of loyal teenage fans would be sitting around some computer or hologram—or whatever they would use to watch movies in the future—to watch the Rosen brothers' masterpiece films, and one would turn to the other and say: *Did you know that their father was on the U.S. Supreme Court?* The other would look back incredulously and say: *No, really, you're kidding!* And then the first would nod and grin and insist: *Really, I'm serious—the guy was some obscure justice in the early 21st century.*

Gideon stood abruptly. "Excuse me, guys. I'll be right back." He escaped into the bathroom, shut the door and splashed water on his face. He hoped his distress wasn't too obvious. He stood at the sink, refusing to look at himself in the mirror.

This jealousy and narcissism, this sense of doom and failure, the comically and utterly clichéd Jewish self-loathing—how could he succumb to it? All this anxiety about his relevance might as well have come from his father's brain. Dr. Seymour Rosen had a wiry body and a bald head, a big bent nose and a closet full of tweed jackets. He used to pace back and forth in their tiny kitchen in West Ridge, practically carving a rut into the linoleum. He would come home at night after working long hours in the uptown office, treating fevers and polio limps and broken noses from neighborhood stick-ball games, or on Saturday afternoons volunteering to treat the "less fortunate negroes" at his down-town clinic. He must have seen quasi-third-world problems down there. He would deposit himself in his favorite armchair, pick up a novel or an issue of *The Paris Review*, or listen to a classical record, or an opera on the radio—always that same avid and nervous engagement with art. *A nonentity.* Surely that's what Sey-mour thought about himself every night of his life. He passed his evenings in silent terror. Gideon had always been able to read the doubt and dread on his father's face. He was a man who worried about whether or not he was capable of understanding "impor-tant" and "worthwhile" artistic creations, or if he would be able to recognize which contemporary artists might someday sit at the canonical table beside Rembrandt, Shakespeare and Mozart. He worried that he had somehow missed the boat, or that he had been too stupid to see which boat was the right one to catch. It didn't matter to him in the slightest that he was a beloved West Ridge GP, or that he commanded respect everywhere he went. Gideon had once walked with his father down the street when he was five years old, and to this day he still remembered the hats doffed at the corner store, the polite questions about Seymour's health, asked by friendly passersby. None of that deference mattered to his father. None of that respect touched him. Nothing was more powerful than his own insecurity, fright and envy. And was Seymour's past neurosis really any different from Gideon's own, right now? The tinny tone and jumpy inflection of Seymour's voice rang in Gideon's head: *That Jascha Heifetz is a wonder, Estelle, one of the all-time greatest, and we'll be lucky to see him do Tchaikovsky next week.* Or: *Don't forget, Faulkner's a revolutionary, our century's Shakespeare, our country's Shakespeare, and I love him, just love him—I'm so engrossed in this book I can barely eat, Estelle, I can't get enough of it!* That was from the summer they rented the beachfront cottage on Lake Michigan, a handsome shingled place, when Gideon was ten. Gideon was jogging through the screened porch past his anguished father, en route to lunch with his mother and sister, when he stopped in shock at the sight of Seymour's sweaty, concentrated face. His father spent the entire two weeks of that vacation hunkered down in the wicker chair, hunched over *Absalom, Absalom*, probably trying to figure out what the hell that book *meant*, while Abigail and Gideon built their sand castles and swam and rolled down the dunes.

But Seymour was right to be so insecure. He *was* a second-rate mind who didn't understand anything. Gideon's mother once told him a story, which had occurred back in the summer of '42, when Gideon was just a baby, and the Chicago Symphony Orchestra had performed Shostakovich's Seventh Symphony for the first time. It was a brand new piece, and Seymour had struggled with his decision about whether or not they should go to hear it. The problem, it seemed, was that there was strong disagreement in the critical community about the symphony's worth. On one hand, the weeping Russian masses and the pro-war American propaganda machine loved it, and said it was the greatest thing since Beethoven, but on the other hand, Rachmaninoff and Virgil Thomson said that serious and discerning ears had no business listening to it, as it was nothing but crass melodrama. A week before the premiere, Seymour still didn't know whom to side with. He paced the house and barked about the undercooked potatoes or the dishes in the sink, and covered his ears whenever Gideon cried. Seymour spent the entire day before the premiere in his bedroom with a hot water bottle on his stomach and the lights turned off, mumbling about how he was a fool and a philistine, how he knew nothing at all about taste or culture or art. Gideon had latched onto that story as the definitive portrait of his father. Seymour was incapable of assessing anything for himself. He used to quote Cleanth Brooks's *Well Wrought Urn* word for word. All of his opinions were derived from his cultural masters, really no different from Gideon with his precious Brandeis this, Brandeis that. So did that mean Gideon was a second-rate mind, just like his father?

Enough. He left the bathroom, returned to his family. He sat on the couch and turned his attention to the film's narrative thrall. The Stasi officer was eavesdropping on the playwright, who was playing a piano sonata.

"Donnersmarck's use of music is as deft as Kubrick's."

Max was scanning the screen with reverence, his bare feet resting on the cushions and his skinny knees pressed against his hagiographic T-shirt. What a comment! Gideon filled with empathic sadness. Did his dear boy feel the same crippling self-doubt that Seymour had once felt, that was plaguing Gideon so terribly right now? Was this a shared suffering, a genetic curse? Was pathological insecurity the real link between Seymour and Max and him? When Max watched how Stanley Kubrick wielded his camera in *Strangelove*, or listened to the thrilling score of *The Shining*, was he primarily seeing and hearing his own inability to create work on that high level?

Soon the credits were rolling. Jacob popped out of his arm-chair, flipped on the lights and stopped the disc. Victoria and Max stretched their backs, their four arms rising parallel above their heads. "Now *that* is a great movie," Jacob declared, glancing back at his somber father, as if taunting and challenging him to disagree. He held up the disc for observation. "And I don't care what anybody else says about it."

Late that night, the storm surging outside sounded like a symphony, played by an orchestra of tall trees' swishing branches, and wind whistling through close-set houses, and windows drummed by fat raindrops. Victoria slept serenely, but under the high rumbling thunder and flashes of lightning Gideon lay awake, constrained by his tucked-in sheet.

There was a suicide in Subic Bay two days earlier. A Saudi prisoner of six years, who had never been allowed to meet with a lawyer or contest his imprisonment, hung himself in his cell. The military had tried to suppress the news, but Amnesty International had gotten wind of it and now it was all over the news. Tonight CNN had been flush with the would-be presidential candidates from both parties outdoing each other with their plans either to close Subic Bay and transfer the prisoners into the United States for civilian trial or to keep it open, and possibly even expand it. Everyone had a definitive opinion. Gideon had watched the news with the volume turned up, although Victoria scowled beside him in bed, trying to read. More attention, still, for his precious case. Now he couldn't turn off his mind.

With *Al-Tounsi* reviving, he considered the prospects of the case realistically. He was a fool if he believed that it would be different from any other status quo suit. If he got to write its majority opinion, his argument wouldn't break any new ground. Any so-called "radical" liberal position would merely call for the maintenance of rulings already codified. It would support precedent and reinforce the existing bright line between war and peace. He could only argue for stasis. What was the point of fighting like crazy to hear *Al-Tounsi* as if his identity rested on it?

No, the only potential for revolution in *Al-Tounsi* was the conservative one: the hawkish redefinition of war and peace. That was the painful fact of his miserable era. Justices who reimagined conservatism for a contemporary context were the only ones with any claim on innovation. Killian Quinn was the architect of that new jurisprudence, the primary justice from the Eberly Court with a legitimate claim on the history books. It was a maddening fact—because although Killian's techniques were clever, his mind sharp and his prose sharper still, his values were retrograde. Why did those principles have to be so cutting-edge? It wasn't fair. Gideon groaned, and it came out louder than expected.

Victoria woke up abruptly. In a fog, she focused on her husband. "What happened?"

"It's nothing. I just groaned. You can go back to sleep."

Victoria lowered her head. Soon her ribcage rose and fell with each long breath.

Gideon stared at the ceiling and imagined talking to Justice Brandeis. *Tell me, then, Louis, what would you do if you were me?*

Brandeis's imaginary advice, so easy for Gideon to conjure, streamed without pause: *Concentrate on what you do best, on what is most needed. Not on futile cases like* Al-Tounsi *that you imagine will be significant. Remember you are the Court's undisputed expert on administrative law, author of that foundational text elucidating "separation of powers" questions in Title 5 U.S.C. 500 et seq. Why not focus on that? Essential administrative cases rise to the Court each and every year, so pour your attention into them, jockey for their opinions whenever you can, instill them with as much creativity and imagination as you can muster.*

I know Administrative law is important, countered Gideon, *but nobody actually cares about it. I want to expand personal rights— constitutionally mandated health care, housing, gay marriage.*

It's overstated, the glamour of our storied individual rights, continued the imaginary voice of Brandeis. *The smooth functioning of our enormous federal apparatus in challenging times is a far more serious problem than—*

"You should really try to get some sleep. I can tell you're not trying."

Victoria's back was turned to him, her mass of thick gray hair splayed across her pillow. She lay motionless, but obviously not asleep. Gideon sighed. He listened to the rain outside, which had lessened into a gentle patter.

He closed his eyes, and there, unbidden, was Ellen, 30 years earlier, when she was a paralegal in Chicago. Her cherubic faced was framed by her teased blond hair, her pale skin powdered with copious blush. Her eyebrows were plucked and penciled into arches, and she had magazine-model teeth, a testament to modern orthodontics. Ellen Granger. Her most appealing feature had been her complete faith in his genius. The night their affair ended Ellen had bought a bit of pot from her younger sister Kay, and she asked Gideon if he wanted to smoke it when he dropped by her apartment, morose and irritable, collapsing into her dilapidated couch. He had been working late at the office on yet another trivial case that he knew would never blaze any new legal ground or accomplish any progressive reforms, and wasn't even all that interesting in purely intellectual terms. *What the hell am I doing on this old cat-hair covered sofa?* Gideon wondered. *Why aren't I lying in bed with Victoria?* He mumbled something about the drugs being a juvenile idea, that he was a 40-year-old man and not a kid, for God sakes, but then for reasons still mysterious to him, he smoked that pot with Ellen—his first and only foray into illegal substances.

Gideon smiled at the memory of what happened once the drug took effect. He was overwhelmed by the past, which suddenly seemed to influence every gesture made and word uttered. The past was all around him, inside him, everywhere, and what a weird state of hyper-consciousness that was. When he muttered some half-phrase to Ellen, nothing more than a brief dismissal of the case he had been working, he heard a huge personal drama inside those words: his childhood vanity, his longing for greatness. He heard his blind acceptance of his mother's proclamation of his genius, the roots of his own arrogance and superiority. Behind another throw-away phrase, Gideon heard himself echoing his father's futile search for meaning through the arts, and then he realized that his grandfa-

ther Moshe must have passed down that desperation and insecurity
to Gideon's father from his own awful childhood of pogroms and
squalor back in Galicia—all that baggage and more in a single
stupid comment! And then, worse still, when Ellen complimented
him on the shape of his haircut, he heard in his lover's calculatedly
playful tone her Iowa-born mother—or rather Gideon's fantasy of
Ellen's mother—a woman who must have mitigated her oppressive husband's foul moods on the farm by complimenting the little
autocrat incessantly on his hair, on his strength lifting bales of hay,
and on his intelligence and dexterity in fixing the tractor. And then,
worst of all, he suddenly understood that Ellen's frequent compli-
ments to him about his intelligence, wisdom and looks were really
nothing more than her aping of her own mother's survival reflex.
All of Ellen's praise for him was a mask for her own insecurity, a
means of guaranteeing that Gideon would find her tolerable and
attractive, and that he would want to keep her around. Her compli-
ments had nothing to do with his actual talents. She didn't think
he was a genius, or rather, she didn't care one way or another. It
was only that she understood him (rightly!) as a proud and vain
man, and that he really liked it a lot when she called him a genius.
He had been duped by his own petty, selfish needs, and by Ellen's.

Gideon's drugged vision made the room spin around a radius
at the center of his nose. His disembodied voice jabbered on, but
he knew, quite suddenly, that he was trying too hard, that he had
always tried too hard, and that he had to stop. He was 40 years
old, and it was time to stop. He apologized to Ellen, took a long
walk home by the shore of Lake Michigan, and in the morning
confessed his affair to Victoria.

What then? The years that followed their marital crisis had
been the most productive of his life. He stopped comparing himself
incessantly, stopped lamenting that Brandeis's important insights
had already been institutionalized and championed by the Warren
Court of the '50s and '60s, stripping Gideon of his opportunity to
be a liberal hero, and he refocused his attention on the present, a
recalculation that cleared away his emotional debris and improved
the quality of his work. Without losing hours in fruitless anxiety,

Gideon stopped laboring on cases and articles, and his associations grew more lucid and precise. His logic distilled into wise and solid arcs, his prose shimmered, his results were undeniably good. He allowed himself to take a year and a half off from his legal practice to write his comprehensive analysis of Administrative Law—how it had functioned in the past, how it could be improved in the future—and the result was that "classic" work, published by a prestigious academic press, still hailed as the single best text on the subject to date. His return to the firm after the book's publication had been equally blessed, as he led a few major cases to successful argument before the Supreme Court. And then, to his astonishment, not long after his return, Gideon was nominated to an empty seat on the Seventh Circuit Court of Appeals in Chicago—and by a staunchly Republican president, no less. All of that success, all of it, was because he had relaxed his insane anxiety and abandoned those paralyzing comparisons with Louis Brandeis. How ironic, how predictable: only by letting go of his striving for status had he been able to achieve something in his life.

And it was in those years that Gideon realized just how lucky he was, how fortuitous and wise, to be married to Victoria Chilton. She never pandered to his vanity like Ellen had—indeed, he had only started that affair because of his weakness and insecurity, his infantile need to feel special. Once Gideon realized it, and denied himself the cheap reward of Ellen's praise, he could all the more appreciate Victoria's refusal to indulge him, her strength in erecting emotional boundaries. She never had any patience for his whining about how today's personal rights cases were only the natural extension of rights already enumerated by others. She absolutely refused to treat him like anything but an adult, and silently insisted that he treat himself like one as well. Oh, how he loved Victoria after his affair! How he still loved her. She kept him above the abyss of his own despair.

A high flash of lightning illuminated his bedroom, and then thunder rumbled distantly. Gideon shifted to his side, reached out and ran his fingers through his wife's smooth, once flaxen hair, still so beautiful, but now the color of polished silver.

"Victoria." She didn't stir.

He let his fingers fall to the pillow. He was indebted to her wisdom in ways he was still discovering. She had never asked him for anything. Except this once. How could he ever forgive himself for the cruelty and selfishness of what he was about to do? Because he knew he wasn't going to leave the bench. He couldn't do that for anything in the world. Not for the happiness of his children, or of his beloved wife. He didn't want to go. He wanted to stay on in his job for another 20 years, 30 if he was lucky enough to live that long. He wanted to die on the fucking bench like Chief Justice Harlan Stone, one of the blood vessels popping in his brain as he read aloud from a dissenting opinion—*Girouard v. United States*, if Gideon remembered correctly. Who the hell wants to retire before he's a vegetable? He would only leave the Court when the doctors declared him brain-dead in his robes, when he had to be wheeled out of chambers in a stretcher, down the marbled corridors lined with weeping colleagues and clerks, past officers of the Court with their hats doffed like the residents of West Ridge for his father, and visitors too stunned and shocked to click their little cameras. He would stay on until the bitter end, fighting with Killian, Charles and Joanna, attempting to win over Talos in a tenuous coalition, struggling with cases, impartial to the achievements of any other justice past or present, having the time of his life, trying to get that one masterful opinion written before he was buried once and for all. Nothing else would satisfy him. Nothing else seemed right. The key ideological war of his generation was raging around him, and Gideon Rosen had been called into service for that epic fight.

3

ORIGINAL SIN

THE SUPREME COURT did the right thing Monday morning by ruling
that an archaic anti-sodomy law from Arkansas was unconstitutional. Although Justice Quinn read a fiery dissent from the bench,
he did not have the votes to prevent the 20-year precedent, which
he had written himself, from being overruled in the landmark 6–3
decision. We think it only fair that Killian Quinn, the Court's most
conservative Catholic, will no longer be the arbiter of what gay and
lesbian people are allowed to do in the privacy of their own homes.
The Supreme Court has finally extended a measure of justice and
civil rights to millions of gay Americans.

Thus sayeth *The New York Times*—or rather the cabal of silver-
spoon-fed editors at the helm of that smug rag, those French-
cuffed, high-heeled, tortoise-rimmed elites who obviously had no
real knowledge of why the Constitution was enacted, or what its
proper function should be in the United States of America. Killian
tossed the insulting newspaper onto his desk and squeezed his
Federalist Society Conference mug with both beefy hands. How
could any big-city, East Coast newspaper feel so comfortable telling the rest of the country *definitively* what justice is and how
it should be served? On what authority did the editors speak?
They certainly didn't have the law credentials. It was astound-
ing—no, breathtaking—to witness the bloated sense of entitle-

ment of that navel-gazing paper. Their offensive pronouncements had set Killian's heart racing, and if only somebody were sitting with him in chambers right now, he would regale them with an extended rant.

Steady, old boy. Tantrums were bad for his health. Killian pinched his nose at its thin bridge, and then drew his thumb and fingertip down to its enlarged tip, a rounded soccer ball of flesh with nostrils. Fat *gaosán* of a ruddy Irish boy. The flesh beneath Killian's eyes pulsed with his rage. Impossible to cork his inner volcano once it got rumbling. He ran his fingers through the tufts of straw-colored hair sprouting behind his temples, all that remained of his once thick and curly mop.

Coyote, a foul-mouthed devil in a red satin cape that Killian drew out of the air in these moments of high stress, hovered over his left shoulder. "Folger," he muttered, through his tobacco-stained teeth, referring to the famous Shakespeare Library on East Capital Street, around the corner from the Supreme Court Building. "You can sit your fat self down in Katherine's armchair and beg her to climb on top." Killian conjured an image of Katherine Kirsch, the Folger library's impish curator of manuscripts— her boyish build, pixie-cut blond hair and icy-blue irises.

"Gloria, Gloria, Gloria," countered the winged angel McGovern, frowning severely over Killian's opposite shoulder, wearing a peace medallion, comb-over and long sideburns. Killian had named this demonic and celestial duo back in the 1970s, when he realized that a conflicted soul would be his life-long predicament, and he decided to embrace and personalize the dual forces of his conscience. Coyote was named in honor of that indestructible and wily antagonist of the Roadrunner cartoons that his kids liked to watch on Saturday mornings. McGovern was and remained the perfect moniker for his angel, because the poor bleeding heart always lost the final vote.

Gloria wasn't a reference to *Gloria in Excelsis Deo*, the primary doxology of the Roman Catholic Mass, although that too would have been an effective appeal to Killian's conscience. No, McGovern was intoning the name of his beloved wife, Gloria

Quinn (née Scarlatti), former high school sweetheart, mother of their six children, and a woman the Justice loved passionately, despite his five-plus decades of adultery and mortal sin.

"She is your soulmate, and you should picture her as she was the evening you met, chaste and pure, standing awkwardly beneath the streamers and balloons at your interschool dance in Mount Saint Joseph Academy's gymnasium. Place her now in your mind's eye. I know you can do that. Do you want to deceive that innocent woman, Killian? Do you want to abuse her trust?"

"Oh, the wife'll be around when you get home," countered Coyote, long-snouted, irascible, and pinching a smoldering cigarette between his lips. "In the meantime, you've got to battle through your exasperating day." He gave the Justice's thick neck a prick with his cartoon pitchfork.

"*Gloria.*" McGovern flapped his white wings and clung pathetically to his harp.

"We're talking here about an unparalleled piece of ass!"

Killian laughed at the banter of his dueling angel and devil, who had once again pulled him from fulmination into joy. He had originally discovered his stock characters while reading Christopher Marlowe's *Doctor Faustus* in an undergraduate Elizabethan drama class at Boston College, back in the spring of 1962, but refined them in his modern, low-brow terms decades later, when lounging in the modest living room of a young woman he had just met and seduced, trying to ignore his guilty conscience by flipping through channels on her cable TV, and alighting on the famed toga party scene in *Animal House*. Larry, a freshman recruit played by Tom Hulce, invited an intoxicated underage girl up to his room, who promptly passed out on his bed without her shirt on, leaving him holding two handfuls of the tissue she had used to stuff her bra. When he regarded the drunken girl and the tissues and considered his options, the angel and devil of his conscience appeared on either side of the screen, whispering their contrary pieces of advice. "Fuck her," rasped the devil, dressed in a cheesy satin cape and holding a pitchfork. "Fuck her brains out. Suck her tits, squeeze her buns. You know she wants it." Killian had laughed out loud, his big belly shaking. All that was good and noble in him disagreed with that devil's advice—a nasty and crude suggestion, to fuck the drunken girl's brains out, a direct challenge to the sacred teachings of his Catholic boyhood, to the morals and values he so treasured—but he also recognized in it his own impulses dramatized. "Bingo," Killian told the television, pointing at it with the remote control. "That's me to a T."

McGovern and Coyote dissipated. Killian put his feet up, crossed his ankles on his desk and tilted his head back to gaze at the stag elk mounted on the wall behind him. A splendid creature, shot on vacation in northwestern Alberta with Clayton Garfield, the present Secretary of Defense, in the dark days of the previous Democratic administration, when Garfield worked as a consultant for an oil company and made a seven-figure salary. Lucky bastard. The elk's huge antlers sheltered his chair as if they were the branches of a rainforest canopy or the wings of a guardian angel. If only life could offer such protection.

He sighed and caught his breath, and then his anger surged again, the adrenaline dilating his veins and whipping his heart into action. How could he have been pushed into the meaningless minority on a crucial case yet again? But there was more to his exasperation than the personal insult of some stupid editorial on *Geitz v. Arkansas* in *The New York Times*. It was also that doggone petitioners' reply brief filed for *Al-Tounsi v. Shaw*, or rather the shocking, sworn declaration attached to that brief by a certain Colonel Michael Inge of the U.S. Navy. Killian had just reread it in the backseat of a Lincoln Town Car on his way into work that morning, half-tempted to roll down his window on the 14th Street Bridge and toss the thing into the Potomac. He didn't doubt Colonel Inge's credentials or even his frank assessment of the CSRT procedures' flaws, but he was astonished that a so-called "patriot" would dream of ratting out his superior officer in public on a matter of such importance to national security. Where was this man's military integrity? Where was the respect? Furthermore, Justice Quinn simply could not understand how the Shaw administration had supplied Colonel Inge with such potent

fuel. How could they have acted so irresponsibly in their regula-
tion of those crucial CSRT procedures? Why did the Department
of Defense not do a better job monitoring fairness? Didn't they
realize the whole world was watching?

And what about the gall of those elite law firms and constitutional rights centers behind the reply brief? Did they really think
they would be able to reverse a denial of cert at the Supreme
Court for the first time in 60 years? And what about the arrogance of Colonel Inge's superior, some jerk of a rear admiral
named Ryan Bonairre? Good Lord, were there any people left
on this planet willing to embrace their responsibilities and limitations, and ready to take the blame for their mistakes? It was
impossible, outright *impossible*, to keep the United States on the
right track in these difficult times when idiots and fools mishan-
dled the reins of power, no matter how noble their ideologies or
principles might be.

The justices were going to reconsider *Al-Tounsi*'s certiorari
in conference that afternoon. In the worst-case scenario, Gideon
would grin in victory, self-satisfied. Justice Rosen, God love him,
was a good man and decent jurist (in his own misguided way),
but never a modest winner. He would laugh and boast; he would
positively gloat; and most important, he would use the Inge declaration to flip Davidson and Katsakis. Oh, yes, Katsakis would
flip—and he was the key vote in this whole thing. They would
grant that case cert, and although Killian might hoot and holler
and make himself sick, there wasn't much that he could do to
defend denial in the face of such explosive new evidence.

His neck veins pulsed. It was bad for his blood pressure to
think about it. There was a clear and correct road for the country
to follow—the guiding lines so freshly painted they glowed in the
dark—and yet the various drunks at the wheels of the judicial,
executive and legislative branches swerved across that right path
like Gramma Quinn's Fiat in her final years, veering toward poles
and trees and perilous cliffs, reducing the helpless U.S. citizens
packed in the back into a heap of sweaty fools. And Killian, who
understood his limited role as a federal judge, was not authorized

to take the wheel from them. He was stuck in the passenger seat, offering futile directions.

There was a party being thrown for departing clerks in the West Conference Room. Most years a comparable event was scheduled for Wednesday happy hour, a long-standing tradition, but for some unknown reason, this year the final party had been switched. Bagels would be served. Tuna salad, coffee, cream cheese. A gathering of young and brilliant lawyers, full of vim and vigor, roughly half of whom would be female. And there would be no discussion whatsoever about homosexual sodomy legislation or reply brief declarations from treasonous colonels in the United States Navy. Killian pulled himself out of his seat and slipped on his jacket. He left chambers and hobbled his large self into the hall, huffing from the effort.

Killian's chambers were located on the southwest corner of the Supreme Court Building's first floor, meaning the Justice had to waddle past the lawyer's lounge and across the marbled Great Hall, decorated with busts of past Chief Justices, to reach the clerks' party. His sciatica fired hot flares down the nerves in his legs, so he walked the shortest possible route. The problem with that plan was that passing through the Great Hall was risky, as it was open to the public. An eager follower of the Court might recognize and detain him with blunt questions about originalism, or with numbskull thoughts on foreign policy, or with pictures of some cocker spaniel named Killian.

The Great Hall was full. Early summer tourists carried point-and-shoot cameras and thick guidebooks. They wore shorts and T-shirts, tank tops, spaghetti-strap sundresses. As feared, a middle-aged man in a polo shirt recognized Justice Quinn when he entered, even though Killian barreled through the hall with his head lowered. The man called Quinn's name. A couple of intrepid tourists angled themselves against the wall to photograph the passing Justice, while others stepped back to gawk openly. Killian absorbed their collective awe with his peripheral vision, sensing the electricity that he had inadvertently injected into the room. It was insane how he was treated more like a famous actor or pop star than a boring federal judge. Although it was sometimes fun to be this revered and reviled, to be considered worthy, it also got old. What was notoriety worth if he couldn't achieve decent legal results for the country? If he was rendered futile by eight other justices? When Killian reentered the restricted zone on the north side of the building, he heard a tourist whispering behind him, "Which one was that?" and another breathlessly responding "Justice Quinn! Justice Quinn!" as if his name were Mick Jagger. At least his fellow Americans now considered his brand of respectful textual analysis important. And maybe there was more to their fandom, Killian thought, as he approached the West Conference Room. He was a colorful and frank personality, and he wrote in pithy phrases.

The oak-paneled West Conference Room was full of clerks and justices. Killian closed the door behind him and made his way over to the buffet table, covered with a white tablecloth. He chose a poppy-seed bagel to spread thickly with cream cheese. Above him loomed the famed, mustachioed former U.S. President and Chief Justice William Taft in a large standing portrait, his right hand tucked into his robe, as if he were hungry and his belly was rumbling. Now, there was a fat man. Good gracious, if Killian wasn't more careful with his food, he would soon reach the splendid rotundity of old Bill Taft, and end up in an early grave. He layered the cream cheese with tomatoes, onions and capers, took a large bite, and nudged the tomato back on his bagel with his pinky. He turned to survey the group. He knew the names and faces of the 36 departing clerks, but a lot of good that would do him, as they would all begin leaving their posts at the end of this week. A new batch of clerks would begin filtering into the Court for their year-long terms on Monday, and right away start reviewing cert petitions and writing memos over the justices' summer holiday. When he returned to the Court in September, Killian would have to learn new names, like he did every year.

Three of Killian's four departing clerks surrounded him, including Isaac Marx, a Canadian from Montreal with a kind, round face, number one in his Harvard Law class, and perhaps Killian's best employee in his 20 years on the Court. Isaac was an Orthodox Jew, never seen without his kippah, even while sprinting down the basketball court on the top floor of the Court building. Isaac had breezed through his work all year, unchallenged by the most complicated questions, as if he had been clerking for decades. A genius, that one. To Isaac's right stood the pale and gaunt Alexa Ruff, number two in her class at Cornell, a dark-eyed and red-haired rail of a woman, fierce and acerbic, the wittiest of Quinn's clerks that term. Next to Alexa stood Martin Croll, second in his class at Yale, bespectacled and meticulously groomed, archly conservative, and frankly a bit of a dud. Martin had a photographic memory, which must have served him well in law school, and also for certain tasks at the Court, but offered little in the way of creativity. Martin would easily slip into the ranks of some corporate law firm, Killian had long ago decided, destined for big bucks but not much legal innovation. The other two, though, could go somewhere big. This trio of young lawyers gathered around him at the buffet.

"Honestly, Justice Quinn, it's going to be difficult stomaching a normal job after this," said Alexa Ruff. "I'm going to fall asleep at my desk in the Justice Department, the work'll be so boring."

"This has been an opportunity of a lifetime," added Isaac Marx. "I'm so thankful."

"Me too." Martin Croll was wearing a golden silk tie with such a big knot that it might as well have been an ascot.

Killian smiled and thanked his clerks. It was wonderful to have such devoted employees, but their praise was really nothing more than an embarrassment and a distraction, an unnecessary ego-stroking that at worst would make him lessen his vigilance, and even at best would do nothing to help establish his jurisprudence. Quinn shook their hands and separated. He ambled over to Justice Sykes, who was standing stiff and still, with a bemused smile on his face, by the end of the buffet table. Rodney greeted Killian with a slight nod, but didn't say anything. His hands were pulled behind his back, as if he were a waiter charged with the responsibility of guarding the food rather than an esteemed Supreme Court justice celebrating the departure of his clerks.

"Howdy, Rodney, I see you've come out to party."

"Indeed. I have put on my party hat."

"Figuratively speaking."

"It should go without saying, Killian, I am not a big wearer of hats."

"Or a big eater. No bagels for ya this morning?"

"I ate before I arrived."

Something about Rodney wasn't right. The man seemed off, comically tired, big bags under his eyes, worry lines etched in his forehead and across his cheeks. Although Rodney Sykes had always impressed Killian with his pseudo-European mannerisms—his half-nod greetings with a tilted head, his gentle fingers on your back when he let you pass through the door, and those interlocked hands pulled behind him—gestures that could have been dismissible as insecure pretentions but somehow read as genuine, today Killian detected the Herculean effort behind Rodney's rigid posture. The brittle fragility beneath his composure was broadcast in his face.

"What's up, Rodney? Gotta say, you don't look yourself."

Justice Sykes fired an angry glare at him, the first time that Killian could remember striking a nerve in the stoic man.

"I assure you, Killian, I am myself through and through, despite any appearances to the contrary."

"Oh, I don't doubt it." Killian took another bite of his bagel. A blob of cream cheese fell off, skimming the Justice's lapel and landing on the hardwood floor with a splat. Killian ignored it. "Frankly, Rodney," he added, his mouth packed full of semi-masticated food, "looks to me like you made the mistake of sticking your head in the washing machine for a cycle or two, and that you haven't been sleeping either."

That joke, at least, made Rodney smile. "No need to restrain your honest opinion, Justice Quinn."

Killian gulped down the oversized bolus in his mouth. "I'm worried about you, that's all. You don't look well. What's going on with you?" He wiped the splotch on his jacket with a napkin, which only seemed to embed the cheese deeper into the fabric.

On the far side of the room, Justice Bryce was talking to a striking young woman in a brocade suit—a real beauty with a mane of thick black hair, smooth olive skin, and perfect legs. The whole package. Killian scanned her up and down, every inch of that fine body. What was an outsider, gorgeous as she might be, doing at a private clerks' function?

"The end of this term has been difficult." Rodney was answering a query that Killian had now all but forgotten. Justice Sykes stared at the rug, looking uncomfortable exposing even this modicum of personal information. "Perhaps I'm overworked. Something of that sort. I'm not certain. Whatever's the matter, I'm eager for the break."

"Well, I'm glad you're going to get one." Killian watched the brocaded woman's naked heel rise from the back of her two-inch pump and descend again into its awaiting cradle, which Killian now wished was his own sweaty palm. "What you need is a beach. Florida or Rehoboth. Or your own native California. Although the water's too cold out there."

Rodney shrugged. "I'm not certain what I need."

It was sad, Rodney's tone, somber and strange and uncharacteristic. He sounded like a crushed man. Maybe that's what happened to everyone in this job eventually; they got worn down and defeated by the futility of writing useless opinions, years of being ignored by the other eight, and by the endless onslaught of mentally taxing work. It was depressing to think about. So maybe he should stop contemplating Rodney Sykes's odd mood, and his own miserable failings, and instead think about that black-haired beauty across the room shifting her weight from side to side on the balls of her feet, and tossing the hump of her taut ass back and forth like a very firm and well-played volleyball. Killian pointed at her.

"That woman over there, talking with Joanna. She wasn't a clerk this term, was she?"

Rodney roused and looked at her. "Oh, no."

"What's she doing here? She's not supposed to be here."

"I believe she's one of Joanna's for next term. As I recall, she's a good friend to a clerk from this year, and so she was invited to the party with Justice Bryce's consent."

"Right." Killian suppressed a sigh. He did not need a whole year with that beauty working in the Supreme Court. Killian had always maintained absolute respect for the firm sexual boundaries separating the aging justices from clerks, secretaries, and other employees of the Court, and had prided himself on never crossing that line—no matter that he had privately lusted after Vita, Kolmann's clerk in 1994–1995, or Tatyana, Davidson's impossibly svelte, Russian-immigrant clerk in '99—but today Killian felt weak, like he couldn't overcome the challenge. He would have to remove himself from an embarrassing situation. He would have to escape from the room before he was caught ogling the new clerk.

Killian's ears tingled from the pulls and pricks of McGovern and Coyote. "Slip over to the Folger for an early lunch," whispered Coyote. An image of Katherine's small breasts and pink nipples flashed in his mind. "I bet you can still get back here with enough time to review cert memos before conference."

"Or you can choose to eat lunch alone in your chambers." McGovern wrapped a white sheet around Katherine's nakedness.

Killian popped the last piece of bagel into his mouth and clasped his colleague's shoulder. "Rodney, I do believe I'm all partied out. I'm like a drunken fraternity boy, four in the morning, pledge week."

Rodney chuckled and shook his head.

"Feeling hateful of the world. Feeling furious at the manifold stupidity and vanity of our species. Feeling judgmental and misanthropic."

"How unfortunate. Although not unprecedented for you."

"Puts me in the mood for *Timon of Athens*. So, Justice Sykes, if you'll please excuse me."

"Certainly." Rodney Sykes offered another slight bow, his tacit approval of Killian's Shakespeare habit. "I shall see you in conference."

The Folger Shakespeare Library—thank the Good Lord in Heaven—was a two-minute walk from the Supreme Court Building. Killian left the West Conference Room and marched out the back entrance on Second Street, his legs smoldering. He affirmed his plan in transit: to visit the Folger's Old Reading Room, request his favorite late 18th-century edition of Shakespeare, and sit with that sacred text, studying the hateful rantings of the abused Athenian Timon, until Katherine discovered him, pulled him into her office, unrolled the blinds, and fucked his brains out. *And how will you feel*, the Justice wondered, as he trotted across East Capital Street and up the library's short marble steps, his brow already dripping, *when you've added yet another mortal sin to your résumé? Another devilish act in defiance of a cardinal virtue, depriving you of God's sanctifying grace, killing and damning your soul to the fire and brimstone of hell?* If he did indeed transgress—and his pull toward sin was so gravitational now that he couldn't imagine avoiding it—then he would find salvation through confession, as he had done many times before, through Father Elko's prescribed penitence, those punishments suffered with gratitude and relief.

Killian slipped through the Folger's art-deco entrance, beneath the marble Mask of Comedy protruding above the glass door. The bigger complication with his plan was material rather than spiritual. His erectile dysfunction, which had bothered him for a decade running, had shifted in recent months from a sporadic problem into a chronic condition, meaning the great carnal sin might prove too difficult to complete. The prospect of failure only quickened his step. The base conditions fueling his desire—all of this stress and anger and rage—hadn't abated. He felt rendered futile by another lost case, another dissent against the majority, another scathing editorial in a liberal newspaper. His intelligence and insight were meaningless in this corrupt world. Heck, being *right* was meaningless. And if the satisfaction of release in some young woman's embrace couldn't be counted on, what would become of him?

Killian flashed his Folger Reader's card to the half-sleeping guard seated at the entrance and then walked the short hallway to the Old Reading Room. He passed through a glass door etched with an hexagonal pattern, like a honeycomb. The tiny green-carpeted Registrar's office was staffed, as always, by Eric, a young and ominous gatekeeper, who took his job of blocking entry to anyone without a Reader's card too seriously. Killian and Eric exchanged tight, closed-lipped smiles. What the hell did it matter if a fellow American without a card wanted to peek in at that beautiful room, so long as they promised not to disturb any of the concentrating scholars? Killian signed his name in the log.

The Reading Room was designed to mimic the great hall of a prosperous Elizabethan house with high-trussed roof, marble fire-place and two-tiered chandeliers lit by dozens of electric candles. The Head of Reference, Dr. Anne Frezel, a spry, elderly woman sporting a gray bob, glanced up from the journal she was reading at the circulation desk and greeted him with her typical formality: "Good Morning, Justice Quinn."

"Dr. Frezel," replied Killian, tersely. There was no good reason for this continuing reserve on Frezel's part; Killian had been com-ing to this same dang library for years, she knew him well, and they should have long since graduated into addressing each other by first names. But no, this eminent scholar on "Women in the Elizabethan Era," who was obviously a knee-jerk reactionary and left-leaning feminist, who fit the mold of a faithful reader of *The New York Times* and *Washington Post*, would never dream of letting down her guard in the company of a demon conservative like Killian Quinn. He was, after all, a crude bigot, a misogynist, an old-school paternalist, who had declared himself a vocal critic of the proposed Equal Rights Amendment back in the '70s and early '80s. How could a man like that ever be forgiven? Never mind that he believed gender rights were included in the Equal Protection Clause of the Fourteenth Amendment.

Killian plucked a white call slip from the neat stack on the circulation desk and scribbled the memorized call number for volume five of his favorite Shakespeare edition. He handed the slip to Dr. Frezel. Although his handwriting was disastrous and near illegible, the Head of Reference never had trouble interpreting his requests. Dr. Frazel nodded and disappeared into the rare book stacks behind the desk. Maybe her antipathy was more personal than political. She must have witnessed Katherine chatting playfully with him in the Reading Room on occasion, maybe even saw them disappearing into Katherine's office, closing the door and turning the blinds behind them. Maybe Dr. Frazel didn't want to see her colleague hurt by a married man.

Good God, if Dr. Frazel ever told a reporter about them, it would all be over, everything, his entire life's work. Killian's spine tingled at the thought. But she could never know for certain. Katherine certainly wouldn't tell.

A dozen or so scholars sat hunched around the oak tables, their desk lights focused on the rare books perched in foam support cradles to protect their fragile spines. None of these quiet PhD students or visiting scholars ever seemed to register Killian's presence. Katherine wasn't sitting with any of them. Killian hoped to spy his lover on one of the twin balconies that flanked the main body of the Reading Room, pulling a book from an ornate, carved shelf, but again he was disappointed.

Dr. Frezel returned with Killian's large book, which she handed over gingerly, both hands beneath it. He nodded thanks and lumbered across the room to his favorite seat, beneath a stained-glass window depicting the Seven Ages of Man as taken from Jaques's famous speech in *As You Like It*. He laid the volume in a foam support.

Killian rubbed his fingertips over the smooth cover of this beloved edition of Shakespeare's work, published at Oxford in 1770. He was fond of its decorative features—the spray motif and raised band along the book's spine; the silken green-and-white headband and smooth gilt edges; the gold-tooled image of Shakespeare leaning against a tower of books that was impressed into its crimson, calf-leather cover—but his main reason for choosing the Oxford edition instead of some other was historical rather than decorative: its date of publication. Nothing like sitting here in the Old Reading Room, turning these fragile pages, imagining that James Madison owned a copy of this same six-volume set in his own personal library. Madison himself, sitting at his desk in his Montpelier estate, fire roaring, candles lit, perusing these pages. It was impossible to conceive of anything like that happening when you were reading a paperback Shakespeare in private chambers or, worse still, a digital version on a computer screen or e-reader.

Killian opened the volume to the first play, *Timon of Athens*, and skimmed the archaic text, the S's printed like elongated F's. Although he loved the entire play, he was not in the mood for the first three acts of *Timon*, which detail the protagonist's generosity to his fellow Athenians and the meaty drama of his downfall: Timon's loss of fortune and subsequent discovery that his so-called friends are fickle and cruel. Instead he flipped to the last two acts, when Timon has retreated into the wilderness as a hermit and misanthrope, unwashed and feral, and berates anyone who visits him.

> *Who dares, who dares,*
> *In purity of manhood stand upright*
> *And say this man's a flatterer? If one be,*
> *So are they all, for every grise of fortune*
> *Is smooth'd by that below: the learned pate*
> *Ducks to the golden fool; all's obliquy.*
> *There's nothing level in our cursed natures*
> *But direct villainy.*

Oh yes, railing against humanity was the right stuff for today. Killian felt like standing on his chair and shouting "Amen!" across the mock-Elizabethan reading room. The vast majority of people in the world really were fools at best, villains at worst, and even the wisest amongst them would happily defer to an idiot if he might get rich in doing so. Justice Quinn's long experience with the law had exposed him to countless cases of greedy plaintiffs and negligent defendants, prodigal children and wicked parents, narcissists, egomaniacs, outright cutthroats. The world was packed full of evil human beings, billions and billions of them, driven by devilish instincts, fallen natures, original sin. Brother turned against brother, friend murdered friend, collaborator stole from collaborator, and together they lied to their investors. People were bad—pretty much without exception. The majesty of the law, especially American constitutional law, was rooted in its mechanism for balancing one group's dark tendencies with another's, equally foul. Competing interests stabilized like immobile rams, their horns locked in battle. They balanced in federalism or triangulated in checks and balances, countering one another to create a stable foundation. Let men be evil so long as the law muzzles their wickedness structurally. If Timon were alive today, he would of course concede the effectiveness of American institutions. Timon would accept the U.S. Constitution, at least how it worked in its root conception. He would understand the truth in Killian's jurisprudential claims, unlike certain unnamed editors of major East Coast newspapers or Ivy League law reviews. Now, if only the other justices on the Court would respect the text *as written* and stop projecting their ill-conceived personal desires onto the nation's foundational source of law.

A set of slender fingers slipped over the top of his weathered page, tiny, like a child's, with impeccably trim and clean nails that had no polish.

"*Timon of Athens*? Again?"

Killian smiled at Katherine. "A person can never have too much Timon."

"You must be in a bad mood."

"Less so with each and every line. Less still with you before me."

The openness of Katherine's expression, her sparkling wide-set eyes, the smoothness of her skin—it was all so striking. She bit a swatch of skin off her bottom lip, but Katherine's brightness shined on, obliterating the dark pits of Killian's anger and frustration. *My mistress's eyes are nothing like the sun*, he thought. *No way Shakespeare had a mistress that looked like Katherine Kirsch.*

"Come to my office." Katherine turned to go.

He kept himself from staring at her ass. He waited until she was gone, and then stood and heaved his book out of the foam support, cradling it with both arms as he approached the circulation desk. Dr. Frezel was studying him with an undisguised, sly squint, and Killian's throat caught. Of course, she had to know what was going on between him and Katherine. Dr. Frezel was too smart not to know.

He laid the heavy book on her desk, tapped his fingers on its leather cover, and offered the Head of Reference such a frank and wide grin that it could be nothing other than a taunt.

"I won't be needing this anymore today, Dr. Frezel." Killian's aggressive stare still dared the woman to speak. "Thank you very much."

Katherine awaited him downstairs, where the ceilings were neither high nor stately, and the decor invoked the 20th century institutional rather than pseudo-Elizabethan court. Fluorescent bulbs in a paneled ceiling, blue wall-to-wall polyester carpet that had nothing in common with the rugs of Shakespeare's era. It would have been nice had Katherine pulled the blinds on her office's interior window and waited for his arrival in the plush armchair, but no such luck; she was standing beside her desk. Killian sighed, closed the door, and took her hand. Katherine slipped it out of his greedy clasp, laughing.

"Not so fast, buster."

He collapsed in the armchair, which expelled a faint cloud of dust, crossed his legs and shrugged, as if to say: *All right, what? What do you want from me?*—the same gesture he offered his prospective clerks in their interviews. "Nice to see you, Katherine. Been a long time."

"Four months."

"Really?" The Justice pulled his brow to feign surprise. "That long?"

Katherine's smile was thin, but she didn't look hurt.

Killian shook his head at the mysterious workings of time. "I'm sorry. I lose track in the spring. End of term, you know. You look well, though."

Katherine showed only the slightest trace of a tremor in the contours of her round face. So calm and even-tempered, such cool composure, leaning against her desk with her arms crossed. She had a way of making him feel he wasn't in control of their relationship, even though he was setting all the terms and limits. She radiated dignity, which had to be the by-product of her wealthy and disciplined childhood in South Carolina, the daughter of a senior vice president at Sonoco, who, rumor had it, was a man of impeccable values and scratch golfing skills. Katherine had once told Killian, with mortification but detectable pride, that her family used finger bowls at their family meals.

"I can't say you look happy to see me."

"I'm quite happy to see you, Killian."

He pressed his fingertips against his lips, but immediately disliked the preposterous gesture, which seemed like something an English professor or psychoanalyst might do when trying to lord his superiority over students or patients. "I've missed you."

"Four months without a word is a funny way of showing it." Katherine unfurled her arms and sat on her desk.

The recessed fluorescent bulbs in Katherine's office were covered by frosted plastic paneling and those ubiquitous ceiling tiles, PVCs—whatever that actually stood for.

"Yoo-hoo, Killian, over here." Katherine waved.

"I'm sorry." Killian sighed. "It's not you. I'm just irritated by work."

"I can tell."

"No, worse than irritated—I'm enraged and infuriated. I'm surrounded by intelligent men and women—bright people who I respect and even like—but every day I'm confronted with greater evidence that most of these esteemed colleagues of mine simply do not understand the proper role of the judicial branch in our triangulated system of government. They don't get it, Katherine, what we're supposed to do and not do. They refuse to let the Constitution function as designed. And it's been like this for the full twenty years of my tenure, as you know, as I've said many times. I've had this argument with them ad infinitum, and the world at large, like some raving Jeremiah, so I wouldn't say I'm surprised by it, but still it's frustrating to have the one or two integral, majority decisions of my career undermined and overturned by judges who rely on such obviously flawed logic. It's depressing. Did you read that *New York Times* editorial?"

"You're really upset about losing."

"I wrote a brilliant precedent twenty years ago that my dear companions on the Court have just thrown into the garbage."

"Why is it that you only come to me when you're feeling bad?" Katherine picked a speck of dark lint off her linen slacks. "You might think about coming sometimes when you're feeling good."

Killian frowned and buried his chin in his fist.

"I'm an interesting person," she continued, with her preternatural calmness. "And fun. You might think about visiting because you *like* me, not just because you want to vent your problems and have sex."

"That's not fair. I'm crazy about you."

Katherine smiled—not quite immune to his affection—but suppressed it. "Look, Killian, you don't owe me anything. I'm not your wife and I'm no idiot. I'm just saying you used to come here in a good mood, and we had lots to talk about. *Lots.* Shakespeare. Marlowe and Middleton. All your complicated cases. Brazil. I'm the same interesting person I used to be."

"I know you're interesting, believe me—I don't have much patience for people who aren't interesting."

"My mind's a wealth of thoughts and references and obscure facts, all interesting to you. Worth its weight in gold."

Killian's jowls trembled. He tried to contort his face into a mask of somber contrition but for some inexplicable reason, he couldn't stop a mirthful chuckle from rising. He covered his mouth and laughed.

"What's funny?"

"I have no idea." Laughter, his favorite thing—where would he be without its clarifying properties? "You were doing that Brazilian dance thing, whatever the heck it's called."

"Capoeira, you jerk."

"Still doing it?"

"Every day except Sunday."

"Your bird is Brazilian, too, correct?"

"A sunburst conure. Alive and well."

"Harry?"

"Hugo."

"Whatever."

"His name is Hugo. Like your personal hero, Hugo Chavez."

"Cute. I was close. Two names that start with H."

"Is this really so hard, Killian? A few simple questions about my life?"

"It is very difficult, actually."

"Why's that? Because all you can think about is that absolute spanking you got in *Geitz v. Arkansas*?"

"Look, Katherine, I don't mean to be a pig. I like you immensely and I *have* missed you."

Katherine hopped off her desk and moved into her chair. "We don't have to talk about my boring old bird." She braced her feet against the side of the desk, pressing her thighs against her chest. "I don't mean that."

"It's just that I spend most of my time thinking about the law, you understand. I'm 18 hours a day thinking about cases, and I'm afraid that if you don't want to talk about them, there's really not much I can discuss at this juncture. Maybe next month, when the term's done and I've got a break, but now? Not so much."

"I want to talk about your case, actually. The gay sex one."

"See, that's just the thing that irritates me." Killian leaned forward in the armchair. "It's not a gay sex case. I mean it's not *about* gay sex. It's about the right of the majority in the state of Arkansas to make democratic laws based on their own moral judgments."

"Really? It's not about gay sex?"

"I never said *I* thought the law was morally correct. Just that it has the right to exist."

"But you *do* think it's morally correct."

"That's beside the point. The state has a right to legislate morality—that's what states have always done—and it's an act of supreme arrogance for an unelected justice to say they are not allowed to do it."

"I see." Katherine's sardonic smile spread. "Well, what about adulterers, then? What if the state declared adultery illegal, made you pay a fine and threw you in jail for visiting *me*?"

Killian recoiled and erupted in laughter, which shook his big belly. "Bravo! Let 'em! Look, from time to time there have been laws banning adultery in this country, and if one of those laws ever reached us on the Court I would say that it was a perfectly legal expression of the people's will, their moral will, and that if adulterers broke the law, well, then they would have to suffer the consequences just like any other lawbreaker."

"So when the police bust in here today and catch you in my arms?"

"Tough luck for me. I broke the law. I'd have to suffer the consequences like anybody else."

That was a good sign: Katherine suggesting that the police might bust in here today and catch him in her arms.

"I'm no hypocrite, Katherine. It's just lucky for me there's no statute on the books criminalizing infidelity in the District of Columbia."

"Doesn't it make any difference to you that gay people have suffered years of abuse?"

"Oh, please. You want a donation for the elite gay folks living their hard-knock lives in their prime, urban real estate?"

Now Katherine rolled back and chuckled, shaking her head in disbelief. "You mean the rich elitists like my brother Kyle, who was offered a full scholarship to University of South Carolina but instead decided to work two awful jobs in Seattle and live in a dump because the thought of passing one more day of his life in South Carolina, a state of thugs and bullies, made him want to kill himself? Who had to cross the country to Washington in order to survive?"

"I'm talking about a demographic, Katherine."

"My brother didn't tell my parents he was gay until he was twenty-four years old because he was terrified that his own mother and father—who he loves as much as you loved your parents, by the way—would never speak to him again. And he was right. They did almost disown him. That must be who you're talking about, because Kyle's got a miserable little one-bedroom apartment downtown in a liberal city." Katherine was positively gloating.

"This isn't about your brother's suffering, real as it may have been."

"But it *is* about his suffering. You talk about the moral will of the majority like it's an abstract thing, but who are the people suffering the wrath of that majority? When Kyle was in ninth grade he was tortured—I mean, Jacobean stuff, Killian, like scenes from the *Duchess of Malfi*."

"He was shown a severed hand and told his entire family was murdered?"

"I'm serious. There was a hall in Calhoun High on the first floor that everybody called the Gauntlet. Every day after lunch the jocks and metal heads and straight-up insecure wannabes, even the math and computer nerds, gathered and pressed themselves up against the lockers and stood there whistling and grinning and ribbing each other until the one group that they had all agreed to torture came by. The gay kids. Then everyone pounced. They shoved them back and forth across the hall like pinballs, punching them in the kidneys and jabbing their elbows into their ribs and generally abusing and terrifying them. The Gauntlet was the only way to get from the cafeteria to the math and science rooms, so kids like Kyle had no choice but to pass through it. The entire population of Calhoun High called him a *faggot* and beat him up—and the slightly less abused kids like the math nerds were the worst."

"Kids can be awful. Everybody knows that."

"It wasn't just the kids, Killian! The school administration gave the Gauntlet their tacit approval. Every now and then some teacher would drop by to scold these abusers, but with a really feeble command to *settle down, settle down*, and a big smile. I think the administration actually liked the Gauntlet. It was the only place in South Carolina other than the football field during a game where black and white students actually mingled with each other, let alone with the outcasts, so the school probably thought it was progressive. Nobody cared about gay kids like Kyle back then. Now you've got me wondering if that hallway wasn't just another version of your Arkansas case. Aren't you claiming that Calhoun students and staff had the unspoken right to pass a law endorsing the Gauntlet? That their sacred hallway expressed the moral will of the majority?"

"No. Your brother was assaulted and harassed in that hall, and there are laws against that kind of behavior, good ones on the books in every state, including South Carolina, and school codes, too, probably in every district, so your high school's administration was wrong, *criminally* wrong, not to enforce them. And you're also wrong to compare the abuse of your brother to an entirely democratic anti-sodomy law. It's like apples and oranges. Legislatures have the legal right to ban certain actions that they think icky, actions like gay sex—and no matter how you spin it, banning a sexual act is not the same as condoning abuse. Then the citizens governed by those legislatures have free choice as to whether they want to engage in those forbidden activities and accept the consequences—which weren't so terribly bad in that Arkansas case, I'll remind you, just a couple hundred bucks and a night in jail—or acquiesce to the moral will of the people."

"How is that not just another form of discrimination?"

"Oh, don't give me that civil rights malarkey!" cried Killian. "These are laws banning *activities*, Katherine, not states of *being*. A man doesn't have a choice if he's black or white or Jewish or Italian, and so the Constitution rightfully says you can't discriminate based on race or religion. Easy-peasy. But having gay sex isn't a state of *being*. It's an *action*. The law says you can't beat up a kid in a hall, and the law also says a man can't have sex with another man. That's the proper comparison, not the opposite. Gay sex is just one of many activities that have been prohibited by democratic will in Arkansas and other places without any real complaint from the populace. Robbery and murder are other examples."

"You don't understand what I'm saying."

"Anti-sodomy laws have been on the books since common law. Nowhere in the Constitution does it say that homosexual sex is a fundamental right, or even what we call a fundamental liberty interest, which would be protected by the Fourteenth Amendment, and would trigger strict scrutiny on a statute."

"You still don't get it." Katherine pulled her feet beneath her and sat cross-legged. "The sex act is so fundamental to peoples' existences they have no choice but to engage in it."

"There's nothing *innate* about engaging in an act. It's a choice."

"Homosexuality is innate. Everybody knows that. That's what I'm saying."

As Katherine scolded him, Killian stared at the wall behind her head, where she had mounted a poster from a recent conference on ancient manuscripts at the British Library. The poster featured a multicolored, medieval illumination of a pair of dainty English monarchs, the king in a flowing blue robe and the queen in a shimmering rose gown, sitting beside one another on tiny thrones and holding their delicate fingers in each other's slender hand. Both monarchs wore crowns and clutched matching scepters, angled outward, like tilting goalposts, which framed their seated figures. Before the royal pair knelt a man in a pied robe of bright red and blue, who was bequeathing the queen a large bound book held together with golden clasps and decorated with gilt edges and a thick leather cover. This trio was surrounded by the tapestry, flooring and frescos of a Tudor castle, which in turn was framed by turrets, columns and stone arches dating from that same period. The image had a narrative, obvious enough: it portrayed the gift of a book to the monarchs of the English nation, and somehow, through the angling of scepters, tapestries and turrets, the image declared that gift as the keystone to the entire empire. The manuscript was the featured element, particularly illuminated, like a beating red heart. It was as if that book pulsed life into the glorious institution surrounding it. *Katherine has got to respect the power of ancient text as much as I do*, thought Killian Quinn. *In her own way, she must.* A surge of love for the young woman sped his aging heart, and he released a weary sigh.

"I give people more credit than that," said Killian. "We can choose where and when we have sex, and with whom."

"Oh yeah?" Katherine leaned over her desk, her wry smile returning. "So what do you think of yourself, Mr. Morality, diddling the manuscript curator while your faithful wife waits for you at home?"

Killian allowed his shoulders to sink, his belly protruding upward and outward like a packed duffle bag resting on his lap. "I sit in severe judgment of myself, if you really must know. I made a choice, you're correct, and I'm quite ashamed of it. I think you're a delightful woman, Katherine, in style and substance, but I know if I were a better man, less sinful, and strong enough to live in accordance with the values I respect and know to be true with a capital T, I would have never gotten close to you in the first place." He shrugged. "There. Okay? I am a terrible sinner, but like I said, no hypocrite."

A quiet settled over her office. Killian stared into his plump fingers, clasped together in his lap.

"I should state what I believe more plainly." Katherine spoke somberly now. "I don't think being honest about your weakness changes my verdict. If you believe that something's wrong and you do it anyway, then you're a hypocrite, Killian. No matter how much I like you, or how much you claim you're not."

"Yes." He displayed a beatific grin. "You're more right than I am."

"Oh, God, don't give me that!" Katherine laughed, loudly, in her thin-walled office. "When I call you a hypocrite, you're supposed to *fight* me, you infuriating man."

Killian laughed along with her. "Oh believe me, I see the flaws in your logic and I could rip it to shreds. But I think you misunderstand me. It's not that I like fessing up to my failure. I hate it as much as anyone. But I hate it more when people don't take responsibility for their choices. There are ideas worth holding onto that are more important than blatant self-interest. Ideas like virtue and morality and the classical 'good.' Redemption comes only with embracing one's guilt. That is a stable law of the universe, and it applies to me as much as anyone else. A criminal might be able to get off legally on a *Miranda* rights exception, but that doesn't mean they *should*. The weasels who weasel out of their responsibilities are corrupting our world with trickery, and worse still, more intimately, they are denying their own poor souls any chance whatsoever for salvation. They damn themselves to hell, both figuratively and, I would argue, literally as well. A weasel cannot stop being a weasel until he admits far and wide that he is one, and then accepts the just punishments accorded to weasely weasel bastards."

"This is not a hypothetical conversation. *You* are the weasel in question."

"An unusually fat weasel."

"So let's not forget that."

"I have not forgotten it."

"Good." Katherine's fast fingers snatched a paper clip off her desk and whipped it at him. It bounced harmlessly off the cushion of Killian's belly. "How can you sit there waiting for me when you believe that?"

"Is that a real question?"

"It is, actually."

Killian sighed. "A little demon convinced me to do it. An imaginary devil who helps me enact my deeply felt psychomachia."

"*What?*"

"Psychomachia—the internal battle for one's soul."

"I know what psychomachia means, but I don't know what you're talking about."

"I'm trying in my stupid way to say I like you, Katherine. I admire and respect you greatly, and that makes me want to embrace you, and make love to you, and confess all sorts of things I have no business confessing."

Katherine's fingertips rapped in quick succession along the surface of her desk. She squinted at Justice Quinn. "Your legal response to sodomy is atavistic and paranoid and full of misplaced fear."

"You know," countered Killian, as he adjusted his tone into a playful lilt that didn't quite go as far as an Irish accent, but certainly indicated the possibility of one, "I much prefer your argument about homosexuality being innate than the rational-basis test professed by Justice Katsakis and adopted by his feeble-minded majority, which as far as I'm concerned just ends up saying that you can't legislate against morality. Where in the Constitution does it say you can't? Aren't there laws against polygamy? No one's complaining about those. And against gambling, incest, public masturbation, bestiality—you name it. Sex *can* be regulated. What are those laws if not moral judgments? It's so absurd I can't even think straight. At least you declare that gay people have a fundamental right to sodomy, based on their innate *gayness*, or whatever."

Katherine stood, slipped around her desk and approached Killian. She cupped his face with both hands, planted a firm kiss on his lips and pressed her tongue into his mouth. He wrapped his arms around the tiny woman's lower back and he pulled her onto his lap to straddle him. With his hands slipped inside the thin cotton of her shirt, he felt the smoothness of her skin, the knuckles of her spine, her ropey back muscles, toned and strengthened from years of Capoeira. Katherine pulled her mouth from Killian's and leaned back, cradling his face and absorbing his image, her cheeks flushed and warm.

"I'll close the blinds. Just give me a sec."

Katherine climbed off him and the musty armchair. Killian closed his eyes and felt the darkness settle on his eyelids. Willing himself—*willing*—but it wasn't any use. He was weak and deflated in the old armchair. No amount of teasing, toying and licking would spur the erection of what most needed erecting. Broken, dysfunctional—an old, limp man, well past his prime, gradually retiring from the heated and carnal battle for his soul, beyond the pleas of a well-meaning angel or the temptations of a sinister devil.

Katherine approached him, unbuttoning the top of her pleated pants. Killian opened his eyes, and shook his head at her. Her brow lifted, and she halted.

"Sorry. I just don't think there's any point."

Killian's bad eating had ruined his bowels and made his visits to the bathroom lengthy affairs. After lunch of a BBQ chicken sandwich and fries slathered in ketchup, he struggled in a private stall in the Supreme Court Building, his pants collapsed around his ankles and tiny beads of sweat dotting his brow, wondering if his failed attempt at lovemaking had crossed the threshold into sin, at least enough to warrant confession. He closed his eyes and visualized the dark blue cover and chunky, golden font of the Baltimore Catechism No. 3, which he had memorized entirely by the age of 12. That stable and true document of Catholic doctrine, although abandoned as a teaching text by primary schools post-Vatican II, contained lessons that Killian still considered the cornerstone of his spiritual education. To quote Father Corrigan from sixth grade: *It behooves a good Catholic to know the text by heart.*

With the formidable power of his memory, Killian tested himself on the toilet. He skimmed Lesson 19 (On Confession) for relevant phrases, recalling question #209: *What sins are we bound to confess?*, which he intoned in a gravelly voice. He cleared his throat and answered with the same bold earnestness he had expressed as a child: "We are bound to confess all our mortal sins, but it is well also to confess our venial sins." Pretty clever to remember both the unusual grammar of the dependent clause and the Catechism's unexpected use of the word *also*.

But was his sin with Katherine Kirsch mortal or venial? It was mortal, of course—a willful turning from God. Then again, a good lawyer might argue it was only a venial sin, since the act itself had been left unconsummated. Ah, the rabbit hole of pedantry, curse of a lawyerly mind. He had transgressed in one manner or another; that was the point. The Catechism was clear that either sin required confession. He resolved to drop by the Church of the Immaculate Conception near his house in Northern Virginia on his way home that evening.

His intestines whined and rolled. He scrunched his face and contracted his abdominal muscles, pressing a sweaty hand against the wall for support, trying to coax his bowels into some reasonable semblance of peristalsis. Nothing coming. He huffed, caught his breath, tried and failed once more. Killian grumbled curses, dabbed his forehead with a folded piece of toilet paper and resolved to wait it out.

"What must we do to receive the sacrament of penance worthily?" Killian recited the catechism with flushed cheeks, shifting his weight from left to right to prevent his legs from falling asleep. "To receive the sacrament of penance worthily we must: examine our conscience; be sorry for our sins; have the firm purpose of not sinning again; confess our sins to the priest; be willing to perform the penance the priest gives us." He mopped his brow, worried that his aorta would burst from the strenuous effort. "Please Lord grant me penance in the form of a good bowel movement."

That question about penance had arisen spontaneously, but he must have read or seen it not long ago, certainly more recently than third-grade Catechism class with Father O'Hagen. Maybe his last conversation with Katherine? He had mentioned the importance of the Baltimore Catechism to his spiritual development, and yes, she had wanted to see a portion of the significant text. When they looked it up online, Katherine arbitrarily clicked lesson 29, question 384—that one about penance—and he read it aloud to her.

"You're supposed to recite it clearly." Killian had hovered over her seat, savoring the residual tang of her passion fruit–scented shampoo. "So you can memorize it, word for word."

"Really? That precisely?"

"It's the official doctrine of the Catholic belief."

"That's intense."

He found her surprise astonishing. Didn't Katherine also believe important text should be memorized? Killian had always assumed that a Curator of Manuscripts at the Folger Library would share his positivist approach to the written word. But maybe Katherine did not hold his same reverence for text. It made him want to

interrogate her suspect epistemology, though he was wise enough
to attack her in a roundabout manner. He changed the topic of
conversation from the Baltimore Catechism to *Timon of Athens*
and the authorship questions surrounding that play—how some
scholars claim Thomas Middleton wrote scenes, while others say
the incomplete pentameter and bad rhyming schemes indicate an
incomplete work, a last-minute addition to the Folio, printed from
Shakespeare's first draft. He tried to bait Katherine into declaring
something affirmative about historicism, how the play's shaky history influenced the value or meaning of its words. Killian longed to
defend his belief that any text had to be assessed by its own artistic
merits, outside the context of its history or composition, without
respect to authorial intent or to its cultural, economic and political circumstances, and certainly without regard to any particular
reader's idiosyncratic feelings and passions. First draft or finished
version, it didn't matter: the text was the text. It was something
that his father, Malachi Quinn, would have said to his classes at
Emmanuel College when introducing students to the ideas of New
Criticism. Actually, it was something Malachi *had* said and written
on countless occasions, while sitting at the dinner table or in his
comprehensive studies of Irish poetry. Killian agreed with his father
entirely, then and now. New Critics had it right.

But Katherine refused to take any affirming stance on historicism. Killian tried to lure her into confessing her adherence to one
of the other literary theories—deconstruction and post-structur-
alism; feminism, Marxism or post-colonialism; psychoanalysis
and queer theory. He would attack any of those as morally relativistic. He would tell her that *Timon of Athens*, like the U.S.
Constitution, meant what it said *plainly*, that it was impossible
to interpret any of its passages consistently if one refused to let
its terms retain their clear meanings. He had prepared a whole
speech on how it doesn't matter what the so-called *purpose* of a
text might have been way back when it was written, or what the
perceived intention of its author (or authors) might have been—as
if that could ever really be known! "The text is what it is," he had
wanted to scream at her.

Again Katherine refused to take his bait. He peppered her with leading questions about the play, and about her implicit preferences in literary theory, but her replies remained bland and noncommittal. She didn't seem to care too deeply about the theoretical status of text, didn't mind if *Timon of Athens* was jointly written by Shakespeare and Middleton or by Popeye and Olive Oyl, and she even indicated that all literary theories were more or less palatable, including Killian's own version of constitutional originalism. People had all sorts of reasons for believing what they believed, she stated, and that while she found it enjoyable and valuable to preserve rare manuscripts, and exciting to enable others to reencounter them at the Folger, mostly she felt that it was okay for some people to have a sacred relationship to text while others maintained a skeptical or critical one. Both stances seemed worthwhile and productive. And when Killian asked how in heaven, with all that aimless apathy, Katherine could have started down the path of a literary profession—"I mean, the whole point of your job," he had barked, "is to preserve and value text"—she replied with her considerable self-assurance, that it had been a pragmatic choice: the students and professors at her college who studied Shakespeare were more quirky and interesting than the boring kids she hung out with in her dorm.

"How can you say that!" Killian was far more irked than he should have been. "Only idiots don't have opinions, and you, Katherine, are no idiot!"

Now, stuck on the toilet, Killian channeled that recalled fury into the contraction of his abdominal muscles, which unrolled a ribbon of stool into the water beneath him. "Lord Almighty." He grunted, held his breath and pushed again, allowing another marginally satisfying voidance of his bowel. It was a nightmare, struggling so, in the U.S. Supreme Court's absurdly marbled, Athenian temple of a john.

He took a break from all that pushing to catch his breath. Sometimes Katherine could be so exasperating. Her opinion on textual matters was clear and lucid—value-neutral, yes, but perfectly valid—and that made him angry. In fact, his anger had kept him away from Katherine for four long months. Was that why he had avoided her? Had he been punishing her for resisting the foundation of his jurisprudence? His face grew hot at the thought. But it was true. It was vital that Katherine agreed with him, even more than it was vital for the other justices to agree with him, although they, of course, had much more influence on his professional success; their agreement alone would lead to the widespread adoption of his textual theory. Oh yes, it mattered! The world could never be at peace unless Katherine Kirsch understood the proper role of text. "Text *exists*, Katherine," Killian mumbled inside his bathroom stall, "and so it very much matters that you are there to interpret it correctly."

But what was the question that Killian had read on the computer in Katherine's office that he felt so desperate for her to interpret correctly? How a person must receive his penance. He must be sorry for his sins. He must have the firm purpose of not sinning again.

So there. He was a hypocrite. Katherine had always known it.

Killian finished in the toilet as well he could, and began working his way through the roll of toilet paper. If the public knew about his hypocrisy, they would crucify him. They would disregard his writings and his opinions, all those reams of text he had generated so precisely, with the dream that future justices would someday understand both his argument and methodology. Gone, his philosophy: that text should be read at face value, positively, without projecting personal beliefs or preferences onto it, without assuming anything beyond what's marked on the paper, plain and simple. They would delight at any excuse to throw it all away, Killian's entire jurisprudence, and with it any chance for the law to grow in dignity and meaning, and provide stability to human life. *And why would I lose it all?* thought Killian Quinn. *Because I can't for the life of me keep my pecker in my pants.* He stood, tossed the last of his soiled paper into the toilet and, with considerable dismay, flushed it all away.

"We've got a motion to rehear 06-1172." Chief Justice Eberly sighed, removed his glasses and polished the lenses with his tie. "This Subic Bay case is back on the discuss list, folks, so let's get it over with. I, for one, have a few words before we vote."

Charles had dropped the usual formality of his leadership role, which could only mean he was angry, and that he didn't want a belabored discussion of *Al-Tounsi*. Although it was tempting to spur on the Chief's rage by muttering, "Go on, Charles! Go get 'em!," instead Killian sat back listening, rubbing his belly in silence.

The Chief returned his glasses to his face and leaned on his armrest. "I trust we're not such a pusillanimous Court as to change our mind on a cert decision because of some hasty declaration composed by the lawyers of an aberrant colonel. Reversing cert would not foster any confidence in this Court whatsoever. That is just not what we do. At this juncture, it would be a great disservice, both to our stature and the country."

Gideon Rosen, who started fidgeting as soon as Eberly mentioned the case, shot an inquisitive glance down the table at Talos Katsakis. Killian caught the slip, but Talos seemed immune to Rosen's scrutiny, or at least had made the choice to remain expressionless. Katsakis must not have told anyone his thoughts on the vote. And Gideon was clearly insecure, which could only be a sign that the case was still unresolved. If the Inge declaration hadn't convinced Katsakis to switch, then Justice Davidson would most likely not change his vote either. No way that old rascal would grant an important case cert if he were certain to lose it.

"Anyone else?"

When it was clear that none of the senior members had anything to add, Gideon raised a finger. Eberly nodded his permission.

"Colonel Inge's declaration has got to be one of the worst rebukes ever laid on an executive claim. It is now abundantly clear to us that the CSRT procedures used in Subic are subpar at best, unconstitutional at worst. This should throw into serious doubt the assertion that *any* of the MCA-mandated procedures are an adequate habeas substitute. Now, we might end up agreeing or disagreeing on whether these detainees are entitled to a habeas substitute, but to declare we have no right to even ask the question, after this, well that's just no longer a valid position to take."

"We haven't reversed on cert in sixty years, Gideon." Justice Bryce's tone was harsh and scolding. "Sixty years."

"We haven't had a declaration like this one laid before us either." Without glancing at Katsakis, although surely fighting the desire to do so, Gideon added: "A declaration that's obliterated this country's legitimacy in the eyes of the world."

Killian fought off the urge to roll with laughter. Shameless Gideon Rosen, going all the way, picking and choosing the exact words to most inflame Talos. Justice Katsakis, for his part, stirred his mug of milky coffee and ignored his colleague's bait.

"Anyone else?" Charles glanced around the Conference Room. "Or can we vote on this thing?"

"Let's vote," said Sarah Kolmann.

"All right. I vote to deny. Bernhard?"

The old man shook his head and drummed his fingers on the table. He must have not known which side Katsakis would take, so he was stuck out on a limb, at the far end of the conference table, having to make up his mind without the benefit of knowing the others' votes.

"Deny," Justice Davidson whispered.

Gideon groaned and shielded his eyes with his hand.

"Killian, your turn."

Killian had never really doubted his vote. Still, as always, he had done his due diligence. He had decided to gather his clerks in chambers after lunch to discuss *Al-Tounsi* one final time, just before the buzzer rang to summon him to conference. When he had asked for their opinions, his clerks regurgitated all the known arguments for denying cert. "The question of whether or not detainees are receiving an adequate substitute for habeas is not even worth asking," Isaac Marks declared, "since they have no such habeas rights under the Constitution or common law." "And even if that question *was* worth asking," Alexa Ruff added, "none of the MCA-mandated procedures have run their full course, which makes it grossly premature for the Court to rule on their constitutionality. The Department of Justice and the American people first need to be given the opportunity to see how the procedures actually function." "You shouldn't give that traitor Inge any credibility," added Martin Croll.

Killian agreed with them, of course. He shuffled his clerks out of his chambers, patted their backs and complimented their sage thinking, and then sat in his chair, waiting for the buzzer, stewing in anger at Colonel Inge and his superior officer, Rear Admiral Bonairre. Or course, this debacle wasn't only the fault of the naval officers at Subic Bay. It had also been caused by President Shaw, Vice President Bloomfield, and Secretary of Defense Garfield, all of whom should have known better, who should have monitored the CSRT procedures and kept them fair, who should have extracted their heads from the rank darkness of their own asses. Killian knew all three men quite well—Secretary Garfield, in particular, was a good friend, hunting partner, fellow New York strip loin consumer, and occasional companion to the Congressional Country Club, where the two of them knocked their blasted little white balls into every water or sand trap that Robert Trent Jones had planted around that devious course. Killian had not been particularly surprised by the President's irresponsibility. Mark Shaw was an idiot, frankly, more like an insecure actor playing the role of President than the thing itself: well meaning, ideologically sound, hoping to do some good, but far too preoccupied with his mountain biking, vocal classes, and personal relationship with the Lord to keep track of any of the mundane procedures used to process terrorists in the Philippine Naval Base. Secretary Garfield and Vice President Bloomfield, however, were no such idiots. They were seasoned soldiers in a multi-generational battle for expanded executive power. Their authority, like Killian's, stretched all the way back to the Nixon era, to an administration in which each of them had held a significant post. Both Garfield and Bloomfield knew exactly how important the MCA-mandated CSRT procedures were to the legitimacy of their argument. They had no right to drop the ball. Killian was so furious with their oversight that he was half-tempted to pick up the phone, call Secretary Garfield at his Pentagon office, and tell the man to get his act together, despite knowing that such a call to a high-profile member of the executive branch, if anyone found out about it, would be magnified into a national controversy that would force Justice Quinn into recusing himself from *Al-Tounsi* and any other Subic Bay cases that rose to the Court. But there was another, less toxic option that Killian could also pursue, he realized, as he sat in chambers, waiting for the buzzer. He could vote to grant cert. He could say that Justice Rosen was now correct, that the Inge declaration was indeed an affront that made the key question of an adequate substitute for habeas unavoidable, and that the Court had no choice now but to hear *Al-Tounsi*. It would shock his colleagues, sure, but more importantly it would be equivalent to publicly scolding President Shaw, Vice President Bloomfield and Secretary Garfield; it would be the same as telling them to clean up their acts *fast*, and it would do so while avoiding the gross inappropriateness of a telephone call. Voting to grant cert didn't mean that Killian had to side with the petitioners in the end. He would vote for the government, of course, when it came down to the actual case. But his cert vote might be the jolt that this administration needed. It might do a world of good.

Killian was still considering the possibility of switching his vote to "grant" when the conference began. He ruminated all through the justices' handshakes and the opening procedures, and even as Eberly and Davidson voted to deny *Al-Tounsi*. No one around the table had any idea just how close he was to astonishing them. It was a delightful feeling, really, to be this unexpected kingmaker, and he treasured his secret right up to the moment when he had to declare his vote.

"Deny," Killian said, betraying none of his inner debate.

"Elyse?"

"I vote to grant cert."

"And Talos?"

Justice Katsakis nodded. "I vote to grant, as well."

Elyse Van Cleve gasped—actually went so far as to gasp. Killian laughed, shoulders shaking. So old two-faced Talos had switched after all! Not even Bernhard saw that coming. Gideon stood up, grinning like a fool, but when he realized what he was doing, he sat down again. Bernhard and Sarah fought off smiles as well; Killian caught them looking to each other for support. Justice Bryce murmured in outrage, and shook her head vehemently.

"Whoo-boy." Killian wiped the tears of laughter out of his eyes. "Drama on the Court!"

Charles glared at him, and then quietly asked Talos to confirm his vote, to assure the entire table that he was indeed reversing his previous decision and effectively granting cert to a denied case for the first time in 60 years.

"Yes. I'm reversing and voting to grant cert."

"Fine. Noted." The Chief Justice retreated into stone-faced professionalism, as if he felt nothing personally about the case whatsoever, and as if Justice Katsakis's switch had been entirely expected. "Rodney?"

"I vote to deny." Rodney was as calm as usual, unfazed by any drama, and his simple answer had the effect of quieting the other justices.

The remaining justices voted as expected: Rosen and Kolmann to grant cert, Bryce to deny.

"We have four votes in favor," intoned Chief Justice Eberly. "We hereby reverse our denial and grant case 06-1172, *Al-Tounsi v. Shaw*, certiorari for next term." He kept his voice low and quiet, pretending nothing unusual or historic had just occurred.

Talos slurped his coffee, hiding a smile behind his mug. So the final decision in this case would, as usual, be Talos Katsakis's. Killian would have Bryce, Sykes, and Eberly in the government's corner with him, while Rosen, Davidson, Kolmann and Van Cleve would rule for the detainees. Katsakis was the only vote in play. The Inge declaration had offended him exactly as predicted; it made the U.S. executive look awful. But Talos's indignity at the initial offense did not ensure his vote on the substantive issues. In the coming months, Killian knew, an army of lawyers for either

side would tailor their briefs to that one man's idiosyncratic jurisprudence. They would all appeal to Talos, which would drive
Gideon crazy and mildly amuse everyone else. And although by
switching his certiorari vote Talos had indeed indicated his openness to the petitioners' side—the man was now most likely leaning toward ruling for the detainees—Killian still felt buoyant at
the prospect of hearing a powerful case on executive power, the
reach of habeas corpus and the breadth of the Suspension clause.
It would be exciting. Heck, it already *was* exciting, the first reversal of a cert decision since the end of World War II. *Al-Tounsi*
would be in all the papers as soon as it was announced.

And it was of the utmost importance. Non-citizen detainees in
Subic Bay should not have access to habeas corpus. If the Court
released them via habeas on some technicality, it would be another
example of guilty people denying their responsibilities, and then
having their denial affirmed by a court of law. And these were not
your average guilty men; they were terrorists bent on destroying
Western civilization. Granting them habeas would send a message
to the millions of people internationally who hated the United
States that the country was weak, that terrorists could proceed
against it with impunity. And Katherine, dear Katherine, held
in his arms, straddled on his lap, would have to understand that
there was no room for hypocrisy on this issue. National security was more important than sex. The inherent badness of those
detainees' characters, which was a whole different category of
badness than his own or his lover's, demanded that they embrace
their own imprisonments if they wanted any sort of penitence or
redemption for their corrupted souls. And if they chose not to
embrace it—the most likely scenario—well, then, at least they
would be locked up, and put out of commission.

The conference moved on to another piece of business. As
he listened to the next case, Killian decided to work with great
effort and passion in the coming year to convince Talos that the
detainees must be denied habeas. He would pressure Talos to vote
for the government's side. Killian had good, sound arguments to
make; he was *right*, and he knew it. Yes, the executive branch

had screwed up their responsibilities, embarrassed the nation, and launched this sordid case into the Supreme Court, but Justice Quinn could still lead the country out of this mess. He could do the work that President Shaw and his subordinates had failed to accomplish. *Al-Tounsi* was on the docket, and Killian Quinn would welcome its challenge.

4

AD OUT

Elyse Van Cleve bounced a tennis ball against the gray clay, picturing Venus Williams's long black arms in place of her stubby white ones. If she could fully visualize those arms as her own, she might harness that great champion's catapulting service motion. She would leap high off the court with her racquet extended, her arm lithe and strong, and then whip down ferociously on the suspended ball, channeling the power of her youthful muscles and the torque of her sinewy forearm into the sweet spot of her strings, just as Venus did that morning to win her fourth Wimbledon singles title. What did it matter that Justice Van Cleve's opponents in this amateur doubles match were a couple of septuagenarian ladies from the Amelia National Golf and Country Club, or that their agreed upon spoils were only bragging rights for a week plus a free round of gin-and-tonics on the patio? It didn't matter that her prize wasn't as grand as kissing the famed Venus Rosewater Dish of the All England Lawn Tennis and Croquet Club, and holding it high above her head for the flashing cameras. Winning was its own reward. Winning anchored existence. It showed how you had outsmarted and outplayed your opponents, and achieved lasting results. It didn't matter if anybody witnessed your accomplishment or celebrated it. Past victories provided you with a reservoir of strength for the difficult tasks of the future. Nothing trivial about that. There were only two possible results from this hour-and-a-half competition on the tennis court: victory or defeat. Elyse was going to win.

Without question, the best way to secure victory was to emulate Venus. While powerful Serena was a better model on most occasions, today would belong to the lithe older sister. Elyse would have to identify with Venus entirely, embodying more than just Venus's physical power and technical mastery. She meant to inhabit her past, her emotional state—her hard-luck childhood in Compton, her lack of a fancy court and tennis club. It meant imagining that sea of white English faces watching her on Centre Court, wondering if she had enough skill to win this match, and if she had the proper grace and manners to act as a dignified champion. It meant considering not only what it took for Venus to win physically, but also the psychological strength she needed to maintain grace and gratitude in that socially conservative arena. It meant committing herself to transforming the values of people who opposed her success because she was a woman, and black. It meant merging with Venus Williams, becoming one person, if only for a few service games on a tennis court of this Georgian country club.

Elyse stood on the baseline bouncing her tennis ball. Her legs tensed, and she held her back straight. She threw the ball in the air and cocked her racquet into her spine, but knew right away that she hadn't tossed it high enough, that she would have to compensate with a quicker swing. Still, she could reach above the ball and drive it down into the service court using Venus's muscles rather than her own.

She spun her racquet around, but not as quickly as she had wanted. The ball hit low on her strings and as the jostled composite frame sent vibrations into her hand, it hurled forward without spin and hit the tape along the net. The ball dropped onto her side of the court, and died after a piddling bounce.

"Drat."

She had been too rash. Nowhere near conservative enough for a second serve.

Justice Van Cleve watched her two elderly opponents in short white skirts switch their relative depths, congratulating each other over the point they had just won. How irritating: their smug satisfaction over such a small win. Not like it took any effort on their part, nothing but crouching for a serve that never came. Oh, they would pay for their conceit, those overconfident old ladies. Elyse retrieved her ball, and returned to the baseline to play the next point in the ad court.

"Thirty-forty." She bounced it again. She would throw the ball higher this time. She wouldn't do anything to defeat herself.

Elyse blotted out her surroundings, focused solely on the ball. A champion cleared her head for each and every point. Nothing mattered but the present challenge. Forget the sea of faces, ignore Venus's arms. Venus hadn't thought of anything when she played that morning. She thought of nothing but the task—a ball suspended in the air, hitting the racquet, twisting down with vicious spin for an ace in the far corner.

Elyse served without error. The ball hit the center of her strings with a satisfying pop and flew into the deep right side of Laura Elmwood's court. Although her serve lacked the severe topspin and speed of Venus's 125-mph wonders, it was still a decent enough facsimile to please her. She crouched for her opponent's return.

Laura Elmwood, the strongest player of the quartet, forehanded crosscourt into the alley. Elyse ran to it and hit a weak, backhand shot to her second opponent, the recently widowed Alma Epp—a woman completely incapable of executing a forehand with any topspin, but who at least had decent placement. Alma bobbed as she ran and mishit the ball, lobbing it high above Karen Feldstein, Elyse's doubles partner. Karen stepped in and volleyed it back, deep to Elmwood's forehand. Another poor shot, a floater, lacking power. It would be maddening to lose the point on that. Crosscourt, Laura Elmwood, relying on a cheap but effective knee brace, bent low and powered through her next shot, but put too much force on the ball, sailing it above Karen and landing it out, two feet beyond the baseline.

"Ah, fudge it!" Laura Elmwood swatted angrily at her tennis shoe with the tip of her racquet. "Come on, now!"

The players reset for deuce. Good, Elyse was working now, and on a roll. She concentrated, tried to repeat the smooth motion of her previous service. Something went off, though. She couldn't leap as high, and hit a weaker, lobbed serve that was driven hard crosscourt by Alma, and then returned into the net by Karen. The point was lost before she had even settled in.

Elyse paused. Her racquet felt like it weighed ten pounds. This game was not going according to plan. One more mistake like that and she would lose her serve. She had lacked consistency all day: two of her past three service attempts had been total garbage. Why? She was known among her peers as a serve-and-volley specialist, not one of those grind-'em-out ground strokers. Maybe her energy had been sapped by the oppressive heat of this muggy Saturday afternoon in late July. Truth was it didn't matter *why*, results were the same. Facts needed to be faced. Her serve wasn't going to power her into this match.

Across the net, Laura Elmwood squatted low with her back curved, bouncing to and fro on the balls of her feet, determined to return the next shot for a winner. But wasn't there frustration in the vigor of her bounce, the near horizontal angle of her back? An overeager stance? Maybe Laura was angry with herself for hitting the ball too strongly two shots earlier. Maybe she was mumbling quietly, resolving then and there not to make the same mistake twice.

Laura's red, hard face resembled Killian Quinn's in conference, whenever he articulated a furious objection to a controversial decision, one of those cases he lost regularly by a single tentative vote. Maybe Laura was like him. Maybe that comparison with Justice Quinn was the key to defeating her.

Elyse walked to the net to retrieve the tennis ball, her thoughts speeding, calculating. Killian's anger tended to ruin his diplomacy and poison his results. Whenever he was overcome by emotion, venom would spit from his pen and lace his writing with sarcastic taunts and jokes, and personal attacks against his colleagues.

Like that affirmative action dissent from '05, the *Duke Medical* case—his blistering sentence had made national news: *I'm sure that nonminority individuals who have been excluded from Duke Medical School by a patently racist policy are thrilled that the less qualified minority students who have usurped their rightful spots are providing the "educational benefit" of "cross-racial understanding" to the school's future doctors, as if Duke Medical has even been the proper forum for teaching citizens how "we should all get along together," rather than, say, church class, or the family dinner table, or the neighborhood kindergarten.* The public had loved that colorful dissent, but not Elyse. She shook her head in dismay when she read it. So unwise. When Killian wrote like that, he lost cases. How could he forget that the point of these legal exercises was to garner five votes? Killian's logic was brilliant, his literary skills were without question the most playful and enjoyable of the nine, and he had the intellectual power to switch that crucial fifth vote in the drafting stage of contentious cases, but he just couldn't maintain his tranquility; he could never tone down the screech in his prose. He was his own worst enemy. And if the comparison of Killian Quinn to Laura Elmwood was accurate, then she would be her own worst enemy, too.

The key, with Killian, was to play into his anger, and make it worse. You had to set him up to overreact. Elyse had done it so many times in conference, on the bench in argument, and with her carefully chosen phrases in draft opinions, that it was barely conscious. It was pure instinct, like a cat torturing a mouse. She would probably do it again this term, when that big habeas case came up in the winter. Just last week she was joking with Carla about it. Carla had come down from Kentucky for the week, and they had been sipping the mojitos Kevin made so masterfully on the Club patio, and tucking into their Caesar salads. Of course Elyse was careful to speak in veiled terms—never discuss a pending case directly, not even with her trusted sister.

"Sometimes conference is not so different from riding a horse." It was a good analogy to use with Carla, who, with her husband, Kenny, owned and managed the Van Cleves' remote Kentucky

horse farm, that rolling Jefferson County compound where Elyse
had grown up. "Same thing: reading moods and inflections,
what's going on underneath, and riding that out. I remember with
Diablo, I'd always *know* when to get firm with him or slacken
his reins, just by the way he walked or breathed. Whether to dig
in and push, or give him room, just by the position of his ears."

"Of course." Carla chomped her crispy bacon. "Every horse is
distinct but predictable."

"Well, people, too. Even justices of the Supreme Court. You
got to watch them for their breathing and gestures. The way they
hold their ears."

They laughed hard at that one. Whenever Elyse talked with
Carla or her brother, Franklin, her accent regressed to its Ken-
tuckian roots.

"A corral of pinto geldings, the nine of us in that room. All
predictable beasts."

"Oh, you don't honestly think that, Elyse."

"I swear sometimes that's what it feels like. Same psychology
at play. There's one case this term coming up—and like all cases
these days, it's going to be determined by Talos's vote. He'll decide
my way, too—I just know it. Because ultimately it's not about what
he believes—I honestly do think Talos could go either way—or
what anyone believes. It's going to be decided by psychology. Just
like horses. It always comes down to psychology. It's an executive
power case. But see, I think the question there is not about constitutional consistency or any firm rule, it's about certain practicalities,
what the situation needs. And when I get around to saying all that
in conference, Killian will go wild. He'll call me wishy-washy, and
claim I haven't got any theoretical center to my reasoning, and that
I'm using the same language I would've used back in the Kentucky
legislature—behaving like a legislator not a judge—which he hates.
But then he'll get carried away and push it too far, see, like saying
something about how the executive should *never* listen to the legislative branch at all. And he'll yell and holler in a way that really
irks Talos. Beause he's irresponsible with his words. And that'll be
it. Killian will win the argument in conference, and it'll looks as if

I'm defeated, and he'll sit back red-faced and passionate and proud, but meanwhile Talos will have just resolved himself against Justice Quinn, yet again. So when it's time for our opinions, Killian'll find himself writing a dissent, while I'll be in the majority again, just like I am 91 percent of the time."

"91 percent?" Carla frowned.

"*The Washington Post* did a study. I'm in the majority 91 percent of time. More than anyone."

"You make it sound like a strategy."

"It's just the way people are, Carla. I know my fellow justices so well now that I can't stop myself or fight it. You let the horse be the horse, and you ride what they give you."

"I can't believe a man as smart as Killian Quinn hasn't caught on."

"Oh, he's caught on all right. Just can't help himself. It's as if his parents never taught him restraint. He doesn't have it in him, kind and smart as he is. I find it amazing the way some people are raised. Could you imagine how Mom or Pop would've responded if we'd spoken to them like Killian Quinn speaks to everybody, with all his sarcasm and personal insults?"

"Or to each other. Or to Johnny and Mitch, or any of the stable boys."

"Don't I know it. Not like those two would've been fazed by a few of our off-color words."

"Pop would've beat us."

"Absolutely he would've, and that's just for private talk. You imagine how he would've come at us had we talked disrespect-fully in *public*, even to the black boys hanging 'round outside Gerry Sangham's?" Elyse tsk-tsk-ed into her salad.

"Shudder to think."

"Well, that's what Killian does every time he opens his mouth or picks up his pen. Just rude, rude, rude."

Standing by the net, remembering that conversation, Elyse squeezed the tennis ball. Her fingers barely dented its yellow fuzz. It still had most of its pressure, so it would bounce high off the clay if anyone hit it hard enough.

She walked back to the baseline. She could play it out consciously. She could capitalize on Laura's weakness, just like Killian's, as long as she set up her opponent properly. Elyse would have to *appear* to lose. She couldn't blast her serves or aim for winners. Even if the ball landed in on her next attempt—a big *if*, this morning—Laura would be waiting for a hard shot, expecting it to remain low against the court, and would be prepared to respond with a quick swing. Laura's anger had predetermined her response. If Elyse was going to set up Laura Elmwood properly, it meant offering her a serve that worked *against* her decision to strike at it with full force—namely, a slow floater, a dinky and amateurish thing that would bounce high off the clay and hang at Laura's shoulders rather than at her waist, far from the ideal placement. Elmwood would see that ball and think she'd got Elyse beat, but she would not adjust her stroke in time. She was not that talented. Laura would follow through as if the ball were low, grunting, smashing it long. Elyse's serve wouldn't look pretty, and it wouldn't feel anywhere near as satisfying as an ace, but it would have a better chance of winning.

That wasn't what Venus Williams would have done. Well, so be it. Elyse would have to abandon her embodiment of the Wimbledon champion. Because any version of herself as one who lost a tennis match was not one worth preserving. Truth was, Elyse was more flexible than Venus William. Elyse was not just one kind of person who did one kind of thing. Flexibility might be a less poetic or romantic character trait in a champion than unwavering talent, but it was all that Elyse had, and it was her way to victory. And that's what really mattered: winning 91 percent of the time.

"Ad Out." Elyse bounced the ball on the gray clay. She prepared herself for a dinky little serve to her opponent, who had sunk deep into her return stance.

Elyse tossed the ball high but came around lightly, tapping rather than hitting it. The ball floated in an arc over the net and landed shallow in Laura's court, so delicately hit that it would have easily bounced three times before reaching the base line if Laura hadn't run up to intercept it. Laura charged forward with her racquet drawn and swung with full strength, hoping to drive a winner into the alley on Karen's side, but just as Elyse had predicted she hit the ball with too much force and not enough topspin, and her shot sailed out beyond the sideline.

"Damn it!" Laura Elmwood clutched her fists to her head. "That was mine!"

Elyse smiled broadly. A sharp pain stung behind her left eye. It was startling and severe. She turned away from the net and hung her head so she might get a hold of it, but the pain didn't diminish. It only increased. It was a cold and intense cramp, as if her brain had been wrapped in ice and then squeezed. The pain radiated through to the back of her skull. Elyse pressed the heel of her palm against her eyebrow and stood motionless, hoping it would pass.

The other three players shifted their positions and waited for Elyse to reset. Elyse didn't move. Karen called her name and asked if she was okay.

"Yes. Fine."

She gazed at the live oaks behind the court. The pain gripped her harder. Elyse squinted at the intensity of the afternoon light, a brightness that now seemed much stronger than it had been even a minute earlier. Sunbeams illuminated every speck of dust, and that dust made the air seem as thick as water. She grew more and more aware of it with each blink. She felt submerged in a warm bath, her skin drenched in light and heat, such an intense and pleasurable sensation that it was difficult for Elyse to tell where the hot sunlight ended and where her skin began. She closed her eyes. Her body emanated rays of light. Elyse suddenly understood that there were two suns in the solar system, one external and one internal—or no, that wasn't right, it was something more magnificent, something greater still. There was only a single sun, but it had been divided into two parts that yearned to connect, that leapt toward one another, their rays touching on the thin, almost transparent surface of her skin. She opened her eyes and noticed that the trees behind the fence were gigantic and ancient, so much grander than she recalled. Their thick branches twisted above the court in an enormous canopy. Most of those branches dripped with Spanish moss. They were living arms, and they wrapped the court, encroaching in a hug. The icy pain in her head began to wane, but then returned to squeeze her brain with greater strength. She looked at the rough surface of the court. Elyse noticed that someone had swept the fallen strands of silvery-gray Spanish moss into large piles in the corners, and that the new, thin white hairs of the moss's seed, which had fallen throughout the day, were sprinkled across the gray clay. The seeds were like a delicate dusting of icing sugar. Elyse distinguished each individual strand of the gathered moss and every wisp of the downy seed. She inhaled. The whole world smelled green and fresh, but also strong and suffocating. It was as if a wet sponge saturated with the essence of Spanish moss was pressed against her face. She inhaled again and realized that she could no longer distinguish a boundary between that all-pervasive perfume and the receptors of her nose. Was there nothing in the world but Spanish moss? It hung from tree branches above her; it surrounded her in piles on the court; it even seemed to grow from the pores of her own skin.

A shrill voice pierced the air somewhere behind Elyse, high and discordant. It spoke a word that Elyse had certainly heard before; but for the life of her she couldn't tell what that word was or what it could possibly mean. The sound was cutting and harsh, quite out of place with the background murmur of the trilling crickets and chirping birds.

The ice pressing against Elyse's brain melted and released but refroze instantaneously, gripping her head again.

Her intense bath of sensory pleasure dulled, and Elyse turned toward the court to face her tennis partners. All three ladies were staring at her with looks of great concern. Laura Elmwood and Alma Epp had lowered their racquets and were now approaching the net.

Elyse recalled that there was a game in progress. She had been busy playing it. There had been some strategy to the game, something that involved Killian Quinn's anger—or no, his red face—or no, something about using that anger to jockey the others for their votes. But how could that be? Killian wasn't here under all this hanging moss and brilliant sunshine. These were only old ladies. And what was that game, exactly? Did it have some kind of purpose? It was something about cutting and limiting one's words, being careful with the language, distinguishing this from that, for the purpose of winning the others over. Something about affirmative something. *Medical school. Black skin.* What did those words mean? *Medical school. Black skin.* Strange sounds. Elyse looked down at her feet and saw a fluffy yellow ball on the clay beside her shoe. She saw that her claw-like hand was holding the rubbery grip of a racquet. This game had something to do with hitting that ball with that racquet. There had been some importance attached to the phrase *Ad Out.* Yes, Elyse was supposed to say *Ad Out* and then hit the ball over the net, she suddenly remembered, but how would that ever win Killian Quinn's vote? And *vote*? What is *vote*? Just another strange sound. It seemed absurd, absolutely ridiculous, to hit a yellow ball and then care about where it landed when there was so much light penetrating her skin, and also emanating from inside her, and such a fresh, sponge-like smell, and so much joy associated with this overpowering, sensory bath, which was all so present, so here and now, and which eliminated the possibility of anything else ever existing. Elyse blinked and tried to distinguish the faces coming toward her. Icy pain pulsed through her eye. A whispered voice in her head reminded her that it was proper to say *Ad Out.*

"Wuuuu wuuu." Was that her own voice? That did not sound right at all.

Her mouth hung slack. Her right arm suddenly felt like it had been turned to stone. The racquet fell from her grip. She gazed down at it, lying on the clay, and wondered how that racquet had traveled so far from her hand so quickly, so many millions of miles away, and then she realized she was swooning, that the sky was below her, that the whole world had been turned upside down and that she was standing on the blue sky, and then she was hitting the ground. The pain from her icy brain distributed across her body, but refocused like a pinprick inside her head.

She blinked and saw gray grit just beyond her nose. The rough clay scratched and tickled her exposed flesh, the grains embedding themselves into her, and now Elyse couldn't distinguish the border between that grit and her own rough skin. She was a piece of sandpaper. Her skin was the craggy bark of the surrounding trees. She squinted and turned her head into the light. She saw panicked, silhouetted faces of wrinkled women hovering above her. They looked so old, all of them.

They have names, these women. Every old face is named. But what are those names? What is the purpose of a name?

Elyse closed her eyes. The fierce sunshine and trilling insects and spongy sweet scent of the Georgian paradise dissipated into a gray haze, a peaceful emptiness. She felt soothed and exhausted by the quiet around her, and she let her body relax. She would open her eyes again only once, fifteen minutes later, to discover she was lying on a stretcher inside a racing ambulance. The voices and sirens, the obnoxious fluorescent lights and bright red beams on the black screens, and all the bumping and jostling of the vehicle in rapid motion—it was all so artificial and overwhelming. And each of those sensations was indistinguishable from the others. Elyse felt fingers poking at her, and metal pricking her skin, and plastic smothering her breathing, and an additional pain in her limbs and head that was much too hot and angry to categorize. She pushed it all away and closed her eyes. And although the last of Elyse Van Cleve's internal organs wouldn't shut down for another 41 hours, she was, for all effective purposes, already dead on that ride to the hospital.

PART 2

ARGUMENT

5

THE UNITARY
EXECUTIVE

Reclining in first class on an early-morning flight from San Francisco to Washington Dulles, Judge Emmanuel Arroyo sipped his coffee and cracked open a new book by his favorite radio host. Four pages in, he grew weary with the pundit's tone, which was cutting and sharp on air, but on paper read more like a semiliterate and puerile screed. He stuffed the manifesto into his briefcase, took out a legal pad and a stack of briefs. Each year it seemed increasingly crazy to have a draft opinion due in early August, when federal courts more reasonable than the "nutty ninth"—as that same pundit called his notoriously liberal Ninth Circuit—were in the midst of their summer recesses. But this would be his last torturous August, thank the good Lord in Heaven, if he passed the test awaiting him in D.C. Manny skimmed his briefs, refreshed himself with the substance of the case, and decided what to write. He scribbled his first draft over the pale desert of western Utah, and only stopped when the flight attendant laid his steaming breakfast before him.

"Would you like more coffee?"

"Why yes, I would. Thank you." Such uncharacteristic polite-
ness. And his omelet smelled a whole lot better than airplane food
should. The world right now was a perfect place.

Just yesterday afternoon, carrying two hot dogs—one for himself, one for Lonny—he had emerged from the dark concrete tun-
nel in the upper tier of AT&T Park into the open air, and felt so
overwhelmed by the world's perfection that he had to stop to take
in the view. The water of San Francisco Bay shimmered beyond
the center-field wall and scoreboard, and the Oakland hills in the
far distance were muted beige silhouettes in the summer haze. He
was at a Giants game with his son, about to eat a hot dog under
a cloudless sky. And finally, *finally*, he had received that call from
the White House.

Manny ate more of his omelet than he expected, and drank
his coffee. His anxiety had receded under the pleasant ache in
his arms and chest, the strain in his shoulders and throughout
his back. He had worked out hard last night in his condo's gym,
and the pulsing, warming throb in his muscles would calm him
all day, just as it had allowed him to sleep soundly last night. He
pinched his shoulder blades together and stretched his traps. He
felt fantastic. Strong, alert, calm.

He was ready for this. He had worked his whole life for this.
But of course he would have to be careful in his interview with
Deputy White House Chief of Staff Gordon Kale. Kale was a
political animal who would read Manny's posture, his pick of suit
and tie, his choice of words, how closely he had shaved. Those
incidentals would be as important as any substantive jurisprudence. As long as Manny remembered he was being watched, as
he did when he was in the courtroom, he would be fine.

His flight landed on schedule. Manny was gripped by faint
nausea as the plane taxied to the gate. He shouldn't have had that
third cup of coffee. As soon as the flight attendant opened the
airplane door, he strode onto the jet bridge and into the terminal.
He discovered a tall, thin limo driver—probably Sudanese—waiting for him by baggage claim, loosely clutching a sign printed
Moreno, the cover Kale had suggested. Manny grinned at the

man's bony, dark-skinned face. Subterfuge was thrilling. They exchanged quick nods and Manny was led outside into the sweltering heat and humidity, toward a black Town Car with tinted windows and government plates, his heart pounding as though he were midway through a set of heavy squats.

They drove into town. Manny half-expected the limo to pull in through the front gates of the White House on Pennsylvania Avenue, but instead it stopped at a curb on 17th Street, by an unadorned entrance to the Old Executive Office Building. No security. The driver put the car in park.

"Here you go."

Manny stepped out of the car, smacking into a solid wall of heat so severe it bent the light into shimmering waves that rose off the asphalt. He immediately started to sweat. He had forgotten that Washington summers had all the fire of Waco's, but worse humidity. The streets were quiet, except for a handful of tourists lumbering through Farragut Square toward the White House, cameras in hand. Two boyish young interns, the sleeves of their dress shirts informally rolled above their elbows and their boldly colored ties knotted tightly around their necks, were waiting for him by the door.

"Welcome, Judge."

Arroyo nodded a brusque greeting.

The interns ushered him into the building and past the security guards, flashing laminated passes, and then into a small elevator inside a roped-off alcove, which was most likely reserved for the executive branch's privileged guests. The two interns stood awkwardly beside him.

"How was your flight?"

He wanted to tell this taller intern to shut up, but instead mumbled "fine." He dug around in the pocket of his suit jacket and withdrew a crumbling tissue, which he used to wipe his sweaty brow. Kale would notice his sweat.

They emerged from the elevator by a doorway with a small plaque that read: *Office of the Vice President*. The interns led him inside, through an empty room with several cubicles, and stopped

at the threshold of a boardroom. They gestured for Manny to
enter, and closed the door behind him.

All the powerbrokers of the executive branch were standing in
the room but for President Shaw himself. Their skin looked pasty
in the fluorescent light, and their eyes drooped wearily, like they
had been standing around and waiting for him all day. But Kale
had said it would be one interview, just "preliminary stuff." He
hadn't said anything about Manny meeting all these people at
once! Manny's fingers tingled, and he closed his hands into tight
fists, his gaze darting from face to face. He was still goddamn
sweating, although this office was heavily air-conditioned.

"Emmanuel Arroyo, good to see you." The White House Chief
of Staff, Jeremy Rimm, showed his horsey teeth, walked around
the table and stuck out his stubby hand.

Manny wished to God that he could wipe his sweaty palm
before shaking anyone's hand.

One by one they came around the table to greet him. Deputy
Chief Gordon Kale was next in line, followed by Attorney General Rolando Nicolaides, White House Counsel Lorna MacKneer
and Vice Presidential Chief of Staff L. J. Batherson. Arroyo took
care to meet each set of eyes as he shook hands, concentrating on
offering just the right suggestion of power with his sturdy grip.
Too strong a clasp might indicate a will to dominance, maybe
even violence, but too limp a grip would expose a timorous
nature. The perfect handshake would show just enough strength
to resist pressure, and indicate his ability stick to a textualist
position in conference. Arroyo's last handshake was with Vice
President Bloomfield, whose fingers felt fat and swollen. Probably
poor circulation. To Manny's dismay, Kale asked him to sit on
the near side of the long conference table while the entire White
House staff shuffled around the corner to sit on the other side of
the table, opposite him. Manny again clenched his hands into fists
in preparation for an old-fashioned grilling, an assault.

"I heard Gordon caught you at a ball game yesterday with his
phone call."

"I was with my son, Lonny. When Gordon asked if I was
alone, I said, yeah, just me and 40,000 Giants fans."

They all laughed—a good sign.

"Giants win?"

"Of course, Jeremy. Barry Bonds homered into McCovey Cove."

Baseball talk put Manny at ease, which was probably what Rimm had intended. They moved on. In 90 minutes of amicable questioning, led by MacKneer and Nicolaides, they asked Manny about key cases on the Ninth Circuit during his tenure, about his strict constructionist jurisprudence, and his opinion on the so-called "rights" that liberal justices and leftist law professors freely espoused, none of which had ever been enumerated in the Constitution. All standard stuff, and he could feel the correct answers slipping effortlessly from his mouth. He only struggled to figure out which of these officials he should be working hardest to impress. Attorney General Nicolaides and White House Counsel MacKneer were the most obvious targets, given their legal expertise and important advisory positions, but Nicolaides bobbed his head like a kowtowing servant, muttering *mmm-hmmm, mmm-hmmm*, an annoying mantra, implying he was a robotic functionary, not an opinionated decision maker; and MacKneer squeezed her wide, owl-like eyes shut and snarled her upper lip in a disfiguring twitch, which indicated some inner reservoir of insecurity and fear. Who in their right mind would let emotional weaklings like those two make Shaw's final pick for the Supreme Court? As for the three chiefs of staff, Rimm, Batherson and Kale, they were clearly sharks, watching him with sly, sidelong glances, searching for his weaknesses, considering points of attack. They were doing what Manny had expected them to do: calculating tangential factors like his vocabulary and how his ethnicity might play, his tone and grammar, his looks and manners. Manny made sure to acknowledge all three of them equally, and addressed his answers to them, even though Nicolaides and MacKneer posed all the questions. But most importantly, he never lost awareness of that ominous presence at the far end of the table. Vice President Bloomfield sat like a king on his throne, in the only chair with armrests. He said nothing, not a word, and hardly moved. Bloomfield was the real authority here. His thumbs up or thumbs down would be as consequential as Nero's back in the day, at least during this early round of questioning—before President Shaw got involved. Manny ceded full authority to Bloomfield, and allowed himself to be the object of the man's scrutiny. He did not turn his own gaze to the Vice President, and he did not speak to him directly. Subtle deference. Only when Nicolaides asked Manny for his take on executive power did it seem right to directly address the Vice President, a man who had built his entire career on that issue. "I think the Court has grossly weakened the executive's proper power in recent years. If I were a member, I would help correct that imbalance." He couldn't have asked for a better opportunity to stare squarely at Bloomfield, to meet him eye-to-eye. The Vice President's ashen face was as bloated as his fingers, but Manny's comment seemed to elicit a faint smile at the corners of his lips.

Kale tossed his pen and notepad on the desk. "Now we need to ask you some personal questions, Judge Arroyo, if you don't mind."

Manny pressed his molars together, crossed his legs under the table. "I don't mind at all."

"Taxes?"

"Always on time."

"Any illegals in your employ? Nanny or housekeeper you pay under the table?"

"Everything's on the up and up."

"I see you're recently divorced."

"I am. In January."

"You know that's not ideal."

"Well, it is what it is."

"Might I ask you why?"

Manny peered at him intently. "Might I ask why it matters?"

Kale sat back, chuckling. "'Cause if you're going be our nominee, then we need to know exactly what bones are buried in your backyard."

Manny nodded. Nothing wrong with challenging a probing question. It showed independence, strength and assurance, all qualities this group would be pleased to see. "Sonia and I had irreconcilable differences."

"Affairs?"

"Just fighting."

"Nothing ever physical, though, right? No hitting or anything?"

"Of course not, Gordon. My God."

"Well, Manny, I've got to ask. The confirmation process isn't a schoolyard kickball game, and the referees don't always have your best interests in mind." Kale picked up his pen again, tapped it against his nose. "On good enough terms with the ex these days that she'd show up with the kids and sit in the front row for a hearing? Dressed up and so forth?"

"Sonia is amenable, yes."

"You say that like you don't believe it."

"It might cost me a bit personally, but if I ask her, she'll show."

Everyone, including Bloomfield, shared a hearty laugh over that.

"Seeing anyone new?"

He shook his head somberly. "I'm single."

"Anything else? Anything at all? Things you don't want to say, but unfortunately have to? We're not fond of surprises."

"That's everything, Gordon." Manny smiled. But that phrase—*I'm single*—lingered in his mind.

He fielded additional questions about his childhood in Irvine, his father's managerial position in a U.S.-owned pharmaceutical company—the reason for his family's emigration to California from Puerto Rico—and his undergraduate years at Baylor. The conversation took a quick detour into the prospects of the Baylor Bears football team this season—another good sign. They all stood when it was time for Manny to go. He shook their hands once again, his palms no longer sweaty, and thanked them individually, but not profusely—no dignity in sycophancy. Manny was released with an assurance that he would be contacted in the near future, no matter what they decided.

The two interns waited for him in the next room and ferried him back down the elevator. The same driver was sitting in the idling limo by the curb. As the Town Car pulled away from the Old Executive Office Building, Manny slouched in exhaustion from his ordeal, and looked out the back window at this city he barely knew. This bureaucratic town might soon be his home.

He closed his eyes and pictured Cassandra Sykes. Last week she had stomped into Manny's condo and collapsed on his sofa, her eyes red and puffy from tears. Her hair had abandoned its tight curl and exploded in all directions, wild and frizzy. Her skin was blotchy, and she had swollen bags under her eyes. She said she had just left her husband, Denny, for good. What the hell was wrong with women these days? If you're going to leave your husband and expect another man to take you in right away, isn't it just common sense to pull yourself together before descending on him? Is that any way to stalk your new prey? You do your fucking hair, at the very least.

Cassandra made a stupid and naïve suggestion that night. She said that she shouldn't move to Washington in the fall, that she should drop her next job as Associate Chief Counsel for Corporate Affairs with the IRS and instead find a job in the Bay area. She wanted to move in with Manny. Denny was an overgrown man-boy, she said, who would never finish his PhD—she just didn't love him anymore. She was ready to move on. She pushed Manny on her plan, but he said it was too serious a decision to make in one night. He told her he would think about it.

Christ Almighty, he had gotten in too deep with that woman. He had been planning to end their relationship as soon as Cassandra moved to Washington in September, but now things were getting complicated. Things were getting ugly. *Cassandra* was getting ugly.

He leaned back against the headrest behind him. The Town Car crossed the 14th Street Bridge into Virginia, heading back to Dulles Airport, where Manny would catch the late flight to San Francisco. *I'm single*, he told Kale, Rimm and Batherson, Nicolaides and MacKneer. He told the Vice President of the United States that he was single. Now he had better make that true.

Manny was unwinding before a shitty cop show the following Wednesday night, eating a bowl of Shredded Wheat and drinking a Diet Coke, when his intercom buzzed. No question who it was. He had been ignoring Cassandra's increasingly pushy phone messages all week, and it was just like her to drop by without warning. He switched the TV off, left his cereal on the side table, and pressed the button on his intercom.

"I need to speak to you."

"You've got to come back another time. I've got three opinions due on Friday."

"Manny, I have to speak to you *now*."

"I'm sure it can wait, Cassandra."

"It's not going to wait. I'm going to stay out here until you buzz me up."

He released the talk button on his intercom. *Christ.* Manny did not want this incensed and possessive woman stalking him on the corner of Berry and 5th while residents tramped in and out of his building. He buzzed her up, went to empty his cereal, and left the bowl by the sink. Maybe he should take some papers out and spread them out on the coffee table to make it look as if he had been working.

Cassandra stood on his threshold, wearing an oversized sweater and leggings, her hair pulled back into a scrappy ponytail and her face entirely devoid of makeup. Manny held the door open for her. He didn't touch or greet her, and then he followed her into the living room.

She didn't sit down. She looked at him, wrinkles pressed between her eyebrows, and she tensed and distended her otherwise soft lips. Cassandra was so far removed from the coy and pretty young lady who had entered his chambers last September, with that bright red belt and red shoes, that sheer silk scarf knotted around her neck, her sweet smile and effortless, casual elegance.

"I'm pregnant."

Manny heard the words, but he took a moment to register them. Sour bile seeped beneath his tongue from the back of his throat.

"Are you sure Denny's not the father?"

"Are you kidding? I haven't slept with Denny since October. You know that."

Out the window, he searched the blackness of San Francisco bay, the yellow lights of Alameda glowing behind it. Rage made those lights tremble and wave in his vision.

"Did you deliberately not take the proper precautions?"

"Oh my God." Cassandra laughed bitterly, walked in a circle and glared at him. "What about you, Manny? Did you deliberately put your condom on wrongly?" Without blush or shadow, her wide-set eyes and broad nose loudly broadcasted her relationship to Justice Sykes—something he had managed not to think about for all these months. It was not an attractive association. "I cannot fucking believe you just said that."

He retreated into the kitchen and stood behind the counter. Putting a reasonable physical barrier between him and this woman seemed like a mighty fine idea right now. He felt like strangling her. He stared at the counter, its green marble flecked with shining bits of quartz, which seemed to pulse inside the stone. "I am *very* angry about this."

"You are such an asshole."

"Calm down, Cassandra."

"I'm perfectly calm, Manny. Do I not look calm to you?"

She didn't move or flinch—just stared at him.

He felt heavy on his feet. He felt hot and suddenly dizzy, cornered and violent—like a tricked animal, like he had been playing some secret game for months that he had never understood, with rules beyond his comprehension. Traps and snares had been set for him. Manny's rage expanded. He wanted to snarl, and bite this woman. Had she done this to him on purpose? Had Cassandra lured him into her lair with fake warmth and girlish deference?

He didn't take his eyes off the green marble counter.

"I'm thinking about getting an abortion."

"You know perfectly well, Cassandra, what I think of that odious practice." He channeled all of his energy into sounding steady, keeping calm. He would be okay as long as he didn't look at her. "I can't believe you did this. You've just put us in a terrible situation."

"*Me?* It's *my* fault?"

"I was under the distinct and clear impression you were taking care of this."

"It takes two to get pregnant, Manny."

Now he had to look up at her. She aimed her teary, bloodshot eyes at him, a bubble of snot in her nostrils.

"You are such an unbelievable pig," she said. Cassandra stormed past him, out of his condo, slamming the door behind her. He heard her cursing in the hallway, all the way to the elevator.

Manny spun around and ripped opened the refrigerator door. Milk and eggs and cheese and fucking deli meat. He slammed the door closed, grabbed the bowl by the sink and smashed it on the floor.

Shards of blue ceramic were scattered around his kitchen, under his refrigerator and beneath the counter. His neck pulsed with rage, but less now, less. He turned on the water, splashed his face, and then looked at what he had done. He had broken that bowl: his actions, his rage. Manny could break another bowl; he could whine and complain and wail—or he could sweep up the mess. It was his decision, his agency. He had been angry enough to attack Cassandra, but he hadn't done that. Manny alone controlled what Manny did. Manny alone had put himself through Baylor and Penn Law; he alone had worked his way up the ladder at Farrow Marsh and made the right friends in that practice—Martin Fieldstone, Gordon Kale, Jeff Haverstein—to earn his Ninth Circuit appointment. No one else was living his life for him. It was all his own responsibility. And now it was his responsibility to calm down. He would figure out what to do with Cassandra, figure out how to seduce the Shaw administration. He would get that fucking appointment to the United States Supreme Court. Manny would do all of it, alone.

Late that night, Gordon Kale called to say that the President of
the United States wanted to interview Manny in person, so would
he mind coming back to Washington immediately, this time for
a few days? Manny assured him it was no problem. In the early
morning, he emailed his secretary, rescheduled a dentist appointment, packed his bag and cabbed to the airport in time for a 9 A.M.
flight—a rush of activity that didn't allow him to think. It wasn't
until he was sitting quietly in the airport's first-class lounge that
Manny considered the severity of his predicament. He had to be
more strategic. He could not have an enemy in his life right now,
or do anything to make his situation worse. He needed to call and
appease Cassandra.

"What do you want." The sound of Cassandra's voice made
his legs tense up.

"I want apologize for my behavior last night. It was far from
exemplary."

"You were disgusting."

"I was shocked. Please let me apologize."

There weren't many people in the lounge, and it was unlikely
he would be recognized, but still San Francisco was a small city.
Some sleepy, geeky guy fiddled with the coffee maker at the complementary buffet, his cheese Danish about to slide off his plate
onto the rug. But that man didn't seem to be listening to him.

"I want to discuss this shared problem of ours in more detail,
Cassandra—"

"*Shared*. Exactly."

"But I can't do that now. My head's a mess, and I need to think
about it clearly. Please, accept my apology and just give me a little
time to calm down."

God, he hating apologizing to his ex-lovers. Manny had called
Sonia last night, begged her to take Lonny and Carmen for the
weekend, and apologized to her as well. He had had to say *sorry*
more often in the past few days then he had in years. It made him
itch all over.

"Fine," Cassandra said. "Call me in a few days." Cassandra's
voice was softer and less enraged now, as they got off the phone.

He could only hope that he had done enough. He couldn't have any kind of public scene waiting for him when he returned from Washington.

Manny squirmed in his airport lounge chair. Could he really have another child? This weekend Sonia would take his kids, Carmen and Lonny, to St. Sebastian's in Mill Valley, as was right and proper, even if he couldn't go with them. His children would sit quietly in the pews, well behaved, lulled by the soporific liturgy, their hair clean and brushed, their skin warming in the red glow of the stained glass windows. Carmen would wear that floral dress with the matching azalea in her hair. Alonzo would wear his blue blazer and sharp, striped tie. Manny's children were beautiful, and he loved them, but he had already raised them. He was happy to be done with all that. Only six months left until Carmen's confirmation.

Many men in his position would push their girlfriends to get an abortion. They wouldn't even think twice about doing it. They would rather murder a baby than show a little resilience. But Manny would never be that selfish. He simply couldn't do it. So he was trapped. Cassandra had known what he believed, and she had fucking trapped him.

He stood and grabbed a Danish from the buffet. He wanted to crush it in his fingers and throw it against the wall, but instead he took a long and deep breath, exhaled slowly, and took a bite. He would have to calm down and clear his mind. He would have to release his anger long before he reached Washington.

The same tall and thin limo driver picked up Manny at Dulles airport, although he had abandoned his *Moreno* sign. The car with tinted windows drove into the city, proceeded through the White House gates and approached the covered entrance to the West Wing—just pulled right up. It was surreal. Manny had always wanted to see the White House and to meet a sitting President, and he had always assumed he would, but it seemed improbable that he was minutes away from doing both those things. Another suited aide opened the limo's door and ushered Manny into the lobby. They passed by the Roosevelt Room, where Manny glimpsed a painting over the fireplace of Teddy in his Rough Rider uniform, mounted on a jumpy steed. The aide led him through a narrow hallway into a wider corridor and stopped before a non-descript door. "Right in here, Judge Arroyo."

Manny stepped into the Oval Office. President Shaw was seated behind the massive and ornate Resolute Desk, chatting with Lorna MacKneer, who stood beside him. The President rose to greet him. "Hello, Judge!" The right side of Shaw's face twisted into a sneering half-smile—that smile that had been broadcast on television countless times. "So good to finally meet you." Mark Shaw's hand was warm and dry, and his smile had a genuine friendliness. "I guess you already know Lorna."

Lorna MacKneer greeted Manny with her big, twitchy grin. She stood behind the President, to his side, holding a large file of papers that were probably all about him.

"Let's have a seat."

The President led him to one of the pale, yellow-striped Martha Washington chairs positioned by the fireplace and took the other for himself. MacKneer sat on the cream-colored damask couch on the President's side. The Oval Office was oddly clean and sparse. It didn't look as if any real work was done here. The President's desk was empty of papers, and a large bouquet of freshly cut yellow roses decorated the coffee table, which matched the soothing palate of the large oval carpet. Photographs and paintings had been set on shelves, side tables and walls with artful precision, as Sonia would have done it, but the designer here knew exactly which colors in those pictures would work well together, and which would clash, and what surfaces needed the light touch of a gleaming silver frame, or the dark heft of a wooden one.

The President left his suit jacket hanging on his desk chair, and wore only a dress shirt with rolled sleeves. His body was trimmer than Manny's, but less muscular. No body fat. Must be his mountain biking. It was an impressive physique, seeing as the President was a good 12 years Manny's senior, and the judge was in great shape. Rumor had it that the 62-year-old could ditch security agents half his age on a steep hill climb if he so desired.

"So I looked at my records and saw we talked on the phone back in 2002."

"I remember it well."

"We got you through the Senate pretty easy that round, huh?"

"You sure did. Guess it's not always that smooth."

"Oh, you better believe it's not!" President Shaw laughed. "You well, generally?"

"I am. Enjoying the Ninth Circuit. Healthy and fit."

"I hear you've been divorced this year?"

"Yes, unfortunately."

"Well, that happens. Catholic base might not like it so much, but we live in the real world, don't we?"

"The Catholic base will likely forgive him," MacKneer piped in, "once they see his voting record."

Manny uncrossed his arms, and squeezed his hands together. He didn't acknowledge the White House Counsel's comment, but wished he could bark back at her that he didn't care one way or another if the Catholic voting base approved of his marital status, that it was none of their damn business. Nor did he like Ms. MacKneer speaking about him in the third person when he was sitting right in front her. But nervousness always made him angry.

"Swinging single, now, are you?" The President nudged Manny on the arm.

"Not so swinging, but certainly single."

"Been told you're not seeing anyone?"

Manny hesitated. It was one thing to mislead advisors, another thing to lie directly to the President of the United States. But then he wasn't going to sleep with Cassandra again, so technically it wasn't a lie to say that he wasn't seeing anyone *actively*. Furthermore, it was irritating to have the entire White House staff, including the President himself, rifling around in his private affairs. It was none of their business, and it wasn't as if Cassandra's pregnancy would influence Arroyo's interpretations of statutes or his reading of the Constitution.

"I'm not actively seeing anyone."

"Think you can keep yourself unhitched for a few months, if it comes down to it?" Shaw winked, like some overly chummy father trying to act cool with his teenage son. "After that you can do what you want."

Manny said yes, he could stay single, and forced a smile for the man. The President didn't have to speak so casually with him. Would Shaw have reminded a white judge to act "respectable" for the senators? On the other hand, Manny reminded himself, President Shaw was known for being comfortable with people of all races, and his multicultural cabinet could never be accused of discrimination.

Sweat trickled down Manny's sides. He hoped it wasn't staining his suit jacket.

"So Lorna, Gordon and the Vice President have all told me you support the Unitary Executive theory. They said you gave a speech about it back in 2000?"

"Yes, for the Federalist Society. My position hasn't changed. I subscribe to the Unitary Executive theory in its strongest form: the president has hierarchical control over the execution of all federal law. That means Congress today oversteps its bounds, pretty much regularly. It also means independent counsels created by Congress to investigate the executive in any way are constitutionally troublesome."

"That's good, Manny. Keep going. You're on a roll." The President laughed.

"I also believe a Unitary Executive is at the apex of his powers in times of war. As soon as Congress authorizes the use of force, the president has plenary power over any decision having to do with that conflict. That's true without exception. Now obviously, Mr. President, I can't talk about any actual cases that might come before the Court, but broadly speaking the theory should apply to situations when the executive, say, wants to interpret treaties differently than Congress does, or when he wants to process captured foreign detainees without being subject to federal court review."

"But that's just your *general* position, right?"

Counsel MacKneer twitched and nodded beside her boss.

"Absolutely, Mr. President. That position has no bearing on how I might rule in any specific case with any of its particular constraints."

"And that's what you'd tell the Senate if they asked?"

"Of course. It's the truth."

The President and MacKneer nodded in concurrence. Manny silently congratulated himself on making a direct reference to *Al-Tounsi* without actually mentioning the case itself.

Out the Oval Office's eastern windows, through the columns along the West Colonnade, there were a hundred ripe red blossoms in the Rose Garden, just as there were supposed to be. Every damned inch of this room was iconic. This office's primary purpose was as a symbol of American power and autonomy. Isolated in the back of the West Wing, with windows facing the South Lawn and the picturesque garden, the Oval Office was a place for the President to sit and ruminate, a peaceful environment imbued with gravitas where he could make his most difficult decisions. It was an iconic room for this heroic figure.

"I think, Mr. President, the fundamental question posed by the Unitary Executive theory is this: What kind of sovereignty does our country demand, and what kind of sovereign? The framers never wanted to handcuff a sitting president with too much oversight, especially in times of war. When our nation is under attack, as it is currently, we can't have Congress or the federal courts second-guessing each and every independent decision the president makes. We need a fully autonomous executive. That's what the Constitution says. Nations, presidents, individual *people* are autonomous. Like it or not, when push comes to shove, we're separate from one another—each as solid and indivisible as an island. The framers knew that, and so they codified natural law. They understood that if you hold a president back with hen-pecking laws and regulations and limitations, our country's enemies, who are as ruthless now as they were in 1787—and who don't have those same moral constraints—will tear us to shreds. They will destroy this country if we choose to restrict an executive with Congressional oversight."

President Shaw nodded forcefully. "And you feel that in your gut?"

"I've reasoned it out, Mr. President, *and* I feel it in my gut."

Later that night, as Manny lay sprawled on his bed in the Mayflower Hotel, watching FOX news on mute and washing down a chocolate bar with the mini-bar's surprisingly decent scotch, he further considered the theory of a Unitary Executive. The profundity of his argument extended beyond constitutional law. Any individual person could be seen as analogous to the executive of the United States. Personal freedom was always under attack, always precarious. Consider Manny's own autonomy, and how Cassandra's pregnancy had threatened it. If Cassandra had behaved in a fully moral and trustworthy manner, she would have taken the damn pill until it was clear both of them wanted to have children. But Cassandra hadn't done that, had she? Her behavior had transgressed the accepted rules of engagement for a budding relationship. Her behavior was an attack—vicious or unconscious, or just plain careless—that hit its target, and had bonded them together for life. Worse, now that she was pregnant, the accepted rules of conduct for Manny, the would-be father, demanded his prudence, admission to the president, and lifelong financial compensation. It meant being constrained by rules of propriety even after his girlfriend hadn't conformed to any accepted rules. Manny was supposed to stand up like a man, raise a baby he didn't want, and put his own professional future at risk. That was obviously the "right" thing to do—Christ, there might as well be a Geneva Conventions governing personal relationships that claimed as much. But Manny had no autonomy left if he accepted those full restraints. He would never be able to defend himself.

Of course, Manny's political philosophy and personal philosophies had the same root. Why should this Executive bow to every absurd clause in the Geneva Conventions or every bit of Congressional oversight when the terrorists flouted the rules of war, crashing commercial airplanes into the twin towers? And why should Manny let Cassandra's pregnancy determine his behavior? She had entrapped and ensnared him with her deceit, but now it was his duty to acknowledge and respect their relationship, and to tell the President about it? No. Sometimes the right thing to do is to refuse to play by the accepted rules. If someone comes at you with trickery, you have to respond with flexibility and autonomy. In the political example, only a strong, unitary executive who isn't under the thumb of Congress or the courts can make the perfectly logical and moral decision to opt out of oppressive "rules" when they are certain to destroy him.

Manny tilted the last few drops of scotch out of the tiny plastic bottle into his mouth. Too much was at stake. This was his only shot at the Supreme Court. There was no way he would let Cassandra's irresponsibility destroy his career now.

In the morning, the brilliantly sunlit Oval Office showed signs of having been worked in. A mostly empty plate of bagels rested beside a bowl of cream cheese, and another platter, with a few chunks of melon and berries left on it, had replaced the yellow roses on the coffee table. Papers were strewn across the Resolute desk, probably Manny's own rulings from the Ninth Circuit. President Shaw, wearing a suit jacket and a crisp red tie, seemed hale and refreshed, but MacKneer, Nicolaides and Kale had haggard faces and bloodshot eyes. Together they reeked of a harsh amalgam of perfume, cologne and sporty deodorant. But beneath those floral and musky scents, Manny could smell the vinegary aroma of their bodies. A long night's work, he guessed. President Shaw ushered Manny into one of the Martha Washington chairs and patted him on the back.

"Manny, we'd like to nominate you to the Court. Congratulations."

Manny gripped the arms of his chair, pressed his lips together. "I accept your offer."

"Excellent. I suspect that's going be your first of many right calls."

Everyone laughed.

"Thank you, Mr. President. I hope you'll be proud of this decision long after you've left office."

"Now, I want to announce your nomination Monday morning. In the meantime, Rolando and Lorna would like to start working with you this weekend."

"Preparation will be intense. It will pretty well have to be your full-time job for the next six to eight weeks." Attorney General Nicolaides leaned his hands on the back of the couch.

"Won't exactly be a good time either." The President laughed. "I'm sure you know the drill."

Manny's heart quickened. Of course he knew about the nomination process, but he hadn't let himself consider it seriously. He would have to visit all the senators in their offices when they returned from their summer breaks, answer their tough questions, and generally be on his best behavior. He would have to fill out the Judiciary Committee's extensive questionnaire, which would require detailed answers, like writing a large memoir. The White House would stage mock hearings for him. The press would be everywhere, poking their snouts into his past decisions, his lectures, his traffic tickets, his whole life. They would want to talk to Manny's colleagues and friends. They would want to speak with Sonia and his clerks. They would speak with Cassandra.

"It'll be a hard process, but you will be confirmed." The President smiled at him. "We have the votes. I guarantee it."

For the rest of the day, Manny worked with Rolando Nicolaides and Lorna MacKneer in the Roosevelt Room, doors closed to everyone but that core contingent originally present in the Oval Office. He collated his written opinions into broad categories, answered questions about his jurisprudence, his private law career, his years at Baylor and Penn, his parents' background and his own childhood. All the while he was unable to shake his thoughts of Cassandra. Would the President drop Manny from consideration if the White House discovered that he had slept with the daughter of his future colleague, Rodney Sykes? And what if they knew she was pregnant? His Senate hearings would turn sordid and comic. His ethics would be questioned, doubted. It would be easier for him if Cassandra got an abortion this week—if she did that without telling him about it, so he wouldn't have to consent. He was adamantly against abortion; he would castigate and denounce her if she asked for his approval, but he would be so relieved if it just *happened*. Then he could break up with her and move on cleanly. Sleeping with Cassandra suddenly seemed like the stupidest thing he had ever done.

At 6 P.M., Gordon Kale ushered Manny out of the West Wing's entrance toward a limo. "We'll leak your nomination to the press Monday morning." Kale opened the car door for him. "So don't tell your former bosses, friends, anyone. Just core family."

"Absolutely."

That night, Manny called Cassandra from his hotel room.

"I'm having the baby," she declared, as soon as she answered the phone.

"Good, Cassandra. I think that's a wise decision."

"You don't sound like you mean that."

"Well, I'm not exactly thrilled about this situation. But I'll help. I'm not a deadbeat."

"You mean you'll give me money as long as the implication's clear I'm the whore, not you?"

Manny gripped the television remote. She was just begging for a fight, wasn't she? But then his *deadbeat* comment was a mistake. It sounded as if he was planning on dumping her. He had to be more careful. God, he wished he could end this ridiculous relationship right now.

"I've been thinking a lot about us, Cassandra, and I don't think you should reconsider your counsel position with the IRS. You should take the job and move to Washington in September."

"That way you won't have to witness my growing belly, or be there to take care of our kid."

"No, quite the opposite. I *will* be with you in Washington in September. We'll have a fighting chance at working through our problems and staying together." That silenced her. "The President has just nominated me to take Van Cleve's seat on the Supreme Court." He threw the TV remote into the air, where it spun on its axis and turned over twice—a perfect double flip and a twist, like an Olympic diver—and landed back in his palm.

"The Supreme Court?"

"The United States Supreme Court. I'm sure you've heard of it."

"But my father."

"Don't worry about him. I'll make peace with your father. It won't be difficult."

"Oh my God."

"They're not announcing it until Monday, so you have to keep it quiet."

Manny fingered the power button on the remote. If only he could switch this woman on and off as easily as he could the television.

"Look, Cassandra, I am really sorry about the other night. I said some terrible things to you. I was under a great deal of pressure. I knew they were considering me, and I was freaked out and preoccupied, and then very surprised by your news. Please don't let my one bout of unwarranted anger ruin us."

Manny tossed the remote on the bed. This was a better approach. He would act like a Unitary Executive from here on out: the rules of traditional relationships didn't apply to him anymore. He would pretend he wanted marriage, stability and permanence until he was confirmed. That meant six to eight weeks. He would avoid any trouble in his confirmation hearings only if Cassandra stayed with him. She would have no desire to come forward with a public confession about their relationship. She would avoid the press to protect him. It was early enough in her pregnancy that no questions would arise about the baby's father until well after his confirmation. This whole debacle would stay secret unless they broke up and Cassandra's fury clouded her judgment. Unless she were provoked into attacking him.

And maybe their relationship would improve temporarily. Back in September, Manny had actually liked Cassandra Sykes. She cracked filthy and dark jokes, worthy of any locker room, and shimmered with vivaciousness. She had myriad faults, certainly, but she was never egotistical or attention seeking. It was possible that Cassandra might even come to enjoy the nomination process, that as his ex-clerk she would feel flattered to help the White House gather his opinions, speeches and articles, and summarize his work. He might suggest to the White House staff that she be involved, not just for cynical reasons. It was true she had been a great aide to him on the Ninth Circuit.

"I don't know if I want to be with you, Manny."

"You want to have my child."

"That isn't about what I *want*. I'm pregnant. I take that as seriously as you do."

"Look, Cassandra, I want you to come to Washington. I want to be with you. We're going to have a baby together. It's incredible. Catch the next flight and help me do this. I need you with me."

He waited for her answer, but the silence between them extended for a few seconds too long. Goddamn it, he had said too much. She didn't believe a word. He had fucked it all up.

"Denny told my brother we're getting a divorce."

Arroyo's breath shortened. "Did he tell your brother anything else? Does Sam know about us?"

"I don't know what Sam knows and what Sam doesn't know. He and Denny are good friends. I can't control what they say to each other."

"What about your father?"

"I don't know, Manny."

"No one should know about our relationship until after my confirmation. It wouldn't be fair to put a spotlight on your father."

Cassandra snorted. "Oh, you're suddenly worried about him?"

"There are many reasons why silence is the right option, Cassandra."

"I'm sure that's true. All I'm saying is my father—Mr. Adolph Eichmann himself—is not the person you're worried about. You're worried about yourself, Manny. No one but yourself."

He twisted the corner of his pillowcase into a tight spiral. If he removed the pillow, he could roll out the cotton case long enough to make a rope. And then he could strangle Cassandra Sykes with it. God, how this woman obliterated his good will.

"Come to Washington, Cassandra."

"I'll think about it."

Monday morning, as Manny rode in the Town Car on its short trip down 17th Street to the White House, the radio buzzed with Kale's leak. The driver had tuned his radio to a liberal pundit's show, a man who sounded thrilled that there was a Latino nominee to the U.S. Supreme Court. He spoke of Arroyo's Puerto Rican heritage with smug satisfaction, as if the inconsequential fact of a justice's skin had somehow transformed the United States into a better nation, and the pundit himself into a finer human being. Christ Almighty, was skin color the only thing these liberal racists ever thought about? Why should a left-leaning radio host be happy about Arroyo's nomination? He should be railing against it, on principled grounds, no matter whether Manny was black, brown, white or green. He should be nothing but dismayed.

Manny stepped out of the car inside the White House compound and discovered the entire West Wing staff waiting by the entrance. They applauded, and he beamed, shaking hand after hand. Younger staffers fixed him with the wide-eyed gawk often saved for celebrities, that hunger in their eyes—their desire to connect to a power broker. It was disconcerting and strange, but incredible; he was the same person he was last week, but now he was decidedly more important.

He was paraded through the halls by MacKneer, stopping to shake hands with one person, then another, and then led into a small office, where he was left alone with Gordon Kale. The Deputy Chief of Staff asked him to recite his short acceptance speech, just once, for practice.

"You got it, Manny. You'll be terrific."

A press conference had been called for 10 A.M. in the East Room. Manny drank a cup of coffee in the Roosevelt Room and chatted with Kale about the upcoming NFL season. Anyone strong enough to beat the Patriots? Only the Colts, opined Gordon, and Manny was feeling so grand he wasn't about to disagree. Ten minutes before the scheduled conference, Kale led Manny into the Blue Room to wait with President Shaw, Vice President Bloomfield and Jeremy Rimm. Manny had gone over his speech a couple more times, and all morning he had felt more excited than nervous, but now, standing here with the most powerful men in the world, Manny shifted his weight from side to side, twiddled his fingers, and fiddled with the paper tucked into his jacket's inside pocket.

"Don't drop that speech," said the Vice President, with a wink.

"Is my family here?" Manny was surprised by the plea in his voice. He knew Carmen and Lonny had arrived with Sonia and his parents late last night, and that the White House wanted to keep them in a separate hotel, to make sure no one figured out who the nominee was a day early. Of course they were sitting out there in the East Room.

"Your kids look mighty handsome and proud. Don't you worry about that."

"And don't be nervous," added the President. He patted Manny on the back. Shaw's crooked smile indicated his ease. Eight years on the national stage, requiring countless speeches and interviews and debates in two grueling campaigns, had made him immune to cameras and publicity. This little press conference would not be a big challenge for the President. "Best advice I've got is don't say *orgasm* when you mean to say *organism*."

Everyone laughed, even Arroyo.

"My mom used to tell me that before my school presentations. Now that's some good advice."

At precisely ten o'clock, Manny stepped into the Cross Hall, flanked by President Shaw and Vice President Bloomfield, and marched slowly toward the blue podium in the East Room. The room was packed with journalists and politicos and was brightly lit. Cameras flashed and clicked. Walking into this scrum felt like an assault, hot and disorienting. As the President spoke at the podium, unfazed, Manny thought about the frank void of the TV cameras' lenses pointing at him, the recognizable faces of the White House press corps, senators and congressmen. He spied Carmen and Lonny sitting a few rows back, looking a little shocked, hands in their laps, postures stiff, well groomed. Sonia had been nothing but accommodating and gracious in this whole nomination circus, flying out to Washington with the kids even though the White House had opted to keep her away from the press conference, given their recent divorce. When he had confessed his big news to her on the phone, Sonia seemed genuinely proud of his accomplishment. Manny's elderly parents sat beside his children in place of his ex-wife, his mother teary with pride. His parents were here, in the White House, for his nomination to the Court! Manny grinned like a fool.

The President finished his introduction, stepped back from the podium and touched Manny's shoulder. They shook hands for the cameras, and he stepped forward. The reporters clutched pens and pads of paper, cameras clicked ceaselessly. Lorna MacKneer, L. J. Batherson and Rolando Nicolaides were discreetly positioned in the back, standing beside a television camera. Manny removed his speech from his jacket pocket, pressed it on the podium's slanted surface. The printed words were enlarged, so he wouldn't have to worry about squinting or misreading them. He rested his palms on the sides of the famous podium, the President and Vice President flanking him like choice wingmen guarding their ace fighter.

"Mr. President, I am humbled and honored by your nomination today, and I thank you for the confidence you have shown in me."

Five weeks later, Gordon Kale crossed the threshold into the Roosevelt Room in the middle of Manny's meeting. The Deputy Chief of Staff was an overweight man with pale skin, a waddling double chin, and a knobby, elongated head that reflected light from the powerful halogens. He never looked healthy. His rounded fat shoulders blurred any distinction between neck and arm, and dark stains colored the pits of his white shirt. He wore rimless, tinted glasses that made him look like a gangster. Red-faced and glaring, Kale pressed his lips together and held his jaw tight.

"I'd like to see you in my office." Kale's breathing was audible and phlegmy like a bulldog's. He had been driving Manny bat-shit crazy these past few weeks, and that had made him all the more physically repulsive. Kale had been autocratic and demanding, and every minor problem was an emergency: the stubborn Republican senator from Michigan who wouldn't commit to voting *yes*, that hiccup investigation into Manny's underpaid tax return in 1996. Now here he was again, angry as hell, interrupting Manny's robust meeting with Batherson and MacKneer with some other manufactured crisis.

"Can it wait, Gordon?"

"No, it cannot."

Kale pushed his glasses up on his nose and disappeared into the hallway. Batherson and MacKneer glanced at each other and shrugged, and Manny tossed his pen on the table. "Excuse me."

The Deputy Chief of Staff was already seated behind his desk. His small office felt constraining on a good day, but today it seemed as tight as a dog cage, even with its expansive view of the trees behind the White House.

"Shut the door."

Manny resisted an urge to tell Kale to calm down and not to speak to him like that. Instead he did what he was told. He sat down.

"We got ourselves a big problem." Kale held up a stapled, three-page document. "This article's coming out in next month's *Vanity Fair*. Claims you've been amorously involved with Cassandra Sykes for eight or nine months running, and that you broke up her marriage. Further accusations of the scandalous sort. Sources double-checked and confirmed. Now the editor wants the White House to comment on it. Or even better—you. They're pretty well going to print this no matter what we say."

He handed over the document and leaned forward onto his desk, defiant, furious. Manny tried to look calm as he read the headline: *Arroyo's Girl*.

"Maybe we could start by telling them that Cassandra is a full-grown woman, not a *girl*. She's an accomplished lawyer."

"I've been dealing with this thing all afternoon, Manny."

"And I've been in the Roosevelt Room, doing my job."

Kale twisted his lips and snorted. "Well, I'm going to let you take a minute or two to read this thing over. That's what I'm going to do." He sat back, squinty-eyed, glowering.

Manny's mounting panic made him want to scream and punch indiscriminately, or stand up and kick down the door. No good would come from staring defiantly at Kale, or acknowledging him in any way. He scanned the document, its print drifting in and out of focus as waves of fear and rage took hold and passed through him. Who the fuck had betrayed him? This journalist had better name names. He focused on the beginning of the article.

Emmanuel Arroyo doesn't look like he's 51 years old. The handsome, olive-skinned jurist has a youth and vibrancy that has acquired legendary status through-out the scattered cities of the massive Ninth Circuit. With his strik-ing physique, slicked back hair, and styl-ish Burt Reynolds-era mustache, Arroyo's the pinup boy of appel-late judges. "Manny's got arms like a line-backer," said one career employee at the James R. Brown-ing Courthouse in San Francisco, where Arroyo has worked since his appointment to the federal bench in 2002. "Big shoulders, bulging pecs—that guy is *cut*."

Emmanuel Arroyo's already commanding presence is about to get even a whole lot more impressive. If confirmed this month as President Shaw's second selection to the United States Supreme Court, and its first-ever Latino, Arroyo's vote would have the power to radically transform American law, push-ing it far to the right on the country's most contentious issues like gay marriage and abor-tion rights. The Court will get younger and bolder, more confident and conservative. And it's not just the law that will change. Some say Arroyo has the potential to spice up the stodgy atmosphere on First Street more than any nominee who

has come along in a generation.

But Washingtonians won't have to wait for Arroyo's confirmation or his presence in the hallowed halls of the Supreme Court Build-ing for sexual intrigue to land in the nation's capital. *Vanity Fair* has confirmed that the recently divorced judge has been dating one of his clerks for months now, a married woman who recently followed him to Washington and is temporarily working with the White House staff on Arroyo's nomination. Her name is Cassandra Sykes. If that name sounds familiar, it's because Cassandra Sykes is the accomplished daughter of his future colleague, Justice Rodney Sykes.

Manny squeezed his hand into a fist under the desk. Coffee burned the lining of his stomach. He skimmed a few more paragraphs. The tone was breezy and lurid all the way through. The article claimed their affair had begun in February, that Cassandra had left her husband for good in July and moved to Washington in August. (Denny, thankfully, hadn't been quoted.) The journalist hadn't missed anything, but nowhere, *nowhere*, did it mention sources—who exactly had ratted Manny out.

He tossed the papers on Kale's desk and shrugged as if there was nothing of consequence there, certainly not about him. Kale sighed.

"Let's be frank with each other, Manny."

"I'm happy to be frank. I don't believe the White House should make any comment about this speculation, or that I should either."

"Is it true?"

"Of course it's true, Gordon. You think *Vanity Fair* would get this far if it wasn't true?"

"When did this thing start?"

"Over the summer."

"Cassandra was your employee."

"Not at the time, she wasn't. We were two consenting adults no longer working together."

"If this started before June, we've got an ethical mess on our hands."

"It's not unethical to date a coworker, even a subordinate. Besides, our relationship began in early July."

"In July, Manny? When she was done with her term and you two were barely seeing each other? You really expect me to believe that?"

"Our relationship started in July."

"I could go upstairs and ask Cassandra myself, mind you."

"Go right ahead."

"Some sworn witness is going to say *February* before the Senate Judiciary Committee. You understand that, right?"

"Look, Gordon, if some liberal saboteur claims they saw me kissing Cassandra under the mistletoe last winter they can go right ahead, but I will swear the contrary under oath, and it will be my word against theirs."

"Goddamn it, Manny, we asked you *outright* if you were seeing someone, and you did not mince words in your denial."

"Who I sleep with is not the business of the United States government. I'm fairly certain that's settled law. Besides, none of this matters. We've got enough votes to get me through."

"Oh, we have the votes, now, do we? It's all smooth sailing from here on in for Manny Arroyo? So I guess you're pretty positive that the President's going to stick with your nomination even though you lied to him outright?"

Manny sat back and crossed his legs. He showed nothing, *nothing*—but imagined having to shuffle up to that podium in the East Room to read another speech in oversized font, before the flashes and television cameras, although without any senators or his family present. Having to stand there and thank the President for his evaporated support. Having to apologize sincerely—*Again! With sincerity!*—to the entire country for fucking everything up. Manny cleared his throat. He wanted to hop out of his chair and pound that fat fuck Kale right in his sneering jaw.

"You have reason to believe my nomination would be in jeopardy over something this trivial?"

"It is not trivial. The President is very upset." Kale picked up the article, scanned it, shook his head. "What's this country coming to?"

"It's a witch hunt."

"It sure the hell is a witch hunt, but it's your own fucking fault." He tossed the article back on his desk. "The President's going talk to you about this today. In fact I'll check in now, see if this is a good time. We got maybe twenty-four hours if we're lucky until this thing gets out national, and then it's going be a tornado in your world—photographers in your lobby, your garage, everywhere, and we need to know exactly how the heck we're handling this before the vultures descend." He stood, the fat old walrus, puffing his chest like an alpha male perched on his stubby back flippers. "You read that thing over carefully because there'll be some hard questions coming your way pretty soon."

Kale left him stinging. Such blatant disrespect. No one believed him anymore; they didn't even want to pretend. Manny rubbed his face with damp palms and picked up the article.

Fresh out of Penn Law, Emmanuel and Sonia returned to Oakland, where Arroyo was hired by the prestigious California law firm of Farrow Marsh. Although he was the only Latino lawyer in a company with few visible minorities, that didn't bother him much. Arroyo had always been more comfortable in the white world of California than in Philadelphia's Puerto Rican community with Sonia's family. "Manny attended every cocktail party and reception we had," said Roger Korn, a now-retired partner at Farrow Marsh. "He always gravitated to the most powerful man in the room, whoever that happened to be. Pretty soon we were actively pairing Manny up with clients who needed a personal relationship. Because Manny could charm anyone, and loved doing so."

It was in those elite cocktail parties and board rooms of Farrow Marsh that Arroyo first met Jeffery Haverstein, the future governor of California, and Gordon Kale, the present Deputy White House Chief of Staff. Kale was working for Fieldstone Consolidated at the time, a corporation that had extensive dealings with Arroyo's firm. Arroyo grew close with both men, and was prescient enough to keep them as friends. No doubt Governor Haverstein and Gordon Kale helped secure the judge's meteoric rise.

Farrow Marsh has a long-standing mentoring policy, assigning each incoming lawyer to a senior partner, someone who can guide the new hire and show him the ropes. Emmanuel Arroyo was rash and pushy, and his mentor couldn't have been a bigger contrast in disposition.

"We rather blindly assigned him to Rodney Sykes," said Korn. "It's kind of incredible now, when you think about it—two future Supreme Court justices put together like that." Sykes was a staid and studious lawyer, 12 years Arroyo's senior, with no real interest in social climbing at Farrow Marsh. "Rodney was a quiet guy who kept to himself. His only real friend was Morris Bayfield," said Korn. "Sometimes I'd hear them talking about opera or wine in the hall, and I know they had lunch together frequently, but they never came to cocktail parties." Not only did Bayfield and Sykes live low-key personal lives, they also shared an emphatically traditional view of law as a set of rules to be strictly obeyed, never circumvented or massaged. "Rodney's skill set matched the needs of our more conservative clients," said Korn, "but we had other clients, too, who were more keen to push boundaries. Powerful companies, mostly. Those were the clients that Manny wanted right away. But he felt he couldn't get access to them while shadowing Rodney Sykes. He was ambitious, and felt hampered by Rodney's temperate manner."

Arroyo's growing frustration with his cautious mentor peaked in a now-infamous confrontation that lawyers at the firm still call "The Eichmann Incident." "About six months after Manny joined us, a group of top partners gathered in a boardroom to discuss one of Sykes's trickier cases," said Clayton Youkalis, another senior part-ner at Farrow Marsh. "Sykes was arguing for restraint and compliance on every issue, as he often did, and you could see it was driving Arroyo crazy. We all noticed it. But then Manny cracked. He started shouting that Sykes's reasoning was slavish, and that it reminded him of Adolph Eichmann's, and that if we left it unchecked it would probably have the same grim results. The whole room fell silent. Manny was so aggressive, and what a shocking thing to say. After that outburst, it was all over between them. Arroyo was reprimanded, and I don't think he and Sykes worked together again."

Sources tell *Vanity Fair* that the animosity between Emmanuel Arroyo and Rodney Sykes has lingered for years, and has never been resolved. One source has even speculated that Judge Arroyo's affair with Cassandra Sykes is motivated by his anger toward her father. Manny Arroyo, he says, has a vindictive streak.

Insiders are now wondering if peace will be possible between Justices Arroyo and Sykes on the Supreme Court. Arroyo's tempestuous past with his mentor and his present affair with Cassandra Sykes might prove too explosive. The justices are required to meet regularly in Conference and work together closely to reach their decisions. If Arroyo is indeed confirmed, what effect would their personal conflict have on the nation's law?

Manny folded the article in half and laid it on Kale's desk. It was worse than he had feared. He smoldered at the characterization: *Rash. Pushy. Social climber.* And now the President of the United States, the U.S. Senate, and his future colleagues on the Supreme Court would all think him a malicious sadist, screwing Cassandra Sykes because of his hatred for her father. Never mind that he didn't hate Rodney at all. He was completely indifferent to Justice Sykes, and he was certain they could work together just fine. Manny wouldn't be Rodney's subordinate on the Court. The unique and intimate circumstances of the job would dampen any explosive potential in their relationship. Justice Sykes, thanks to his ridiculous repression and ovine conformity, would never make a scene.

How dare they malign him! Cassandra had been a stellar applicant for his clerkship, regardless of her last name. She was sexy as hell when she arrived in his chambers, unhappy with her marriage, eagerly searching for a way out. She had seduced *him*, not the other way around. With her blood-red, come-fuck-me lipsticks and grab-me-by-the-neck scarfs, Cassandra had thrown herself at Manny long before his divorce had been finalized. She had known all about that Eichmann incident and her father's antipathy toward him, so if anyone was guilty of revenge tactics or sadism, it was Cassandra.

"The President wants to talk to you alone." Kale had silently reappeared in the doorway behind him.

Alone. Didn't seem likely. The entire West Wing staff would be waiting in the Oval Office—all the commanders of a regime that liked to face adversity with bellicosity—Batherson, Rimm, MacKneer and Nicolaides. Maybe Press Secretary Orrin Gray? It would be reassuring if Orrin was there, because that would mean the President wasn't going to sack Manny right away, and instead thought of this situation primarily as a communication problem, requiring deft messaging, the right spin.

Kale ushered Manny into the Oval Office. He sighed in relief at the sight of the President standing alone, resting his weight against the Resolute desk, his arms crossing his chest like a disappointed school principal. President Shaw greeted Manny curtly, moved to his chair and offered the judge a seat across from him.

"Now I don't believe it's ever wise to get angry at someone." The President's lip rose in his usual half-smile. "But I need to get some facts straight here. This relationship with Cassandra started in July, right? You sure about that?"

"Bring her down here and ask her yourself if you doubt me, Mr. President."

"Now hold on, Manny, you don't have to get testy. You can just answer the questions I ask. Because remember, we have to focus on the big issue here, which is employer–employee ethics. I need the whole truth. I need your word." President Shaw's slow, deliberate speech made Manny feel like a child. "You can give your word on this?"

"Of course, Mr. President." Manny tried to calculate the time-line for Cassandra's pregnancy. Conception mid-to-late June. Baby due in early-March. No one would be able to figure out the exact math for months, until well after his confirmation. "I give you my word."

"What about this February thing?"

"It isn't true."

"So you're telling me there is no ethical issue? Might not look pretty to some, but you and Cassandra are consenting adults, and you say July, and that's that."

"That's correct."

"All right." The President nodded slowly, like he didn't believe him. He laid his palm flat on his iconic desk. "But here's the thing, Manny. We can't work like this. It's just not how it's done. We can't be expected to get you past the Senate unless we're properly prepared, and we aren't able to do so unless we have ourselves some good, solid information." His condescending tone invoked the moral rectitude and folk wisdom of an old time Texas Ranger. "So I'm just going to come out and warn you. You can't misspeak like that. I don't see how I can continue with your nomination if you misspeak."

"Yes, sir." And Manny heard in his *sir* something he hadn't intended—an echo of what the younger Emmanuel Arroyo had once said in another precarious situation, when he felt similar cowed humiliation. Dragged into Doug Carrodine's corner office at Farrow Marsh, overlooking the Bay Bridge and downtown San Francisco, like a dog who had just pissed on his master's carpet and now had to suffer the insult of having his nose thrust into a pool of urine and scolded. All because of that ridiculous Eich-mann outburst. Manny's comment had apparently broken the bonds of Farrow Marsh's self-righteous Ethical Code of Conduct, a policy that was flagrantly ignored by everyone who actually mattered around the firm. Yes, sir, Mr. Carrodine—ears hanging, tail between his legs—he realized his mistake, and no, sir, Mr. Carrodine, he hadn't meant what he'd said, and yes, sir, of course, Mr. Carrodine, he would apologize right away to Rodney Sykes. Manny knew that his Eichmann comment was in bad taste, and too harshly delivered, but Rodney was a milquetoast of a man, Eichmann-like in every conceivable way, who forsook his own critical thought in order to follow the law mindlessly. Rodney Sykes was bad for the firm. Why should Manny, the one lawyer on staff brave enough to tell the truth, be reprimanded and humiliated and forced to eat crow? Where was the sense in that, Mr. Carrodine, *sir*?

"Is there anything else you need to tell me, Manny? Any more surprises?"

He was sweating profusely. It felt as if he had taken a shower in his shirt, slipped his jacket over the swampy thing, and waltzed right into the Oval Office. This experience was goddamn degrading. And now he had no choice but confess everything to the President.

"Cassandra has recently informed me that she's pregnant." His voice sounded weak, more like Cassandra's limp-dick ex-husband's than his own.

"Pregnant? With a baby?"

"I should think so."

Mark Shaw raised his brow, laid a hand on his lips, and laughed. "Well, fuck a duck."

He called the core of his staff into the Oval Office—Rimm, Kale and MacKneer—to discuss this unexpected twist and decide what should be done about it. They all gathered around President Shaw, their expressions dark and grim. Manny sat and listened to them, but he would not participate in the shameful weighing of his personal life. Sleeping with Cassandra might rub against the morality of certain sanctimonious prigs, but his sex life was none of their damn business. The Senate should investigate one single question in their hearings: was he qualified to be a Supreme Court justice, to assess the constitutionality of U.S. law? Nothing else. President Shaw's staff looked angry, like they were on the verge of dropping him. At the very least, they would insist that he play the game on their terms, which meant eating crow on a very big platter. He grimaced and waited for orders.

"Maybe Cassandra's pregnancy makes this situation better, not worse." Gordon Kale marched back and forth, chewing a fingernail. "We can release a statement exposing their relationship and the pregnancy. Stun the world and scoop *Vanity Fair*. Tell everyone the whole damn thing."

MacKneer shook her head. "An affair with a younger staff member and a pregnancy out of wedlock?"

"We've been over the conservative base, Lorna, and they're not half the problem you worry about. They don't care about divorces, affairs, any of that shit—only votes on the cases." Kale leaned against the back of the couch. "Judge Arroyo and Cassandra Sykes have been seeing each other since July. They're consenting adults in a serious relationship working toward marriage."

Jeremy Rimm nodded, standing beside the President like a Secret Service agent. "Of course, we consult Orrin for precise wording."

Manny sat up stiffly. This idea was catching on with members of the staff, maybe even with the President. This approach wouldn't mean groveling before the whole country. Quite the opposite.

"Cassandra and her husband were in a dead marriage. Manny was divorced. They fell in love, and wanted a new family, children. Where's the scandal in that? It's a blessing."

"The scandal, Gordon, is the existence of Rodney Sykes. Judge Arroyo here is about to be the father to Sykes's grandson."

"With all due respect, Mr. President, your father was Chief Executive of this country not long before you, and that hasn't held you back, has it?"

The President chuckled and shrugged his agreement.

"So what's the big deal? This is a private matter. We knew about it beforehand and respected their privacy. Happens all the time—people fall in love, raise a family. Make *that* the story. Something the senators on the Judiciary can get behind."

Manny nodded vigorously. "I couldn't agree more."

Gordon turned on him angrily. "But if we do this, Manny, you and Cassandra have to play this thing *exactly* as we say, word for word, using the script *we* write. You don't even *grunt* if that grunt hasn't been planned in advance and fed to you by *us*, or you're out, Manny—just *out*."

"Temper." Mark Shaw held palms aloft, like a serene portrait of Jesus. "Come on, Gordon."

"Judge Arroyo needs to speak with Cassandra," said Lorna. "Before we go any further."

"Absolutely. I can do that, right away."

The President agreed. Manny was dispatched along with Kale to the second floor of the West Wing, where Cassandra was redacting and correlating Arroyo's writings on executive power, the Commerce Clause, affirmative action and abortion—study sheets to be used in his last round of confidential mock hearings, and then his Senate confirmation. But before entering the small Office of Political Affairs, Manny stopped at the door to the men's room, and thumbed toward it.

"I need a second."

He sequestered himself in the toilet stall and pressed his forehead against its cool metal door. This was the only reasonable plan, to talk to Cassandra, but it was excruciating to have to appeal to her again. He was desperate to end this charade. It had already been weeks of apologizing, holding his nose, pleading with Cassandra to please, *please* come with him to his Watergate condo just for the night, because he missed her tender touch, and fantasized about her, and wanted her. More than anything, he had said, he hoped and prayed that she would move in with him as soon as possible, right after his confirmation. Oh, why had he bothered with those lies? It wasn't as if Cassandra believed him. She had only acquiesced to his lame seductions once since she had come to Washington, because she needed the fiction of their continuing relationship as much as he did. One round of awkward, halting, self-conscious sex. She had only fucked him out of fear of what would happen to her when their relationship crumbled, fear of being pregnant, separated from Denny, terrified of hurting her father and fighting with her brother, all-around petrified at the prospect of being a single mother. In bed, in this office, everywhere—that woman was nothing but a statue of steely passivity and silent judgment. Approaching her now, begging her to play along with Kale's grand plan, to do him yet another favor—he didn't know if he could do that. He didn't have the strength. Manny banged his forehead against the metal door. How was this any better than going home and castrating himself with a kitchen knife?

He left the stall, pissed in a urinal, splashed water on his face. Looked at himself in the mirror. It would be just a few more days. A couple of rough weeks. And then he would have a lifetime appointment to the Supreme Court. Nothing but autonomy and freedom.

He left the men's room, smiled at Kale and followed him down the hall to the Office of Political Affairs. Kale asked everyone but Cassandra to leave, and then left them alone. He closed the door behind them.

Cassandra was sitting at the large round table, wide-eyed and pale with panic. "They know about us, don't they? They know everything."

Manny nodded. "There's an exposé coming out in *Vanity Fair*. A real meaty history on me and your father, including details of the Eichmann incident at Farrow Marsh. The article suggests you and I are together because I want revenge."

She lowered her head into her hands.

"I had to tell the President and staff that you're pregnant. But it's all right. We've developed a plan to turn this in our favor."

Tears streamed down Cassandra's cheeks as Manny relayed the details of the White House's approach, and their need for full cooperation from both of them. He kept talking and talking, although taciturn Cassandra looked exhausted and just blinked at the wall.

"I need to know if you emailed or spoke to anyone about our relationship before July. I mean *anyone*, Cassandra."

"I didn't."

"One text or scribbled note that you forget now means I could get caught lying to the Senate and likely won't be confirmed."

"My father is going to be devastated and humiliated."

"Your father is the least of our problems."

"You don't understand what this is going to do to him. He has pride and dignity. He hates you."

"He doesn't *hate* me."

"He *hates* you, Manny. I'm sure about that."

"Well, he's going to have to get over his hatred pretty damn soon."

"I'm going to be called a slut and a whore in every newspaper in this country. I will be dismissed as a serious person forever."

"Cassandra, focus on the real problem here."

Cassandra's glazed eyes ignited, and flared with an anger that she had somehow managed to keep in check for weeks. "The *real* problem? Do you mean your concerns more *real* than my father's? Or *mine*?"

Manny sighed and lowered his head. A SCOTUS nomination was the culmination of his entire life's work, and yet Cassandra wanted him to defer to Rodney's wispy ego and her own greedy needs. Was her family really so embarrassed and fragile—such poor, suffering innocents, such tender little birds—that they needed special consideration? Only Manny Arroyo's livelihood depended on what happened next.

"You know, I have a pretty strong sense that I'm as *real* as you," Cassandra continued.

Steady now, steady. *I'm sorry*—that was his correct response, the proper rule of engagement. That was what the White House expected him to say. Manny needed to offer her another unsavory and pusillanimous reply to accompany his *yes, sir* to the President. He had to make this work.

"You're right, Cassandra. I'm sorry."

"You're not in the least bit sorry. You just want me to play along. God, I wish you could hear yourself."

"We're in this together, Cassandra. We have to present a united front."

She nodded in exaggeration, mocking Manny mercilessly.

"We need to make a strong statement. We should announce we're getting married or at least getting engaged."

Cassandra started to laugh, a harsh, bitter chortle. "Wow, you are without a doubt the most cynical person I have ever met."

"Every fucking intern in this building knows how politics works."

Manny faced the wall, closed his eyes and tried to calm down.

"I understand what you're up to, Manny," he heard Cassandra whisper behind him. "You don't deserve to be on the United States Supreme Court."

White light encroached on the periphery of Manny's vision, and his hands began to tremble. He spun around, pointing at her. "Listen, you bitch, if you fuck this up and so much as a goddamn *blink* at the wrong time or in the wrong way, I'll spend the rest of my natural life systematically destroying yours. I'll smear your name all over this goddamn country, and you'll never again work at a meaningful job, and don't you goddamn think I can't or won't do it."

Cassandra stood, tears welling, her jaw locked. "You nauseating pig."

"Shut the fuck up."

She leaned over the table. "Oh, there is no chance in hell I'm going to shut up *ever*. If you and your President want me to play the good little pregnant wifey, then you damn well better get me out of this disaster with a job in the White House or the Justice Department. You give me exactly what I fucking ask for or I will not play your game, Emmanuel. I'll tell the world the whole truth about how we started our affair back in November, and plenty of other juicy insights into your golden character, and I'll make damn sure you are *not* confirmed to the United States Supreme Court. So don't you fucking threaten me, you dickhead."

The door opened. Kale's red face peeked into the room, panning back and forth between them. "Oh Lord."

"This woman's a poisonous snake." Manny backed away, hands raised.

"Hold up, now." Gordon stepped between them.

"Just watch where threats get you!"

"Okay, stop it!" Gordon touched Cassandra's shoulder, made her and Manny sit down on opposite sides of the room. He made them take deep breaths. He asked them to stay quiet for a full 20 seconds, which he tracked on his watch. In the awkward silence, with his eyes pressed shut, Manny let the relief of Kale's interruption seep into his knotted muscles. His body wilted with exhaustion. He might as well withdraw his nomination, hop the next flight to San Francisco, and pray that he would still be allowed to finish his career on the Ninth Circuit without getting impeached and disbarred.

But then Gordon Kale took over. He spoke softly. His southern-twanged inflections and colloquial speech had a soothing effect. He gestured back and forth between them, saying all the right things: *I'm not gonna pretend you two are gonna kiss and make up, here. We just gotta calm this fire down a few degrees. What do we need to do for you, Cassandra, to make this right?* Manny tapped his fingers on the wooden table, and said nothing. He hadn't felt this helpless in years. It was more profound than impotence. He was being subjected to forces much larger than himself.

But still, he knew this feeling. When he had first met Sonia in his Penn Law days, she used to drag him up to Fairhill on Sunday afternoons for those long dinners with her extended family. She would lead him into the dining room to speak with her maternal *abuela*, who was a hilarious old woman—blind as an earthworm, and with skin as pale and juicy. She puffed through her packs of Virginia Slims and felt Sonia's skirts and blouses to make certain they revealed just enough skin, but not too much. That *abuela* grilled Manny about his long-term goals, how he expected to make a living, what his intentions were toward her beloved *Sonita*, and about his family background. Manny had to just sit there and take it. *You're from California, but Puerto Rican? What kind of community do they have out there where none of us live? What kind of Puerto Rican kids go to school in Texas? Only Mexicans go to school in Texas!* His every answer was *yes, ma'am, no ma'am, I don't know, ma'am*—infallibly polite, because everyone in Sonia's family deferred to this tiny, wrinkly, phlegmy little matriarch like she was a goddess incarnate, and if he gave her lip even once he would get turfed out of their house unceremoniously. Sonia had 16 *tíos* and *tías*, and so many damn cousins Manny couldn't even begin to remember their names. He had to defer to all of them as well. One group of wiry *tíos* trapped him for hours in the backyard, plying him with beer, talking in excruciating detail about the benefits and drawbacks of this or that combustion engine. All those families lived within the same six-block radius in Fairhill, none of them had a decent job or education, they all charged through their *abuela*'s one-story house like it was Grand Central Station—and Manny was completely at their mercy. Even then he had dreams of graduating into the Unitary Executive of his own life. Sitting beside Sonia, holding her hand in his lap, saying nothing but *please* and *thank you*, he dreamed of absconding with his astonishingly beautiful girlfriend out of Philadelphia, out to the West Coast, where he wouldn't be subjugated to and overwhelmed by the tectonic forces of her extended family—forces too big for him to manage, too powerful to fight. He felt the same thing as that—right now, right here, in the White House Office of Political Affairs. That same desperation and need for endurance. He tuned into Kale, who was still appeasing Cassandra.

"We won't abandon you," the White House Deputy Chief of Staff told her. "You've got our full support. Starting with today's press release, we'll make sure you're portrayed as a competent professional, one of two consenting adults. Not some tawdry whore or seductress. You can take your time, Cassandra, and after your baby's born, when you're ready, you can come back to work. You have my promise we'll work out something for you professionally—a great job in the White House or Justice Department, if you'd rather have a position here than in the IRS."

He was standing behind Cassandra, rubbing her slumping shoulders, a real high school coach. He was laying the folksiness on thick—his Arizona, Alabama or Arkansas folksiness. The man grew up in a small town in one of those A states, but Manny couldn't remember which.

"We got to be brave, here, okay? We're going to get through this together. We have got to stay calm. All right, Cassandra? You calmer?"

"Yes."

God, Gordon was savvy.

"And how about you, Manny? You with me, too?"

"Absolutely."

Manny felt his anger fading away—all his fury toward Cassandra, and toward Gordon, which he had been holding onto for weeks. It was incredible how Kale had managed to soothe both of them simultaneously. No wonder he held such a powerful position in the Shaw administration. He was great at his job. Manny sighed, and his chest warmed with an emotion he hadn't felt in years: gratitude. Thanks to Gordon Kale and no one else, he might still have a chance at making it onto the illustrious Supreme Court.

"Good morning, Judge Arroyo." Lionel Mahoney sat behind the senators' raised bench in room 325 of the Russell Senate Office Building, ready to begin his allotted half-hour of questioning. "I'd like to begin today with an inquiry into your views on the Unitary Executive Theory."

Manny tensed his back, leaned his elbows on the green tablecloth. He locked his fingers together, sweating under C-SPAN's camera lights.

The senator removed his glasses and leaned into the microphone. "The Shaw administration has used this peculiar Unitary Executive theory to justify their dubious tactics in the war on terror, including imprisoning American citizens in Subic Bay without charge or trial, holding non-Americans as enemy combatants, and authorizing torture. Judge Arroyo, you have repeatedly supported the theory. That greatly concerns me. Would you allow this administration to ignore settled law by invoking a Unitary Executive, who rules without subjection to court review?"

"Well, Senator, I think we need to step back for a moment and clarify our terms. Because I'm pretty sure there's been a larger misunderstanding here. There are two kinds of questions being conflated when you invoke the Unitary Executive theory. The first questions—which you're asking now—address how much power the executive actually has. Those are *quantitative* questions. Can the president do this, that, or the other? Are certain actions within the scope of his constitutional powers? Those are open inquiries, and the answers are up for debate. But there are secondary questions as well, which arise when a power is firmly understood to be maintained by the executive. Who exactly *within* the massive executive branch holds a declared power? Which person or group? Those are *qualitative* questions, Senator, and they are the only ones that the Unitary Executive theory has explicitly addressed. All the theory claims is that the president alone holds the reins of powers ascribed to the executive branch. He is our unitary leader. That's what's written in the Constitution, and that's the reading of the theory I have long maintained."

Manny sipped his water. It was a perfect answer, delivered without stuttering or self-doubt, exactly how Attorney General Nicolaides had instructed him in their clandestine mock hearings in the White House press room.

"But that's not true. Justice Bryce's dissent in *Bakhish* explicitly mentioned the Unitary Executive when she argued for an expanded *scope* of presidential powers. The theory addresses more than just your secondary questions. So the American people need to know, Judge Arroyo, if you had decided *Bakhish*, would you have joined Justice Bryce in her radical dissent, or would you have stuck with the majority opinion—written by Justice Van Cleve, by the way, whose seat you will fill if confirmed?"

"Again, Senator Mahoney, I don't believe the Unitary Executive theory addresses *any* questions about the *scope* of the executive's powers in—"

"Justice Bryce says it does."

"I don't recall Justice Bryce using the term 'Unitary Executive' in her dissent in *Bakhish*."

The senator's face reddened, and in his aggressive and showboating style he reaffirmed that Justice Bryce had indeed used that loaded term, and then he expounded on the full implications of the Unitary Executive theory, how it would remove independent counsels and be used to maneuver around precedents like *Myers* through *Humphrey's Executor, Frank* and *Planter*. Good. The more Mahoney took the bait, and wasted his half-hour lecturing the world on useless tangents, and padding his own ego, the fewer difficult questions Manny would have to answer.

"We cannot allow the war on terror to continue unregulated under this administration's terms, with its never-ending timeline, dubious logic, and the entire world declared as its—"

Arroyo pressed his thumbs together. He tried not to blink too frequently. There were only seven of 18 senators left on the Judiciary Committee to question him after Mahoney. Four of those were solid Republicans. So he was entering the home stretch. Manny hadn't done half-badly. He had addressed their substantive questions with aplomb, and weathered the Democrats' tepid and politically motivated probing of his relationship with Cassandra without talking back and making it worse. He always kept in mind one basic fact: he had the votes to win.

Manny was buoyant that night, at one in the morning, humming a favorite saxophone riff as he rode the elevator up to his rented Watergate apartment. He texted *sleep* to Gordon Kale, a mock answer to Kale's question about his plans for tomorrow. Manny pocketed his BlackBerry as the elevator opened, having already fielded calls from Rimm and MacKneer, from Vice President Bloomfield and President Shaw, who had all praised him for how he had handled his second and final day in the Senate's hot seat, the committee's inevitable abortion-rights questions, their Second Amendment and Commerce Clause attacks, and of course Mahoney's tirade on executive power.

His apartment was dark. He threw his keys on the small table in the foyer and went into the kitchen. He poured himself a large glass of milk and downed it in a single gulp. Cool, sweet and creamy— exactly what his body needed after a long day under the lights. He put his glass on the counter, and his eyes caught a flash of pink in the living room. He squinted and hit the switch for the corner lamp.

Cassandra looked small in his giant leather chair. She was wearing a gray stretch-wool suit, a large-collared pink blouse and a pale pink belt, as if she had been working in an office all day. Her eyes still retained hints of black mascara, but she had washed most of it off, along with her lipstick. She had removed her heels, probably left them in the extra room where she was sleeping. Her feet, with the toenails painted red, pressed flat against the wooden floor.

Manny moved closer to her, and rested his weight against the counter. For the first time since Cassandra had moved in with him—on the White House's request—she didn't escape into her room when Manny entered the apartment.

"It's done. The Senate has dismissed me as a witness."

"I know. I watched."

"Thought it went pretty well, considering."

Cassandra didn't agree or disagree. "Are they calling any witnesses tomorrow who could get us in trouble?"

"I don't think so. A few professors and colleagues. Looks like they're willing to let us be."

Cassandra nodded, but she didn't look pleased or relieved. She certainly wasn't about to congratulate him.

"Looks like you went out tonight," Manny said.

"I went to dinner with my brother."

"I noticed he hasn't been sitting with the press. I looked for him today."

"The *Post* pulled him off your hearings. They didn't think it smart for him to cover his sister's lover."

"They never had a problem with him covering his father."

"He would have drawn focus."

Manny nodded. "How's he doing?"

"Angry."

"Still?"

"He'll be furious at me for the rest of his life."

"I'm sorry to hear that."

"Yeah, well, I can't exactly blame him."

Cassandra stared out the window, beyond the brightly lit Kennedy Center, into the murky blackness of the Potomac River. She looked calm but drained. She had been living in limbo, really. No longer working on Manny's confirmation, but not yet ensconced in her new position at the Justice Department. Stuck, at the White House's request, living in Arroyo's Watergate apartment, biding her time until after his confirmation, when she could move back into the dinky Dupont Circle apartment she had rented. Forced, as per instructions from Kale and Rimm, to leave the Watergate complex once a day, if only to go to the grocery store, so that any papers, networks, blogs or magazines could snap pictures of her if they so desired and confirm their cohabitation. Her sole job these days was to be the future Justice's trophy girlfriend, to maintain the fiction of their romance. That must have been pure torture for an ambitious and educated woman like Cassandra Sykes. Harder than Manny imagined.

Without anger contorting Cassandra's expressions, she was pretty. Her hair, pulled back straight, allowed her cheekbones to rise in prominence, and the bright pop of her pink collar suggested color in her cheeks. This woman was pregnant. Manny's third child was growing inside her. His heart sped up as he thought about that, and he pressed his palms into the kitchen counter, tensing his triceps. He had been too goddamn busy, too preoccupied with his confirmation hearings to register that incredible fact. He was going to have another child, a brother or sister for Lonny, with his tubby belly and never fully brushed buck teeth, his ridiculous knowledge of obscure baseball stats. Another sibling for perfect Carmen, so beautiful and bright. A new baby: little feet, downy head, a tiny nose. Every child was a miracle—there was no more appropriate word. Manny felt like crying with relief that Cassandra hadn't aborted their child or promised it up for adoption.

"I have never properly thanked you, Cassandra."

Cassandra cocked her head in surprise.

"I know this process has been difficult. And I know you don't share my religious beliefs. I'm grateful you decided to have this baby."

"Thank you for saying that."

"Although I'm surprised."

Cassandra considered that. "I guess I am, too."

"Why are you going through with it?"

"I don't fucking know."

She pulled her feet up and sat cross-legged on the chair. Cassandra was so somber tonight, so unusually calm. She gazed placidly over the water, which was a black void at night, although punctuated by the bright red warning lights atop the buildings in Rosslyn, for planes flying low into National Airport.

"I miss my mom."

Of course. Cassandra's mother had been dead for only a year and a half.

"It's going to be especially hard for me when the baby's born. I get teary thinking about it. But I also get excited. I want so badly to hold this child and look into its eyes. I guess it's obvious that having a kid is a disaster for my career and life, but I still want to do it. I'm alone, Manny. I don't have a family. I've alienated my brother and Denny. I could use someone on my team."

"You have your father. Rodney is on your team."

Cassandra shook her head. "No, he's not."

"Why don't you call him, Cassandra?"

She chuckled, sadly.

"I've been sitting in this chair for hours thinking about my father. I can't call him. You compared him to Adolph Eichmann. I knew what had happened between the two of you, but that didn't stop me from sleeping with you. I humiliated him, Manny, and now the whole world is party to that humiliation."

"It's too bad it worked out this way, but you couldn't have foreseen these circumstances."

"No, that's just it. I thought about sleeping with you as soon as I interviewed in your chambers. I considered it seriously and dismissed it as a crazy idea, specifically because of your past with my dad. But then after my mom died, and I started working for you, I suddenly knew I was going to do it. It's like I *had* to do it. You and Sonia were finished, and I could tell you would do it, too."

"Don't read too much into it, Cassandra. We were attracted to each other. That's all."

"No, there's more. I did it at least in part because of how my father behaved. He sat in that funeral office with the funeral director and he had to pick a coffin off the menu. The guy asked him to pick the coffin, not me, not Sam, because Rebecca was his wife, but my dad kept saying *whatever you kids prefer*, over and over, and smiling, too, like it was all nothing to him. Like he was just ordering lunch, and it was pleasant either way. *How would you kids like to handle the service? Bagels and tea and coffee back at the apartment, or shall I get it catered by Giordino's? Perhaps a two-day shiva or six? Either would be fine with me. Why don't you children decide?* Not once did he howl or cry or scream. I even screamed at him once—which I've never done before—that I didn't fucking care one iota if the funeral was scheduled for eleven or one. Even then he said, *all right, whatever you prefer, Cassandra. And what do think your mother would've wanted?* I just couldn't stand him. He had no fucking spine. My mom was dead, and it meant nothing to him. She didn't even know if he loved her."

"People deal with grief in all sorts of ways."

"There was never anything in my father to hold. He is a nothing man. He's nonexistent. You weren't wrong to compare him to Eichmann."

Cassandra stopped talking suddenly. She turned away, stooped her shoulders, astonished at herself. "I don't mean that."

"You're just upset."

"I can't believe I said that."

"Yeah, I know the feeling."

Cassandra looked at him and smiled—an actual smile. For him.

"And then back in San Francisco, there you were: decisive, clear-headed, present. I remember saying to myself: *I think I would prefer, Rodney, since you have no real objection to anything, to fuck this man you hate right on his desk.*"

"Cassandra."

"*How would you feel about that, Rodney? Would you, perhaps, mind? But then who can say, who can say?*"

"Stop it."

Cassandra paused, chuckled at herself. "We were perfect for each other, you and I."

"Just call your father. Make peace. It's not that hard."

Cassandra crossed her arms and sank deeper into the soft chair.

"My father's not doing well. Sam saw him last night. Apparently he missed lunch with Morris Bayfield—I mean, missed it for no reason. They talked and made plans, but then my father just forgot. Didn't show up to the restaurant or call."

"That doesn't sound like Rodney."

"No. And Sam had a similar experience with him last week. Sam called and left him a message, but my father didn't return his call for days. Usually he'll call back in ten or 15 minutes. And when they finally had dinner last night, my father was like a ghost. Tired and very haggard."

"Do you think he's sick?"

"I think he's humiliated. Sam said he small-talked the whole night about some water pipe the city's installing in Connecticut Avenue, how it'll improve the pressure throughout his neighborhood. Things like that. The cleanliness of the carpets in the lobby of his building."

"It will get better for Rodney when my confirmation is over."

"Did you know that journalists have been calling his chambers to ask him how he feels about his daughter sleeping with Manny Arroyo? Can you imagine what that must be like for him?"

Manny bit his lip. He moved around to the kitchen side of the counter, picked up his milky glass and rinsed it. Cassandra wanted him to think about what this experience was like for Rodney Sykes? Except it was not Manny's job to worry about Rodney's feelings, or anyone else's. *That's fucking life*, he wanted to say. *Everyone gets humiliated and fucked over. And everyone has to find the strength to endure their suffering, alone.* But he didn't say anything. He put his glass in the dishwasher.

"Manny, will you be kind to him?" Cassandra's voice cracked. "You're going to work with him for years in very close quarters. You don't have to like him, and God knows you're right about his faults. He's too slavish in all the ways you say. But he's not a bad man. He was a terrible father, and he's probably a terrible justice, but he means well. He has always meant well. I can't bear for him to suffer."

Cassandra rested her feet on the floor. She leaned forward in the chair, facing Manny, pleading for a father who had long angered her and let her down, just because of her relationship with him. The sacred bond between children and their parents. Carmen and Lonny would likely do the same for him, no matter if he fought with them, berated them, and controlled their lives. Would his unborn child fight for him, too, if Manny were so attacked? *I can't bear for him to suffer.* Oh, the unbridled joy, the back-tingling, blinding pleasure of being a father again.

"I can promise you that I'll be civil to Rodney for the rest of my life. I feel no animosity toward him whatsoever."

Cassandra nodded. "Just don't attack him unnecessarily. With sarcasm and all that."

"Well, I'm going to disagree with him, and dissenting against wrong opinions is part of my job."

"Just don't make your attacks personal. That's all I'm asking. Let your criticism be principled without being mean. You know the line. Go for his jurisprudence, not his character."

"Rodney has a thicker skin than you think."

"I'm sure he does, but I don't care. Just give him some respect."

Having said her piece, Cassandra sat back in the chair. Somehow she seemed vulnerable and aggressive simultaneously.

"All right," said Manny. "I'll try."

Not until Manny stood beside Chief Justice Eberly in the Supreme
Court's private conference room, with his right hand raised and his
left hand lying flat against a leather-covered Bible, did he consider
the significance of the two oaths that he was about to take. The full
Senate had hastily confirmed him a day earlier, 73–25, which he
watched on CNN, but had only briefly registered. He was too busy
organizing chambers, reading briefs, furiously trying to catch up on
cases to be argued in the next weeks, and he had even spent his night
interviewing young lawyers for his two remaining clerkships—they
had to get started right away. Now Eberly's long, jowly face was
visible before him, and never again would Manny be interviewed
or assessed for a job. Never again would he be held accountable to
a more powerful person's standards of decorum, right thinking,
or suitable approach. He would have eight equal colleagues on the
Court, but no one above him, not even the Chief, for the rest of his
life. He was on the verge of becoming a Unitary Executive of the
most unusual sort, in certain ways more powerful than any president, governor or mayor in the land. A lifetime appointment.

"Repeat after me," said Charles Eberly.

Eberly intoned the lengthy general federal oath, phrase by
phrase, which commanded Manny to swear his allegiance to the
U.S. Constitution. Manny repeated it slowly, standing up straight,
speaking in his deepest voice. Nothing quite like this satisfaction,
his kids and parents watching from the far side of the conference
table, standing beside his buddy Tommy Wellens from Baylor,
Gordon Kale, and even Sonia, with her hand resting on Carmen's
shoulder.

He finished his recitation. Eberly congratulated him, shook
his hand. "Now we go downstairs." The Chief led him toward
the door.

Manny's mother approached before he could leave the room,
teary-eyed, wanting a hug. "Not yet, Mama." He held her small

shoulders and gently thrust her away from him. "Nothing's official until I take the second oath downstairs."

His mother hugged and kissed him anyway.

"You don't have to be so superstitious, Emmanuel. It's happening. You can't jinx it."

On the stairs, Jeremy Rimm jogged up to meet him halfway, and then turned to walk down beside him, whispering. "I got Cassandra to take a seat in the front row. Give her a smile when you enter."

Manny chuckled, shaking his head. "If you still need us to keep up the fiction, Jeremy, she should have been upstairs. You White House guys are off your game. That's the kind of thing the press notices."

"She was late. We had no choice."

"Well, it certainly doesn't matter to me."

Dozens of cameras clicked as Manny followed the Chief Justice into the East Conference Room. A couple of powerful standing lights were positioned in the back corners of the room, bookending a wall of reporters. The place was filled but for a few empty chairs in the front row, reserved for Arroyo's family. Cassandra was already seated in that row, wearing makeup and a dark green suit, with an inscrutable smile plastered across her face. Manny smiled and nodded at her, as requested.

Chief Justice Eberly stood with him before the huge fireplace, beneath Rembrandt Peale's portrait of John Marshall. Eberly cleared his gravelly throat and launched into his set speech about how Manny's official investiture would occur at an upcoming date, but that he was taking the judicial oath today so he could launch right into his copious work for the Court.

"Can I have the Arroyo family up here, please?" Manny's mother, father and children approached, Lonny rocking back and forth with embarrassment, Carmen, as usual, happiest in the spotlight, beaming her broad smile, breaking hearts already, just shy of 15. His mother took the Bible from Eberly's outstretched hand and held it out for Manny to place his left hand on. Again the future Justice raised his right hand in the air.

"Repeat after me," grumbled Charles Eberly.

Manny swore his second oath, this one taken exclusively by federal judges, to administer justice without respect to persons, to give equal rights to poor and rich alike, and to faithfully and impartially discharge and perform all the duties incumbent upon him as an Associate Justice for the United States Supreme Court. It didn't take long, a minute at most. Manny finished and hugged his mother, earnestly now. Everyone in attendance stood and applauded, and someone whooped, Texas-style—had to be Tommy Wellens, that rascal. Eberly fanned them down and announced to the quieting crowd that there would be a reception down the hall in the Lawyers' Lounge. He invited everyone to please join them to congratulate the new Justice.

As the room thinned out, Cassandra approached, tugging her green skirt down towards her knees, although it was hardly hemmed high. "Congratulations, Manny." She gave him a brief hug, and he hugged her back. They had been civil to each other since that night—a brokered peace, of sorts—but he still wondered if was this a performance for the cameras. Or could it be genuine good wishes for a man she said didn't deserve to be on the Court? She pulled away abruptly. "I have to go. I'm sorry."

"Not at all, Cassandra. Thank you for coming. I'll see you at home."

She tucked her purse tight against her side and scurried out.

Manny turned to follow the Chief Justice into the Lawyers' Lounge, but then he caught Rodney Sykes's wide-set, squinting eyes across the room. It was a shock to see Rodney, even though it had occurred to Manny that he would be at this ceremony. All the justices were present. Rodney was grayer and older than Manny remembered him—it had been years, after all—but it wasn't just time's passage. Justice Sykes looked older than he did in the Court's annual photographs, and in his occasional C-SPAN appearances, and in his pictures in the papers. Rodney wore a handsome tie and navy jacket, his hair combed impeccably. No trace of tumult or humiliation, no obvious distress at being in the room with his scandalous daughter—who had probably not called him, and probably hadn't said hello to him—or with Manny. Rodney approached, smiling opaquely. Photographers clicked away around them, capturing their meeting, pictures sure to be shared all over the Internet in a few hours, or printed in the back pages of national newspapers tomorrow morning, gossip columns, and SCOTUS blogs.

"Justice Arroyo." Rodney shook Manny's hand. "It is so good to see you again. My sincerest congratulations, and welcome to the Supreme Court."

6

A PERSON'S A PERSON NO MATTER HOW SMALL

"We can cancel," said Justice Sarah Kolmann, as her seated husband bent over their oak breakfast table and pressed his forehead against the surface, something she had never once seen him do in their 52 years of marriage. "We absolutely do not have to do this."

Jonathan's fleshy nose flattened against the wood, and Sarah—to her own horror—imagined that table as a coffin pressing against his face. But of course it wouldn't be like that; Jonathan wouldn't be lying facing down in his own grave. Sarah closed her eyes, blotted the terrible image from her mind.

"We can't cancel," her husband said into the wood.

"I'll call them and say you're not feeling well. They'll understand."

"The lamb's cooking."

"We can freeze the lamb, Jonathan."

"That'll ruin it."

Jonathan lifted himself off the table, but slumped in his seat like a weary child. He brushed wisps of gray hair to the side of his forehead, picked up his big round glasses and slipped them on. He shaded his gaze with both palms, tunneling his vision, as if he couldn't bear to look at Sarah, or at his beloved kitchen. "It's not just that." The fragility in Jonathan's voice was so shocking that it shortened Sarah's breath. "I mean, cancel for *what*? So I can sit around here and mope?" A dab of olive oil was streaked across his forehead. Flakes of dried mint were stuck to the skin above his eyebrows, and hanging from the hair he had just brushed away.

Sarah had been standing at the counter making salad. She wiped tomato viscera and seeds from her hands with a dish towel, and moved into the breakfast nook. She sat across from Jonathan and brought the towel to his head. "You have some oil and mint, Jonathan, right here, on your—"

"I don't care." He swatted his hand at the encroaching dish towel as if it were a bothersome fly—a reckless gesture for this dignified man.

"It's a lot for anyone to absorb." Sarah squeezed and wrung the cloth in her lap. "You're not expected to get back to normal in a day. I do think we should cancel tonight. That'll give us time to process it."

"I don't know."

"Well, *I* want to cancel, Jonathan. I don't think, I . . ." Sarah cleared her constricting throat. "I doubt I can do this myself." She was whispering now, and her shoulders sagged. An attacked porcupine would roll its spine, collapse inward and lie on the floor in a ball. Her face flushed. To think like this, to demonstrate no strength at all—it was such an embarrassing response to misfortune. This meekness, this trembling, fiddling her bony old hands in front of her, she didn't want to do it, didn't approve of it. But Jonathan wasn't like *this*. Jonathan was ebullient and gregarious; he charmed senators and business tycoons, stockbrokers and justices, stage actors and socialites; he was sanguine in adversity, and never so morose as to require her support. What was happening to him? And her? Could they crumble under the weight of misfortune? How could Jonathan, of all people, think about canceling New Year's Eve?

He peered at Sarah through his oversized glasses. Jonathan's eyes reminded her of that odd double-barreled cannon outside

City Hall in Athens, Georgia, which Sarah had seen after her lecture at Georgia Law: twin barrels aimed at her. She imagined them firing. Suddenly, Jonathan reached across the table and snatched the cloth out of her hands. He brushed his forehead and hair, rubbing the oil into his skin, sprinkling bits of mint onto his lap. "You'll be fine tonight." His voice sounded steadier. "We're not going to cancel." He was bolstering himself. He hadn't been angered by her show of weakness. He was reviving, now, as of course he would—becoming himself again.

"I don't know." But Sarah knew that wasn't true. The strength had already returned to her limbs.

"I've made my decision. We'll go on as expected."

"It's not a law we have to do it."

"It's a tradition and that's important. Did I get all the mint?"

Sarah pointed to a missed flake on his forehead, and nodded once he had wiped it away. Her husband deftly folded the dish towel into a perfect square, and stuffed it into the breast pocket of his jacket. "There." He stiffened in his seat, and offered her his warmest smile. The thick, cotton towel bulged absurdly, its light blue stripe clashing with his navy silk tie. "How's that?"

"Elegant."

"Did you expect anything less?" Jonathan yanked the cloth from his pocket and tossed it on the table. "We'll have a fun night. I promise that."

"You don't have to fake anything, Jonathan."

He nodded, unconvinced. "Do me a favor, will you? Take the lamb out in five minutes, coat it with that vinegar-mint, and put it back in the oven. Maybe lower the heat 25 degrees. I'd like to lie down for a bit."

"Of course," Sarah leaned across the table and kissed her husband's forehead.

As Jonathan shuffled toward the swinging door, Justice Kolmann retreated to her knife and cutting board, mimicking equanimity. She chopped tomatoes until she was sure he wouldn't return, and then put her knife down and pressed her hands flat against the board. The refrigerator hummed, the oven's fan whirled. Her modest kitchen had never felt larger. What would it be like to cook in here without him around, without his jokes or *joie de vivre*, without the luxury of his instructions? How would she know what to make? She picked up the knife and scraped chunks of tomato into a juicy red line. Better to wash and cut the endive than to succumb to these morbid imaginings.

The thing no one understood, thought Sarah, as she removed the steaming pink lamb from the oven and brushed it with her husband's marinade, was how much she depended upon the open communication of her marriage for her happiness and sanity. "Normal people would crumble under your pressure," her friend Norma had said, years ago, while flipping through a pile of hate mail that Sarah received in response to an abortion rights opinion—one of her strident affirmations of *Roe v. Wade.* "Oh, that stuff's just part of the job," Sarah replied, aware of how casual she sounded. "You get used to it." "No, *you* get used to it," Norma countered. "That's exactly how you're different from most people: you weather these things unfazed." But that wasn't right. Norma, her best friend, didn't know her at all. Neither did her colleagues or relatives, who made similar observations now and again about Sarah's strength and independence, her apparent contentment with her isolation when traveling or working in chambers. The truth was Sarah didn't weather anything by herself. The day Sarah received those death threats, she scurried home, panicked, painfully self-conscious, and gabbed at length to Jonathan, lying in his arms at two in the morning, trembling and unable to sleep, asking him if they should install bullet-proof glass in their apartment windows, if she should be worried about venturing to the grocery store unaccompanied, if perhaps she should ask her clerks next term to do all her errands and domestic chores until the threat died down. At that moment she did not resemble the great feminist lawyer who had shattered the glass ceiling, the progressive advocate for women's rights and preeminent judicial mind. Even a friend as close as Norma Schechter probably could not conceive of Jonathan stroking her hair and patting her back in bed, whispering in his rolling, smoky voice: *Don't panic, Sarah. Pro-life groups are all bluster. You've got to have a little strength.* If Jonathan died, Sarah thought, as she extracted the good china from the dining room's credenza, Sarah feared she would respond as her mother did when her father died, by sleeping only two hours a night, waking in a panic that the plants weren't properly watered, or that the furnace was leaking toxic gas and would kill her as soon as she fell back asleep. Wondering if she could accomplish even the smallest tasks without his support. Of course, like her mother, Sarah would appear to carry on as normal, venturing to Court, aggressively interrogating lawyers from the raised bench, negotiating in conference and ruling stridently on cases, neither complaining nor acknowledging any inner angst. Her mother returned to work in the family's tiny *shmata* store the day after she had buried her father, smiling at customers, soldiering on. *His death didn't even faze her*—that's what Sarah overheard a neighbor saying in their Brooklyn neighborhood. All the neighbors probably thought the same thing. Her father, David, must have seemed like an insignificant man, like a sleeping dog in the corner of *Silverstein's*, with his bad heart and wheezy breathing and even worse business acumen, greeting customers with his meek little nod and *welcome, welcome*, which he repeated every time a person entered their store. Devorah was the obvious boss, servicing customers, budgeting, hiring and firing the occasional employee, ordering inventory and paying bills, while David was merely the host. The two rarely spoke to each other during the day. So how bad could it have been for her when he died? She might have been relieved, for all anyone knew. But Devorah Silverstein, much like her daughter, the famous Supreme Court Justice, drew strength from her husband's steady love, his stoicism and optimism, his quiet, sage advice delivered late at night in bed, his magnificent cooking and housekeeping. She relied on him in all sorts of ways that never quite matched the gender stereotypes of her era, and she never recovered from his death. Nightmares, panic attacks, insane worries about poorly watered plants and faulty furnaces, meteors hitting earth, ax murderers, tropical viruses, all of that and more would plague Sarah when Jonathan died and left her alone for good. Justice Kolmann knew it. She was sweating and fighting back tears as she set their table with their Jensen Cactus silverware.

She arranged the crystal glasses, goblets and silver candlesticks. Preparing the table was something that they had always done together. Once the work was finished, she peeked into their bedroom. Jonathan's short, stocky body lay on the covers, his head propped on a pillow, his silhouette illuminated by ambient light from the cracks in the blinds.

"You all right in there?"

"Yes." Jonathan's voice was just a whisper.

"Are you just suffering in silence?"

"I'm okay."

"Sure you don't want me to cancel? There's still time."

"Don't cancel. You did the lamb?"

"I did, and it's cooking."

"Don't worry, then, I'll be out in a minute."

"Okay," said Sarah. "You're certain?"

"I'm fine."

She retreated into the kitchen to further bolster herself with busywork: chopping more tomatoes, plating the crostini that Jonathan had prepared earlier in the afternoon. Gradually, she relaxed, and allowed herself to consider a recent dissent, half completed, that she still had to finish. It stated that a clause in the Medical Equipment Amendments Act of 1969 should not be allowed to preempt a common-law tort suit from Michigan. Why had she been so insistent on dissenting in an otherwise unanimous case? No one else on the Court had found any federalism conflicts with 21 U.S. C. § 854h(b)—neither Gideon nor Bernhard. Might her objection be at least partially rooted in her deep mistrust of the multinational corporation that had manufactured the malfunctioning medical instrument in question, a distrust based on its rank history as the inventor and producer of an intrauterine birth control device that had once upon a time resulted in the deaths of three young women and the unnecessary sterilization of another 34? If so, then her objection on federalist grounds was insincere, and didn't fulfill her sworn oath to administer justice impartially. Sarah rearranged the crostini so that they were angled away from the center of the platter, fanning outward and spiraling like a flower. Of course it was easier to bat around legal minutiae than it was to worry about Jonathan, alone in the dark, suffering. Easier than thinking about him dying.

The doorbell rang. "They're he-re!" Sarah approached the entrance, conscious of the delight in her tone, that bald indicator of her relief. She would no longer be alone with her fear. She opened the door to discover Killian's and Gloria's beaming, round faces, wet with melted snow, and their arms bearing gifts: a bottle of Pinot Grigio, Gloria's famous tiramisu wrapped in tinfoil, and a couple of plastic bags with ice-packed venison steaks. The unfortunate elk was shot by Killian's son Gabriel in November, Justice Quinn said. Sarah was aware of hugging her guests without clasping them too hard. What she really wanted was to hold them tight and not let go.

"Somehow doesn't feel right to eat the steaks if I don't shoot the animal myself." Killian dropped the heavy frozen slabs in Sarah's arms. "I miss the trip, I miss the meat—that's my motto."

"Oh dear me." Sarah held the bag away from her body while imagining the bloody deer meat within. "These must still have the bullets in them."

"Half of that's ice. They were frozen so fresh you can eat them raw, if you'd like, Sarah. Like a mountain lion."

"Maybe I'll just put them in the freezer." As Sarah carried away the gift, Killian was already clutching Gloria's puffy parka and his own cashmere trench, and his wife was opening the closet door next to her.

Justice Quinn's huge presence filled their apartment, and what a blessing that was. Even as Sarah fiddled around in her kitchen, her friend's infectious boisterousness, his desire to find jokes in any sullen situation, pepped her up. "Am I to assume that rule of yours, Killian," she called out to him, as she re-wrapped the venison in a thicker plastic bag, "means you have to go out and kill some poor cow whenever you feel the need for a steak?"

"What, you're going to interrogate me, counsel?" Killian and Gloria entered her kitchen now, rid of their overcoats. "I plead the Fifth."

"Hey, where's Jonathan?" Gloria glanced around the kitchen, no doubt expecting to find him finishing his lamb in his stained Washington Opera apron, just like he did every year. Her supple facial muscles stretched and contorted as she panned the room, broadcasting surprise on an operatic scale.

"He's getting dressed."

Lying, even subtly, by omission, made Sarah's sinuses pulse. It put distance between Sarah and her beloved guests, a chasm; it felt like the opposite of giving the Quinns a hug. If only she could confess the bad news and cry, and let her guests subsume her in their bountiful warmth and girth. But she couldn't make that decision alone. It was Jonathan's night to endure, his decision to inform or conceal.

Gloria wore one of her matching outfits, this one in an entirely purple palate, straying toward eggplant hues at its lower end (her mauve wool tights) and toward crimson-plum ones at its upper (her plastic hairband). She accented it all with a pair of polished amethyst earrings and a long agate broach. She looked terrific. Her tweed skirt was cut above the knee. Most devoutly Catholic women in their late 60s didn't show off their fine and shapely legs. Her firm round calves, thin knees, and muscular thighs looked like they belonged on a 40-year-old athlete, and those short skirts of Gloria's had been the source of numerable jokes and risqué banter in their years of friendship. "Oooo, smells like Jonathan's lamb!" Gloria jut her jaw forward. "Wonderful!"

"Hope it won't disappoint!" Jonathan had stealthily entered the kitchen behind the Quinns. His big smile radiated warmth. He took Killian's hand and shook it hard, and then kissed Gloria on both cheeks. Jonathan had changed his clothes, and wore a budding red rose pinned to his lapel—his signature style for any special occasion—a French cuffed shirt, his large round glasses, and a handsome gray silk tie. Of course, this sartorial elegance and soothing amicability was all part of Jonathan's nature, and he

wasn't going to abandon it now. He loved offering guests his genuine hospitality, even when he was feeling personal pressure. He
would never have succeeded so magnificently in his management
consultant business, or in his many advisory positions as a cul-
tured patron—member of the Trustees' Council for the National
Gallery of Art, the Madison Council of the Library of Congress,
and an executive director for the Kennedy Center of the Performing Arts—if he weren't so comfortable in social situations. Still,
it was impressive to watch him access his lightness, and his joy in
hosting the Quinns, after such a shattering afternoon.

While the Kolmanns and the Quinns chatted in the kitchen,
eating *hors d'oeuvres* and uncorking a bottle of Châtêau Mou-
ton—better with the lamb, Jonathan claimed, than the Pinot Grigio that the Quinns had brought—Sarah's isolation crystalized.
The couples drifted into the dining room to eat, where Jonathan
bloomed in the warmth of their banter, embracing his hosting
duties, ushering out successive dishes to his guests' appreciative
gasps, describing ingredients and cooking methods, and filling
emptying glasses with just enough wine. The brittle and icy lone-
liness at Sarah's core expanded, slowing her blood, freezing her
into her seat. She tried to relax and feel more connected with
her guests but couldn't do it. She sipped her Bordeaux—maybe
getting drunk would help. Why couldn't she just tell them the
awful news? This polite conversation was excruciating. Jonathan's ability to cheerily ignore the bad news for the night cast
her into the uncomfortable role of his accomplice. She listened to
herself performing well enough as they spoke at length about a
recent production of *Richard III* at Washington Shakespeare, the
improvement plans for the National Gallery, and an upcoming
gala ball for the Cystic Fibrosis Foundation, organized by Gloria,
to be held in the Kennedy Center—thanks to Jonathan Kolmann's
magnanimous intervention. It was hard. She was only partially
present. But when the conversation drifted toward recent events
on the Court, as it inevitably did on New Year's Eve, she temporarily forgot about Jonathan's predicament and cracked through
her frosty shell into a more lively presence. Gloria asked Sarah

how the Court was handling the new addition of Justice Arroyo and the loss of Justice Van Cleve.

"Well, the testosterone levels in conference have increased noticeably."

Killian pushed back from the table and laughed. "Yeah, and the guy is so unbelievably fit he makes me feel like a sumo wrestler." He patted his big belly.

"Gideon's fit, too. It's just that Manny is noticeably muscular and strong. I'm half expecting him to move his desk out of chambers and replace it with one of those weight machine contraptions."

Killian was still regarding his big belly. "You know, maybe I should start hitting the gym."

"Not a terrible idea." Gloria leaned in toward her husband and nudged him. "Twenty minutes twice a week would make a huge difference."

Killian raised his brow at her. "Gloria! I was joking! No way am I starting in with the gym. I'm way too old for that foolishness. And too ornery. I can't stand the fitness nuts everywhere these days. The blasted Manny Arroyos."

"Let him be, Killian," chastised Gloria.

"Running on the treadmill like a hamster in a cage, lifting weights for no good reason, counting calories like a teenage girl. Ah, whatever, to each their own. More power to him. He'll live to be a hundred and twenty."

"Stop making fun of him, Killian."

"I'm not saying anything bad, Gloria. He's doing fine so far. He looks comfortable and thriving. He's far more confident than your average new Supreme Court justice."

"I find Manny too confident, actually," said Sarah. "He has too much swagger. He's certainly capable intellectually, and his writings are very clear, but I have doubts about how good one can be as a justice with so much confidence. Even you, Killian, you never had that bluster, or that belief in your opinions as correct in a pure way, as opposed to just deeply felt and well-argued points of view."

"No, my opinions are objectively *right*." Killian's wry delivery spurred a round of chuckles. "Any neutral observer will tell you plainly I've written nothing but a series of true and outright brilliant statements in my storied career."

"Well, fine, of course—but that said, Killian, you also understand that your perfect reasoning and generous spouting of the *Truth*, as it were, has originated in the mind of a fallible human being. Hence your lack of swagger. Now, I think it's fine for you to fervently believe what you believe about the law, but it's that self-assurance, that arrogance in Manny—I don't know, it's something new."

"Joanna's the same. We've seen this before."

"Yes, but that's what I'm talking about. It's this new generation of fervent, right-wing believers. They're all so bold, so unwilling to compromise on their personal behavior as well as in their jurisprudence. Joanna was the first in that new mold. Now we have another. And replacing Elyse, no less, the ultimate compromiser. So it's a trend. I only fear their attitude will increase the divisiveness in our rulings, and in time might cause palpable tension in conference."

"Killian hasn't mentioned any tension," said Gloria.

"Oh no, it's all very cordial. A few colleagues have bristled in small ways at their tone in conference, but that's only now and then. Mostly, I'd say that Joanna and Manny have been generous, never obnoxious. Even the relationship between Rodney and Manny has been amicable. And I was expecting it to be the worst relationship on the Court in the last hundred years. At least since the 1920s, when those awful four horsemen had to deal with an actual Jew. So perhaps I'm overreacting."

"You're only upset because Manny and Joanna are about to shift the law in a way you despise."

"Now, that's not fair, Killian!"

Killian, reddening slightly, shrugged and giggled. "All right. I'm taking it too far."

"You *are* taking it too far. I'm not objecting to their jurisprudence, ominous as it may be. I'm talking about their *style*. I find that swagger new for a federal justice, or really for any person with our kind of knowledge and understanding about the limited role of the judiciary."

"Sure," said Killian. "I agree."

Jonathan sipped his wine. "You say Rodney's handling the transition well?"

Sarah shrugged. "I don't really know. He's a very opaque man."

"I have my doubts," offered Killian. "I think the high drama of Manny's confirmation, the affair and all that, affected him badly. He looks like he's aged a decade. He's the same old rigid-thinking, decent Rodney, but I don't know. He looks unhinged to me in conference."

"Yes, to me as well. But I've been worried about him ever since Rebecca's death."

Hunched at the table, Jonathan ran his index finger in quick circles around the rim of his wine glass. Her husband's smile was thinning, a sure sign of his nervousness, a crack in his façade that only Sarah could detect. She suddenly knew that when the Quinns left them alone just after midnight, Jonathan would collapse. She imagined him unclipping the wilting rose from his lapel, undressing silently, turning out the light before she had even finished scrubbing pots. His effervescence gone. She would be alone in their dark apartment, brushing her teeth, dressing for bed, with no one to offer her company or solace.

Sarah sipped her wine. "I do love Rodney, dearly. I hate to see him suffering."

"I'm finding Rodney's writings increasingly stale this term. That's what worries me most. That recent opinion of his—wait, *Holbrook*'s released, right? I never check these dang things. I'm not breaching, am I?"

"No, no, Killian. *Holbrook*'s out. It's fine."

"Okay, so take that case, for example. *Holbrook*. It's recent, and not a major issue—a jurisdictional question on an environment suit, no reason why you guys should've heard about it. For complex and stupid reasons that have to do with the shoddy overlap between the Missouri legislature and Congress, there ended up being three pieces of legislation proscribing different rulings. The case forced us to decide which of those three laws is best. Not to interpret what's written, see, or what's actually *there*—each point of view has good textual proof—but just to decide which one is right. No way out from taking a stand in *Holbrook*. And so Rodney gets the assignment, and what does he do? Hems and haws, and then finds the reading that's most *cited* by judges, lawyers, law reviews, et cetera, and says that must be the correct one. As in: the biggest number wins. As if the correct statute should be the result of a popularity contest, or an equation. Heaven forbid that he might have an *opinion* about which of those three choices might be best based on meaningful criteria, whatever he thinks makes sense. No, he refuses to admit that there are actual minds involved in any aspect of law-making. He wants the law to be nothing more than a computer-generated algorithm read in all instances by another computer."

Sarah nodded somberly. "You're right. He's taking his restraint too far."

"You know what it is?" Killian inched forward in his chair, and rested his elbows on the table. "You know what really bothers me about him? His blatant terror at being human. He's so mistrustful of anything that smacks of mortal thought or effort it's astonishing, and so he restrains himself to an absurd degree."

"Well, I think he's been stung. The combination of his wife passing, and his daughter sleeping with Manny, and then all that publicity, for such a private and dignified man? I think his hurt is just so deep that he's become extremely cautious. You can almost see him wither away in certain situations around the Court. I was eating with him in the Dining Room a couple weeks ago—just Charles, Talos, Rodney and I—and halfway through our meal Manny joined us. We started talking about how Manny's adjusting to Washington, and then Talos asked him directly about Cassandra. Right in front of Rodney! Is her pregnancy proceeding smoothly, and is he excited for the baby? Talos was just trying to be nice, of course—"

Killian groaned, and shook his head. "Talos can be so unbelievably stupid."

"And you know they're not living together, right? Manny and Cassandra. They don't even like each other. Well, Manny got very diplomatic, and said Cassandra was doing fine, and he's very excited for the baby, but he didn't once look at Rodney, or acknowledge him in any way. And while you can't expect Rodney to say or do anything in that situation, his physical language changed markedly. He got stiff as a board. Before Manny arrived Rodney was already quiet, monosyllabic in every comment, adding nothing of value or interest to our conversation, but after, he seemed to shrink away to nothing. It was awful to witness. He's wounded. He doesn't show his pain overtly maybe, but he's wounded deeper than any of us can see."

"He's lost confidence in himself," Killian said, "and in all humanity. He's absurdly suspicious. It's as if he thinks our fragile brains can't be trusted, and that a person is too unstable a thing to be relied upon."

"Well, a person *is* unstable, that's true. But I don't think that's what he really—"

"Whoa, whoa!"

Everyone started groaning and laughing.

"Hang on, Killian."

"No, no, no! You're not getting off that easily."

Sarah, laughing, shrugged at Jonathan. Every year on New Year's Eve their conversation devolved into a playful battle between Justices Quinn and Kolmann over some legal or philosophical issue. Their spouses spurred them on, and loved it. Why should this year be any different?

"Killian, don't get distracted. I'm just saying that Rodney—"

"Forget Rodney! We're done with him. You just said a human being is too unstable a thing to be relied upon. You *said* that. I heard you!"

Sarah recoiled in her chair, laughing still. Jonathan, patting her back, poured more wine in her glass. "I think you're going to need this, dear."

"Drink up quick!" Killian pointed at her wine. "You've got some 'splainin' to do."

Sarah took a long sip and let her head gently swirl. She so rarely drank like this, but her lightheadedness, her slower and deeper heartbeat, the way her back muscles eased and relaxed from the alcohol, it was all so welcome tonight. "You know exactly what I'm referring to, Killian: the category of personhood in law. Its tumultuous history. And because the law never sits still, at any given moment personhood is an unstable concept. It was born as a fictional category, and it continues to be one. That instability is active and developing, that's all I meant. I wasn't making any epistemological rulings on the judicial mind. It was a minor, tangential thought."

"Uh-oh." Killian nudged his wife in the ribs and nodded authoritatively. "People are fiction, Gloria. Bet you didn't know that. Means you're not really *here*. What'll I tell the kids?"

Gloria laughed with her mouth wide open, as if her bountiful joy had far too much force behind it to be channeled through a smaller opening.

"You know as well as I do, Killian, that constructing personhood has always been one of the principal actions of law. It's particularly important for women to recognize that process, Gloria—more so than men—because the *person* that the law long assumed us to be was a decidedly *male* creation. For centuries, we didn't qualify."

Killian groaned. "Oh please."

"Well, it isn't now, of course, but it certainly *was*. Personhood was engendered in a way that's largely invisible to men."

"That's done, Sarah. It's a resolved question in every Western nation."

"But constructing and limiting personhood didn't stop with suffrage or the Nineteenth Amendment. It's an ongoing process. That's my whole point."

"Your bat mitzvah speech, Sarah." Jonathan was swirling his wine at the head of the table. "Tell them about it."

"I was going to. So when I was thirteen, I had a bat mitzvah in an observant synagogue, which was a rather unusual thing to do at the time, because only boys were supposed to receive bar mitzvahs, you see, not girls. But I made a stink to the rabbi and the president of the congregation, and got a petition together, and won. I think I was just too interested in Jewish learning for them to ignore me, and it was New York, after all, and so ultimately what were they going to do? These weren't the *haredim*. Anyway, there I was, reading from the Torah, the first girl in my *shul* to do so."

"A pattern that you'd repeat rather brilliantly in your career," Killian piped in.

"Well, that's no matter. The Torah portion I was assigned was *Yitro*, which is taken from Exodus, and includes the Ten Commandments. Now, I had to give a *Dvar Torah*—that's a little talk or lecture you deliver during your bat mitzvah about the meaning of something in your portion—and so naturally, I wanted to give mine on the Ten Commandments. My plan was to argue that there is much more to those commandments than a mere set of moral laws about what a Jew should believe or do. What they really are is a set of *definitions* about what it means to be a legal person in the first place. You see, I thought the commandments had a more primary function in Jewish law, something deeper than moral rules, and more basic. Well, the rabbi didn't like that idea very much, and he told me I couldn't do it. He was very paternalistic and condescending about the whole thing, really. I said I would indeed do what I wanted, and then he said no, I said yes, and so on and so forth. He wasn't going to budge. So what I finally did, then, was write a separate *dvar* on some boring and traditional topic, and showed that to him, but when my bat mitzvah actually came around and I got up on the *bimah*, I read my original *dvar*, word for word. I remember the rabbi turning green in the pew, but he didn't stop me. He couldn't. A lot of other people in the congregation didn't like what I said either. Too bad for them. Well, the next week the rabbi asked me and my family to come visit him in his office, and he told us in a very cold manner to please find another *shul* for all our religious needs. My parents pretended they were angry at me, but actually I could see they were quite proud, and they really did support me in the end. So we found another *shul*."

"The Ten Commandments," said Killian. "You were saying."

"What I argued that day was that the Ten Commandments offers us a set of increasingly specific definitions of personhood. They build off each other, one through ten. So when you start at the beginning, you are nothing—I mean not a real *person*, just a living *thing*, and then as you proceed through the commandments in chronological order, you add another key aspect to your personhood, one by one, until you're complete. Only when you've acquired all ten definitions can you be called a true *person* in the Western sense of the word. So I'll explain. The first one is—"

"*You shall have no other gods before me.*" Killian sat up tall, and took obvious pleasure intoning that commandment.

"Why, yes, thank you. Now the traditional reading declares that's about monotheism, of course. But in my alternate reading— as the first definition of legal personhood—the commandment says that a person is a singular, unitary *thing*, not multiple things or multiple people. You are one. You are contained. That is a very Western idea. In many cultures, community exists before singularity, so a monotheistic command or definition like this would not at all be the first in any consecutive series. But in the Judeo-Christian tradition, we always begin by assuming that a person is as unified as is our God. So now let's move on. The second commandment, Killian?"

"*You shall not make for yourself an image in the form of any-thing in heaven above or on the earth beneath or in the waters below. You shall not bow down to them or worship them; for I, the Lord your God, am a jealous God, punishing the children for the sin of the parents to the third and fourth generation of those who hate me, but showing love to a thousand generations of those who love me and keep my commandments.*"

Jonathan laughed. "Good lord, Killian, how do you remember all that?"

"I don't know how he does it." Gloria shook her head in wonder. "He remembers everything,"

"He does the same thing in conference with statutory language. It's scary. The entire U.S. Code."

"Party trick," added Killian, with obvious glee.

"Let me summarize," Sarah continued. "*No worshipping graven images*. That's fine. Now, graven images are *things*. See, that's how this defines personhood—a person is not to be confused with a *thing*. A person is a unified creature, we've already learned, but now we add this second definition: there is more to a person than his or her material body."

"Blasphemy!"

"I'm talking about a secular reading, Killian. Not a religious one. Now, what's the next commandment?"

"*You shall not misuse the name of the Lord your God, for the Lord will not hold anyone guiltless who misuses his name.*"

"Thank you. So, to be a person—definition number three—means you have to live within a system of language. I think the name of God, here, functions as a synecdoche, standing in for all of human language. It means you have to follow linguistic rules and respect those rules. And that's true, right? How can you be an active legal person without first agreeing to participate in communication? All contracts, rights, writs, commands, they're all dependent on language. So this says that being a legal person is to be a servant of language, and never its master, no matter how deftly you might mold and bend it."

"Nice. Continue."

"We have three legal definitions so far. One—a person is unitary. Two—a person is not to be confused with a material thing. And three—a person lives inside language, and has to respect its rules. Now we reach legal definition number four."

"*Remember the Sabbath day by keeping it holy,*" Killian chanted. "*Six days you shall labor and do all your work, but the seventh day is a Sabbath to the Lord your God.*"

"Okay, enough. I don't need the whole thing. Definition number four has to do with time. The life of a legal person exists in structured units, the sequential time of yesterday, today, tomorrow. Remembering the Sabbath day means acknowledging that you exist in this universally agreed-upon temporal system, and that you respect its units—minutes, days, weeks, et cetera. Past and future. Now, think for a moment. Contrast that temporal state of being with one of living inside the perpetual *present*, as, say, an enlightened Buddhist might do, or a mystic in any tradition. See, mysticism has always explicitly attacked legal institutions—in Judaism there's been a conflict for millennia between the rabbinic tradition and the mystical one, the *Halachah* and the *Kabbalah.* You see traces of that conflict all the way back to the Sadducees and the Pharisees. The main aspect of mysticism is abandoning personhood, losing the self, and one of the most important components of that loss is the abandonment of sequential time. Across cultures it's the same. But what this definition number four describes is the *opposite* of a mystical journey. This is a normative one. We must gain time, not lose it. We are building up our personhood here instead of tearing it down. You must adopt sequential time if you want to adopt personhood."

"Oh, you are clever." Gloria shook her head. "I suppose we should know that by now, but sometimes it's overwhelming."

"There's more."

"My brain's beginning to melt." Jonathan smirked in jest at her.

"Well, I can stop, Jonathan."

"No way," said Killian. "Continue. We'll mop up your husband's oozing brains once we're done. Honor your father and mother. That's next."

"Just get to the point about gender, Sarah." Jonathan rolled his hand.

"Well, I'll skim the next few. Honoring your mother and father should be obvious enough. A legal person is defined by his or her familial and personal relationships, by interpersonal context. As a person, you are a mother, brother, sister, friend, what have you, within the society of people. Those and other relationships further define you legally."

"Wait a second." Killian held up his hands, stopping her. "Everything you have said about these commandments is equally applicable to both genders."

"You're right—so far, all of our definitions apply to any person, male or female."

"You said ancient personhood only defines men."

"I'm getting to it, Killian. Be patient. Tell me what's next."

"No murder."

"In so many words."

"*Thou shalt not!*"

"Yes, and after?"

"No adultery, no stealing, no—"

"Okay, stop. Those three. No killing, no cheating, no stealing. They're all functionally the same. A legal person has to respect limits regarding the other people surrounding him. Because a person lives within society. Now, those three particular prohibitions mentioned in Exodus are basic to many legal systems, but not all of them. And there could be other specific prohibitions. In the American tradition, for example, a legal person can't kill or steal, but adultery's certainly not regulated. That doesn't change the basic point, that there are various acts in society that a legal person can't do to other people. There are limits upon his actions."

"And how about after that?" asked Killian. "*You shall not give false testimony against your neighbor.*"

"Now, this is where we get more refined and subtle. Which one is this, Killian? Number nine?"

"Nine it is."

"Good. This commandment says that a legal person has the capacity for deceit. For lying. In definition number nine, the law now understands each of us to have a hidden self. This says a person has both public and private qualities, and the law must make a distinction between the two. *You shall not give false testimony* means that only the public self will be regulated by the law. For now, it says nothing about the private self."

"Oh no." Killian groaned. "Please tell me we're not going to get into privacy. I don't for one second believe the Bible says anything about the legal self getting an abortion."

"Killian," scolded Gloria.

"I don't think the commandments have anything to say specifically about abortion."

"Fine. Then we can continue."

"A person's *acts* can be regulated. But commandment number nine says nothing about his thoughts or inner life. That's all. This definition of legal personhood merely refines the earlier ones about limits on a person within society. It distinguishes between what a person says or does and what he *thinks*. But now we get to my big point. Finally. Killian, please, drum roll—the last commandment. Number ten!"

"*You shall not covet your neighbor's house. You shall not covet your neighbor's wife, or his male or female servant, his ox or donkey, or anything that belongs to your neighbor.*"

"There: You shall not covet your neighbor's wife."

"Or his house, or his donkey." Killian wagged a finger at her. "Let's not forget that donkey lovers are disallowed."

"Your neighbor's *wife*. That's what I objected to way back when in my bat mitzvah. But my goodness, there's so much in this one. It's difficult to unpack. Most significantly, commandment number ten claims that a legal person *can* have his thoughts regulated. Yes? *Covet* deals with thoughts. That is a truly shocking statement to our modern ears. We disagree with it on instinct. But also, along with that rather restrictive limit on a legal person's thought, this definition assumes that our subject is *male*. It's the only such indication in the Ten Commandments, but there it is, clear as day. A person is *male*, a straight male."

"Or a lascivious lesbian. Hiding in the bushes, coveting our wives."

"Somehow, Killian, I don't think that's what they had in mind."

"Well, no, the key word there is *covet*." Killian crossed his arms and frowned, as he did in conference when he disagreed with a colleague. "Not *wife*. Your definition just means that a legal person, male or female, shouldn't covet anything or anyone—his neighbor's wife, or husband, or whatever. Don't covet the teenage nannies and buff trainers either, for that matter."

"I think it's significant that this authoritarian and obstructive definition of personhood ends the series. This is the only one of the ten that wants to prescribe not just the legal person's *actions*, but also his *thoughts*. And I think it's no coincidence that this same intrusive and violent definition of personhood also distinguishes between masters and slaves, and between women and men. There is violence and hierarchy in this definition. That's because what we have here is the *pre-modern* definition of personhood, one that claims you must be a master and land owner to even exist. If you are owned, in other words, you cannot be a legal person. That was certainly true for a long time. You can't be female either and be a person. Right? The curse of womanhood excludes you from that precious legal club. So what we have here is an arcane definition of personhood, pre-democratic, that says *not all individuals are created equal*. Some are superior to others. Some are excluded from the major category. Moreover, thoughts can be regulated. Slavery is sacrosanct. Gender bias is a cornerstone, enshrined. And, remember, this is the crowning definition of personhood in ancient law! What could be more basic than the Ten Commandments? All of the previous nine definitions were basic, and this tenth one was thought to be just as important as the others. So I think that should give us some indication of how crucial sexism was to the initial conception of legal personhood. I have long believed that those sexist and violent roots are still buried in the soil of the Western legal tradition. It took centuries to excise most of them out, but some traces are still there. And still today personhood is growing and changing, and always at risk of recidivism. That was my big point in my bat mitzvah speech."

Sarah sat back and sighed. Killian started to applaud.

"Bravo! Really, Sarah. Brilliant. Although I happen to think you left out several grave implications for donkeys and oxen. But still, impressive. Unfortunately, though, your magnificently constructed argument supports a bunch of relativistic nonsense. I admire you immensely, and disagree with you entirely."

"Thank you, Killian. That's very kind."

"And since you've invited me into your lovely home, plied me with superior wine, and fed me the choicest of lambs, I will not eviscerate your argument publicly, although I would like to reserve the right to do so at a later date."

"Again, generous, but I won't accept it. I don't believe we should leave this important matter unsettled. If you're so set against my argument, Killian, why not put it to a vote? Of all present. All who heard the argument."

"Interesting. Why not? What do we do in case of a tie?"

"What we always do, Killian. The decision of the lower court stands. In this case, that would be the traditional view of the Ten Commandments as a moral and religious guide for already established, contained selves."

"So the odds are in my favor."

"We'll see."

"Agreed. But I get to play Chief Justice, for once." Killian cleared his throat, and then adjusted his voice into a gravelly approximation of Charles Eberly's. "All those in favor of Justice Kolmann's heretic, relativistic, morally bankrupt albeit beautifully argued point that the Ten Commandments are nothing but a patriarchal power play in the sordid tradition of Michel Foucault, please raise your hand."

Laughing, Jonathan and Sarah raised their hands high, but Gloria hesitated. She blushed under the pressure, but then, sheepishly and slowly, raised her hand. She squeezed her eyes shut. The Kolmanns roared in pleasure.

"Gloria Scarlotti Quinn!"

"I'm sorry, Killian!" Her hand was still aloft.

"How *could* you?"

"Sarah made a great point."

"My own wife! Thou who art required to cleave unto me!"

"The audacity," gasped Sarah. "Women these days."

"Don't you insane people realize there's a precedent here? A two-thousand-year-old precedent that you're about to overthrow willy-nilly after too much wine?"

"You don't have the votes, Killian," chided Sarah Kolmann, as she lowered her hand. "You lose."

"But these two fools here aren't even Supreme Court justices!" Killian thumbed toward the two spouses, amidst the general laughter. "They don't count."

"Too late to change the rules, Justice Quinn. Our vote is cast. And now, as the senior justice in the majority, I get to assign the opinion. I choose myself. I've got a firm hold on this argument, so you better look out. It will be blistering."

"Well, I have every intention of writing a vigorous dissent. And you can count on me reading it from high on the bench—or rather deep in your couch, assuming I can maintain the sobriety to do so."

"Deal."

When the laughter died down, all four of them sipped their wine, and settled into a short silence.

"Well, that was fun," sighed Gloria.

Sarah sat forward again. "But we've gotten away from my main point. Personhood, as a legal category, is still actively developing, and in ways that I think are troubling. There is the combination of a too-rigid exclusion on one end of the spectrum and a too-liberal inclusion on the other. So, for example, the borders of personhood are much too strict when it comes to the rights of gay and lesbian and transgendered people, and much too liberal when you consider the absurd expansion of corporate personhood."

"Uh-oh," said Killian. "You said a dirty word."

Gloria and Jonathan chuckled.

"And now that we have Justice Arroyo in place of Van Cleve, it means we're going to start seeing a radical expansion of what the corporate person will be allowed to do and be."

"You don't know that," said Killian.

"I do know it."

"Like what?" pressed Jonathan.

"Well, first and foremost, we'll take Killian's bugbear for corporations—free speech. He's been fighting for that right since he was a young pugilist up on the First Circuit, haven't you, Killian? Now it's just a matter of time before he gets his way. In three or four terms at the most, we'll be ruling that a corporate person has the same right to free speech that we've long granted only to natural persons. And that will be a disaster for this country. No more restrictions on campaign donations, political funding, buying votes. You name it."

"Nonsense, Sarah. Any free-speech ruling we make would apply equally to unions and nonprofits, or to any incorporated gathering of like-minded individuals, so it would all balance out in the end. It would never be a license for only the right wing."

"But neither a corporation nor a union is a *person* in the same way as a living creature. They don't have desires and appetites, physical limits and accountability. And, most importantly, Killian, they don't have a conscience. So free speech for those groups would be an entirely new expansion of personhood, and a dangerous one at that. Oh, but enough, enough, I hate talking about this subject!"

"You're getting all worked up."

"I'm glad you think it's funny."

"It's especially funny because you're going to lose on free speech."

"Absolutely hilarious."

"I find it positively delightful."

Killian punctuated his teasing with a naughty, oversized wink. Although Sarah let him off with a wag of her finger, she realized, as she did it, that Killian's prankish ways had increased in recent months. He had been cracking racier jokes in conference and taunting the Marshal in the court chamber. On one occasion, Sarah had caught him dancing a heavy jig in the hallway of the Supreme Court Building, trying to force their sourpuss Chief Justice into attempting moves from the Blackbird set dance, despite Eberly's clear protestations about his bad leg. Killian seemed happier than ever, and there could only be one reason: Manny Arroyo's vote had replaced Elyse Van Cleve's. Regardless of whether Killian liked or disliked Arroyo as a man, the new Justice was shifting the law sharply toward Quinn's jurisprudence. *Al-Tounsi v. Shaw*, for example, scheduled for argument in February, would most likely switch from a 5–4 ruling in favor of the petitioners into 5–4 ruling for the government, and that was assuming Talos Katsakis remained with the liberal wing. Killian Quinn, who would have certainly written a blazing dissent when President Shaw's side lost, might now reasonably expect to write the majority opinion—and this for the most important case on presidential power in decades. Killian wouldn't need to compromise on merits, or tone down his rhetoric, not that he was capable of doing so. Arroyo, Bryce, Sykes, Eberly and Quinn—five votes for the respondents, that was guaranteed.

"Our recent Subic Bay habeas corpus cases exist at that other end of the spectrum—where personhood is too restricted. Although I thought we had long ago decided that the right to the Great Writ applies to all persons, here we are, potentially limiting that right, deciding whether or not habeas should be applicable to a particular set of people in Subic Bay."

"That's not a question of personhood, Sarah. It's a question of jurisdiction. You know that."

"No, Killian. Ultimately, it *is* about personhood. Denying habeas is putting a limit on a fundamental human right, a right that should belong to all persons. If we say that habeas applies only to American citizens or non-citizens held in sovereign U.S. territory, that's no different than limiting the general scope of personhood. Tightening its definition. Maybe not directly, but I think it's related."

"We shouldn't talk about Subic Bay. It's an active case."

Sarah nodded. "You're quite right."

They sipped their wine and waited for Sarah's little breach to pass over.

"Well, if corporations are going to be granted expanded personhood," added Jonathan, brightly, "maybe they too should get habeas corpus rights."

The four of them laughed at that.

"Oh, I'd like to see that case," said Sarah.

"Now we're just getting silly." Killian grinned. "Too much to drink."

"What a headache it would be," Justice Kolmann continued, "if the warden at Riker's Island was suddenly obliged to bring a corporation's actual body before a judge—its living *corpus*, certainly, because the writ is very clear in its construction about that requirement, isn't it, Justice Quinn? What would our poor warden do? How would he get the living and breathing body of, say, the Stanley J. Stinky Corporation, a free-speaking and fully delineated citizen of the fine state of New York, before, say, a particular district court judge of Lower Manhattan?"

"Stanley J. *Stinky*?" Killian's astonished gaze darted back and forth between Jonathan and Gloria.

"Seeing as Mr. Stinky has long been an amorphous person, located on the 3rd to 7th floors of an office tower on 6th Avenue, Manhattan, as well as in several warehouses scattered around the continental United States, along with a few other subsidiary offices in Boston and Los Angeles and Washington—"

"Okay, okay, enough." Killian pushed his big belly forward and stretched his back.

"And also in twenty different subcontracted factories peppered across the globe from Bangladesh to Morocco, India, China and the Dominican Republic."

"I want my wife's tiramisu." Killian pounded playfully on the table. "I believe that's my right as a guest in this home."

"Indeed, it is." Jonathan pushed back from the table, and went into the kitchen to fetch Gloria's famous dessert. Sarah watched him go, and couldn't help but wonder: what will New Year's Eve be without Jonathan? Their meal would be catered, certainly, and the conversation would be less fun. Jonathan's vanishing from the world was shockingly easy to imagine. Each person is a thing too fragile, too small. Sarah closed her eyes and saw herself lying on Cathy's lavender bedspread, years ago, in their Cambridge home, her five-year-old daughter tucked inside her favorite sheets, clutching her big stuffed moose, the one purchased on their trip to Booth Bay Harbor, Maine. Booth the Mooth, she'd named it. They were flipping through pages of that Dr. Seuss book about the kind elephant, Horton. A phrase reoccurred throughout the book, and every time that Sarah read it, Cathy liked to repeat it. *A person's a person no matter how small.* Horton the elephant saved a miniscule city on a speck of dust, which the mean kanga-roo wanted to destroy. *A person's a person no matter how small.*

Jonathan returned. He praised the tiramisu as he cut and passed around generous slices. He continued praising the dessert's smooth texture as the bitter and earthy scents of coffee and cocoa pervaded the dining room. To Sarah, this was the smell of New Year's Eve, as it had been for over 20 years. But what would happen next year? Would Gloria still bring her tiramisu? Would Sarah be able to savor the acidity of the Marsala wine, or the creaminess of the cheese, without Jonathan here to praise those same qualities? She would never want to eat tiramisu again. A single bite into her dessert, Sarah laid down her fork and watched the others finish their por-tions. Why couldn't she just tell them about Jonathan?

Killian, the first to finish, sucked the final streak of mas-carpone off of his spoon. "Oh, what this stuff does to me." He waved his utensil at his wife. "Gloria, you're a genius. A culinary Michelangelo."

He reached his hand over and gave Gloria's a big, warm squeeze. It was a perfect example of why Sarah loved Killian Quinn so dearly: not once had the Justice made a negative com-ment about his wife. He had only ever praised and complimented her volunteer work, her stay-at-home mothering, her culinary accomplishments. He treasured Gloria. It was odd, really, that the union between these two, certainly the most traditional and conservative marriage of any of Sarah's friends, was also the strongest, and one she admired a great deal. If Sarah had met the Quinns as a younger woman, when she had been a more ide-ological advocate for equality between the genders, she would have had a harder time imagining that such fairness was pos-sible within the confines of traditional marriage. But of course it was—under certain exceptional circumstances. Anything is *pos-sible*. And that harmony, really, was testament to Killian's integ-rity more than Gloria's. There *was* equality between the genders inside the Quinn home, as far as Sarah could tell, and it was due to the immense respect that Killian had for his wife's intel-ligence and work. He could have dismissed or disrespected her in any number of ways—offhand comments, vaguely misogynist jokes—and done so with total impunity, chalked it up to *the way men dealt with their wives*. It was doubtful, however, that Killian harbored a single negative thought about Gloria. Sure, he might have spent his days drafting opinions and dissents for the United States Supreme Court, but in no way did he consider that work superior to Gloria's. It did not matter to him that society might rank their achievements; *he* didn't.

Killian reached over to Sarah's abandoned tiramisu to spoon himself another bite. "You don't mind, do you?"

"No, please, go ahead. I'm too full."

"This is how I get fat." He hovered the loaded spoon before his mouth. "The thin people leave their bloody desserts on the table."

"It was delicious. I just couldn't. I don't know."

Killian put his empty spoon down. He reclined, cocked his head, and looked at Sarah carefully. "Something's bothering you."

Sarah shrugged. "I just think you should need to be a physical, flesh-and-blood person to exercise your right to free speech. You need lips to utter freely spoken words, or hands to sign them, or at least an aide who can interpret your intent, if all you can do is blink your eyelids in Morse code thanks to some dreadful motorcycle accident that you suffered in your youth. And if you want the right to keep and bear arms, then you really should have hands to hold your weapon, and fingers to pull the trigger. And if you want to practice your religion freely, as an individual, as is your constitutional right, well, then, you should have a digestive system that can consume kosher meat, or a tongue to accept communion, or a forehead that can prostrate itself five times daily in the direction of Mecca, if that's what you believe. You can't be an observant Jew or Catholic or Muslim or anything else without a body. And if a person finds herself imprisoned, and needs to exercise her right to habeas corpus, then she needs to have a body that can stand before a judge, a flesh and blood body, with sweat on her brow, and fleshy lips that can declare *I was wronged, your Honor*. We all know this is true. A person is an 'I'. An *I* is a body."

"Sarah."

"I know, Jonathan. I know." Sarah heard herself speaking with increasing softness, and she felt more than ever like weeping. "I'm sorry. It's just that I'm increasingly aware of how fragile and tentative we are as people. Our so-called stable selves are so easily destroyed. Our lives are based on nothing but a few willful delusions. Biological systems. Legal systems. The big fiction of permanence. I think I'm just feeling that fragility more forcefully than ever these days." And here she turned and noticed Jonathan's lowered head, his fingernails picking at the loose fibers on the tablecloth, his refusal to look at her. "I'm getting old. And at a certain point in life one has to face the stark reality that you are not a permanent fixture of this world. You are a passing creature, and very small, and you will soon be gone."

"Indeed," said Killian. "Happy New Year."

When the chuckles died down, Jonathan raised his gaze from his empty plate. His eyes were red, fighting tears. "If Sarah seems especially shaken tonight, it's because I found out this afternoon that my cancer has returned, and it's terribly advanced and aggressive. There is not much anyone will be able do about it."

"Oh my." Gloria pressed her fingers to her mouth.

"We haven't told Cathy or Mark yet. We haven't told anyone. I don't know what I'll say to them when I have to. I don't have long to live. Six months. Maybe a year."

"Jonathan, I'm sorry."

"No, Killian." Jonathan held up his hand, and wiped his eyes with the other. "Please. I didn't want to dominate this evening with something that you can't say anything about, or do anything about. It's bad news, bad as anyone could get, and we all know it."

"It's my fault." Sarah watched her own hands trembling on the table. "I should've never said all those morose things about aging."

"No, it's fine. You didn't have a choice. It's on your mind. I just . . . I . . ." Jonathan threw up his hands. "There's nothing really to say, now, is there?"

"I can say it's terrible. I'm sorry."

"Thank you, Killian. It is terrible. Yes."

Silence opened up between and around them, as they stared red-faced at the smeared chocolate on their plates. Confessing

Jonathan's illness didn't make Sarah feel any closer to Killian or Gloria, and it didn't make her feel any less like an actor playing the part of happy hostess. Her few bites of tiramisu revolted in her stomach. Jonathan, the first of the frozen group to move, adjusted his glasses and glanced at his watch. "It's 11:53," he said, brightly. "Who wants to watch the ball fall over Times Square?"

They moved into the den—or floated, really, as Sarah could hardly feel herself walking. She stood pressed against the large window, shivering from her proximity to the cold glass. Jonathan's confession had the dual effect of intensifying her sensory experience and deepening the isolation of her thoughts. Her husband turned on the TV, and then stood back from it, remote in hand. On the screen, a couple of heavily made-up and hair-dyed announcers yelled into their microphones, projecting their voices above the cacophonous crowd of Times Square. All that screaming grated on Sarah's nerves; it was insufferable, even with the sound set low. Neon lights flashed. A rock guitarist played screeching notes while a rapper chanted what sounded to Sarah like obscene versions of elementary school rhymes. The camera passed over the crowd, across the blues and reds of the revelers' dresses, jackets and hats—all so garish, so unwatchable. Sarah turned away from the television and saw Gloria stroking her husband's upper back with two fingers through his shirt. Gentle, little strokes along Killian's shoulder blades. The only peace that Sarah could find right now was in watching the tiny rhythm of that gesture.

"One minute left."

The gaudy crystal ball slowly descended on its track atop One Times Square, and then burst into light, illuminating *2008*. In the din of a screaming mob, Killian and Gloria kissed, and Jonathan quietly moved beside Sarah. He wrapped his stocky arm around her shoulder and kissed her on the temple. "Happy New Year, Sarah," he whispered, certainly for the last time in his life. Sarah Kolmann closed her eyes and leaned against his chest.

7

SOVEREIGNTY

"I'll be blunt," Justice Sykes said to his clerks, who were all packed together on the couch across from him. "I remain unconcerned if these review procedures are an adequate substitute for habeas. Maybe they are, maybe not. Our opinions do not matter. It remains premature to address the question, as DTA-MCA review has not yet run its full course. So I see no other choice but to show restraint."

Kyle and Samantha, two of Rodney's even-keeled clerks for the term, nodded in favor of his pronouncement, but Jessica Klein, a bold and original legal thinker and a rising superstar, pressed her index finger into her temple and contorted her lips.

"You disagree, Ms. Klein, but I am certain."

Jessica moved a stack of briefs from her lap onto the coffee table. "I think you have to assess the procedures themselves, Justice Sykes, because the Suspension Clause applies. If the procedures aren't adequate, then the detainees are entitled to constitutional habeas."

"The Suspension Clause does *not* apply to non-citizens imprisoned outside the sovereign United States."

"According to *Bayat*, Subic is subject to U.S. jurisdiction."

"I disagreed with Justice Kataskis in *Bayat*, and I do again now."

"But either way, Subic Bay is de facto—"

"There are no *buts*, Ms. Klein. De facto this, that or the other—it does not translate into the letter of the law. Subic Bay is on lease from the Philippines. Legally, the base is not under the sovereign control of the United States of America. De facto rule it might be, but we cannot interject what we personally think about an issue when the law itself is so clear."

Ms. Klein, who was only 25, spoke with the cool composure and confidence of a fellow justice. She would never back down from an argument with her boss. Instead, she leaned forward to confront him more directly. "It all turns on what we mean by sovereignty. Seems whether you agree with *Bayat* or not, sovereignty was definitively resolved in that case. Subic is squarely under the D.C. Circuit's jurisdiction, and that's as much a part of the law as any lease agreement with the Philippines from a hundred years ago."

Rodney shook his head vigorously. "No. I don't like it, and I won't do it. I will not play fast and loose with definitions. Sovereignty means what it means: it informs us who is the owner of that land, by law, de jure. Does that land belong to one nation or another? Can we draw a bright line? Yes. Subic Bay is part of the Philippines, and subsequently leased, meaning it is owned by the lessor. We cannot start questioning who de facto has power, or if sovereignty is affected by de facto status. If we begin to think of sovereignty as a gray concept, up for debate, then any time there's a tiny dispute occurring outside the confirmed sovereign territory of the United States, this Court will be asked to determine jurisdiction. And we will have cornered ourselves, Ms. Klein, and be under an obligation to take those cases. Ominous and absurd that would be, determining what *sovereignty* means on a case-by-case basis, as if we were somehow judges of international law, not to mention elected officials charged with the task of deciding political questions. We are not qualified to say what sovereignty means internationally. We have been *told* what it means, and that is enough for us. End of our story. And if that still does not satisfy you, if you are eager to open up a can of worms and get into the business of questioning clear terminology, let me remind you of what happened to this Court in the 1960s when we decided to pry open questions around the term *obscenity*. Our brethren wasted countless hours of their precious time investigating the nooks and crannies, so to speak, of every piece of smut imaginable—*does this pornographic image differ substantively from that one? How much of a woman's or man's privates must we witness for it to be obscene?* and so on and so forth—while holed up in the basement, room 22-B, in fact, watching dirty movies like a pack of sex addicts. Moreover," continued Rodney, over the laughter of his delighted clerks, "after all those hours behind a flickering film projector or huddled around an explicit magazine, our greatest contribution to the understanding of what obscenity might actually *be* was Justice Stewart's infamous *I know it when I see it*. Tell me, Ms. Klein, do you find that legally helpful? Do you know *sovereignty* when you see it? I think, perhaps, we should have a more straightforward guideline, something along the lines of a definition. So if we open *sovereignty*, do you not see what that does to the law? What that does to you, or rather me, as a judge? No. *I* cannot do it. The cost is too great. I am unprepared for such a price."

Rodney sat back in his armchair, and straightened his lapels. Why was he inflaming himself over a minor disagreement with Jessica Klein about *sovereignty*? He was not obliged to explain his logic. He had solicited the opinions of his innocent clerks, received them graciously, and now he should be able to move on assuredly without further drama. Yet here he was, raising his voice, on the verge of slamming his fist down on the coffee table like a judge in the movies, demanding his clerk's full acquiescence. Order in the Court! Order in *my* Court!

He thanked and dismissed them. He locked the door and turned his *Do Not Disturb* sign against his secretaries and clerks. He rotated the venetian blinds on his windows downwards. He straightened the stack of the cert briefs on his desk beside his blotter, cases to be considered for next term, to be decided in this afternoon's conference. He had to get to work. Instead, he sat at his desk, motionless, staring at the portrait of his dead wife. He turned it over, face down, and picked up his phone and buzzed his secretary.

"Jenn, would you please ask Ms. Klein to bring in her notes on *Cartman v. Tennessee*?"

Rodney unlocked his door, and returned to his desk before the clerk arrived. When Jessica entered chambers, he tried to look as if he were reviewing a cert petition, immersed in its questions. He glanced up at her expectantly, albeit with irritation at being interrupted.

"How's that opinion progressing?"

The clerk showed him the draft in her hand. "Very well, Justice Sykes. I've added the footnotes you requested and key citations, but I think other than that it's close to circulation."

Rodney thanked her, and returned to his reading. She began to walk away, but he stopped her.

"Surely, Ms. Klein, you understand my point on sovereignty."

Jessica stood behind an armchair. "Of course I do, Justice Sykes. But I still think you need to review the DTA procedures. Habeas applies, regardless."

"How can habeas apply if Subic Bay is not part of sovereign U.S. territory?"

"It applies because the Military Commissions Act was written and signed inside the territorial United States. That's what matters, not the status of the detainees. Habeas has to be understood as a fundamentally different right than the ones enumerated in the Amendments. There's more to it than an individual entitlement. The Suspension Clause is Article I, so I think that it is intended primarily as a limitation on Congress, and not as a positive right that's granted *to* citizens like free speech or the freedom to bear arms. I think the framers thought of habeas as one of our few unalienable natural rights, and therefore it could only be acted on *negatively*, taken away, and not granted. Obviously only in rebellion or invasion, as the clause so clearly states. So I think anybody in the world, if they're imprisoned by the U.S., has the technical right to habeas in our courts. I mean, the text of the Constitution, look—is habeas ever enumerated as such? No. It's assumed, right from the start. So on the constitutional level, at least, it doesn't really matter if the prisoner in question has standing or is a citizen or is detained inside U.S. territory or anything like that. What matters is only that one key question: is Congress trying to limit constitutional habeas without offering a proper substitute?"

"And so therefore we have no choice but examine the procedures themselves?"

"Absolutely."

"And when we complete our examination? How do they hold up?"

"I find them deficient in all seven ways that the *Al-Tounsi* petitioner's brief so eloquently outlined."

"I see. Thank you, Ms. Klein. I appreciate your candor."

She left him alone. His clerks last year wouldn't have challenged him like this. Cindy Chin, in particular—no, she wouldn't have done it, with all her deference, her insecure voice that raised sentences into questions. This term only Jessica Klein had such fight. And yet she was the one clerk he had invited back into his private chambers, whom he wanted to debate. If Cindy Chin were in chambers today, he would have dismissed her along with the others, without a thought.

He picked up a cert brief and read it, but the words jumbled together, a linguistic mush of legal terms, clauses, stock phrases. Rodney stood. He put on his jacket, checked the time, and fetched his overcoat from the hanger by the door. In the entrance to chambers, he told his secretaries that he was venturing outside for a bit but would soon return, and would they please be so kind as to hold his calls.

He exited onto 2nd Street through the small back entrance to the Supreme Court Building into the biting cold of a late February morning. The frigid air stung his cheeks. Rodney walked south on the near empty street, past the colorless administrative building for the Library of Congress, toward the only bustling neighborhood in the near vicinity, on Pennsylvania Avenue. Icy hillocks of snow rose out of the pavement here and there, blackened with exhaust and grime. He passed burrito shacks and banks, a prosperous Capitol Hill lounge, and a convenience store, the only business open before 10 A.M. An elderly man sat on an upside-down bucket in front of the store, arms crossed, huddling in the cold. His propped sign rested against a chewed-up Dunkin' Donuts styrene cup, its words engraved in ballpoint pen that was running out of ink, on a piece of scrap cardboard. RIGHT HERE, said the sign, in blunt block letters. Rodney stopped. The beggar's coffee cup sat on the gum-spotted sidewalk. The tips of the man's two shredded running shoes stuck out on either side of the cup and the sign, with bits of his threadbare socks and toes peeking through the holes.

Rodney squinted and removed his glasses. The beggar wore an old down jacket that was missing most of its feathers, a dirty pair of work pants, and a maroon knit cap emblazoned with the Redskins profile logo. He had a bushy mustache and uneven stubble. Patches of his gray facial hair were on the verge of overtaking the black.

"Hey, brother." The beggar nodded at him.

"Pardon me." Rodney pointed at the sign. "*Right here?*"

The man looked down, as if he wasn't aware of what he wrote. "The cup. 'Cause that's where you wanna put your unwanted change and spare bills. Make it easy on you, man, so you don' miss a thing."

"I see."

"Just pointin' it out direct."

"You're not saying it about yourself?"

"What?" The beggar cocked his head in consideration. "Well, I ain't sunnin' myself on Miami beach, now, am I?" He laughed. "Just here like you." He laughed again, with enough force to shake his body, and offered Rodney a shrug. He picked up his styrene cup and shook it at the Justice. A few nickels and dimes rattled.

"Feel like tappin' that deep pocket of yours, doctor, for a couple of them quarters? Help a brother get right?"

Rodney fished around in his trouser pocket, but found only lint. As he had just undertaken a grand gesture of searching, now he had to offer something. He retrieved his wallet and deposited a couple of bills into the man's cup.

Before the beggar could thank him, Rodney turned in the opposite direction and headed northwest on Pennsylvania, passing the businesses and restaurants waking for the day. He marched toward the Capital and veered out of the short commercial district onto Independence Avenue. The small stores were replaced with foreboding, block-sized government buildings enclosed by heavy iron fences. He walked faster now, blowing into his hands, and steered up toward the Capital on a gravel pathway. The neoclassical dome loomed before him. He skirted the building itself, and kept to the surrounding gardens. He passed giant white ashes and white oaks, gnarled Yoshino cherries once gifted by the Japanese government, and approached a grove of enormous magnolias hugging the western steps. When he reached the marble terrace, Rodney stopped to survey the Great Mall before him. He regarded the Ulysses S. Grant monument, erected before a small reflecting pool, but from this angle he saw only the rear end of that general's bronze horse. In the distance, the Washington Monument resembled a giant toothpick stuck into the ground. The last time he had stood in this place was on the second inauguration of President Shaw, three years earlier. He hadn't stood on this terrace exactly, but was seated above, in temporary bleachers on the western steps. From that vantage point, Rodney and his fellow justices surveyed the crowd, and a more expansive view of the Mall.

Today the gray city was compressed under heavy clouds. None of the deciduous trees had leaves, and the wilting evergreens shivered in a sharp, icy wind. The Great Mall's lawn, so lush and green in summer, had browned. Huge swaths of it were covered with thin sheets of murky ice, too chunky and pock-marked to offer the appearance of glass. These last frigid days of winter could be so dismal. It felt like the world was coming to its end.

Cold air pricked his lungs. His non-negotiable duty for Friday mornings, between ten and noon, after that meeting with his clerks, was to review the week's cert petitions. With the conference scheduled for one, he needed to be prepared. But cert petitions, like so much else these days, made little sense. Or no, their sense was clear, but their purpose felt diminished. Procedures, rules, questions of standing: more and more they felt like arbitrary barriers, a type of technical sophistry. Rodney had always thought of statutes and clauses and common law as tools to help him fight off the siege of incoming cases, to hold the line against the inevitable challenges, attacks and encroachments, but now his rulings, stricter than ever, made him feel directionless. As a result, his effort, attention to detail and self-discipline were slackening. His vigilance had waned, as indicated by this, right now—walking around aimlessly in the middle of a busy day. There were too many opinions and dissents, more and more streaming in from the circuits every day: *you may do this, must not do that, the law shall only allow you to go so far, wide, and deep. You do not have standing on questions of sovereignty. My goodness,* thought Rodney, *has the time had come for me to retire?*

Long after his secretaries and clerks had left for the weekend, Rodney worked in dark chambers under a single desk light, catching up on his endless reading and fiddling with the wording of an opinion, until someone knocked on his door. "Yes?" He pulled his attention up from the revision to *Cartman v. Tennessee,* expecting Linton, a custodian who had been at the Court for 35 years, to enter and gather the week's garbage, or perhaps a court police officer, making his final rounds.

"Hey, Dad. Working?"

Rodney smiled, slid his chair back and pushed his papers aside. "Come in, Samuel, please. Just final touches on a minor case."

Samuel's lengthening dreadlocks gave him the unflattering appearance of a Portuguese Water Dog. Along with that ratty leather jacket, peeling at the elbows, Rodney's son certainly did not resemble a typical *Washington Post* reporter. But then Samuel had tempered the slightly edgier elements of his outfit and personal style with a light blue button down shirt and a pair of khaki pants. He hung his jacket on a hook on the back of Rodney's door and collapsed onto the low black couch. His shoulders looked broader than Rodney remembered—perhaps he was going to the gym. He snatched a pillow to prop his head, and slouched on the couch with an ease and comfort unthinkable for any clerk.

"To what do I owe this pleasure?"

"Thought we could catch some dinner, if you're free." Samuel crossed his ankles. "I don't have any plans."

"Aren't we scheduled for tomorrow evening?"

"We don't always have to stick to schedule, Dad. Look, if you can't do it—"

"No, no," interrupted Rodney. He stood from his desk and sat across from Samuel in one of the arm chairs. "Dinner would be delightful. Giordino's?"

Samuel was studying him, the type of probing look that a psychiatrist might use on a patient he suspects has abandoned his medication. This was the drawback, Rodney supposed, of his son's pronounced attentiveness, which had begun months earlier, during that torturous circus with Arroyo and Cassandra. The positive effects had been obvious: they now had dinner together every two weeks, and Samuel called him regularly. Nonetheless, Rodney would have to inform his kind but nosy son to stop worrying so much about him. Rodney was in no danger of falling off a cliff, he was absolutely fine. Perhaps he was a bit tired, and overcome with tasks that seemed ever more futile, but the Arroyo scandal had passed, and he had made it through that mess with his dignity intact. There was nothing more to say about his present situation, nothing to investigate.

"I don't recall seeing you with the press in argument this week, Samuel."

"I had to go to Montreal. Just got back this afternoon."

"How lovely."

"Yeah. It's freezing up there, but they know how to make a bagel." Sam kicked off his shoes and put his feet on the coffee table. "How're you doing, Dad?"

"I am fine, Samuel. Thank you for asking."

"Have you talked to Cassandra recently?"

"I have not." Rodney crossed his legs tightly in the armchair. "Why don't we go to dinner? I can wrap things up here." He stood and returned to his desk to gather his papers for the weekend.

Samuel did not press his investigation as they left the building, nor while driving up Massachusetts in his old Volkswagen. Rodney sat and enjoyed Samuel's silent company, the passing cabs and traffic lights, the swish of tires on a wet road. They passed the Islamic Center on Massachusetts, with its tall minaret and pale blue Arabic inscription, and the bridge over Rock Creek, the embassies of Great Britain, South Africa, and Brazil, and the fortressed grounds of the Naval Observatory, official home of Vice President Bloomfield. This stretch of road was one of Rodney's favorites in the city, and it seemed especially peaceful and picturesque in the lightly falling snow. They drove up Wisconsin Avenue until it crossed Fessenden, and then Samuel found a parking spot in front of Giordino's. Rodney and Samuel were recognized and greeted by the young hostess, who led them to the Justice's favorite booth. Ray Giordino emerged from the back in his tucked-in shirt. As usual, he wore his belt a notch too tightly, so that his stomach bulged above his waist.

"But I have you for tomorrow!" Ray shook Rodney's hand and patted Samuel on the back. "What in heaven's name is going on here, Justice Sykes? You don't change Saturdays! You don't do that! You've got me all confused!"

"A slight alteration, which I hope does not preclude me from visiting you twice in a single weekend."

Ray assured him that it would not, and asked what they wanted. Ray suggested a new Chianti, the perfect accompaniment for Rodney's chicken cacciatore, but something that would not overpower Samuel's eggplant parmesan. Rodney agreed, waited for Ray's return, tested the wine, and approved the fine choice. Samuel watched this whole interaction in silence. After Ray had poured their glasses and departed, Sam sat forward and spoke.

"How's the mood on the Court these days?"

"Amicable." Rodney smiled politely.

"Arroyo?"

"He's a qualified professional."

"You guys talking at all?"

"We speak when it's required. In conference. During our discussion of cases."

"And that's it?"

"I don't see why you should be surprised by that, Samuel. There is nothing strange about it. I have the same relationship with all of my other colleagues."

"Okay." Samuel sighed with impatience. He unrolled his cloth napkin, and then draped one corner of it over the middle fingers on his right hand, tucked a second corner into the gap between his thumb and forefinger, and a third between his ring finger and pinkie. He fiddled and fussed and shaped the cloth. When at last he raised his covered hand, Samuel had transformed his napkin into a bright red, floppy-eared rabbit.

"I want cawwots," said the rabbit. "Cawwots pwease."

"*Samuel!*"

Samuel tossed the napkin onto the table, grumbled inaudibly, and took a big sip of wine. "Come on, Dad. You see Manny every single day. What's that like? Is it all just formal and restrained and with everything under the surface? Tell me what you actually think and feel about sitting in the same room with the guy. What's it like to decide cases with him?"

"I have no complaints with the man."

"Please, Dad. Listen to me. I am begging you to tell me something substantial about your life."

"Why? Does *The Washington Post* need a new piece about the great Supreme Court scandal, six months hence? Are you that eager to have even more salacious gossip for your pages?"

"It's not for the record. I'm not going to write a story. I want to know because I'm your son. Simple as that." Samuel's innocent, open smile made him look 16, in spite of his manly shoulders.

"If you must know something, I will tell you this. I dislike Justice Arroyo's jurisprudence. I dislike it immensely. There. You may take your mental notes."

"I don't like it either."

"Except that is not a personal verdict, Samuel. That has nothing to do with any old nonsense about Cassandra, or the man's past indiscretion with me. It is entirely a function of his present opinions and dissents. I find them odious, and deeply problematic. Sometimes, as I sit in conference listening to Justice Arroyo blather on with his shocking arrogance, and I feel tempted to engage him in battle—which I resist, mind you, always—I feel more like a weary law professor faced with an unruly first-year, know-it-all student than a Supreme Court justice confronted with a colleague. Emmanuel Arroyo is a mean-spirited and over-entitled bully who has somehow forgotten that the basic purpose of law is to balance two equally valid, opposing needs, and that inevitably in each case someone worthy must lose, and moreover the possibility of loss in any given instance is right and good. That it is, in fact, better in the aggregate for everyone to suffer a tiny bit when entering into an adversarial legal proceeding than for one side to always win. Incredibly, Manny Arroyo does not seem to grasp this most basic lesson of fair play. With him, any unwelcome ruling is sour grapes, an unfair request, an improper denial, or faulty logic. He is incapable of dissociating his bald, egotistical desires from the will of the people as embodied by statute. From democracy. Frankly, Samuel, his behavior reminds me less of what a justice's should be, and more of an entirely partisan player in the political branches. It's as if Vice President Bloomfield himself has joined us on the bench. Or worse. In his narcissism, he's like your Uncle Marshall, writing childish screeds locked away in his prison cell."

"Ouch."

"If you must know everything, Samuel, then I will also add this. I cannot bring myself to look at his self-righteous face when he speaks. I catch myself staring off into space, or pondering the tip of my pen, anything. The books on the shelves. Sometimes I pretend to take notes. I loathe that man's thinking. His presence, Samuel, and the knowledge that he will remain my colleague for many decades, has me quite despondent."

"But none of that, of course, has anything to do with the fact that your daughter and this man just—"

"It is a principled response to his jurisprudence! That is *it*. Now I'm done talking about it."

Rodney sat back hard and pressed his hands into fists beneath the table. He should never have taken his son's obvious bait. Like his late mother, Samuel believed that diving into the murky swamp of one's emotions was a productive exercise, and often necessary, but Rodney believed differently. To Rodney, it always seemed like an indulgence, a futile exercise. Why talk in depth about a situation that could not be changed or altered in any meaningful way, only endured? He gritted his teeth. He had been enflamed unnecessarily, and damn Samuel for pressing! He turned away from his son, toward a mounted poster of the 2006 Italian National Football Team, its players posed joyously in three successively higher rows, the striker holding aloft the small World Cup trophy. He studied their open glee of victory. The poster was framed by two hanging scarves, emblazed with the Italian team's tri-colored shield and the bold phrase "*Forza Azzuri.*" His anger wasn't fading.

"If you must insist on pressing me about Arroyo and your sister, then I would rather cut short our dinner tonight."

"Fine. So we won't talk about it." Samuel pulled one of his feet onto the upholstered bench beside him, and rested the weight of his outstretched arm on his knee. "There's something I want to tell you about Montreal. I went up there for a story I'm writing for Monday's paper. It's been timed for the *Al-Tounsi* argument. I got an email at work awhile back from this kid, an engineering student up in McGill, named Athir Al-Tounsi. He's your main petitioner's eldest son. Really bright guy, got a scholarship to study up in Canada, and off he went. This was a couple years ago. So he's third year, now, acclimatized to North America and all that. Obviously, he's been concerned about his father, and he's a diligent guy—done all sorts of research, talking with his father's lawyers, consulting law professors at McGill, and you wouldn't believe what he's put together. He's treated this a like a full-time job while also holding down his considerable schoolwork. He figured out I was your son, read my articles, and emailed me to say he wanted to meet. I think, really, more than anything, he wanted me to work on you, subtly, to try to get you to—"

"Stop it!" Rodney's face heated. "I will not talk to you about an upcoming case!"

"I'm not asking you to talk about it."

"Don't you know how deeply unethical it is for you to try to convince me of anything?"

"Look, Dad, I'm just telling you some information I learned that I think will be of some interest to you. Okay? It's stuff you'll see on Monday in the newspaper, anyway, which I know you'll read before argument, so why don't you consider this a personally directed, last-minute amicus brief? The guy made a big impression on me, and I want to tell you about it. I was thinking about you the entire three days I was up there talking to him." Samuel removed his leg and leaned on the table, toward Rodney. "Also, you're wrong, Dad. There's nothing unethical about me trying to convince you of something, although that's not even what I'm doing. Presenting an argument is what everyone around you from the lawyers to the clerks to the other justices do. It's your *job* to be convinced, Dad. That's kind of the whole point, isn't it?"

"This is ex parte, Samuel. Entirely unethical."

"I don't care. Will you please just listen?"

Rodney crossed his arms and waited.

"You know the facts of the case, obviously. Athir repeated his father's claim—that he never had anything to do with Al Qaeda, he was just a visiting engineer in Istanbul when he was arrested, and had nothing to do with plotting bombs in embassies or train stations or anywhere else. Never on a battlefield in Afghanistan or Iraq, never arrested or watched by the police back in Cairo. Just a decent, educated family man somehow caught up in a ridiculous mistake, and treated as a scapegoat by the Turkish government, ignored by his own, lumped together with dubious detainees, and assumed to be part of some big plot."

"Mr. Al-Tounsi knew those other men before he arrived in Turkey. He knew them in Cairo. He admitted that. He gave them money. Those are established facts. And also quite beside the point, legally speaking."

"Well, everybody knows unsavory people, doesn't mean *you* are unsavory. Look, Dad, you're right, it doesn't matter whether or not Majid Al-Tounsi played some minor part in a plot to blow up buildings, even unwittingly, or got involved with bad people—loaning money to a dumb friend. I don't know the man's conscience. I don't really care. Regardless of what he did or didn't do, Majid Al-Tounsi and these guys were sent halfway across the world to the Philippines and have since rotted away in a Naval Base without being charged with any crime for six years, six *years*, and there's no end in sight. Al-Tounsi's shady combat status tribunal claimed that somebody, somewhere— we're not even allowed to know *who*—told the military, proba- bly under duress or torture or something, that he gave money to a terrorist, and that's it! That's all they seem to have on him, and it's hardly an established fact. His lawyer wasn't even given an opportunity to question that information, let alone his absurd 'enemy combatant' status. God, he wasn't even *allowed* a lawyer at that time. None of this makes any sense, Dad, and you know it. It's crazy."

"There are other legal issues in play, here, Samuel."

"I know, I know—the MCA, the DTA, the Suspension Clause, the historical reach of habeas, fine. I don't want to talk about any of that. You've got your opinions, and I respect you. Well, I respect you, but not really your opinion. In this case, I don't really respect that at all. I think you're missing the point, colossally, and I can't just sit back without saying something about it."

"And what do you think is the *point*?"

"That there is this man, and other men, who are being detained by the United States government without due process. A human being named Majid Al-Tounsi, who is far from you physically, and is completely obscured by all the dry intellectual gymnastics that the nine of you like to perform up there on the bench and in back chambers. He's an engineer. A father to Athir and three girls. A husband. He's mixed up in something way bigger than his own innocence or guilt. By his son's account, he is sweet and generous and kind, and incapable of violence. Not that any of that makes a difference when it comes to due process."

Sam reached into the inside pocket of his worn leather jacket and removed a small photograph, which he slid over to his father's side of the table. In the picture, a tall, middle-aged Arab man with thinning hair stood before the Sphinx in Giza, his gangly arms wrapped around the shoulders of two children, a boy of about 13 and a girl of eight. He wore a light tan jacket, worn slacks, a button-down shirt. His waist was so thin that Rodney suddenly imagined the trouble he must have finding an appropriate belt, at least without having to punch new holes in it himself. His long face, which was faintly pock-marked, and his large crooked smile radiated happiness. The children slouched on either side of him— that weariness of being dragged into a picture with an over-eager parent—but their half-smiles and gleaming eyes also indicated an underlying pleasure, a lack of real resistance. How bad could it be to have their eager father wanting to take his picture with them before the famed Sphinx? Who wrapped his elastic arms around them and pulled them close?

Samuel pointed to the children. "That's Athir and his sister Nyla. Taken with their father just before he left for Istanbul, maybe 2001. That was the last time they saw him."

Rodney peered at Majid Al-Tounsi's grinning face, this man who had no idea of what horrors were about to befall him. Or no, perhaps he did have some idea. Perhaps he knew exactly.

"Athir told me all sorts of details about his father and his mother back in Cairo, the whole extended family. How desperate they are to get him back. His mother's two jobs, what his sisters are studying in school. I won't bore you with it all, but I will say this: that kid, Athir—and he's really just a kid, maybe 20 years old—was so methodical and clear in his legal arguments, so obviously *right*, that I was left speechless. He wasn't even asking for Majid to be let out of Subic Bay. He said if his father really did have something to do with an Al Qaeda plot, then he should stay right where he was. Just that this black-hole situation, without declared proof, without charges laid against him, and most importantly no habeas corpus to even begin to examine—"

Rodney held a trembling palm in front of his son's face. When Samuel stopped speaking, Rodney lowered his hand. "What exactly do you think you're doing here?" Anger shook his voice.

"Here's the thing, Dad. I almost never see the people in your written opinions. I mean, the ones who are actually affected by your rulings. I see a disconnect between the human beings and the law. So I thought you should see one of them, and learn a bit about him."

Rodney leaned forward, his nostrils flaring, his face burning. "You don't see the *people* in my opinions? And you think I don't realize that? You think that would be something *new* for me to discover, some great revelation?" Although Rodney was tempted to crumple the small photograph, instead he turned into over and pushed it, face down, toward his son. "Every case I hear on that bench has a picture like this one behind it, or a set of pictures, or on occasion a whole *class* of them. My job, as you damn well know, Samuel, is to rule on the law and to clarify it, to be an *impartial* judge. You want to inform me that Majid Al-Tounsi has a face? Very well. Show me his face. His child has a face just the same. And my, my, here they all are, so happy, with their bright faces, posed before the Sphinx. Well, the poor souls killed on September 11th had faces, too, and so did their orphaned children. There are countless faces attached to every one of the thousands of petitions that we get on the Court every year. There are so many damn faces before me that I could be looking at, and lamenting, and witnessing, if I let myself, and for what? *What?* What does that precious picture of yours say that I can possibly address from the bench of the Supreme Court in my limited position? That Majid Al-Tounsi was kind to his family, that he loves his son, that his son loves him? Oh, I believe you. And what does that matter?"

Rodney sighed. He tried to take a deep breath, to take a pause, but he was too angry to stop his rant now.

"There are limits to my job, Samuel. Limits that I take very seriously. I am charged with deciding whether or not habeas corpus should be granted to non-citizen petitioners under wartime circumstances as specified by a joint resolution for the Authorization of the Use of Military Force. There are statutes, constitutional clauses and common-law decisions that are quite relevant to this case, but the face of Majid Al-Tounsi is *not*. How *dare* you, Samuel Sykes!"

Rodney pinned his son with his glare, and did not let him go. If Samuel wants so badly to see a face, let him look upon his father's enraged one, which will not be mocked or taunted or played for a fool. Let him look on *this*.

Samuel, nodding slowly, pulled the photograph of Al-Tounsi closer, and slipped it into his pocket. "Sorry," he whispered.

"I think you need to learn a thing or two about self-control. That was an absolutely *disgusting* display of indiscretion and puerility."

"Okay!" Samuel squirmed with sheepish embarrassment. "Your job is insanely difficult and complex, and I just belittled it. I'm sorry, believe me."

The waitress approached with a large Greek salad and two side plates. She halted, and glanced back and forth between them. Rodney forced himself to smile at her, and only then did the waitress put the food down. He thanked her with as much composure as he could muster, and she left hurriedly. For Samuel to assault him in a restaurant like this, in *public*—why, that just made it all the worse.

Rodney let his simmering anger cool. He served two portions of salad, sliding one over to his son. Samuel hung his head and thanked him almost inaudibly. They ate in silence.

Samuel pushed his lettuce around on his plate with his fork. "They're putting a lot of pressure on me over at the paper. There's a dozen big cases in your Court, I know, but the editors only want stories on Subic Bay. It's an international situation, Dad. When they run something on Subic—anything about it, suicides, the hunger strike, the CSRTs, the bloody weather in the Philippines—the article's picked up by half the papers on the planet.

And this *Al-Tounsi* case, Dad, this final habeas test—it's bigger than the rest. It's like every government in the world's that's got habeas on the books, or can trace its comparable provisions back to the *Magna Carta*—which means what? every nation but Syria and Iran and North Korea?—they are all looking to this case as some kind of test, to see how far they'll be able to push their own security and detainee procedures while still claiming to be honest and respectful of their original habeas principles—"

"*Al-Tounsi* has nothing to do with the provisions or requirements of other countries."

"I know that, but still. It's being treated at the paper like some kind of international precedent. It's the legal D-Day. A battle that's getting hashed out in one courtroom, but for the benefit of the whole world. Let alone what it'll allow or disallow for the United States in the future. I get a hundred times the hits I usually do on these stories I'm writing about Subic Bay."

"I am well aware of the importance of this case."

Sam nodded, and took a bite of his salad. "May I say something else?"

"Of course."

"I'm worried about you."

Rodney put his fork down and stared into his feta.

"I have never seen you get as angry as what I just saw. There's a new fury in you, Dad. I don't recognize you."

"I am not angry."

"You *are* angry, all the time. Will you please tell me why?"

Rodney sipped his wine.

"Will you please say something?"

Rodney cleared his throat, and paused as he tried to think of what to say. "I was woefully unprepared for conference this afternoon. I did not review our certs before it began. To be perfectly honest, Samuel—and I trust this information won't find its way into the back pages of *The Washington Post*—I cast my cert votes today exclusively on the assigned clerks' recommendations. I had no other recourse." He allowed that confession to sink in, and then glanced at his son for the first time since their fight. "Are you shocked by that admission?"

"No."

"I have not done that once in my seventeen years on the Court."

"I don't think it's such a big deal."

"I was certain I'd be discovered. But my irresponsible methodology failed to raise my colleagues' suspicions, which I don't believe is to their credit."

"What are you trying to say?"

"I'm saying, more and more, I am thinking of retiring from the Court."

The strangeness of declaring that aloud gave Rodney pause. He pushed aside a piece of lettuce with his fork, and focused his aim on a sliver of red onion. He pressed the tines into it.

"I am no longer certain of what I'm doing there. My jurisprudence is a mystery. I don't know if I even agree with it. I cannot see how such an unmoored individual has any place on the Supreme Court."

"I can think of ten or so justices off the top of my head who've gone through a crisis like that."

"Not the same."

"You're evolving."

"I'm not *evolving*, Samuel. I'm not a Galapagos finch. I'm confused. And yes, I'm angry, you're quite right about that, but I don't know why." Rodney spoke with softness, now, steadily. Another mystery, this—how the rage he had just declared as his own immediately receded into something foreign and inaccessible. "I have been thinking more and more about *Kosterman v. The Regents of the University of Oregon*," he said. "Do you remember that case?"

Samuel nodded.

"Of course you would. It's only reason I was appointed to the Court, isn't it? I've been mulling it over. Certain aspects of it I still find odd and thorny. Although it's the same basic problem with all affirmative action cases, really, including the more recent ones. Justice Rosen calls them the hardest to decide."

"Why are you thinking about it now?"

"Farrow Marsh only assigned it to me because I am black."

Sam scowled and tried to flick a piece of fallen lettuce off the table. It hit the salt shaker and stuck to the glass. "Your strict legalism had something to do with that assignment, as well." He peeled the leaf off the glass. "Not just your skin."

"My fidelity to the law certainly earned me the love of the Republican establishment, and then led to my appointments, Circuit and Supreme, but I doubt it had anything to do with the initial assignation itself. It was just a coincidence that I happened to agree with the plaintiff. No, my blackness was the important feature. I was the image of something useful to project. The negro who could argue a disenfranchised white man's position against affirmative action convincingly before the United States Supreme Court. I was a representative of the new breed of African-American men, who didn't have to rely on affirmative action, who certainly didn't sanction it, who maintained only strict fidelity to the law. What a wonderful symbol I was. And yes, the law was and remains clear: you cannot discriminate based on race, whether your skin is white or black or green. Affirmative action, no matter how well intentioned, as it was in that Oregon case, should never be allowed. All are equal. I remain agnostic as to whether that decision should have been justified through the Equal Protections Clause of the Fourteenth or Title VI of the Civil Rights Act."

"So then it's not as if your opinion has changed."

"No, that's not it. I have been thinking about something else. The sustained arrogance—for lack of a better word—that I discerned in the Regents of the University of Oregon, and their lawyers, and their briefs. It was remarkable. They were all so sure, in a particularly liberal way, that they were doing the right thing when considering race in their admissions policies. Even when the Court ruled against the university, and they gracefully acquiesced, they did so with this air of self-satisfaction, as if a mere court ruling could never touch their deepest self-confidence, or the rightness of their cause. They remained positive of their ability to do good and be just, regardless of how any individual case itself was resolved. Yes, that's it—that's what really bothered me. Their assumption that it was possible to be good and just."

"You don't think it was?"

"No, I don't think it ever is. I suppose that's what I've been mulling over these days. Trying to align that disturbing and disorienting skepticism of mine with my legal rulings—not a possible task, of course, and really not the point either, I should add, when you assume any position of strict fidelity to the—"

"Don't get sidetracked, Dad. Stay on topic."

Rodney smiled, pointed his fork at Samuel. His son responded with fresh laughter, and suddenly their meal felt less tense and somber.

"I think there's an assumption, Samuel, we make in law that an individual or a group—whatever unit is named in the suit—is somehow capable of being good and just, and that it has full control over its decisions. It's a position that comes from the Enlightenment, but it is, in fact, a form of faith. Faith in the reasoning abilities and moral integrity of an individual self. But I don't think that is an accurate understanding of reality. How can the University of Oregon Law School, for example, ever decide upon an entirely moral or just set of admissions criteria when there are so many conflicting demands upon it? All those young and eager applicants imploring them: *let me in, let me in, I am demanding that you look at me, I beg you to answer my call.* There are only so many spaces. A limited number of bodies can fill their seats. So the University of Oregon Law School is really no more able to be just and right and moral, in pure terms, than it is able to admit every resident of Beijing into their first-year class. Agreed?"

"Yeah, but law and morality are separate things. You always say that. The legal question is what's *allowed*, not what's *right*."

"Yes, of course, I think that, but what disturbs me is that the law itself poses its questions in such a way that it *assumes* the possibility of morality, of goodness. Just think of the questions here: Who should be accepted into the school? What criteria should be used to determine admission? These questions both assume that a right answer is possible. But it's not. The only truly ethical answer cannot exist in our compromised world. Everyone who wants to be admitted to the law school *should* be admitted, without exception, without consideration of his or her grades or ability. Anyone who wants to receive a legal education should be allowed to study at any law school they want at any time. It is an ethical *requirement* that those in power of the school's admissions accept each and every applicant."

Samuel whistled. "Damn. You are hard core."

"Of course you see the practical absurdity with that. There aren't enough teachers, buildings, money. There won't be enough jobs in the profession to support the graduates. It does not make any sense to accept everyone. On the contrary, accepting them all would only lead to heartbreak and disappointment. So then what could the school do to be more fair? I have considered that in depth. Perhaps they might install an open admissions policy, accept every applicant for the first year, and then cut the huge number who do not achieve at the required level. Let the candidates earn their places through present work. Sounds better, yes? However, I would argue, it only delays the injustice. It's a fraction less cruel, at best. The students who have requested a legal education would still be denied their fair appeal, and only for callous external reasons like available jobs, money, number of chairs in the room, number of teachers to grade them."

"Right," said Samuel.

The waitress approached cautiously, a full plate in either hand, and laid two steaming meals before them. "Here you go." She topped off their glasses with wine.

Rodney unfolded his napkin and laid it on his lap. "Perfect. Thank you." He carefully sliced a bite of his chicken, placed it in his mouth and chewed.

"I'm waiting, Dad." Samuel was smiling at him, but not yet eating his eggplant.

Rodney finished his bite. "Yes. Most people want to ask: what is the moral and just way to admit students into law school? But I have decided that question has a dangerous and false assumption. The real question should be: what is the least *unjust* way of admitting them? What is the best way of minimizing *harm* rather than maximizing *good*? You see, Samuel, the proper question is never about the right thing to do, only the least wrong thing to do."

"So you assume a negative starting point instead of a positive one."

"Precisely. Or, more accurately, we should make the assumption that a flawed institution is behind every decision rather a perfect one. An institution that can never really have any right answer."

"I love it." Samuel slid forward on the bench, and pinched off a large chunk of eggplant parmesan with his fork. He put it into his mouth, but then grunted in pain and opened his lips. His mouth emitted a faint wisp of steam. "Hot," he murmured.

"Perhaps you shouldn't eat so fast."

Samuel, ignoring his father, swallowed the troublesome bite. "What's the effect on your decision, then? If you start from the negative like that, how does your result differ?"

Rodney shrugged. "I don't know if it differs at all. Perhaps the starting point changes nothing substantially. We must still weigh the same factors, and most likely will end with the same decision we would have, had we proceeded traditionally, trying to do what's right. The real difference, I suspect, can be found in the arrogance that I objected to initially. It is a difference of tone and attitude rather than of substance. It's about the color of one's response. I suspect an administration that thinks of itself as doing the least amount of harm rather than the most amount of good will be more humane and understanding to the huge majority of applicants whom they have no choice but deny—the unaccepted multitude. Such an administration will understand fundamentally that every acceptance letter they offer forces them to send ten or more denials, and that the injustice of those denials far outweighs the justice of the acceptances. Everyone is equal before the law, yes—I believe that, and more. Everyone is equal, period. There can be no ethical criteria for accepting one person into school over another. None whatsoever. Neither race, nor intelligence, nor grades, nor test scores. Birth order is certainly not just, nor is wealth, nor class—one's ability to pay. Admission policies of *any* sort are limiting acts of injustice committed on worthy people at a staggering and ferocious pace." Rodney paused, and considered how he wanted to conclude his unexpected tirade. "Would the tone of acceptances and denials change, if the schools in question realized that each letter sent was an act of injustice? Would the relationships between accepted students alter if they understood that their success and happiness was predicated on an injustice committed to other people? Would those students treasure their good fortune in a different manner? Would they treat those less fortunate with more respect and understanding? Would they learn humility, and develop a more honest perspective of themselves? Would any of this alter the egoism, narcissism and arrogance of the accepted, and especially of those who made the decisions?"

Those like Emmanuel Arroyo. But he didn't say that. Rodney shrugged instead. What did he know? Maybe yes, maybe no. He couldn't answer these questions. He was no expert on human behavior. And moreover, he was finished speaking. He plunged his fork into his chicken, and realized he was hungry.

"I've got to say, I'm impressed. I like what you're saying, Dad." Samuel took another bite.

"It's what I've always believed, although I've never quite been able put it into so many words. It is a belief that has been at the root of my reticence, and my strict adherence to written law. I have never been one to think *I* know the answers, that *I* am so intelligent and wise as to pronounce the truth. I have always doubted my ability to make fair decisions. But, you see, it's this anger, Samuel—and you are quite right to call me on it—this anger I feel, my present distraction, so overwhelming, and so furious . . ."

"At what, though, Dad?"

"At arrogance."

"Arroyo's?"

"More than his. I don't know."

Rodney indicated to the passing waitress that he wanted to speak to her. He praised the cacciatore, as perfect as Ray always made it, and asked for a cup of coffee to accompany his meal. He watched as she topped up his glass of wine.

Something else was bothering Rodney, sharper, as yet untouched, right at the root of his anger, churning inside him. He sipped his wine, the warmth spreading through his chest. He could not access it, but for the nagging guilt, the feeling of being accused.

"He is Egyptian, isn't he? This man, Majid Al-Tounsi."

"Yeah," said Samuel. "His family has lived in Cairo for years. Generations, I think. Egyptian passports."

"Al-Tounsi, though, doesn't that mean *The Tunisian*?"

"I think it does, yes."

"I find that interesting."

"It makes sense, when you think about it. Why would someone be called *The Tunisian* if he lived *in* Tunisia? If everyone else around him was just as Tunisian as he was? You use a name like that only if you're a foreigner, an outsider in the neighborhood. If you are a Tunisian surrounded in all directions by Egyptians."

Rodney did not sleep well. He rose from bed at 5:30 A.M. and wandered into the kitchen, feeling oppressed, as if he wanted to crawl out of his skin. Out his window, Connecticut Avenue was dark and empty but for the large plastic trash bins dotting the sidewalk at regular intervals. He went back into his bedroom and dressed in warm layers, long johns, a pair of 20-year-old, rarely worn jeans, and a heavy sweater. Wool hat and ski gloves. He rode the elevator to the lobby and stepped out into the cold and darkness. He took a deep breath. Such satisfying silence. A passing cab slowed, its driver flashing him an inquisitive look: *Need a ride, buddy?* Rodney shook his head, lowered his shoulders, and walked.

Thanks to years of gentrification, Washington, D.C., was no longer the murder capital of the nation, as when he had first arrived. Still, Rodney wondered if it was safe to wander the streets aimlessly before dawn. But it was fine, he told himself; he lived in the relative peace and harmony of an affluent Northwest neighborhood, and the air, his movement, the lack of a destination—it gave him more peace than he could find lying in his bed or sitting in chambers. He walked toward Chevy Chase, and twice rounded the circle, the border with Maryland, before veering southwest along Western Avenue, passing red brick homes with their front porches, columns, and white shutters. He reached Wisconsin Avenue.

He picked up his pace now, focusing only on his steps, through the luxury of Friendships Heights and past Giordino's, through Tenleytown, and beyond the Sidwell Friends School. He turned right into Maclean Gardens, where he could merge with the upper portions of Glover Archibald Park, which would be safe to walk through once the sun had risen. It was after seven now. A biker in a balaclava zipped passed him on the path. A handful of old Chinese ladies, in layers of mismatched sweatpants and sweatshirts, pinks and light blues and steely grays, with their hats pulled low on their foreheads, perched on the frozen grass, and practiced *tai chi*.

By 8:30, after crossing Reservoir Road, the long and narrow park deposited Rodney at the Potomac River. He powered south through Georgetown, beneath the Whitehurst Freeway, staying as close to the water as possible, and avoiding the busier commercialism of M Street, up the hill. No one recognized him. He cut up to K Street when the bulk of Georgetown was behind him, crossed Rock Creek on the bridge, and merged with a walking path that ran parallel to the Parkway. He did not slow his pace as he walked back down to the river. A handful of intrepid Canadian geese flew low toward the wilds of Theodore Roosevelt Island, perhaps regretting that they had not journeyed further south this cold winter. Rodney watched them disappear into the denuded trees of the memorial park.

His feet ached. His fingers were frozen, as was the tip of his nose. Hunger churned his belly, thirst dried his mouth. He tried not to let any thoughts invade his motion, but for the occasional realization that he needed this walk, that it was an extension of the walk he had begun yesterday from the Court, for whatever that was worth. He approached the Lincoln Memorial, and cut away from the river, trotting up the long steps on its back side. He passed through the monument itself at mid-morning, with tourists taking pictures of the great, seated 16th President, and emerged on its eastern side, at the top of the iconic steps, overlooking the reflecting pool and the Washington Monument. Rodney breathed heavily. His lower back pulsed with a dull pain, and the ligaments on the inside of his knees ached and throbbed. His heart beat low and fast. No doubt he would have trouble walking tomorrow. In the far distance, on the other side of the mall, the Capital loomed, and behind it, invisible, the Supreme Court building. This was the opposite view of yesterday's, he realized: the Great Mall from the west, rather than the east. Why had he returned?

He was standing in approximately the same spot where Martin Luther King delivered his famous *I have a dream* speech, 45 years ago this summer. Rodney remembered that day well, 14 years old, watching on the old black-and-white screen wheeled into his high school classroom by Mrs. Kraft. He didn't know what to feel about Dr. King and his radical civil disobedience back then, the Montgomery bus boycott, the marches and protests, the flagrant disregard for law. Some mixture of pride and shame at black people asserting themselves like that. He was young, and so no one asked him to take a stand either way. He had oscillated his whole life between an admiration for Dr. King's moral certainty and a deep mistrust of it. Things are always more complicated than what the believers proclaim. As soon as a person disobeys the law, problems arise—always—and those problems will come back to bite that person in ways that he or she does not foresee or expect. That remains true even when the law is unjust, as it undoubtedly was in the Jim Crow South. Laws are the bones of society—without them, there is nothing capable of holding society up. Without law, anarchy ensues. No, there are better ways to force change than by breaking the law. The American political system has mechanisms embedded within it that allow for reformation. Hadn't Thurgood Marshall proven that definitively? Thurgood Marshall never led marches or disobedience like Dr. King, but instead quietly challenged and rebuilt the law from within the system. He played by the rules and won. These days everyone celebrated Dr. King unthinkingly, but was that rash and often arrogant man really the person who caused the biggest change? In clear-eyed retrospect, wasn't Thurgood Marshall the true hero of the Civil Rights movement? Wasn't Sarah Kolmann the hero of gender equality as well, and not those well-meaning but ineffective women marching out in the streets? How could any person truly change law if he or she did not speak its language?

It was nearly 11 now, and for the first time in hours Rodney had stopped moving. His vision felt compromised, spotted, and overexposed. Darkness pressed in on the edges of his retinas. He was light-headed. He would need to find a carton of orange juice, perhaps a Pepsi. He felt in some danger of fainting.

Thurgood Marshall. So ornery and unpleasant on the one occasion when Rodney had met him. The man was dying then, of course. He had just had a stroke, and had lost any desire to behave with political tact. He didn't even care for himself physically anymore, as evinced by his peeling dry skin, his bushy mustache and unshaved chin. Glaring at Rodney with watery, sad eyes through his thick glasses, Justice Marshall grumbled that Rodney was the "wrong kind of negro" for promotion to the High Court. In a news conference earlier, he warned the rest of the country that they should all watch out because "there is no difference between a snake white or black—both'll bite ya." He castigated Rodney for his position was in *Kosterman*. Yes, Thurgood Marshall was stuck in that old way of thinking about affirmative action—that African-Americans needed the state to break the law against discrimination in their favor in order to right historical wrongs. Dr. King, of course, Rodney had never met. He would have met him, certainly, had the man lived. Rodney would have sat down in chambers with the elderly minister, and listened to Dr. King's recommendations on how the law should be adjudicated. What would the great Martin Luther King have told him? Rodney tried to imagine it as he looked out at the half-frozen reflecting pool. He might have quoted Thoreau's *Civil Disobedience* in his most self-righteous voice. *May I suggest you read that text, Justice Sykes, and consider when and how a decent man must break the law?* It had been decades since Rodney had perused any Thoreau. Not since first term of Berkeley undergrad, precisely.

"Excuse me."

A middle-aged African-American couple was standing beside Rodney, wide-eyed, stunned.

"I'm sorry to bother you, but are you Rodney Sykes?" asked the mustachioed man, who wore ear warmers, boots and a thick parka.

Rodney smiled at him. "In the flesh."

"Oh my." The diminutive woman put her hand up to her lips.

"Well, I cannot believe it." The man laughed joyously. "I just cannot."

"And where are you fine folks from?"

"Akron, Ohio," said the woman. "Akron. In Ohio."

"I have heard of it, believe me. Welcome to Washington, D.C. Magnificent city, isn't it? Even in the winter."

"Lisa!" The man glanced over his shoulder. "Lisa, come here!"

A girl of about ten in a puffy yellow jacket, who had been weaving back and forth between the memorial's tall, round columns, lost in some game, now skipped toward her parents and stopped beside them. She nestled bashfully into her father's side.

"This is my daughter." He put his arm around her. "This is Lisa."

"Hello, Lisa." Rodney's dizziness made the girl seem to wobble on the marble floor.

"Lisa, this man here is Rodney Sykes. He's a great American. A justice of the United States Supreme Court."

The little girl obviously had no idea what a *Justice* was, and was not especially impressed by the stranger that her parents seemed to hold in such reverence and awe.

"How do you do." Rodney stuck out his hand to shake the girl's, and Lisa offered her limp hand in return. "A pleasure to meet you." Perhaps, someday, she would remember this encounter, when she was older and realized who that elderly stranger was. Or perhaps not. Probably she would never care. But what did it matter, if this moment was meaningless to her? He released her hand, but remained standing before the family.

"We had a long weekend." The mother was still looking at him incredulously. "We just decided to drive to Washington."

"We never, ever expected this," said her husband. "We're lawyers, see. To meet Rodney Sykes!"

Rodney's stomach ached and churned, and his head spun. A kind and engaged couple, with their beautiful daughter—these visitors from Ohio. The little girl reminded Rodney of Cassandra. He smiled at her. Oh, but it was exhausting to be so open with these people. He needed to end this encounter, and he hoped that no other loitering tourists had overheard their conversation. He did not want to repeat the scene with another family, and another after them. He wanted to get a drink, and keep walking, and be alone.

"The Honorable, the Chief Justice and the Associate Justices of the Supreme Court of the United States," called the Marshal, as Rodney slipped through the red curtain at the back of the court chamber and took his seat on the raised bench. "Oyez, Oyez, Oyez! All persons having business before the Honorable, the Supreme Court of the United States, are admonished to draw near and give their attention, for the Court is now sitting. God save the United States and this Honorable Court!"

Chief Justice Eberly leaned into his microphone and intoned with his gravelly voice, "We'll hear argument this morning in case 06-1172, *Al-Tounsi v. Shaw*. Mr. Silver."

Niel Silver, attorney for the petitioners, stepped to the lectern, ten feet before the centrally positioned Chief Justice, and began his argument slowly, enunciating each word. It was a technique Mr. Silver had mastered over his 17 cases argued before the Court. He was an old pro, never trapped, and rarely confused by the often-aggressive questioning.

"Mr. Chief Justice, and may it please the Court." The lawyer's bald head gleamed in the light. "Majid Al-Tounsi and accompanying petitioners have two strikes against them. First, they have been detained in Subic Bay for six long years and counting, without charges laid, and without any clear declaration of the grounds for their detentions. Second, they have been denied a fair forum to challenge their imprisonment, and under the present ruling of the D.C. Circuit, they will continue to be denied any forum."

Eberly interrupted with a first loaded question: *What about the DTA procedures passed by Congress? Didn't we rule in* Noori *that they were a valid forum for U.S. citizens?* Mr. Silver did not think so, and he answered the Chief admirably. That only led to other, more detailed lines of inquiry. Justice Kolmann asked why the Court should consider the merits of the procedures at all, instead of just declaring the petitioners' constitutional right to habeas corpus and then remanding the case to the D.C. Circuit. Bryce followed by pressing him on the relevance of the length of detentions: shouldn't any question of constitutional validity be the same if the detainees had been held for one day instead of six years? Rodney listened and sipped his water. He preferred to limit his own intrusions to no more than one or two questions per argument, as most everything he needed to know was already written in the briefs. No need to grandstand. Justice Quinn, to Rodney's right, squirmed and shifted until at last he found his perfect moment to attack.

"So what you're claiming is a common-law constitutional right to habeas corpus independent of statute."

"That's correct, Justice Quinn."

"But where, *where*—anywhere in the history of the United States, can you find me a case—or, no, I'll go further—anywhere in the history of the British Empire *before* the Constitution, can you find me a case granting habeas to an alien captured and held outside the sovereign territory of a nation?"

"There are several."

"Oh, I doubt that very much."

"There are, Justice Quinn."

"I'd like to see the proof. Please, counsel, show me."

Someone coughed in the packed Court chamber. Rodney pulled his attention away from Mr. Silver, who was now describing an exemplary case to Justice Quinn. Len Stellick, the youthful Solicitor General, dressed in the long morning coat that Court tradition required, sat at the Respondents' table, absently playing with one of the ceremonial quill pens that was left for each arguing lawyer by the Court staff. In distant rows, men and women in stiff naval officers' uniforms, black with gold buttons, brilliant white hats, were interspersed with senators—Missouri's Jay Hackenbert, Claire Bessek of Maine, Lionel Mahoney from Illinois. Yes, an exceptional case, with international implications. Because the arguing attorneys were positioned so close to the bench, with the other attending lawyers seated at tables just behind them, Rodney often forgot about this larger audience, let alone the reporters in the press section and the public at large. On the far side of the chamber, Samuel sat in that recessed press box, which was framed by the room's tall rounded columns. He was scribbling his notes, probably about Quinn shooting down Niel Silver's attempts at analogous cases. Quinn and his theatrics always made for good press.

Samuel had matured into quite a fine young journalist. *There is an open contradiction between the amiable and kind father portrayed by Athir, and the calculating fundraiser and terrorist described by the government. But unless Majid Al-Tounsi is granted a constitutional right to habeas corpus, there will be no way of telling which of those portraits is more accurate.* Samuel's succinct article in the *Post* verged on an opinion piece, more spirited and definitive than his usual writing. He must be finding himself, his beliefs, and standing behind those convictions with fresh confidence. Majid's picture at the Sphinx with his children appeared on the front page. Samuel must have convinced the editor to take that risk, which couldn't have been easy to do.

"Nope." Justice Quinn scowled and shook his head. "That case doesn't hold either. The courts in *Swedish Sailors* may not have been inside the Crown's dominion but they were certainly part of sovereign territory. I mean, come on, Mr. Silver, is that the best you got? You're leaving me wanting."

After the laughter receded, Niel Silver tried with yet another case that Quinn shot down. There was a brief lull, which seemed to Rodney like the ripe opportunity to ask his only pressing question. He leaned into his microphone. "Section 1007(f) of the MCA claims that the United States does *not* exercise sovereignty over the Naval Base at Subic Bay. That is the express determination of the political branches. How can we rule on the merits of habeas given that fact?"

"Actually, I agree with Congress on that," answered Mr. Silver. "Subic Bay is not technically in sovereign U.S. territory. However, Justice Sykes, I don't think sovereignty should be seen as the determining factor here. For one, at common-law sovereignty wasn't even the right test—just look to what Lord Swansea expressed in *Candeleigh*. Also, we have to consider that sovereignty had a looser definition back in 1789. So we have some flexibility, here, about what the term means in this case."

"The definition is quite clear," countered Rodney.

"Today it is, Justice Sykes. Yes. But our present situation—in which the United States has quote unquote *complete jurisdiction over the base*—would have *meant* sovereignty at common law. The relevant question back then was: is this individual a *subject* of the crown? Not does he presently reside within the sovereign *territory* of the crown?"

Rodney sat back against his chair, smoldering and embarrassed. Stupid to raise that issue. This experienced and knowledgeable lawyer had offered the precise answer that Rodney should have dreaded, had he been better prepared, and more clear-headed. Mr. Silver had successfully opened the definition of *sovereignty* by playing with its historical limits, and had established a question where a clean answer should have remained. Rodney tucked his hands into his lap. He would contain himself for the rest of this argument. No more interruptions. Let the others hash it out. He would sit and listen. Nothing out, nothing in.

Rodney suddenly felt absurd. Who did he think he was, resting content and secure on the high mahogany bench in Taft's ornate Temple of Justice, the law his impenetrable armor, the dictionary definition of *sovereignty* his gleaming shield? What did that word *sovereign* really mean? He had looked it up before argument, just to make sure: *Supreme power or authority. Ability to self-govern. The contained and absolute leader.* If Subic Bay was sovereign, then nothing could touch it; the law would never reach. Did Rodney think himself sovereign as well? Did he really believe that he was so independent that nothing could reach him?

"Mr. Silver." Justice Arroyo spoke from the junior-most Justice's seat at the far end of the bench. "Any declaration we might make about sovereignty, subjugation, or jurisdiction in Subic Bay would have a significant impact on international relations. Let me remind you that it is considered an act of war for one nation to assert jurisdiction over another's sovereign territory. It is the very definition of war. But that is exactly what you're asking the United States to do."

That boor should really get over himself. As if the Philippine government hadn't realized that it had lost effective control of Subic Bay a hundred years ago when the United States built its base. As if granting habeas to the trapped detainees in Subic would be the sudden shock that precipitated war between the world's only superpower and a third-world nation. As if the Philippine people would be anything other than pleased with a liberal ruling on this Court. What a manipulative bully, that Emmanuel Arroyo.

But then Rodney realized: both he and Justice Arroyo had reached the same conclusion. Was Arroyo's argument, in substance, any different from his own?

Rodney removed his glasses and rubbed his eyes. Niel Silver was addressing Arroyo's question, but Rodney didn't listen to his answer. He wanted to shut out Niel Silver and the petitioner's argument, wanted to cover his ears with his palms, blot the entire case of *Al-Tounsi v. Shaw* from his mind.

Mr. Silver's voice was insistent and pleading—and then suddenly, unexpectedly, it made Rodney think about Stone, his neglected cat, mewing and scratching at the side of Rodney's bed each morning, calling out for attention, for some food and care. Calling out for Rodney.

Timothy's letters from Vietnam, all those years ago, had also been pleas for Rodney's attention. Whenever he received one of Timothy's envelopes, packed with shocking stories of violent combat and stifling jungle heat, his pained confessions of drug usage—both his own and the other soldiers'—and descriptions of his confusion and feelings of loss, Rodney was quick to respond with a letter of his own, full of encouragement, support, love and advice. Rodney took great care to write his brother eloquent letters that were as long and substantive as Timothy's—because what else did Timothy have? No one else could hear his brother's desperate appeal from the other side of the world. Of course, Rodney could do nothing to alleviate his brother's suffering, but still Timothy needed him. He needed to hear Rodney's voice in those written replies, needed to know his own pain had been heard by the one person who loved him unconditionally. Rodney understood Timothy's call, and he had never once failed to respond.

But all those loving letters to Timothy had amounted to nothing.

Rodney's throat caught. Timothy. Certainly it didn't feel like 38 years since that awful morning in 1969 when the marine sergeant solemnly knocked on the door of his mother's tiny house in Oakland. *Killed in Vietnam, a fierce battle in the A Shau valley near the border with Laos.* Rodney sobbed so ferociously on the drive down Telegraph from his Berkeley dorm, just after his mother's call, that he almost steered his old Datsun into a pole. Sobbing, and sitting alone on Tim's twin bed in the humble green bedroom they had shared for their entire childhood, gazing out their warped window past the gnarled old rose vines onto that stunted lemon tree in their backyard. Never before and never since had he cried like that. One night, when they were kids, lying in their neighboring beds unable to sleep, Timothy had asked why that tree had never issued more than a handful of wrinkled, juiceless fruits. How did Rodney answer? With pure nonsense, no doubt, but spoken in his most authoritative and paternal tone. Anything to give that beautiful brother of his a bit of stability in their fragile, unhappy home.

Rodney wanted so badly to be able to picture Timothy in his mind. But he hadn't had his photographs out in decades. He had banished them from his walls, his desks, his offices.

He could see Majid Al-Tounsi perfectly, though. The smiling, skinny, well-dressed man, standing with two children in the sand by the Sphinx, the Egyptian citizen with a Tunisian name, who might or might not be a terrorist. Yellowing teeth, dry hair, pock-marked face. Majid Al-Tounsi, *precisely*—an individual, held hostage, calling to be brought forth and witnessed by a judge—*you shall have my body*—albeit in the distilled voice of legal argument. A call executed though briefs and hearings, through his federal court case and its subsequent appeals. Yes, right here, this was the faint trace of Al-Tounsi's plea, with just enough power in it to infect Niel Silver's monotonous legalese with passion. Right now. This present argument was the final, personal appeal of *that* particular man, *that* face in the photograph—who was not physically present in this illustrious Supreme Court, who might never be in the room where his fate was determined, and whom Rodney would never meet.

Rodney leaned back in his chair. Adolph Weinman's marble friezes loomed above him, the carved portraits of great lawmakers from all human history, mounted into the recessed ceiling. Here was Blackstone and Hammurabi. Mohammad and Confucius. Moses and Solon of Athens. King John and Lycurgus. Each demanding that Rodney—that every justice on this Court—live up to their noble examples.

Rodney had turned over Majid Al-Tounsi's image in the booth in Giordino's only to find it broadcast large on the front page of *The Washington Post*. He turned over Rebecca's picture most mornings, upon entering chambers, although he would turn it right side up again at the end of the day, before he left. It hardly mattered. He always saw her face. She haunted him. Rebecca's olive skin, even when wrinkled and spotted with age, was a holy compromise between gold and green, a godly gift to the Judaic people. How many times had he touched her face, caressed that cheek, stared into those almost black, coffee-colored eyes? How many times had he kissed her? Thousands? When was the last time? Months before her death? Years? Perhaps it had been that long, because of the tension, the stiffness. Their declarations of mutual sovereignty—implicit, really—and then the cold war that followed. He would imagine her clearly for the rest of his life, but would never actually see her again, never touch her cheek or caress her. She was gone. No chance of relief, no habeas. What was left of her body to bring forth before this judge? Her flesh by now had rotted into the earth, decayed, dust to dust. A basic fact. He knew that, of course, but somehow it had never sunk in. He knew it, but didn't know it—never completely.

His wife, Rebecca, his dear bride, his love, was dead.

"First you should grant constitutional habeas corpus," argued Niel Silver, in response to an unheard question of Justice Katsakis's.

No habeas corpus for the dead.

Rodney blinked and blinked, sipped his water and blinked again. He swallowed hard, felt the discomfort of his body beneath his black robe.

"And then I suggest holding hearings in the Court of Appeals," continued Mr. Silver, "which can be done either under the All Writs Act or 28 U.S.C. Section 2347c . . ."

Rebecca is dead.

Rodney refused an invitation to join his colleagues for lunch in the Justices' Dining Room. Instead he hurried back to chambers, greeted his clerks and secretaries as politely as he could, and retreated into his office. He locked the door, picked up the phone, and called Cassandra. Her high voice startled him, and quickened his pulse. He had called her on impulse, and had not quite considered the possibility of her answering.

"Did I catch you at a bad time?"

"No," Cassandra said. "I'm not doing anything."

"I can try again later."

"I'm just at lunch."

"I see." Rodney paused, flustered, and fiddled with a paper clip. "Then are you able to talk?"

"Yeah."

"How is your apartment?"

"Fine."

"And work?"

"Also fine."

"You are enjoying your life in the Justice Department?"

"It's fine."

He should have prepared himself for these dead-end, one-word replies, as they were precisely the barrier to their previous conversations, most notably that disastrous holiday meal Samuel had arranged for them in December. His few tentative prods that night were met with a similar series of *good*s and *fine*s, which soon gave way to Samuel's wild attempt at banishing the awkward silence—his nervous chatter about the woeful Redskins and Wizards. Rodney had drunk too much wine, and Cassandra feigned nausea. She left before nine. He had spoken to her only once or twice since then, briefly.

"Why are you calling me in the middle of the day?"

Rodney uncoiled the paper clip into a straight wire. "I want to know how you're feeling."

"Like I said. Fine."

"Your pregnancy?"

"Everything's fine."

He paused, thinking. Cindy Chin, the day Stone died, had entered his chambers to ask a routine question, nothing but a clarification of two past rulings, and he had shocked her with his unwarranted sobs. Her grammar devolved, she gave him that ride to the vet, cooked him that feast, and then he told her so much, about Marshall and Timothy and his mother, things he had never told anyone. Now he received emails from her monthly, detailing the slog of her life in a Chicago law firm, with pictures attached of Cindy and her fiancé hugging on the beach of Lake Michigan, and hints that Rodney would soon receive an invitation to their wedding. He did nothing to encourage such affection, and wrote only quick, formal replies. It would be his first invitation to a clerk's wedding. All of her emotion, the inclusion in her life events, her love and respect, it had opened like floodgates, and washed over him, because he had unwittingly released a few tears. His response to his cat's death and his openness with Cindy Chin had seemed silly at the time, a breakdown of boundaries, a mistake, but Rodney was undeniably pleased with the results.

"I was thinking about your mother."

Rodney waited for a reply. He turned over the picture on his desk and shifted it so he could stare at Rebecca's image, 45 years old, bare-shouldered by the pool at the Morrisons' house—if he remembered correctly—her faint crow's-feet accenting the charming squint that appeared whenever she laughed.

"Your poor mother."

"What about her." Cassandra sounded cold.

"I miss her."

"I do, too."

"I was thinking about her."

"And what?"

"In argument."

"You were thinking about mom in *argument*? You mean while sitting on the bench?"

"I couldn't stop myself. I was thinking about her instead of listening to the attorneys, and then, well, then . . ."

"Did something happen?"

"No, not really. But I was thinking that it must be difficult for you. Without her. I mean, now, with the baby coming."

Cassandra was silent, not even the sound of her breathing. Rodney started bending the paper clip into a circle.

"Yeah. It is."

"It must be terribly painful."

"Are you trying to get me to cry in the middle of the deli?"

"No. I'm sorry, Cassandra."

"That's only part of my problem, though. Missing Mom. If you really want to know."

"What is the other part? Emmanuel?"

"Yes, Manny. Of course, Manny."

"Have you seen him recently? Are you on speaking terms—"

"We're on speaking terms, yeah. But ever since I moved out it's been clear to both of us that we're done with each other. We just exchange necessary details and that's about it. It's a relationship of logistics."

"But is he going to—"

"He's going to pay child support, if that's what you mean, of course. And we'll work out some custody deal. He's acting cordial and mature, but the more distance I get from him, the more I realize how much I dislike him. I'm more or less shackled to him in some way or another for the rest of my life."

"What about Denny?"

"He wants nothing to do with me. Can you blame the guy? Look, if you want to know about Denny, ask Sam. I think they talk to each other all the time."

"Cassandra, are you free to speak openly like this? I mean, where you are?"

"Nobody's near me. Don't worry so much."

Rodney sat still at his desk, his shoulders twitching, his legs aching from his marathon walk, and tight with tension.

"Are you really okay, Cassandra?"

"Oh God." She paused. "Do you know what'll happen to my emotional state if I really answer that question? I'm fine, yes, given that I'm terrified, and seven and a half months pregnant, and single, and don't know what the hell's going to happen to me, or how I'm going to get through this nightmare without ruining a child's life. Plus the fact that I'm pretty well considered a cheap whore by anyone who recognizes me, which happens to be every single person wearing a suit or heels in this miserable bureaucratic city."

"Your mother." Rodney hesitated, and considered seriously what it was that he wanted to tell her. "She hated being pregnant."

"What do you mean?" Cassandra's voice was taut and thin.

"It was terrible, both of her pregnancies."

"Why?"

"I don't recall exactly. I think the unfairness had something to do with it. That it was all on her, not me. The physical burden took a toll. But also us, I think. Our relationship."

Rodney had now contorted the paper clip into a more or less compete circle, but he could not get the ends of the thin metal bar to line up exactly. He pressed the wire on the desk, pushing the raised end down with his fingernail, but still, it would not touch.

"I suspect the rules between couples change at that time. Or rather, they did for your mother and me. Before pregnancy, she was independent, entirely, and eager to remain that way. Independent from me. It was a large part of how she thought of herself, and I, of course, loved and expected that quality in her. This was our relationship. But after she got pregnant, I don't know what happened. Perhaps hormones, or the precarious nature of the experience, or some combination of the two, or merely the anxiety of our impending responsibilities . . ."

"Did something happen between you?"

"I don't know."

"*What* happened?"

"Nothing *happened*"—Rodney heard himself say—"that I can put my finger on. We did not fight. I did nothing that was technically wrong. I was *there*, of course, in *body*, but—"

"Not what she needed?"

"Well, I always returned to the house after work, and I *did* work late, of course, but that's not it. What am I saying?" He pulled the paper clip wire apart, shifted its structure, and again pressed the ends toward each other. "What do I mean? I was somehow not present. I had no idea what I was supposed to do or say. Whatever it was, I did not do it. I did not think it was my job. The husband of an independent woman. But ultimately, I was not there. This did something destructive to us. I'm not sure what exactly it did between us."

"I know what it did."

"I suppose you might, yes."

"I saw it every day."

"The fact of the matter is, we never really went back to how we were before her pregnancies." Rodney was sweating now, and feeling quite nauseous. "That is what I wanted to tell you."

He waited. Cassandra sighed, and he hoped that it might release whatever it was that so enraged her. "I have to go, Dad. I have to get back to work."

"All right."

"Thanks for telling me that, though. And for calling."

"You're welcome."

Rodney waited for her to say *goodbye* and hang up. She didn't. He tossed the incomplete circle of a paper clip into the garbage.

"I don't know how to make this better for you, Cassandra."

"You can't make it better."

"I don't know what to offer you. I am beyond words. I am in over my head, here."

"That makes two of us."

"I'm thinking about you all the time. I would like to call you again. I *will* call you again. Soon."

"Thanks."

"And if you ever want to call me, Cassandra . . ."

"Okay, Dad. Thanks."

He hung up the phone. He squinted at the static image of Rebecca. His mantle clock's ticking was quiet and soothing, a gentle reminder of time's passage: steady, subtle, regular. Refusing to rush, no matter what the world was doing outside of his private room. That same clock, once upon a time, had graced some magistrate's office in colonial Williamsburg, no doubt soothing the worries of its bewigged, snuff-snorting owner with its soft *tk tk tk*. Now it was here. Rodney slumped, and then realized that his daughter hadn't used his name, and that instead she had called him *Dad*.

PART 3

OPINION OF THE COURT

8

ODD PAIRINGS

Gideon Rosen burned in envy of Manny Arroyo. He studied Arroyo's upper body, with his rounded shoulders and meaty pecs, which more resembled a professional linebacker's than a Supreme Court justice's. There hadn't been a physique like Manny's in this Conference Room since the early days of Byron White, and old "Whizzer" White actually *had* played halfback for the Detroit Lions. Justice Arroyo sauntered back to the conference table after closing the door—his casual but purposeful walk consistent with his build, like an athlete approaching the locker room before a big game. That guy could crush any hand he gripped. But Arroyo's physical strength wasn't really the source of Gideon's envy. What truly mattered was his colleague's power, the ability to obliterate 50 years of precedent with a single vote.

Manny joined the others, who had gathered around Davidson's chair for their ceremonial handshakes. Gideon tried to smile as he shook Manny's hand, but he found it hard. Today's monumental conference on *Al-Tounsi v. Shaw* had been rendered into a mere formality the moment Justice Arroyo replaced Justice Van Cleve. Justice Katsakis no longer mattered: the government respondents had Eberly, Quinn, Sykes, Bryce and Arroyo on side. The case was all but over. Still, as Arroyo sipped coffee and uncapped his pen at the far end of the table, Gideon's feet tapped, his fingers twitched and he sniffled in quick sets of three. He probably should have been embarrassed by all these nervous tics, but Gideon was too damn anxious to care either way. His tics intensified during the routine dispensation of cert cases, until Eberly announced, at last, that they would discuss cases argued on Monday, February 25, 2008, beginning with number 06-1172, *Al-Tounsi v. Shaw*.

"My big problem," started the Chief Justice, "is the question of reasonable substitute. I could go either way on the question of sovereignty, and if the Constitution applies to these detainees, but second-guessing procedures put in place by the political branches? Just can't see it. CSRTs with review at the court of appeal passes muster for a habeas substitute, absolutely, especially given the limited requirements necessary for enemy combatants abroad in wartime—I mean, look at our precedents. These procedures might be ugly, but they don't trigger the Suspension Clause. Doesn't say anywhere in the Constitution they have to be pretty."

Chief Justice Eberly finished his point and ceded the discussion to Bernhard Davidson, who let loose with his opposing view on the CSRT's deficiencies. Gideon scratched in the margin of his yellow legal pad *BD no longer constrained by cert limitations*, which was an obvious point, and so he scratched out the stupid comment immediately after writing it. God, his nerves: anything to keep his pen moving until it was his turn to speak. The justices' comments on the case proceeded in descending seniority. As expected, Killian's fairy-tale faith in some pure constitutional past focused his attack on the historical reach of the habeas writ, and how it would have never applied here. But there was something other than the usual originalist outrage animating Quinn this morning. He was speaking with an uncharacteristically joyful tone, and he punctuated his remarks with a meek smile. Saving his vitriol for the written word? Or maybe this was how Quinn looked when he was tasting victory in a major case—a rare occurrence, before this term. Victory had dampened his righteous anger. Why should Killian roar furiously at Bernhard when his side would so obviously win?

There were no surprises from Talos Katsakis. Colonel Inge's declaration had pushed Talos's once crucial vote over to the petitioners' side for good—which was predictable, otherwise why would he have granted this case cert back in the summer? Justice Katsakis claimed he was untroubled by ruling for the petitioners here, even though that ruling countered the authority of Congress and the President. The debacle with the CSRTs, he said, was just too embarrassing for the nation; he could no longer worry about bolstering the prestige of the other branches given these kangaroo tribunals, the subversion of the Geneva Conventions, and the blatant disregard for the Court's earlier rulings. By that did he mean the executive's disregard for Talos's own concurrence in *Hajri*? Was there something personal here? Justice Katsakis did not make a complex argument, but he had a way of layering it with obscure details, and blabbered on and on, which had Gideon shifting in his seat. Less than a year earlier, Gideon would have been thrilled to hear Talos speak like this about *Al-Tounsi* and then to have him vote with the petitioners—this very same speech would have made Gideon giddy with joy. But today Talos's vote was meaningless. Instead, Gideon focused his attention on Talos's unusual accent, which had been molded by the twin forces of his early childhood in Thessaloniki and his All-American, valedictorian adolescence in Astoria, New York. Gideon tried to picture Justice Katsakis delivering that favorite lecture of his—*The Revolutionary Bill of Rights*—to some pack of undergrads in whatever state university was willing to offer him the opportunity. Gideon had suffered through that talk once, down at University of Virginia. Maudlin piece of claptrap. Talos driving off to engagements in the sparkling, late-model Cadillac he seemed to love as much as his children.

When Rodney began to speak, Gideon closed his eyes and wanted to bang his head on the table. Rodney's typically stale legalistic argument addressed the unassailable sanctity of sovereignty—Subic Bay was owned by the Philippines, so how could the Court grant these detainees habeas?—but during his soporific monotone Rodney suddenly rolled his head and furrowed his brow in a curious, troubled way. What was the meaning of that? And then Rodney said something truly shocking.

"I don't like it."

Just like that. A flat declaration of dislike. Gideon leaned forward.

Rodney pressed his lips together, as if he were trying to hold back what he wanted to say next. What the hell was going on here? Around the room, Gideon's colleagues all watched Justice Sykes with equal surprise.

"Upon close examination," continued Rodney, "I can see that the CSRTs are gravely deficient. I find the desire of the political branches to strip habeas via the MCA, without offering any humane substitute, bizarre and cruel. That said, I do of course understand the question here is not whether I *like* the law or not. I remain convinced that Philippine sovereignty over Subic Bay is a jurisdictional barrier, that both *Eisentrager* and earlier precedents insist on our denying habeas, and that the law is settled. Therefore, any examination into whether the CSRTs are good or bad, adequate or not, is unnecessary. The government is correct, and so I vote for the respondents. I would be happy to write an opinion addressing the jurisdictional sovereignty question, or to join someone else's opinion on that matter." Rodney hesitated—something big was coming. Gideon held his breath. "But I suppose I'm saying something more than that. There is a limit for me. I doubt I would join any opinion that went so far as to extol the CSRT procedures themselves. I have a very strong distaste for them."

Gideon smiled, and covered it with his hand. Incredible. That Rodney Sykes would admit there was an *I* in the room capable of not liking something! Immediately, Gideon's mind started racing. Was this a possible opening? Rodney had used the word *distaste. A very strong distaste*—that was the juicy phrase. How could Gideon further degrade the CSRTs for Justice Sykes so that their putridity would grow stronger, so Rodney's *distaste* would strengthen to the point that he had no choice but reject the legality of the procedures in disgust and force the necessity of granting habeas? How could Gideon get Rodney to reverse? There must be a way. Rodney had decided to indulge in his personal feelings in conference, so didn't that mean he was pleading with the others to convince him? But that was incredible! Here was a genuine surprise: Rodney's vote might be in play.

Gideon strategically considered Rodney Sykes as he articulated his own position, and was still thinking about him as the remaining justices offered their opinions and votes. Gideon almost didn't care when *Al-Tounsi* was provisionally decided for the government respondents, 5–4. Chief Justice Eberly split the majority decision and assigned it to two writers—part one to himself, on the validity of the CSRTs as a habeas substitute, and part two to Justice Quinn, on the root question of a constitutional prohibition—but that division just opened up more questions about whether Eberly's section would be a majority if Sykes didn't join it, and what would that mean for the opinion as a whole? The case was starting to look like a mess, so everyone agreed to wait and read the draft opinions before deciding anything further.

And then something even more magnificent happened. The four dissenters agreed on the superiority of Gideon's well-articulated logic, and Justice Davidson granted him the treasured assignment. Gideon Rosen, he said, would write the primary dissent in *Al-Tounsi* for the others to join. Nodding quietly as Bernhard announced the decision, Gideon wrote *got it!* on his legal pad in big letters. But got what, exactly? A dissent in this major case wasn't good enough for him; there was suddenly an opportunity to go further. Rodney Sykes didn't *want* to vote for the respondents. Rodney was acting under some sort of cowed compulsion to his sworn jurisprudence and stale legalism, and he had gone so far as to say *I don't like it.* That meant there was a chink in Sykes's armor, a soft spot or weakness, and so with the right weapon, well yielded, Rodney could be pierced and transformed—like Darth Vader lured back to the light. Rodney switching sides would be enough to transform Gideon's fiery dissent into a majority opinion. Not just any majority, but the revolutionary opinion he had dreamt of for God knows how long. Gideon was almost where he wanted to be. So: what twisted logic could argue pure sovereignty for the Philippines and yet still grant the

Subic Bay detainees habeas—an outright contradiction? On what grounds could Gideon have it both ways?

Gideon left the conference room weighing points of attack like a general, and was still pondering various strategies the following Saturday morning, the first of March, when the winter's final cold spell broke across the nation's capital, and spring's incipient warmth crept north across the Potomac. Longing to focus his jumbled ideas, Gideon clipped his biking shoes into the locking pedals of his treasured Eddie Merckx cycle and rode out of the city, veering off Wisconsin onto River Road, pedaling north into Maryland, slow and steady for miles, past Kenwood and the Holton Arms School, through Potomac Village, all the way out beyond the big suburban estates and budding spring forests of Seneca. With his legs churning and his breathing slowed he sorted his thoughts, and by early afternoon, turning back, cruising the twists and turns of MacArthur Boulevard beyond Glen Echo into Washington, Gideon had refined his "functional test" reading of the precedent cases so that with the right wording, strict sovereignty might be expanded to invoke the Suspension Clause, and then Rodney would see that he could join the four dissenters and yet still maintain his principled position. Now all Gideon had to do was write it down, circulate his draft, and then spend some time massaging both the opinion and Rodney until the man had agreed to switch sides.

Home at last, he collapsed on the couch in his sweaty bike shorts and started talking at Victoria, who was reading a novel in the armchair, about how sovereignty defines the exercise of power *inside* Subic Bay rather than describes the base's simple status, and by sovereignty he meant *strict* sovereignty, and Rodney, who was eminently reasonable, and who really did want to find a rationale for switching sides, would certainly comprehend that logic, wouldn't he? Only if Gideon stated it persuasively. But he could do that, couldn't he? And what did Victoria think? And although it sounded crazy and unlike him, Sykes would definitely turn on this case—that was all but guaranteed, you should have heard him in conference with his blunt *I don't like it.*

"You're getting the couch all sweaty." Victoria peered at him above her narrow reading glasses.

"I'd pee on this couch if it would make Rodney switch."

"I doubt that would help."

"Are you listening to me, Vic?"

She took off her glasses and laid them on her book. "I find it hard to imagine Rodney going for anything like that."

"I did, too, but in conference he was begging to be convinced. And it's happened to other justices late in their careers." Gideon was too excited to sit still. He tried to pull himself off the couch, but his back and legs were too tired, and they rebelled. He winced, and stayed where he was. "Do you realize what it would mean if Rodney were to switch sides? I mean, if he were to have some kind of consistent change of heart on major cases? We could start reaching for the meaty ones again—gay marriage, righting the Commerce Clause, God knows what would come down the pipeline if we get a Democrat in office in November. We would have our coalition back—well, there'd still be Talos, of course—but basically we'd spend our time worrying only about him again. Which would be annoying, but fantastic. Like it used to be, with Elyse."

Victoria's face looked less like flesh than a porcelain mask: hard, cold and pale. Gideon stopped talking, and dread set in. She must be processing the implications of his chatter. All his talk of benefiting from Rodney's switch, of tackling big issues, meant he was considering at least five to ten more years on the Court.

"I'm disturbing your reading, aren't I?"

"Not really."

Ah, hell, sometimes, this woman. Why didn't Vic just come out and tell him outright that he was disappointing her? That he hadn't once mentioned his retirement since her surprise visit to his chambers last year? Why the hell did she have to resort to her repressed and steely silences? Gideon bent over and unfastened his cycling shoes, taking longer than the clasps warranted. He pulled them off and laid them side by side on the carpet. There was simply no way he could make an imprint on the law and build a coherent jurisprudence on presidential power in a single year. The law is an incremental business. It could be another decade or so before Gideon was finally satisfied with the thoroughness of his work. He ought to bite the bullet and just say that to his wife.

Victoria's skin was pale from a long winter indoors. Her whiteness highlighted the tiny wrinkles around her mouth. They seemed more pronounced, those wrinkles, as did the ones fanning from the corners of her eyes. A placid face, older than he remembered.

"What is it?" she asked him, calmly.

"Nothing."

Victoria nodded once, picked up her novel and pretended to read.

Maybe it was just his electrolyte imbalance, as Gideon hadn't biked so vigorously or far in months, but he felt queasy and dizzy, dangerously close to throwing up. His muscles pulsed in rebellion. He pried himself off the couch, favoring his left knee, and peeled off his biking shirt as he limped out of the room. He hesitated with the wet shirt covering his head, so he wouldn't have to look directly at Victoria. He caught his breath in the kitchen, leaning over the counter. Gideon strengthened a bit after drinking a glass of Gatorade, then lugged himself upstairs, showered and changed, and locked himself in his study. It didn't take long for him to stop worrying about Vic. He pulled his chair close to his desk, itching to work on *Al-Tounsi*. His back and legs ached, but he was eager now, excited. Of course, he couldn't complete his dissent until after reading and responding to Eberly's and Quinn's drafts, and of course he would need to get his clerks to research precedents, annotate his writing, and probably even suggest complementary approaches when his argument hit a wall, but he had earned his basic clarity while biking, and now he could attack the central questions with gusto. He knew how to begin. He powered on his computer, opened a new document, and typed.

Gideon hummed *My Funny Valentine* as he paced the entrance room of Justice Sykes's chambers. Rodney's two secretaries concentrated on their work, but they glanced at him occasionally, while a trio of Sykes's clerks gathered in the doorway to gawk at him incredulously, as if Gideon were a polar bear trained to sing arias. Word would rocket around the Court that Justice Rosen "dropped in" on Rodney for a little chat, and that had to mean *Al-Tounsi*. Soon Bryce, Eberly, Arroyo and Quinn would pump up their efforts to keep Sykes on their side. A damn risky endeavor, this. He could have just phoned. But, as Abe Fortas once told him in chambers, for the most important cases, nothing beats working on a colleague face to face, consequences be damned.

Rodney opened the door to his private chambers. He didn't look happy at all to see Gideon; in fact, he assaulted him with his dour severity. Justice Rosen froze, stopped humming, and knew right away that he had made a big mistake.

"Please forgive my delay." Rodney's expression was stern; he clearly lacked contrition. "I was on the phone."

He refused to lead Gideon to the couch in his seating area. Instead Rodney retreated behind that ancient desk of his, and made Gideon sit before him, as if he were a clerk. Not a paper or pen was out of place on the mammoth surface, and there was a photograph of Rebecca, Rodney's poor wife, dead in that terrible crash on I-495. Rodney wove his fingers together and rested his forearms on his desk. He released a weary sigh. Right. Disaster.

"I assume you've come to discuss *Al-Tounsi*," began Rodney. "But I don't believe I have anything to say about that case. I have read your dissent, which is very strong, and now I am considering my position."

Gideon's cheeks heated. "Forgive me."

Rodney raised his brow. That was the closest this polite man would ever get to an overt condemnation. "I do understand your concern, Gideon. It is indeed an important case."

"I don't mean to be disrespectful to you or your process. I know you'll make up your mind responsibly, and in good time."

Justice Sykes nodded, not one to hold a grudge. "I am also partially to blame for this. I'm aware of the mixed messages I have given this Court, and the opportunity I've presented for your appeal."

"Still, I should know better than to come here like this. We've got our unwritten rules, and I should do a better job of respecting them."

"But there is no damage done, is there?" Rodney was smiling, now. "Besides, it is rather nice to see you privately, Gideon."

Gideon nodded in defeat and changed position in the hard chair. Justice Sykes's chambers were so austere and conservative compared to his own. By the window, thick crimson curtains were tied back with tasseled golden rope, the raw silk hanging long against the recesses of the window frames. There was an ornate, dark Italian rug, and a wall of degrees, honorary and earned, in matching frames and matting. The painting above Rodney's desk was a cheesy landscape, the Parthenon in ruins, goats ambling before a young shepherd, executed by an insecure, second-tier American artist from the 19th century—a generic choice, a shorthand signal for "democracy." Everything was just so—like a TV version of a justice's chambers. There was no personality here. Impenetrable Rodney.

"You haven't ever been in my chambers, have you?" Rodney had seen him looking around.

"I think I stopped by once at the start of my first term, when I was making my initial rounds."

"A long time ago. I don't believe it's changed."

"I don't remember all the details." Gideon pointed to the photograph on Rodney's desk. "She was lovely, Rebecca."

"Yes, she was."

Rodney possessed such humbling fortitude and stoicism. He was far too rigid and guarded a man to expose any of his suffering. He had a kind of awe-inspiring resilience that Gideon encountered now and again, usually in people who had been born into impoverished or disenfranchised circumstances, but then went on to succeed wildly.

"Is your family well, Gideon? Victoria? Your sons?"

"Everyone's great. Max and Jacob are out in Hollywood, trying to make movies. They just sold a screenplay."

"That's wonderful news. When will we see it in the theatres?"

"Well, they tell me it's unlikely it'll ever get made. Apparently, those studios buy way more screenplays than they can ever produce. But still, it's a start."

"Excellent."

"Victoria is pushing me to retire." Gideon paused in amazement at his own admission. "She wants a bit of freedom and time together. She doesn't want us to grow old confined to Washington like Bernhard."

"That's understandable." Rodney's expression was blank, his stare cold.

"I haven't told anybody."

"Are you considering it?"

"I've got no choice but to consider it. Except I don't want to retire. I'm absolutely clear about that."

"I must say, of the nine, you are the one I'd least likely peg."

Gideon laughed. "I do love this job."

"Yes, I've noticed."

"And I don't feel like I've done enough in my career to retire. At least not yet."

"I know what you mean. It can be a frustrating business. Convincing the other eight."

"I still have this niggling worry that I'm a fraud and a fool."

Rodney scratched a fingernail at an ink spot on his blotter. "I doubt anyone here feels entirely authentic. Well, except Killian, of course."

Gideon laughed again. "I was about to say . . ."

"And perhaps Justice Arroyo. I suspect he feels quite authentic, even in his limited time."

"Don't forget about Joanna."

"Ah, yes. Her, too."

"So maybe it's only me," said Gideon.

"Not at all. You are not alone. I am also insecure. I often feel I need an anchor in this work, for fear of drifting out to sea. I cling to the law as written, you may have noticed, tooth and nail."

"That's a principled stance. Hardly desperation."

"It is principled, Gideon, yes, but it's grown more complicated of late. You see, I've aged like Socrates—only in that I've learned rather painfully how much I still don't know."

"That's a good thing. Long as you don't go drinking hemlock."

Rodney chuckled. "Never fear. Not my style."

Gideon sighed and shook his head in wonder. "God, everyone's problems are so relative. I know the troubles plaguing most people dwarf our own, but still, here I am, worried about what I've accomplished in my career, what my work *means* in the big picture, and if I should heed my wife's call to retire. Because when I'm in the middle of this work, it's so all-consuming. It's hard to see past my own perspective. Life is subjective. Everyone is limited by their own point of view. How could it be any different?"

"Well, the consequences are quite severe for others if we don't move beyond ourselves."

"Of course they are, Rodney. Of course."

Rodney angled his chair away, and looked out the window. "Did you read my son's articles in the *Post*?"

"On *Al-Tounsi*?" Gideon blinked with astonishment. "Yeah, I did."

"They bothered me. But still, I have been thinking about them. Or rather, about those hundreds of prisoners locked away in Subic Bay. Along with the thousands of widows and widowers, orphans and grieving parents, scattered around the country. The victims of terrorism. Our soldiers in the field. And future prisoners, as well, whose fates are determined by precedent, either way we vote. I feel somewhat differently than you, Gideon. My problems—which, as you wisely say, are nothing next to theirs—have always been rather vague in my mind. A kind of distraction or nuisance. An obstacle I must overcome on the path to justice. But I wonder now if there isn't some kind of irony, here. The more I let myself feel the burden of other people's problems, and the more I acknowledge the encumbrance of their pressing needs, the more acutely aware I am of myself as an individual, who has his own considerable problems and needs. Yes, it's ironic. I am less and less overwhelmed, and more and more inside my skin, with each added burden."

The phone rang. Justice Sykes answered, and immediately the woman on the other end of the line started talking fast. She spoke loud enough for Gideon to hear the panic in her voice, if not her actual words. Rodney stood up behind his desk.

"What? *Now*?"

Rodney moved toward the bookcase and faced away. The cord on his ancient telephone stretched taut across the room, and the body of the phone slid to the edge of the desk. Gideon grabbed it before it hit the floor.

"*Me*?" Rodney's eyes opened wide with panic.

Rodney rotated toward the window, twisted back toward his desk, and then jerked back toward the bookshelf, so that the cord wrapped around him. It was comic and absurd—the cord would snap off if Gideon didn't release the phone. But when Gideon did release it, the phone dangled in the air, hanging off Rodney's leg.

"Yes, of course. I'll come, right away."

Rodney held the receiver away from his head, and then searched confusedly for the body of the phone. "Oh my. Look at this."

Gideon rushed over to him, took the headset from Rodney's hand and helped Justice Sykes disentangle himself. "Everything okay?" Gideon dared to ask, as he placed the phone on Rodney's desk. "Was anybody hurt?"

"No, no." Rodney spoke over his shoulder as he ran toward the door. "Cassandra is having her baby and she wants me to come."

The columns and tiers of the U.S. Capitol dome dominated the view from Gideon's chambers. Two birds circled, coasting lazily on air currents, dipping close to the bronze Statue of Freedom atop the dome, and then pulling away to catch the breeze again.

Eventually, Gideon supposed, they would land on the statue's eagle headdress.

It was funny to have said all that personal information to Rodney today, like they were old friends instead of impartial colleagues.

Gideon wondered about the truth of what he had said. Did he really did feel like a fraud, or was that just a performance, an act of staged humility, to open Rodney up and win him over to his side? Was Gideon's confession an act of political manipulation, a means to an end? These were the problems of having an actor's disposition. Sometimes, when overwhelmed by ambition and drive, and performing at his peak abilities, not even Gideon could tell whether his emotions were real or reproduced. He often lived submerged in mimesis, hopelessly riven from himself.

Rodney had described an irony he felt. He claimed to be more inside himself when he was thinking about those outside himself. Gideon supposed that he had experienced that same irony, but in the opposite direction: Gideon felt more outside himself whenever he tried to think about his innermost anxieties. In fact, that's how Gideon felt right now—outside himself—and all the more trapped by his own pressing fears.

How to get back inside? Justice Brandeis had a method. Brandeis used to claim that he could get a year's worth of work done in 11 months, but never in 12. Because to stay sane and grounded (in himself, Gideon supposed), Brandeis said he had to spend a month canoeing down the Ausable River in the Adirondacks, and forget his work. The only thing that would keep Louis Brandeis grounded was to surround himself with birds and trees as he paddled down a river carved into a chasm of ancient New York rock.

Venturing into nature: that was not so different from what Victoria wanted him to do—except Victoria wanted Gideon to go canoeing on that proverbial river permanently, not just for a month. Gideon sighed.

If Victoria were standing beside him now, binoculars in hand, she would peek at those circling birds and say, blandly, *crows*.

Victoria was the only woman who had ever made Gideon forget his ambition. On occasion, when he was with her, Gideon would forget his work and feel what Brandeis must have felt while canoeing on the Ausible—grounded in himself. Victoria was the only person in Gideon's life who had ever enticed him to put down his pen and take a walk in the woods and look at birds. Birds, of all things! Did Gideon even like birds? He didn't know. That was a discomforting thought. What if all his bird-watching over the years had been just another performance of sorts, to win her over?

Gideon returned to his desk, picked up his phone and called his secretary.

"Will you please send a small box of Dominican cigars over to Justice Sykes's chambers for tomorrow? Nothing too expensive. And I'd like you to get a card inscribed: *Congratulations, from Gideon.*"

He sat quietly at his desk after hanging up. Sending cigars to Rodney Sykes was another performance, certainly, but it was also a deeply felt gesture. It was both things, simultaneously. Should he be disgusted with himself for his craven outreach, or pleased with himself for offering honest good wishes to a colleague? Most likely something in between.

Gideon never got chummy with his clerks. He was cordial and professional with them, but he didn't make jokes, and refused to allow his chambers to devolve into a place where they could goof off. Young lawyers had to realize that federal appellate law was a serious business; they were his employees, and he was their boss. Order was essential. When Gideon wanted a reference or string of cases on his desk ASAP, he needed to be able to say *go get it* and know they would do it, right away. If he didn't have that air of seriousness in his chambers, he would be quickly swamped by the endless work. Gideon's clerks, all eager and brilliant lawyers, didn't just suffer in his chambers, either.

They benefited greatly from their relationship with him. Writing on their CVs that they had clerked for a Supreme Court justice would get them hired by any law school faculty, prestigious constitutional firm or governmental department that they wanted; it positioned them for illustrious careers. Gideon's own career had begun inside this building, clerking for Abe Fortas—bless that poor fool with all his shady moral lapses—and that had served him very well. Gideon had no compunction working his clerks very hard. He found that his clerks appreciated the challenge and remained devoted to him.

This year's batch, two women and two men, were on especially friendly terms with clerks in other chambers. They played together on a softball team called *The Supremes*. Their games were held every Wednesday night in spring against the interns and low-ranking staff of other federal departments—like the Department of Agriculture, Health and Human Services, and the Department of Justice—on diamonds near the Lincoln Memorial, beside the FDR memorial. It seemed *The Supremes* had chatted with each other last night between innings, and let some important information slip, because when Gideon's clerks came into work this Thursday morning, they requested an immediate meeting with him in his chambers. They stood around his desk, eager to talk, not bothering to take seats.

"Justice Sykes is switching on *Al-Tounsi*," said Franklin, who was only 26, but already completely bald.

"You sure?" Gideon leaned forward onto his desk.

"His clerks confirmed it," added Tannisha. "We asked if he was joining you—I mean, we assumed it—but then they just got cagey. It sounds like he's joining some parts, but not the complete opinion. We don't know the details yet."

"It's possible he's writing a concurrence."

"But he's joining in part?" Gideon inwardly winced at his naked plead. "My dissent's going to be the official opinion?"

"We don't know exactly," said Neal.

"Well, find out!"

His clerks laughed.

"I mean, come on, guys, you come in here with the biggest news I've heard in years, but you know it's incomplete. I need to know this stuff as soon as possible. If these detainees get habeas, everything changes. Please do a bit more digging."

He sent his clerks on their way and made phone calls.

"It's very good news," agreed Davidson, who had heard the same from his clerks. The old man didn't know any details, like whether or not Rodney planned on writing a concurrence or joining Gideon's majority. Talos had more information, though—one of his clerks was sleeping with one of Rodney's. Talos had heard that Rodney was writing a concurrence, but when Gideon pressed him on that, Talos admitted he didn't know anything for certain.

Gideon peered out his window between calls. The trees by the Capitol were budding with light-green spring leaves. Maybe Justices Quinn and Eberly, when they got hold of this news, would panic and start petitioning Rodney directly, plying him with hard facts about the historical reach of the writ, pushing him into maintaining his traditional view of strict sovereignty. It was possible that they would win him back. But not necessarily. Justice Sykes was stubborn. Once Rodney had decided on a position, no amount of lobbying from the Chief or anyone else would convince him otherwise.

So it was also possible that Gideon's rather brilliant reframing of sovereignty had won Sykes over. That would be glorious! Gideon would be the justice who had limited presidential power, who had realigned the bright line between war and peace after the Shaw administration's irresponsible blurring in its "war on terror." Gideon's opinion would fight against the administration's unnecessary military conflicts in Iraq and Afghanistan and their slow erosion of civil rights at home. The Court would assert habeas rights for non-citizen detainees in territory over which the United States does not exercise sovereignty for the first time in history; the country would right itself, and the history books would have no choice but to show that it was *his* opinion, *his* logic, that had reestablished the dominance of peace. Could that really happen today? Perhaps Sarah would know definitively.

"Sorry," said Justice Kolmann. "Don't know anything more than you."

"Well, should I call Rodney? I could just ask him directly."

"You should do nothing of the sort. You need to sit back, Gideon. Rodney will do what he does, and you can't do anything about it."

"Right."

"Although it does sound like he's committed to our side. But that is all the more reason why you shouldn't pressure him. We'll just have to wait and see."

"Of course. We'll wait and see."

Gideon paced in his chambers and made tea, but he couldn't bring himself to drink it. He slouched on the black sofa, finished gnawing one thumbnail down to its nub before moving on to the other. He had so much work, but he couldn't concentrate. He paced again, counting steps out, nine to the left, nine to the right—like that woman in that Beckett play he saw in Chicago years ago—and then he called his clerks back into chambers.

"Anything new?"

"We'll hear more at lunch," said Tannisha. "Once we get his clerks alone."

"I strongly suggest you take your lunch right now."

Again his clerks laughed. Gideon did not usually command them to skip off for an early meal. They left him alone. Gideon returned to his desk, switched on *Don Giovanni* and his computer, and tried to focus on a lesser opinion he was drafting. His thinking was all over the place. He made a mess of the draft, and erased most of his work.

The clerks knocked on his door after lunch.

"It doesn't make sense," said Franklin. "He's joining a section of your opinion and a section of Justice Quinn's, and also writing a concurrence."

"What do you mean both? What sections? Quinn's *and* mine?"

"From your opinion, it sounds like he's joining two sections, five and six, all parts."

Gideon rifled through his memory. Sections five and six—that was where he offered proof that the DTA-MCA procedures did not provide an adequate substitute for habeas. It was a good start, meaty stuff to join. "What about Justice Quinn's?"

"That's where it gets really strange," said Cynthia. "He's joining Quinn's section two, A and B."

"Section two? Which is that?"

"It's on the historical reach of the writ. The part where Quinn says habeas would never extend as far as non-citizen detainees in Subic Bay, and where he unequivocally denies them a right to the writ."

"He's joining Quinn on *that*?"

"That's what we've been told."

"So he's saying habeas doesn't extend, but also that the DTA-MCA procedures don't substitute? He's saying *both*?"

"Yup."

"Well, that doesn't follow. That doesn't make any sense."

"We know," said Tannisha.

"Because he's joining our ruling, right? And we're remanding the case to circuit, with instructions to grant habeas?" Sykes's logic was too bizarre. Gideon had to spell it out slowly, to see if speaking it out loud made any more sense.

"Apparently, yes."

"That's insane. You can't deny the legal right to habeas, but then grant habeas. That's a logical fallacy. That's not something one does. It makes no sense."

"We know," repeated Franklin. "None of us understands how it could be."

He thanked his clerks and let them go. They must have gotten something wrong. There must have been some breakdown in the clerks' gossip, an egregious case of broken telephone. There were certain fundamental principles of jurisprudence that linked opinions as diverse as Justice Quinn's and Justice Rosen's, Hugo Black's and Elyse Van Cleve's, Roger Taney's and Louis Brandeis's, and the most fundamental of all those principles was that each opinion had to make sense. It had to present a discernible chain of reasoning, which worked to convince the reader that its proposed ruling followed the law according to traditional rules of logic. If Rodney intended to join a bizarre combination of irreconcilable sections in two opposing opinions, which would not withstand the weight of a cursory reading by a first-year law student, then Gideon did indeed need to call him. Because Rodney had to be making some terrible miscalculation about what those sections actually meant. Someone needed to set him straight before he embarrassed himself.

But was it better to call or wait? Rodney never appreciated meddling. Gideon spent another agonizing few hours alone, skipping around on his computer from opinion to opinion, doing a bit of work on one and then another, until the day was almost over. At last he picked up the phone, dialed and reached Justice Sykes on the first ring. Rodney sounded calm, and well. Gideon suffered through a spate of quick pleasantries—*How is Cassandra? Yes, that did seem like quite the startle. She had a boy, that's wonderful, you must be so pleased!*—and then asked his fellow Justice outright about *Al-Tounsi*. Was Rodney writing separately?

"Yes, and I am about to circulate my concurrence. You should receive it within the half-hour."

"But you're concurring with the ruling? Meaning we're granting habeas?"

"That's correct."

"My clerks have told me you're joining part of my opinion and part of Killian's. Is that also right?"

"Indeed, it is. I'm joining your sections five and six, and Killian's second."

"Killian's second section on the historical reach of the writ?"

"That's correct."

Gideon waited for Rodney to offer some kind of explanation, but he didn't.

"Rodney, I don't see how that makes any sense."

"No, I imagine not. It is a rather surprising pairing, I do admit."

"It's more than surprising. It doesn't make any sense."

"You'll have to read my concurrence in order to understand my logic, Gideon."

"Well, can you give me some clue? I'm really struggling here."

"You will have my full explanation on your desk before the day is through, and so I would like to say no more about it now. There's no point in expressing myself in a messy and incomplete way when you will get my complete reasoning on paper soon enough."

"Of course." Gideon waited again for Rodney to offer more. "Okay, then. I'm looking forward to receiving it."

After the phone call, Gideon sank into his seat and rubbed his hands through his thin hair. The silence of his chambers dampened his mood. Rodney's opinion, a concrete thing, would arrive in due course, and either condemn Gideon to irrelevance on the most important case of his career or enshrine him in glory as the author of a majority opinion. Waiting was terrible. Gideon's career lingered in purgatory.

At last, Gideon's secretary brought in the sealed manila envelope, *From Justice Sykes's Chambers* scribbled on its cover. He clutched the envelope in his fist until his secretary had left him alone, and then at last ripped it open.

Rodney's concurrence was a concise 14 pages, although that would extend when reformatted into the Court's official layout. It had three sections. The first was an explanation of how and why Rodney could join such an "odd pairing," in his own words, of two radically opposed opinions. It wasn't anything all that groundbreaking. It just said that Rodney agreed with Gideon on one major point and Killian on another—with Rodney's own strict reading of sovereignty the issue tying them together. Rodney remained adamant that Subic Bay was subject to the Philippines' control, and that that designation barred the Court from offering any legal habeas relief. He attacked Gideon for relying on a "cherry-picked" definition of sovereignty to suit his needs. Ouch. Rodney also attacked Gideon for his "functional test" reading of precedent, the logic that Gideon had used alongside his definition of sovereignty to explain why habeas applied. *No applicable "functional" tests can ever apply constitutional rights to extraterritorial foreign nationals*, Rodney wrote, *because formal sovereignty excludes them by definition. Sovereignty means precisely what it says.*

So Justice Sykes had set up a giant and inescapable contradiction for himself. There was simply no way to grant habeas under the terms of that first section. It was impossible. Gideon read on.

Rodney's second section addressed that insurmountable problem. As Gideon read it, he began to feel weak. His mouth dried, and his legs softened. He read the whole thing quickly, doubted himself, went back and read it again. It couldn't be right. He read it a third time more slowly, stopping to read certain sentences over and over to make sure that they actually said what he thought they did. It was astonishing. Rodney was proposing an entirely new legal doctrine: the doctrine of subversion. That was the word he used. A willed and conscious *subversion* of the law. Subversion? Really? In a legal judgment from the highest court in the land? Rodney wrote that his doctrine should be invoked only in the rarest circumstances, those terrible conditions when the written law was clear and unequivocal and yet undeniably *wrong*—and here, unbelievably, Rodney dared to offer a list of conditions for how and when a justice might determine that a law was *wrong*, the legal conditions necessary for invoking this new doctrine. And the doctrine, itself—incredible! It was self-consciously moral. It allowed a justice to look the law in the eye, so to speak, and say: *I understand your terms, but will not follow you on moral grounds.* It was a kind of justified criminality. Or rather, since it came from a justice's pen and was therefore part of common law, this doctrine of subversion was a proposal to legalize an overt illegality, oxymorons be damned. In short, it was the most lunatic and brazen thing that Gideon had read in his career, and that included the full, complete works of Louis Dembitz Brandeis.

Gideon read part three of Rodney's concurrence. He finished the section and read it again, and then a third time. It was just a short few paragraphs, pure *dicta*, led by a succinct quote from Henry David Thoreau, but it was also the kind of soaring, elegant writing of undeniable moral force that countless Americans would quote for centuries. *The other branches of government have not fulfilled their sworn responsibilities*, Rodney wrote. *That does not mean I must ignore mine.*

Gideon's neck was peppered with sweat when he finished reading the concurrence. His stomach contracted once, tightening into a hard and painful ball. He put it down and stared at his painting of racing yachts. He picked it up and read it through once again. The worst part about Rodney's majestic and suicidal work was its brilliance. He spoke about responsibility in terms that Gideon had never before seen in a legal opinion. He spoke about the individual responsibility of a justice as a *person*, a living breathing *human* who just so happened to be on the bench, a man or woman who was burdened with the unique responsibility of hearing the call of a suffering petitioner. A justice, in Rodney's opinion, was more than a representative of the law. But even with this defiant claim, this slap in the face of legal tradition, Rodney supported his argument with traditional technique and precedent. The wider implications were immediately clear to Gideon. It was a proposal that extended well beyond this one particular instance of habeas rights granted to a small group of suffering people stashed away in Subic Bay. It pertained to *any* abuse of the law by the political branches of the federal government, and could easily be extended to any individual state. The doctrine of subversion would, in theory, be just as valid a tool in an abuse of tax law, family law, tort or criminal procedure. It knew no boundaries. It dared to attack, head-on, the biggest moral problem that arose for judges, time and time again, within the wider justice system, namely: *What must we do when the law is unjust, and no elected officials dare to correct it?* Rodney answered that question directly, responsibly, productively. It was not an answer that would stick with the others on the Court—that was certain—but if it was ever invoked or used, even hinted at by any other justice in the future, in any circumstance, it could offer a radical redefinition of the correct reach of the law, its justification, its validity, and an insertion of ethical thinking into the American system in a way that Gideon had never before imagined possible. It was beyond brilliant. It was revolutionary.

No other justice would dare sign onto such a loony-tune concurrence. It was worse than lunacy. Rodney would be raked over the coals by liberals and conservatives alike. He would be met with complete derision by everybody except the most out-there legal professors in radical schools, accused of not fulfilling his oath, not doing his job. Who knew what kind of trouble he was setting up for himself? It was career suicide. But wait, wait—was Rodney *right*? Was he *just* in the true meaning of that word?

Oh, God, thought Gideon. Yes, he was.

Rodney's concurrence was more right and fair than anything Gideon had read in years. But what did that mean? What should he do about it? Could Gideon dare sign onto that concurrence? Could he give it the power of two justices' signatures, a far more potent and weighty force than Rodney's single voice? Would Gideon be willing to put himself on the line along with Justice Sykes, to stand behind Rodney's insane and risky proposal?

Again, Gideon's stomach knotted, the pain doubling him over now, chest to knees, the sweat flowing from his pores. When it eased, he moved to the couch and lay down. He kicked his shoes off and fussed with the pillow. Another contraction compressed a small, hard ball inside him. Gideon groaned. If only he had stashed a heating pad in his desk drawer, or better yet, a hot water bottle.

Anyone who signed onto Rodney's concurrence ran the risk of going down in history as one of the greatest crackpots to ever sit on the Court, second only to the author himself. Rodney's concurrence wasn't legal thinking, in the terms they had accepted and had all sworn to uphold. No, Gideon couldn't sign it. But then, Gideon realized, like any risk taken, the potential reward was so huge it was beyond imagining. If, in time, others bought into Rodney's bold logic, if his doctrine of subversion was adopted and used by other judges on any level, its importance couldn't be overestimated. Of course, the odds of that happening were beyond slim; they were minuscule. If Rodney submitted this thing, he was most likely dead. But no risk, no reward.

The pain in Gideon's belly rolled through him in waves. A hot water bottle would offer him more than heat; it would have heft and force, the equal distribution of soft plastic against his skin. If only Gideon could fast-forward 50 years into the future and see with certainty what would be made of Rodney's concurrence, whether justices and lawyers would write it off as a crackpot aberration or root it firmly as the seed of a new jurisprudence—if only! Gideon curled, semi-fetal, and moaned in pain, and then suddenly realized that he was doing the opposite of fast-forwarding into the future; he was receding 65 years into the past, back to the summer of 1942, back to the bungalow in Chicago, with a darkened bedroom substituted for his Supreme Court chambers, and with Rodney's concurrence replaced by Shostakovitch's Seventh Symphony. Gideon was Dr. Seymour Rosen reincarnated, he realized with horror.

He bolted upright. He winced through another contraction and slipped his shoes back on.

What did it matter if Gideon signed Rodney's concurrence or not? It was Justice Sykes's brilliance either way; it would never be his. By signing onto that concurrence, Gideon would expose himself to almost inevitable derision but receive none of the potential acclaim. For Gideon, it would be all risk and no reward.

Gideon suffered through another painful contraction. So he would do nothing. He would file his own opinion as is, and let Rodney concur with this crazy document. That decision would let the detainees receive their treasured habeas, albeit on grounds that could never be extended to any other case, a ruling that would have no power over other circumstances, because Gideon's opinion would be a plurality, not a majority. But still, Gideon would win his precious case; the right side would win. The detainees would get habeas. And Gideon would be cheered on by those progressives who lacked an ability to see the extent of Rodney's revolution. He would be celebrated for a brief period of time, but then forgotten. Life would go on.

He stood from the couch and went to his window. He had been waiting years for this victory, and now it felt hollow. His opinion suddenly meant so little to him, and would mean so little to the world. What he had thought was bold thinking was not so bold at all. Out the window, five o'clock, the sun was high in the sky. The glory of spring was rising. A bright-red cardinal landed on his ledge, chirped once at him and flew away.

Victoria, last December, at her going-away party, stood before her weepy co-workers and thanked everyone in her office for their support. She kissed Angie, hugged staff, carried a box filled with photographs and papers from her office into the car. Victoria was home right now, reading a novel, or gardening. Waiting for him to retire. And so deeply disappointed.

Justice Gideon Daniel Rosen of Chicago, Illinois: that was who he was. A good man, and he had a decent career. For 15 years running, Gideon had served as an associate justice of the United States Supreme Court. And so if a Democrat was elected President in November, he would serve another term, and then in June—a year and a month away from now—at the time of greatest convenience, he would hand in his resignation.

9

INTERMISSION

Justice Kolmann lingered on the Kennedy Center's balcony as blinking lights and harmonic chimes announced the end of intermission. She sipped her ice water, the glass trembling as it touched her lips. The night was warm and clear, and the sweet perfume of late-blooming azaleas scented the mild breeze. Sarah felt such relief to be out on this terrace overlooking the dark water of the Potomac River.

"I can't go back for another act."

Rodney nodded grimly, as if he had expected as much. He was disappointed surely, and for good reason, as Mussorgsky's *Boris Godunov* was a rare and challenging treat, and no one could possibly sing the part better than the Russian bass whom Washington Opera had flown in from the Kirov. Rodney was grinning with childlike joy when he left the auditorium after the first act, and he raved about the production during intermission.

"You should go and watch the rest without me. It's terrific, Rodney, and I can get home fine."

"I wouldn't dream of it." He sipped his wine.

How stupid, stupid, stupid of Sarah to have come to the opera tonight! Why had she let Cathy and Jonathan convince her to use her tickets, and then to invite Rodney in place of her husband? It should have been obvious that this experience would be crushing.

We'll be fine, Jonathan had said. Go and enjoy. Yes, they were fine back home, but what about her? Cathy was probably knitting her sweater on the sofa, or bringing Jonathan his blanket, or aiding him in the washroom—and Sarah needed to do those things. She had no desire whatsoever to sit quietly in a stiff velvet chair in the Kennedy Center's Opera House, lost in the musical trials and tribulations of some 17th-century tsar, when she could be useful at home.

In the lobby, the last stragglers threw melting ice cream bars in the garbage, abandoned half-empty glasses on counters, and hurried into the auditorium before the ushers closed the doors.

"Last chance, Rodney."

He stayed beside her. Sarah leaned on the railing, and heard beneath her the roar of cars zipping along on Rock Creek Parkway. The balcony was suspended above the busy road, bordering the Potomac. Even standing this close to the water, she could only see hints of the river, as the Kennedy Center's lights shined brightly behind her.

Rodney leaned his elbows on the railing next to her. "Do you want to go home now?"

"Soon. Not yet."

"All right. We can stay here as long as you like."

"I don't like leaving Jonathan alone when he's so sick."

"I understand. But Cathy is happy to help you, yes? That is, after all, why she came into town."

"I know it's fine. I'm talking about me, not them."

"She probably wants some time alone with her father."

"I know, I know, you're right, and Jonathan wants it, too." Sarah sighed and closed her eyes and felt the soft warm breeze against her cheeks. How many times had she stood on this terrace with Jonathan, either between acts of an opera—hundreds of them—or at fundraising events? Jonathan moved seamlessly between prestigious British theatre directors, bank executives and senators, charming them with anecdotes about his friendships with Edward Albee or George Soros—but never dropping names for the sake of his ego, never showing off. He would stand out here on the terrace, gazing north toward the infamous Watergate building, and tell stories that would make everyone laugh. Jonathan always put those people at ease, whereas Sarah made them freeze in terror and—frankly—in awe. They were reticent and formal around her, nervous to be near a Supreme Court justice, and eager to slip away. How could Sarah be social without Jonathan by her side?

"You're awfully quiet," said Rodney.

"The only thing Jonathan eats these days is soup."

He sipped his wine, but said nothing.

"I've been making him chicken broth with macaroni, and sometimes a watered-down miso. I make beef stock for him too, but I think that's too rich. Jonathan doesn't like it. And he can't eat anything solid or meaty, nothing you have to chew. His teeth hurt, and they bleed. His jaw muscles are losing strength."

"I'm sorry to hear that."

"Of course I don't make him any soups from scratch. They're all broths that he's made himself and put in the freezer, or something I've bought. He would never eat my awful soup. The man still has his standards."

Rodney chuckled, and balanced his wine on the railing. Sarah imagined pushing it over the side with her pinkie, listening to the glass shatter on the curb of Rock Creek Parkway beneath them.

"It doesn't matter how much Jonathan eats, he continues to lose weight." Across the river, on Theodore Roosevelt Island, an owl hooted softly and ominously. The sound faded as it flew away. "Let's talk about something else. Tell me about your grandson."

Rodney smiled. "He's beautiful."

"Gideon told me that your daughter invited you into the delivery room?"

"She did indeed. I suppose he also told you about the surprise phone call I received in chambers? I was quite shocked when Cassandra asked me. Certainly if Rebecca had been alive it would never have happened like that."

"Small blessings, then."

"Yes, indeed." Rodney was still smiling at the memory, staring out into the night. He looked content, running his fingertip along

the edge of his wine glass. Sarah couldn't remember the last time
she had seen Rodney look so relaxed and at peace. It had been
years, certainly. "To be honest, I think Cassandra panicked. I
think she asked me to come help her on the spur of the moment,
and perhaps regretted it as soon as she hung up the phone. But
once I was there in the delivery room with her, I provided some
comfort. I do think I did that."

"I'm sure you did, Rodney."

"Oh, Cassandra was a wonder! Strong and brave. It was like
nothing I could have imagined. I didn't get see my own children's
births, of course—you know how fathers were prohibited from
the delivery room in those days, or discouraged."

"It sounds like this was an important experience for you."

"It was. It shook me. I stood beside Cassandra, holding her
hand, through hours of labor. I don't know quite what to say
about it. I would like to say more, but I'm at a complete loss for
words!"

"Sometimes words don't do the trick."

Rodney laughed. He put his arm around Sarah's shoulders and
squeezed. She stiffened under his pressure, raised her brow, and
eyed him curiously. A gesture of connectedness, even with a close
friend, was so unlike Rodney Sykes. When his laughter petered
out, he released her from his grip and they leaned on the railing
again.

"You know, Rodney, I am rather surprised by your concurrence in *Al-Tounsi*."

He nodded. "You're not alone."

"It's quite a strong statement. You're aware it's going to cause
a big storm when we release it?"

Rodney polished off the final sip of his wine and smiled into
his glass.

"It would have been much easier and more prudent for you
to sign Gideon's opinion along with the rest of us who disagreed
with Killian."

Rodney rubbed his face. "You know I could never do that,
Sarah. Sign an opinion with which I fundamentally disagree?

Impossible. Remember, I did not sign your dissent in *Pinkleman*, either."

Sarah nodded. She remembered it well, both the case and Rodney's refusal to sign on with her. *Pinkleman v. Watson Carburetor Company,* was Justice Kolmann's most prized dissent, probably the most impassioned case of Sarah's career, written at the end of last term, and she had lost it by only one vote. Rodney's vote. The Democrats presently running for president were outdoing each other on the campaign trail with promises of passing new legislation to amend Title VII of the Civil Rights Acts, so that it would force the law to comply with the logic Sarah had proposed in that dissent, against the Court's niggardly ruling. That was *her* word, *niggardly*, which the candidates repeated ad nauseam on TV. If Congress really did that, and if a new president proposed and signed that law—why, it would be a monumental day for women in the workplace, and one of the proudest achievements of Sarah Kolmann's life.

"I didn't sign your *Pinkleman* dissent because I believed the wording of Title VII is precise and clear," said Rodney. "Gwen Pinkleman had 180 days to file her complaint to the EEOC regarding her employing company's discrimination, and she did not do it. She failed to fulfill her obligations for an active suit."

Sarah sipped her water. "Except the Watson Carburetor Company engaged in a gradual and clandestine form of sex discrimination, which limited Ms. Pinkleman's promotions and reduced her pay raises over many years."

"I know that, Sarah. I am not questioning whether or not Ms. Pinkleman was mistreated."

"She was mistreated, absolutely, and her situation required a subtle reading of precedent and an adaptation of Title VII to the conditions at hand."

"That's what you say."

"Yes, that's what I say. One of the explicit purposes of Title VII is to prohibit discrimination on the basis of sex. I believed the conditions Ms. Pinkleman faced in her place of work were covered by Title VII protection, and that given the company's clandestine dealings, her situation required a flexible reading of the statute." Sarah was angry now; she couldn't stop herself. "In particular I felt the courts needed to better define what constitutes an act of discrimination under Title VII; what *precise* acts should fit into the 180-day legal period for filing a claim with the EEOC. You disagreed with me then, and still do now. You think the wording of Title VII prevents that interpretation. Fine. A majority of justices agreed with you. I don't see your larger point."

"Congress will probably change Title VII to embrace your claims."

"I hope they do. They should."

"They will, once this country is run by a new administration. And when they do that, I will support their new law wholeheartedly."

"Of course you will. I know that about you, Rodney."

"Because I agree that Ms. Pinkleman was treated unjustly. I can see that. And the new law will be better. It will close loopholes like the one Ms. Pinkleman slipped through."

"Indeed it will."

"But Sarah, do you really believe Title VII, as it stands today, and as it did last year—the particular wording of that statute— includes protection for Ms. Pinkleman? That it includes the exact protection you claim it does?"

"Of course I do, Rodney! That's why I wrote my dissent!"

"And yet you still think Congress should pass a new law? One that will make that already evident protection more overt?"

"Only because the Court ruled against me. As a practical matter, yes. Because my reading wasn't accepted and adopted into law."

Rodney shook his head. "So there's my problem with your *Pinkleman* dissent. It's the same problem I have with Gideon's opinion in *Al-Tounsi*, with all its talk of "functional tests" and redefining sovereignty. I just do not understand that willful flexibility with the written law. The way both you and Gideon have toyed with the wording of statutes, and with the Constitution itself."

"You don't understand it? Really? You're that naïve about law at this point in your career?"

"I understand the difference between a purposive view of statutory interpretation and an absolute, textualist one. I understand the subtle philosophical differences between those positions. But what I don't understand, Sarah, is how you, or Gideon, or anyone else, could actively *search* for ways to stretch the law so as to make it include the readings you prefer. That you could so boldly hunt for outlying precedents, exceptions, bends in the rule, when the primary reading is so clear. The MCA declared, in plain language, that Subic Bay exists under Philippine sovereignty and therefore habeas rights cannot extend to the detainees. That is the written law. A sixth-grader could understand the meaning of those words, just as a sixth-grader could understand that the proper reading of Title VII stands against you in *Pinkleman*. I think both points are obvious from the text of the statutes. They are absurdly obvious. And I think both you and Gideon know that, too."

Sarah stepped away from Rodney and faced him, angrily.

"Are you accusing me of deceit, Rodney? Are you saying that I am willing to break the law to get the answer I prefer?"

"Unfortunately, I am."

"Well, that offends me deeply. I am not deceiving anybody. I really do believe that good jurisprudence includes reading outlying precedents, and adapting *any* law to make it fit with exceptional situations. And that is exactly what I did to justify my interpretation of Title VII."

"In other words, looking for loopholes. Ways out. Cracks in the wording."

"That is what every single lawyer or judge has ever done in the history of law. That's what it means to advocate for a position. To stake out an opinion."

"And I think all of that is abuse. Every act of stretching or manipulating the clearly written law, of finding a way out, is abuse."

Sarah groaned in disgust, and then stood beside Rodney in awkward silence.

"Forgive me," Rodney said. "I have gone too far. I have no business accusing—"

"No, it's my fault." Sarah touched Rodney's arm, and let her anger pass. "I asked you about your *Al-Tounsi* concurrence. You're only defending yourself, which is fair enough. Even though you're goading me on, you evil man."

Rodney chuckled. That was better. "You are right to question me, Sarah. You see, in *Al-Tounsi*, I found myself at a terrible impasse. I agreed with Killian's interpretation of what the law says, and yet I simply could not sign onto his opinion, which denied those detainees their last chance at habeas corpus. I was stuck. That is why I wrote my 'strong statement,' as you say. I have never been in this position before."

"Well, that's my real question, Rodney. Why were you suddenly stuck in this case and not others? Why now?"

"Too many reasons. I can't explain. I'm not sure I really understand why myself."

"Maybe you can try."

Rodney took a moment to consider. "I believe something radical shifted inside me, Sarah. I see signs of it everywhere in my life."

"I see it, too. I see it in the way you're behaving tonight."

"I feel it all the time. For a year or so, it's been mounting. Here's a good example. This term I have a clerk in my chambers, Jessica Klein—"

"Oh, yes, the brilliant one. I tried to get her, too."

"She's a remarkable woman. But in past years, I would never have hired her. I would have thought her too brash and opinionated, too brilliant. I would have encouraged her to go to your chambers. She does not have enough respect for the written law for my taste. I saw all of this in my first interview with her."

"You have always preferred more modest clerks."

"Do you remember Cindy Chin?"

"No."

"No matter. I was fond of her. She was my more typical choice: modest and hardworking and intelligent. I'm attending her wedding this summer."

"Lovely."

"When I compare Ms. Chin to Ms. Klein, I stand in wonder at the difference. I am still not certain that Ms. Klein is the better clerk—although she will certainly have the more illustrious career—but I am certain that hiring someone like her, with all her talents, is an example of this shift you see in me. It is a sign of what has changed."

"That's a good thing, Rodney."

"Is it? I fear the change puts me on a crash course with the law. It's likely that I am heading for disaster with my *Al-Tounsi* concurrence. I suspect a man like me isn't supposed to be so bold."

"I still don't understand why now. Why didn't you write a concurrence like that for *Pinkleman* if you thought the ruling was unjust?"

"The circumstances of the two cases are not at all the same."

Sarah growled with impatience. "What happened to you, Rodney?"

"I was called." Rodney made a fist and pounded it lightly on the Kennedy Center's railing. "I had no choice. I had evaded the call for too long, and I couldn't do it anymore. I thought I made all this clear in my *Al-Tounsi* concurrence—called by particular circumstances, having no choice but to respond. What I felt happen to me when I wrote *Al-Tounsi* was exactly what happened to me when I received Cassandra's phone call to come to the hospital, just like that. I was called and asked to be present, to take responsibility for what was happening in front of me. I could not ignore it. Doesn't that make sense?"

"I think so."

"When Cassandra was in labor, there wasn't much for me to do in the delivery room but watch. I could only stand there and be present, holding her hand, making sure she wasn't alone. At first I was rather uncomfortable with my limited duties, but as the hours clicked on, I started to think maybe my presence was the point. It was my entire task—to be present as a human being. I am Cassandra's closest kin, her father—and there is a bond between us, whether she likes it or not, whether I like it or not. There are certain obligations that come with my position. I felt certain I was fulfilling my side of that human bond—finally, after years of being so negligent—just by being there. So that is the answer to your question. My role in *Al-Tounsi* required more activity than simply my presence, of course—that comes with being a justice of the Supreme Court—but in principle it was the same response."

Rodney stretched his arms wide and laid his hands on the railing. He was a diminutive man, and he usually stood with his hands behind his back or modestly clasped in front of him, but not now. This posture made him look more like a president than an unassuming justice. He looked commanding and strong.

"I had a strange thought in the delivery room with Cassandra. I imagined myself being sculpted into a man. It was as if I were comprised of clay or stone, and circumstance was chipping away all the bits around me, removing everything that was *not-Rodney*, or perhaps building me up from scratch. That process made me distinct and alive. I felt remade as Cassandra's father, as this new little boy's grandfather. It was as if I were being born again. My daughter's call sculpted me into Rodney Sykes. Merely because I stood still in the right place at the right time for as long as it took!"

Sarah erupted in tears. She leaned over the balcony with her elbows on the railing, heaving and crying, and Rodney wrapped his arm around her shoulder. "He's going to die." Sarah removed her glasses, wiped her eyes, and returned them to her face. She gradually caught her breath. "I understand you, Rodney, and I think that's very eloquently put, but I disagree with you. I profoundly disagree. You weren't called. That's not what happened to you. You read the situation, you changed your mind, and then you *acted* on your decision. You did the same thing I did when I wrote my *Pinkleman* dissent, or when I signed onto Gideon's opinion in *Al-Tounsi*. You decided that the law wasn't correct by some criteria of your own, and then you were active with its boundaries."

Rodney released her shoulder from his grasp.

"Jonathan is dying. That circumstance didn't call me. It didn't choose me. It's just what's happening. What defines me is what *I* choose to do inside that circumstance. I have chosen to take care of him. Every time I bring him water, or help him roll over, or make him soup, I am making that choice again, and each time what I'm really choosing is to love my husband. I have not been sculpted into myself by some force outside of me; I am *choosing* to be myself, to be Jonathan's partner and wife and dear friend, just like I choose every day, when I go into work, to be Sarah Kolmann, the Supreme Court Justice. I know I could hire someone to help me with Jonathan's illness, and I would still be his partner and wife, but I also know that if I did that, I would be a different kind of partner and wife than the one I want to be. I would be a different person, profoundly. So not only do I get to choose my role, but also the particulars of that role. I choose the idiosyncrasies of myself. It seems I'm the kind of person that rolls the covers down a certain way, or warms up chicken broth badly. And I don't want Cathy or anyone else to do that for me any differently than I would. It is my choice to be *me*. That's what you did, Rodney, both by going to Cassandra when she called you and by writing your concurrence in *Al-Tounsi*. You made yourself. I don't see that as some kind of negative space chipped away. *You* were the carver, Rodney. *You*."

Cathy insisted on washing the dishes, although she must have understood perfectly well that Sarah wanted to be alone with Jonathan. Cathy said there was just no way she could leave her father's unwashed soup bowl, plus her own used teapot, cup and saucer in the sink. If Sarah wouldn't let her sleep on the couch, then the least Cathy could do was leave the place spotless before hurrying off to her hotel. Sarah hovered beside her daughter at the sink, watching. It was simply out of the question to let Cathy stay the night. Sarah didn't need help with Jonathan.

"So was he coughing much?"

"It was nothing serious, Mom. Although he did seem more tired than he did last time."

"Well, he is more tired, Cathy, that's not unusual."

"Okay, I'm just saying."

"Nothing happened in particular? He ate all his soup?"

Cathy had finished her last dish. She wiped down the wet counter with a dish towel, rinsed and wrung it out, and hung it up to dry.

"We had a perfectly fine evening here. You should've stayed at the opera."

"It wasn't a good production. There was a young bass who couldn't sing Godunov at all." Sarah grabbed a fresh dish towel from the side drawer, and dried the wet dishes her daughter had left in the rack. "I don't see why I should bore myself just for the principle of going out."

"Fine." Cathy shrugged. She jiggled her jaw from left to right, as she did when she was a kid, exasperated by her mother. "Do whatever you want," Cathy added, over her shoulder, as she escaped into the front hall.

Sarah smoldered in hot shame as she finished drying the dishes, and putting them back where they belonged. She was behaving terribly.

"I'm going now!" Cathy called from the entrance. "I'll come by for breakfast before I head back to Boston."

"Hang on." Sarah couldn't let her daughter leave like this.

Cathy was wearing her light coat, clutching her purse and a plastic bag that held yarn and knitting needles. She stood in the threshold, tight-lipped and pale. Cathy had propped the door open with her foot, as if there were a fire in the apartment and she was ready for a quick escape. She did not look eager for a hug.

"Thank you for your help." Sarah embraced her anyway, reaching up to pat her taller daughter's back. "I'm sorry I wasn't able to enjoy my evening."

Cathy didn't hug her back. "Dad's sleeping well. I wouldn't disturb him if I were you. I'll come around eight, if that's okay."

After she had gone, Sarah hurried into the bedroom to check on Jonathan. His bedside light was on, rotated toward the wall, casting the room in a faint yellow glow, and darkening Jonathan's face in shadow. He was sleeping quietly, as Cathy had promised. He had kicked off most of his blanket, and only one leg was covered. Jonathan's skeletal body all but swam in his favorite blue pajamas, now several sizes too big. His Adam's apple bobbed with each slow inhalation. His cavernous eye sockets, the protruding cheeks, the blunt curve of his skull as it dipped into his temporal bone—all of this was visible through his skin. Jonathan lay very still, so that he reminded Sarah of a mummified body dug up in Pompeii, cemented into the fetal position—a terrible image. She pushed it from her mind, extracted the twisted blanket from under her husband's leg and covered him up to his chin. He looked more comfortable now. He looked less exposed.

She left the light on. Standing in the hallway, not knowing where to go or what to do, Sarah spun her wedding ring around her finger. Speaking with Rodney had somehow relaxed and irritated her simultaneously. She had articulated her motives for caring for Jonathan and connected them to her work on the Court: in both situations she made decisions, conscious choices, and declared herself through her actions. In those choices she decided what was *right*: actively caring for Jonathan was similar to actively interpreting Title VII in favor of Gwen Pinkleman. But Rodney Sykes did not sign onto her interpretations, literally or figuratively. He balked at her activist language, her so-called meddlesome approach to the law. That was unsettling. Rodney probably thought her approach to caring for Jonathan was meddlesome. Cathy seemed to think it was. And there was no doubt some truth to that claim. Tonight's production of *Boris Godunov* was terrific; on any other occasion Sarah would have stayed and enjoyed it. She had only left the opera because she couldn't bear to loosen control over Jonathan's care. Sarah needed to be part of the solution; she needed to be caring for Jonathan right now. She had none of Rodney's patience. Rodney wrote in his shocking *Al-Tounsi* concurrence that he waited until "every available state or federal court denied jurisdiction" before daring to interfere with the written statute and the Constitution. He was right about that. He did not insert himself too soon. He waited until he was called.

Jonathan coughed a deep, phlegmy rattle. Sarah hurried into the bedroom and found him struggling to prop himself up in bed.

She moved his pillow and rested it against the headboard so he could lean back comfortably. He coughed again, and it sounded terrible. She grabbed a tissue from the side table and forced it into his hand. Coughing still, he brought it to his lips, spat wads of phlegm into it from deep in his lungs. Sarah shrunk, wondering if his cancer had spread to his lungs, or if this was the beginning of an endgame bout of pneumonia. That prospect heated her face and set her heart pounding.

She took the tissue from Jonathan's hand as he caught his breath. He gave her a harsh glance. "What are you doing, here? Why aren't you at the opera?"

"I couldn't." She checked the tissue for blood. Nothing but a thick and milky mucus.

"For Christ's sakes, Sarah." Jonathan tensed his body as he tried to roll onto his side. It was too much of a struggle, so he stopped.

"What are you getting mad at me for?"

"I don't need your constant attention. You're going to burn yourself out if you don't give it a rest."

"If I want to stay here, that's my choice," Sarah said, sharply. "My choice, and I can make it."

Jonathan erupted in a second fit of coughing. His face reddened, his body shook—he didn't have the strength for this! He needed to see a doctor right away!

"Jonathan, sit up. I'm going to take you to the hospital."

"No!" He coughed and coughed. He spoke again when his fit had eased. "You'll do no such thing. I was lying down and my lungs filled up a little. I'll be fine in a moment."

"I don't want you to get worse in the night."

"Back off, Sarah!"

Jonathan heaved his weight and turned onto his side. His breathing eased, and he took a deep breath. Slowly, his body settled into the mattress. If his coughing got worse again she would take him to the hospital whether he liked it or not. Jonathan reached for his blanket, padding around for it behind him—and here Sarah resisted every impulse she had of directing his hand to

the edge, and helping him pull it up. He found the blanket eventually, and drew it over his shoulder.

"Could you turn off the light, please?"

"Of course."

She left him alone, and then sat on the couch in the living
room, stunned. Jonathan's irritation was perfectly timed, a per-
suasive argument for Rodney and Cathy's position that she meddled too much, that she inserted herself too early, and didn't wait
to be called. Was she doing the same thing with the law as she
was with Jonathan's care? Had she been too brash, too active in
her opinions and dissents? Was Rodney's attack valid? Had she
meddled unnecessarily for her entire, distinguished career?

Sarah closed her eyes and sighed. She recalled the night she had
met Jonathan, back in 1955, attending a cocktail party for first-
years at Harvard Law. Jonathan was standing at the bar with four
other students, none of whom Sarah had met. She approached as
they talked about their notoriously difficult 1L Contracts course,
exchanging anecdotes they had heard about the professor. She
joined their conversation and then several students—all men—
insinuated that both Contracts and Civil Procedures would be
far too difficult for Sarah or the other six women at Harvard to
pass. Jonathan made a joke—something about women having
had plenty of experience negotiating contracts with men—and
soon after the others, who did not laugh at his joke, left the two
of them alone.

Sarah said she hadn't seen him in any of their classes. Jonathan admitted that he didn't go to Harvard Law or to any school.
He had sweet-talked his way into this exclusive party, open only
to Harvard students, because he wanted to meet the men and
women who would someday rule the world. He wanted to make
connections, he said. He was going into business. Sarah liked him
immediately. Jonathan asked her if it was difficult to be one of
the only women at Harvard Law, and if chauvinists were typical
of the student body. "They are typical," she admitted, glumly.
"They don't understand me. They certainly don't want me at their
party."

"No," Jonathan replied, and he offered her a big smile—his first in a lifetime of beautiful smiles. "I suspect you'll have to barge into their party every time."

Sarah got up from the couch and peeked into the bedroom. Jonathan was sleeping again, snoring faintly. She stepped inside gingerly. There was a small pile of laundry in their hamper—his pale green shirt, his socks, his underwear. Perhaps she would wash and iron his clothes. It wouldn't take her long and it might even relax her. And then if Jonathan woke up coughing in the middle of the night, feverish and scared and needing to go to the hospital, she would have that shirt ready to slip over his bony shoulders.

10

TO KEEP AND
BEAR ARMS

Killian Quinn lay naked on a hotel bed stripped of its covers. A different man might have been ashamed by his girth, and tried to cover it with a blanket, but instead Killian knocked his flab from left to right, watched it jiggle and tremble, and then settle like Jello. He loved his big old belly, his lust for life embodied, his relish for food and sex—and good Lord, the finger-tingling, back-wrenching sex he had thrown himself into since Dr. Gurlick had prescribed him his treasured, orange, almond-shaped pills, that manna of modern medicine. Nothing was more fun than the good hard illicit fucking that had him flipping pillows off beds and burning his knees on rugs, grunting and sweating like a Russian weightlifter, marching all over this hotel room with Katherine's legs wrapped around him. And nothing was more satisfying, more grounding, than his more intimate lovemaking—the slower, quieter, under-the-covers intercourse he so treasured with Gloria, his dear wife. Maybe this belly would kill him someday, maybe that day would come soon, but what better way to leave a fallen world for the pure arms of the Lord than with your whole body rejoicing in God's gift of living passion? Katherine certainly didn't find his oversized belly distasteful, and neither did Gloria, so why should he?

Katherine was in the bathroom, taking a shower. The clock read 6:46. Soon he would head home for a late dinner with Gloria, and then stay up drafting *Wallace*, a Second Amendment ruling so unexpectedly in favor of gun rights that the votes astonished every justice in conference. What was supposed to be a minor statutory case had suddenly turned into the most significant ruling on gun rights in a century. Not even the NRA had considered a victory of this scale possible, so they hadn't offered any financial support for Jason Wallace's suit, and had refused to submit even an amicus brief. *Wallace* would reinstate an American citizen's unadulterated constitutional right to keep and bear whatever arms he or she so chose—and it was Killian's majority opinion, the official verdict of the Court.

"What are you smiling about over there?" Katherine had emerged from the bathroom wrapped in a towel, drying her ears.

He shrugged. "Nothing, just work."

"It's not nice to refuse to answer my questions."

Killian frowned. Nobody outside the Court knew anything about *Wallace*, and certainly no one expected the radical results.

"I'm thinking about the goofy lives of the justices of the United States Supreme Court. We'd make a good reality show."

"Could you be more specific?" Katherine sat at the foot of the bed.

"Rodney Sykes."

"Justice Sykes is *goofy*?"

"Believe me, he can be." Killian rolled onto his side, leaned his weight on an elbow. "There's one case this year—unfortunately I can't say which until the term's over—but suffice it to say, it's a biggie and contentious. I wanted to win it by a large margin, so I spent weeks trying to persuade Katsakis to my side, even though I didn't need to. I wanted to secure every section of my opinion, and I thought Talos might swing on it. Turns out, I was wrong."

"You, wrong? Impossible."

"Hard to believe, I know, but it happens on rare occasions. Katsakis stayed unmoved and resolved against me—and against what's right, too, I should add. But there I was, like a stupid dog the whole term, braying uselessly at the unmovable moon, Talos."

"A stupid horndog."

"Indeed. May I continue?"

Katherine snickered.

"I offered to bring him tea from the cafeteria, and to do his homework for him, and to carry his bags to school and the like, and all the while I was entirely missing our real target. Because Rodney Sykes was silently planning the most outrageous rebellion and Benedict Arnold–style 'turncoatery' that you can imagine, out of sight, without anyone's knowledge. I didn't spend a second of my precious time talking to him, or trying to shore up his vote."

"'Turncoatery'?"

"Your beloved Shakespeare invented words whenever he wanted, so why can't I?"

"You can, of course, but when there's *treason* and *treachery* and *betrayal*—"

"And *sedition* and *perfidy* and *mutiny* and *duplicity*," interrupted Killian, "and the point is Rodney Sykes is guilty of all those, and worse, and I need a new word to express it. I didn't think the guy had it in him."

"People are surprising."

"Rodney is not surprising. Rodney's steadfast and predictable, that's his whole thing."

Katherine stood and dropped her towel, which proved enough of a distraction to abandon the topic of Justice Sykes. She slipped on her underwear and fastened her small bra, now and then acknowledging Killian's hungry gaze in the mirror. Lord knows he didn't mind the show.

"You don't seem too upset." Katherine stepped into her linen slacks.

"About what?" The only thing he could imagine being upset about now was the pending disappearance of her bare legs into those pants.

"About losing your case."

"Well, the ruling hasn't been filed, so I haven't lost yet. But I am upset about it. It'll be a disaster for the United States if that case goes the way it's heading. It'll cause irreparable damage to our peace and security, if you really must know."

"I mean personally upset. Usually, losing eats at you. Like *Geitz* did last year."

Killian lay back, pressed his head into the pillow. That was an astute observation. He tucked his hands behind his head, and spoke up to the ceiling.

"Well, every case falls into a larger context. *Geitz* was one more loss in a long string of failures, and another indication that the Court did not fundamentally agree with my jurisprudence. I saw no hope of the tide turning. But now Elyse Van Cleve, bless her poor soul, has left our world for a better one, and we've got Manny Arroyo on the bench, so I suddenly find myself in the novel territory of being in the majority on almost all the important cases this term. The truth is, Katherine—and please do not repeat this until we announce our decisions—of the eight or nine cases that actually matter this term, I mean those that are contentious and somewhat ideological, I'll be in the majority for all except this one I'm talking about. That has not happened to me since I joined the Court. So you're right, I'm not that upset, even if I lose this big case. The Court has turned. The law is developing as it should—finally—and it looks like that'll continue for the foreseeable future."

Fully dressed now but for her jewelry and shoes, Katherine leaned against the hotel desk. "I'm not so sure I'm happy to hear that."

"Don't worry, your brother can still have gay sex in Arkansas."

"For the time being."

Katherine's cheeks glowed red, and her dark blond hair framed her face, wet and full. She was a beautiful woman. The succulence of her youth, so precious and fleeting. What was she doing wasting her bloom on a fat old judge like Killian Quinn? Sudden shame cascaded through him, so he pulled himself out of bed and started to get dressed. The question lingered in his mind. What was he doing? What was Katherine doing? The truth was that his relationship with her had settled into something calm and peaceful, a period of harmony and stasis. It could not develop any further from here; it could only calcify and decline. They had been meeting twice a month since he had started Cialis in January, always in this same hotel off Capitol Hill, for a couple of glorious hours of lovemaking and light conversation. That was the extent of his commitment. He would never commit to more. How could that arrangement be satisfying for her?

He buttoned his shirt, taking his time. Something was shifting inside him, a profound adjustment, and it was caused by his change of fortune on the Court. Did he really want to lead a double life with Katherine? He had everything and more that a man could reasonably want without her: a rich and rewarding profession, substantive work of consequence, a near-perfect wife (who remained blissfully ignorant of his failings), six ideal children—well, four ideal children, one daughter who was irritating but good enough, and a son, poor Carl, who would just have to remain a work in progress—plus a gaggle of grandchildren, so many beautiful little souls that he had a hard time recalling, on the spot, which kid belonged with which parent. He had his health, appetite and libido, and now—with Arroyo on the bench—a bright future. The Court's turning in his favor was an unexpected gift in his already blessed life. His affair with Katherine was delightful and gratifying, but maybe it was more than he deserved and, importantly, more than what he needed to be content.

Killian snaked his long belt through the loops of his pants beneath his hanging belly. He tossed his tie on the bed and leaned his dampening palms against the edge of the dresser. He hung his head. The dresser groaned. Katherine asked if he was all right, with some concern.

"I am all right, Katherine. Yes."

She sat on the bed, hands in her lap. "You're breaking up with me."

"I didn't say that."

"You said it quite clearly, just not with words."

"I'm considering it."

"Why? Things are great between us."

He sighed. "That's exactly why, Katherine. I'd rather do it now, when there isn't anything wrong, when my reasons can't be dismissed by either of us as some problem we have to work through. When everything's blissful."

Killian pulled his weight off the dresser. Saying those words out loud only confirmed his impulse to end their relationship.

"The fact is, Katherine, I love you. If I were younger, I could easily imagine wanting to build a full life together: kids, marriage, the whole thing. But I can't offer that. I'm already taken, and too old, and I have no business prolonging our relationship, no matter how much I enjoy our conversations and passionate embraces. I hope you know I enjoy it."

The skin around Katherine's eyes tensed and tightened as she oscillated between anger and pain and something else, maybe stalwart acceptance or relief. "Fine."

"I should be entirely blunt and honest with you, Katherine. I don't think you have any business being with me. You are a young, beautiful woman in the prime of your life, and you should be with a man who you can build a future with. Frankly, you can do better. You need a real commitment."

All emotion drained from Katherine's face, leaving her placid, almost peaceful. "Fuck you."

Killian blinked. "Well, you might not agree, but I know I'm right."

"But you don't have the right to say what's good or not good for my life."

He held his hands up in the air. He was just airing his thoughts, but so be it, she could respond however she wished. She had no requirement to heed his advice only because it was good.

"That is so unbelievably condescending."

"I am not condescending to you, Katherine." Killian snatched his tie off the bed and strung it around his neck. He turned towards the mirror.

"You don't get to say."

"All right." He spoke to her reflection.

"You don't get to say what's good for me, that's part of our little deal here."

"I heard you the first time."

Katherine retreated into the bathroom, quietly shutting the door behind her. She wasn't crying; she would never do that. She probably just needed a moment alone. Killian hurriedly tied his tie, slipped on his suit jacket, and suppressed the ache in his chest, the painful realization that he would never again hold Katherine's slender frame against his own. *A dram of perseverance is oft required of a Quinn,* whispered the mischievous voice of his father, Malachi. His son Gregory, who was a second lieutenant in the Marines, would have handled this breakup similarly, saying the necessary words, standing tall, moving on with life. A real stoic. *Man up, sir. Not like you're going for a tour in Afghanistan.* Oh yes, Gregs was one of the noble kids, that was for sure.

When Katherine stepped out of the bathroom, she stood steadier, her face opaque. She grabbed her purse off the desk chair. "Let's go, Killian. There's no point sticking around here forever."

He frowned and moved toward her, but she recoiled well before he could touch her hand. "I don't want to hug you. I understand what you're saying, and I want to go."

"I would very much like to hold you, Katherine."

"Well, you don't get to."

He stood there stupidly: an awkward faceoff on the drab rug. There was clearly nothing more to say or do, but Killian didn't feel right leaving her alone. Their usual arrangement, after both had dressed, was for him to give her half the money for their room, always rented in her name. He would disappear down the side stairwell, slip out from the unmarked entrance in the alley, climb into his Lincoln, innocuously parked on C Street, and zip onto I-395 for the drive out to Virginia. Katherine waited the requisite ten minutes before leaving the building, which she did however she liked, even by the front entrance, and why the heck not? A single woman is free to have a hotel rendezvous with any mysterious stranger she likes, not that she would be seen. The

Capitol Hill Hotel on C Street had two buildings, and Katherine always requested the second, accessible only by a room key, without a staffed lobby. Off they would go on their separate ways: *Finita la Commedia*. Still, it seemed distasteful and crude to part forever in the usual manner. It lacked even a pretext of chivalry.

"I'd like to walk you down to your car."

Katherine rolled her eyes.

"Sneaking out of here like a couple of thieves doesn't give our relationship the dignity it deserves."

"That is one dumb idea."

"Look, unless you insist on denying me, I plan to walk you to your car and seeing you off just once."

"Suit yourself."

They went into the hall together and rode the elevator down in miserable silence, staring at the illuminated buttons all the way to the lobby. He trailed his former lover as they exited the building. Killian squinted in the light. The day was bright and hot, although it was well past seven. He laid his hand on Katherine's shoulder, who was marching a step before him, and then he glanced up and saw Samuel Sykes standing on the sidewalk—right there on the sidewalk—wearing a ridiculous leather jacket. Samuel's eyes bulged.

"Justice Quinn?"

Killian dropped his hand off Katherine's shoulder.

"Samuel. What are you doing here?"

"My girlfriend, uh, lives . . ." Samuel pointed off in the direction of 3rd Street, but his eyes darted back and forth between Killian's face and Katherine's wet hair. Her blasted wet hair.

"Well, good to see you." Killian pressed his palm firmly against Katherine's shoulder. He gave her a tiny nudge. She didn't move.

Everything slowed. In a first floor window in the apartment building across C Street, through half-parted curtains, a woman in her 60s or early 70s, with her back to him, unhooked the industrial clasp of her big bra and exposed a slab of flesh not as tender or as young as Katherine's. This situation was ridiculous and pathetic. Killian's heart pounded. His idiotic fantasies of youth were finally going to catch up with him.

"Hello." Katherine smiled at the young man. "You look familiar."

"I'm Samuel Sykes." He tucked his hands into his pockets. "I cover legal stories for *The Washington Post*." Beneath those faux-Jamaican hair knots, lanky young Sykes blinked and blinked, basking in the heat of his mammoth discovery.

"Oh, right, of course. I've read your articles, they're excellent." She extended her hand without hesitation. Killian fought an urge to intercept it and yank it back. "I'm Katherine Kirsch, curator of manuscripts at the Folger's Library."

Samuel's eyes widened. "Hi." And then the blasted journalist son of Rodney Sykes took her hand and shook it.

"I assume you're here to discuss *Al-Tounsi*." Rodney Sykes sat stoically in his armchair, surrounded by this absurd mockery of a Lake Como villa that he called his chambers.

"Indeed." Killian squirmed in a second armchair, fiddling with his slick and sweaty fingers. Few experiences were as destabilizing as dropping in on another justice in his private space, especially Rodney's, Mr. Protocol himself.

"I'm not changing my vote." Rodney's legs were crossed tightly, as if Killian's brilliant plan for convincing his colleague was to kick him in the groin.

"I don't expect you to. I don't play people like that. I'm here for something much bigger. I think your concurrence is magnificently eloquent—actually I found it quite moving—but I've got to say, Rodney, it's also the only opinion I've ever read that's actually *illegal*. I'm concerned for you. I think you're in breach of your oath. Remember, the applicable words, here, are that you're to *faithfully and impartially discharge and perform*—"

"Yes, yes."

"—*all the duties incumbent upon you as*—"

"I know the judicial oath, Killian."

"You're breaking the law."

"I'm establishing a new doctrine to assess the validity of laws. Which is also part of our job."

"It's grounds for impeachment. Think about it. Out of office in a whirl of shame and scandal."

"Rather dramatically put."

"Well, it's the truth." Killian sat back, tapping his bulbous nose. "Rodney, I'm beyond trying to win over your vote in this case. If your conscience is so bothered by terrorists not getting a shot at habeas, fine, do what the others do, establish some legitimate legal grounds, no matter how tenuous, and give them their blasted habeas. You don't even have to do that work yourself. Just sign on to Gideon's and be done with it!"

"As I've told the others, I profoundly disagree with Justice Rosen's opinion."

"I do, too. That's not my point."

"Then I'm surprised that a man of your strict principles, Killian, would suggest anything like that."

"Like what? Obeying the law?" Rodney's smile hardened, and sealed his mouth tightly. Sarcasm would never move Justice Sykes. "Do you really believe what you wrote?"

"I do."

"You're comfortable saying the law means X, but we should still rule Y?"

"If the law does not conform with justice, the law should change, not justice."

Rodney gently swayed his crossed foot, swinging it back and forth, to and fro. He seemed unaffected by Killian's impeccable reasoning. Good for him. Justice Quinn couldn't help but admire the man's fortitude. *The law should change, not justice!* Since when did Rodney Sykes become this great spokesman for justice, this modern day Oliver Wendell Holmes? It was heartwarming to see, actually, the kind of simple and direct declaration that Killian wanted to hear more of from his colleagues. It was a statement with some backbone, some moral force. But still, his concurrence was crazy, and it planted the seed for a damaging precedent that might someday be applied equally to all branches of law, beyond this Article I question of presidential power. It was like a weed, Rodney's idea, his absurd doctrine of subversion, and if it took, unlikely as that was, it would be near impossible for subsequent justices to root it out.

"You understand I'll have to put a section in my dissent that addresses your concurrence, and I won't be gentle in my wording."

"I would expect nothing less of you, Killian."

"I'll say your logic is unfounded and illegal, and that you should to be censured, maybe worse."

"Yes."

"Any response?"

"Not at the moment."

"Of course that's nothing to do with what I think of you personally."

Justice Sykes nodded. "According to your bond, no more, no less."

Killian laughed. "Look, Rodney. I like you. I hope you know that. But that doesn't change my legal responsibility here. I'll tear you a second asshole and call for your impeachment."

"Oh, I won't be impeached, Justice Quinn." Rodney was so unfazed by the prospect of impeachment that he almost chuckled in response. "For a solo concurrence, unbinding? The only material consequence of my writing will be to limit any precedent for granting habeas, and narrow the grounds to this one instance in Subic Bay, which is unlikely to repeat. My concurrence here works more in your favor than if I were to join Gideon and push him into the majority. So why do you object so strenuously? You should let it be."

"Rodney . . ."

"There is no chance I'll be impeached. You understand? The threat does not touch me. My other votes, opinions and dissents this term are all strict and legalistic."

Killian considered, and nodded. "Right you are."

"So, Justice Quinn. Anything else?"

Killian threw up his hands and shrugged. "Not unless you want to talk about switching on *Wallace*."

Now Rodney laughed, as Killian hoped he would. "The District of Columbia's gun laws are perfectly frank and clear in their wording, and so I see no need to disrupt them with your constitutional claims."

"Now, that sounds more like the old Rodney Sykes."

"There is plenty of him left."

"Last chance? I'd love your vote."

"You already have your five."

"Six is a much prettier number than five. Rounder." Killian stood and grimaced, and shook his leg, which had numbed in his seat and now ached from his activated sciatica. "Oh dear Lord, I am possessed." He massaged his burning thigh. "A demon's got me in its teeth."

Rodney, infallibly polite, had already moved toward the door, which he intended on opening for his guest. Killian hovered by the chair, stretching and lengthening his monster leg. Once he'd stopped shaking, he feigned remembering something.

"Oh, hey, guess who I saw on C Street, yesterday?" It was important to remain casual—he had to sound casual. "Your son. I was there for this interview. My daughter has this friend, this longtime friend, who works nearby, and wanted some legal questions answered. You know I hate those things. But my daughter was asking, so."

Rodney's hand was resting on the door knob. He didn't look suspicious.

"She rented a conference room over at the Capitol Hill Hotel, which was a real waste, if you ask me, but she said it's just around the corner from her place, and she knows the owner or something. Didn't cost her. You know that hotel?"

"I don't think so, no."

"Your son's girlfriend lives over by C Street?"

"I didn't know Samuel had a girlfriend, on C Street or anywhere else."

"Well, maybe he made it up." Killian winked at Rodney, and then moved to the entrance and patted him on the shoulder. "Hey, thanks for seeing me, Justice Sykes. I know this is not the usual way of doing things, but I appreciate it."

Rodney offered Killian that stilted, bowed-head gesture of his, and then opened the door like a valet.

Killian paused in the threshold, eying his colleague. "I'm not the first to visit you about *Al-Tounsi*, am I?" He grinned openly, and wished Rodney's temperament allowed him more leeway to joke. Still, Killian thought it smart to reemphasize the pretext for his visit.

"No, you are not. Gideon came first, then Charles, now you. Nor do I suspect you'll be the last."

There was nothing all that special about the Church of the Immaculate Conception in Reston, Virginia, which was exactly what Killian liked about it. The plain wood siding, painted white, blended seamlessly with half the neo-colonial houses in this wealthy suburb. He parked his Lincoln in the church's massive, half-empty lot, and then marched through the modest portico into the plain sanctuary. The stained glass windows colored the sunlight and invoked God's grace, but they had a paint-by-numbers quality, and their themes were run-of-the-mill: Annunciation, Crucifixion, Christ at home in the bosom of the Lord. Nothing elite or pretentious here, no striving for significance that hadn't been earned. Killian rested his hand on a pine pew that looked like it could have been purchased at IKEA and assembled in this room—that is, if IKEA had had a *Church, Mosque, and Synagogue* department, which, come to think of it, it might. There was an older couple sitting quietly in the back who didn't seem to recognize him. Killian spied Father Elko sitting alone in a front pew, facing away, his head lowered, probably waiting for any supplicant who desired confession in this allotted two-hour period. He approached and called Elko's name.

"Well, hello, Killian." The priest was reading a fat book. He closed it and pressed it against his stomach with one hand while shaking Killian's with the other, exposing the book's spine: *War Letters: Extraordinary Correspondence from American Wars.* Father Elko was a patriot, yet another thing to like about this priest and his unassuming church.

Elko asked after Killian's children, inquiring especially about Gregory's safety in Afghanistan, and Gloria's health. Elko's dappled gray hair was swept back and wavy, a dashing mien for a suburban priest, and he wore a pair of modern, steel-gray glasses. His trim and muscular body looked a decade younger than his age, perfect for a religious leader in this community, as the congregation here would have always secretly suspected the moral standing of a priest fatter than his flock. Elko had once told Killian that he worked out on his cross-country skiing or elliptical machine at 5 A.M. each morning except for Virginia's rare snow days, when he would bind himself into actual skis and take to the rolling trails of a nearby forest.

"Have you come for confession?"

"If you'll hear me, Father."

Killian followed the priest into the confessional, and waited for the screen to slide open on the other side of the grille. He knelt, crossed himself, asked for forgiveness as a penitent. It had been several months since his last confession. And what sins had he to confess? *Here we go*, thought Killian Quinn.

The good priest Elko must have heard many a wretched plea from pedophile, tax evader and wife-abuser alike, from all sorts of corporate embezzlers, political liars and cheats, and maybe even a murderer or two, because he had long since proved immune to Killian's lustful escapades and was quite non-judgmental personally, although of course he had his limits professionally. Half the reason Killian had come today was the finality of his break with Katherine, which allowed him to confess his blissful weeks of romping in one fell swoop and mitigate his blatant, conscious sins with an honest admission that he had put that affair behind him. But even after Killian had finished relating the details of his lustful sins and received his instructions for penitence, he found himself lingering, kneeling. He felt miserable, and realized that he was trembling.

"Is there something else?" whispered Father Elko.

"I'm subsumed by anger, Father. I'm furious."

The priest asked him to elaborate, and so Killian told him about his break-up in the Capitol Hill Hotel, walking Katherine to her car, and their unfortunate collision with Rodney Sykes's son, *The Washington Post* journalist. "I haven't spoken with Katherine since, but my anger toward her hasn't abated at all. She was hurt, and clearly wanted to get back at me. She told the guy her name, and where she works. Told this to a reporter from *The Washington Post*. He obviously knew what was going on between us. I don't understand how she could have done that. I'm someone she cares for, someone she knows loves her in return. I'm stewing in anger, Father. I'm terrified that I'll be exposed and humiliated before my wife and family and colleagues, and I have to tell you, I don't think I deserve that. I have always been as honest as I could have possibly been given the basic deceit of my sinful weak soul and physical needs. I've respected my wife's dignity, and shielded her from unnecessary scandal, and moreover, I think, if she did learn about my sins, she would in part understand them. I know Gloria, and I don't think I'm stretching. She would be hurt, sure, but knowing me, loving me as I am, with my huge appetites, she would get it. But not if *The Washington Post* wrote about my affair. Not if a woman's name and face were put to those deeds. If reporters hounded us, or parked on our lawn, or if all of Gloria's bridge partners and the cashier at the grocery store could look at her and know. *That* she could never forgive, and I don't blame her, neither would I. I don't think I deserve that, Father."

Father Elko's silhouette stirred on the other side of grille, and resettled.

"You know what else makes me angry? What this'll do to my work. See, I've been toiling for decades, Father, in a futile attempt at righting the screwy jurisprudence in this country, trying to put it on some reasonable ground. My methodology has been controversial to some, and there are vested interests railing against me—newspapers, media, the liberal elite. If this stupid affair is exposed, they'll call me a hypocrite and a liar; they'll use one irrelevant personal fact to undermine the whole body of my forthright and important work, destroying it, and just when I'm starting to turn the corner into the majority. I've got the most important cases of my career this term, dissents and opinions, but if this thing comes out now, in our tawdry climate, it'll dwarf everything I've done, *everything*. People won't be talking about the rightful limit of habeas corpus in wartime, or the proper meaning of the Second Amendment; instead they'll be saying that my opinions can't be trusted because I slept with some young woman, and that makes me furious!"

The priest waited until he was certain Killian was done, and then answered him quietly. "Your anger is not a sin. In your situation, it makes sense to be angry. I think both you and your ex-lover have reasons to be upset, valid ones. Your pride, however, is far more troubling than either your anger or your lust."

Killian rocked back and forth on his ruined knees, hanging his head, listening.

"Even those of us lacking in pride by nature are sometimes overcome with its toxicity, especially those of us astute enough to justify our actions, to understand and explain them and to limit their negative consequences. You might be right—you were always careful, and good and decent to other people, and responsible in your work, and yet you could still be afflicted with overweening pride. You are prideful to think you've been wronged. Our each action has consequence. The Lord sees your every thought, deed and sin. So the problem here is far larger than whether some reporter from *The Washington Post* has discovered your affair. You deserve everything and anything that the Lord cares to send your way, every blessing and curse, no matter how good you might be, no matter how right or righteous. In other words, you deserve nothing."

Father Elko gave him further instructions for the absolution of his pride, although prayer alone it seemed would not do all the work. Sick, spent, and humiliated, Killian thanked the priest, who was right about everything, and then he lumbered out of the confessional, moving as quickly as he could, hobbling toward the door, before Father Elko could emerge from the other side. The last thing Killian wanted right now was to see that priest's face. He pushed through the metal door of the portico and barreled into the parking lot, the asphalt radiating heat, the air heavy and humid on this late evening in June. What kind of idiot was he for not considering pride, that most obvious sin, the one that took down all the heroic and nimbly overeducated men, the stock and trade of the great plays, most of which he knew backward and forward, line by line. What next for Killian Quinn? Must he grab his Swiss Army knife and gouge out his eyes like some modern-day Gloucester, Oedipus or Pozzo? Hubris, of all blasted things. Hubris! Him!

He stood by his car, weak and ashamed, as tiny McGovern materialized by Killian's side to recite Shakespeare's verse, poetically, overdone, like Laurence Olivier, conscious of iamb and trochee alike, stressing key words, rolling his consonants, and sliding his silky vowels:

"He that is proud eats up himself: pride is
His own glass, his own trumpet, his own chronicle."

It was a nasty trick of McGovern's to use the beloved bard against him, so Killian wracked his mind for another biting quote that would put that angel in his place. But as he considered his vast and memorized stock of Shakespeare, Coyote, pitchfork and all, appeared beside his life-long foe.

"Killian, you dumb ox, check out that sunset!"

Rich orange and pink clouds smeared above the tall poplars and pin oaks adjacent to the church's parking lot. The smog, heat and exhaust from 18-wheelers running south on I-66 had browned the edges of the sky like it was a piece of old paper. A textured air of particulate matter, carbon monoxide and sulfur compounds—the perfect medium for the sun to execute its brilliant setting. A light breeze shook the tops of the trees, a sudden drop of heat from the coming night, and a kiss of relief from the hot day. God, he loved sunsets. Loved the rain, too. The fog, and the mist. Miserable gray, chilly mornings up in New England, blinding dry scorchers when he visited his cousins down in Arizona. Weather of all kinds. Killian loved day and he loved night, and every half-dim, wishy-washy state in between.

Coyote spoke right into his ear. "So you're a little too proud? You're too fat, also. Who gives a shit?"

Killian laughed, and rested his palms on his car. He lingered in the parking lot, savoring this perfect evening until its colors waned, and then he unlocked his car, started the motor, and drove home to Gloria.

In section II, part A, of Justice Quinn's triumphant opinion for *Wallace v. The District of Columbia*, midway through his evisceration of Justice Davidson's dissent, Killian decided to add a quick rebuke that compared Bernhard's logic to the Red Queen's in *Through the Looking Glass*. Once he had written it, he sat back, chuckling. The old man's dissent was a poor attempt at twisting the text of the Second Amendment into declaring something other than what it plainly said—that is, that *the right of the people to keep and bear arms shall not be infringed*, which was exactly something the Red Queen would have done in his place. Killian had been reading the Lewis Carroll classic to his granddaughter, Ellie, a chapter or two each Saturday night, when she stayed with them. He had just gotten to the funny part where the Red Queen tells Alice to stop twiddling her fingers, and to curtsey while thinking, because that "saves time." Ellie had listened closely as the Red Queen redefined common words like *garden* and *hill*, and said they meant something other than their obvious definitions, transforming *hill* into *valley*, and *garden* into *wilderness*, and all sorts of similar nonsense. Yes, that Red Queen was much like an adept justice in the relativistic Brennan-Davidson line, playing willy-nilly with her terms until she got the result she liked. And with her monarchical title, she had just the right upbringing and pompous self-regard to feel at home at cocktail parties thrown by Hollywood directors and hedge-fund billionaires alike. So few people in this sordid era maintained any good old-fashioned common sense when it came to words, the kind of straightforward wisdom that Alice displayed with such abundance in those Wonderland books. Ellie, giggling and snorting, had understood Carroll's main point plainly, as any kid would, because that point was so simple and obviously right.

An email landed in Killian's inbox, his computer chiming. It was from Katherine Kirsch. Not once had she tried to contact him by phone, email or letter in their entire relationship. *Call me*, it read.

He looked around chambers, as if there could be someone here to spy on him, and then he deleted Katherine's email. The Court's central server, although famously private, would have a record of the transmission. A hacker could someday locate and publish it. But the email wasn't incriminating, was it? It only proved that a relationship of some kind existed between them. Killian locked the door and sat in an armchair. He called Katherine from his cell phone, greeting her coldly.

"I got a message today at work from Samuel Sykes. He wants to talk to me."

"Well, what did you tell him?" Killian's stomach felt both empty and full at once.

"I haven't returned his call."

"You must have expected this, Katherine." He tried to strip his voice of anger.

"I didn't expect anything. I told him my name without thinking."

Killian restrained his urge to say *I don't believe that for a second*, to berate her, and to fight.

"I know I owe you an apology."

"What you did was cruel."

"I know it was, Killian. I think I did it to be cruel. Although not entirely consciously. You were being so outrageously patronizing to me."

"That is no excuse."

"It is an excuse. You do not patronize me. Ever. It demeans me. I never told you to lose weight. I didn't tell you that all my rich life experience has taught me it's really not so smart to sleep with a much younger woman behind your wife's back, and that you might in the future reconsider that decision, did I? So please pay me the same courtesy, and treat me with some respect."

True, Katherine had never intruded into his decisions, never judged him at all. She didn't presume to know how he should live his life, so why should he think he had that right with her? Killian's anger, his constant companion for days running, faded into a duller frustration, something remote, and foreign.

"Are you listening to me?"

"I am. You're right."

"I know I'm right. You don't need to tell me that."

"Well, then, I'm sorry. I can still say sorry, can't I?"

"Yes. I accept your apology." Katherine sighed, paused. "Oh, God, he wants to talk to me, and he's going to ask everything."

"He'll never write about us. Not after seeing his own father and sister suffer in that stupid Arroyo scandal."

"I think he will."

"He's not a gossip columnist."

"Either way, I have to call him back."

Killian's elk, mounted to the wall, was watching him impassively. Who the heck was Killian kidding? Why wouldn't young Sykes write a story about his affair? It was a scoop for a liberal journalist. And what did he know about Samuel's intentions or his ethical limits?

"I lied to his father." Killian stood up and paced as he talked. "I told Rodney I saw Sam on C Street, that I was there because I was being interviewed by a friend of my daughter's in our hotel, that she had rented a boardroom there because she knew the owner and could get it for free."

"Wow, you said *that*?"

"What's wrong with it?"

"You're a bad liar."

"He didn't suspect anything."

"Why the hell would this mystery woman interview you in a board room?"

"Because this fictional woman lives around the corner from the Capitol Hill Hotel, that's why."

"But I don't live around the corner from the Capitol Hill Hotel, and that fictional woman is *me*. And why would the curator of manuscripts from the Folger Library want to interview you in the first place?"

"I don't bloody well know why she would want to do that. That's this fictional woman's problem, not mine, isn't it?"

"Come on, Killian."

"You interviewed me because my massive knowledge of Shakespeare is public information, and of interest to members of the library."

"Then why didn't I interview you in the Folger? It's right around the corner from the Court and it's not like a quiet room there would be any problem."

"I don't know why!"

"I don't know if I can say that, Killian."

"I'm not asking you to say that, am I?"

He retook his seat in the armchair. If he wasn't asking her to lie, then what the heck was he doing repeating all that crap he told Justice Sykes? Merely encouraging her along with a passive-aggressive nudge? He should cut the bullshit. Killian wanted Katherine to cover for him; he wanted her to lie, and lie some more, and lie again! To repeat the same lie, over and over, only better. Work on it, make it real. Killian had rarely wanted anything more than this, yet he couldn't just ask Katherine to do it outright, not after what she had just said.

His thoughts turned to *Wallace*. Justice Kolmann had written a second dissent to accompany Davidson's, which approached the problem of gun control from another angle entirely. She cited statistics, sociological research, murder rates and accidents. She referenced abundant studies that proved, *without a doubt*, that handguns killed Americans at an extraordinary rate and

thus needed to be regulated on pragmatic grounds. She did not
address the wording of the Second Amendment as Davidson had,
and refused to engage in the basic textual problem at the root of
Wallace. Justice Kolmann argued for the *purpose* of gun control laws. She wanted a certain result, thought her solution was
right and good, and so argued for it. Killian had read her dissent with some sympathy. It was not nice at all that guns killed
so many people, but even if her statistics were correct—and he
highly doubted that—that didn't touch the fundamental problem
of her approach—namely, when it came to interpreting the law,
it did not matter what she wanted. If the law enumerates an individual right, a justice is required to respect that right, even if he
or she fundamentally disagrees with it. The Constitution declares
Americans have the right to keep and bear arms, but it does not
say you have to *like* it, or agree with it. It only says you can't touch
it, no matter how noble your purpose might be.

"Killian? Hello?"

Didn't Katherine have an equal right to their story? She could
tell anyone she wanted about their affair, or she could deny it,
that was her right—even though her choice, right now, felt like a
loaded gun pointed at his head. Killian was not Justice Davidson
or Rosen or Kolmann. He would not resort to fancy wordplay or
his personal desire to weasel out of a legal ruling that he didn't
like. He believed in the principle of the individual's rights, and so
he was going to stick by the ruling. *You, too, Katherine, have the
right to keep and bear arms.*

"You know I'm very worried about the effect of our affair
on my work. I don't want to be publicly embarrassed either. I'm
terrified my wife will find out about us. But still, I'm aware, Katherine, this is your decision to make. You were, and are, my equal
in our relationship. I hear you on that. And so I really do think
it's up to you to handle Samuel Sykes however you wish. Repeat
my bald-faced lie, if you want. Make it better, if you can, or tell
him the truth—that you were screwing me in a hotel room, and
that it's something we did every two weeks, and that I loved every
second of it, which I did. And if I'm asked in turn by Sam Sykes

or anyone else about what you said, well . . . I guess I'll first say *no comment*, as I always do to reporters, but then if I'm forced to speak by subpoena or whatever, I'll confirm whatever it is you've chosen to say. Your exact words, even if that damns me forever."

"Really?"

"Yes. Although I don't know why I'd be subpoenaed, as there's no law against adultery. But we've been over that, haven't we?"

"I don't want to talk about the law."

He crossed his feet on the coffee table. *Take that, Pride.* It felt good to submit to a correct principle, to allow himself the strength of what he believed. Lord, he wanted to slip out of this mess unscathed, but if he didn't, if Katherine couldn't bring herself to say anything but the truth, or if young Sykes proved a worthy journalist, skillfully interviewing the hotel manager and extracting some damning information about biweekly rentals in the name of Katherine Kirsch, or skipping over to the Folger and chatting with Dr. Frezel, then at least Killian would take solace that he did not go down patronizing or manipulating a woman who deserved his full respect.

Killian sighed. "So what are you going to tell him?"

"I don't know. I guess we'll just have to wait and see."

Killian leaned against the marbled wall by the door of Justice Kolmann's chambers, clutching a slender manila folder that held an edited version of his dissent in *Al-Tounsi v. Shaw*. His distilled section was still quite long, and might take a half hour to read from the bench. No matter. He was going to force every journalist and spectator in that room to listen to his vociferous objection to the Court's granting habeas corpus to terrorists held in Subic Bay. This ruling was front-page news. With it, the United States would be seriously diminished in its ability to fight terror. Those Subic Bay detainees were sly fanatics and manipulators, working in concert with the best bleeding-heart lawyers in the country, hailing from institutes like the Constitutional Rights Center and top Washington law firms. With their newly granted habeas rights, a portion of those bad men would soon be released, and subsequently travel right back to the battlefields of Afghanistan and Iraq, planting roadside bombs, staging vicious assaults and suicide missions against U.S. forces. For all Killian knew, one of the detainees who was going to be released because of today's grossly irresponsible ruling might eventually set the IED or fire the bullet that would kill his son. And if that was the risk this Court wanted to take, well, then they would darn well have to sit back and listen to Killian berate them from the bench for however long he deemed appropriate. Military families across this nation would certainly understand his resolve. They would appreciate it.

Sarah Kolmann emerged from her chambers, stopping suddenly before Killian. Her smile wasn't forced, but it wasn't wide either. Her skin was pallid and ashen, and she seemed smaller than usual.

"What are you doing here?"

"Thought I'd check in. Grab a moment together on our walk over to the Court."

Sarah touched his shoulder kindly and walked on. Killian carefully matched his pace to hers.

"How's he doing, Sarah?"

"Not well. I've never seen him like this. Did you know we moved him into palliative last night?"

"Yes, I got your email. Gloria and I are very sorry to hear it."

"It's easier to care for him there, but it's not good for him mentally. It makes him want to give up. Can you blame him, really? And that look on his face when he rolled into the room." Sarah shook her head. "Knowing he's going to die there, that it was a place he'd never leave. He might be sleeping most of the time, and look like a skeleton, but he hasn't lost his mind, Killian, and that's just what makes it—"

Sarah stopped speaking, quickened her pace and clasped her small hands together before her. "I don't want to talk about this anymore."

"You don't have to."

"I don't know what I'm going to do next week, when our term's done and I don't have this place to distract me."

"I'll come visit. Gloria and I aren't going anywhere for a while."

"If it wasn't for Cathy and Mark, who are both being heroic, I don't know what I would do."

They reached the door of the Conference Room, but paused before entering.

"I said I didn't want to talk about it anymore."

"No, no."

"So stop making me!"

"My apologies." Killian frowned at the red carpet fixed to the marble floor. It was near impossible to imagine Jonathan—that lively, robust, playful man—on the verge of death.

Killian followed Sarah into the Conference Room, and then through another doorway that led them into the Robing Room, a small, oak-paneled chamber with a row of nine adjacent closets and no windows. There was a brass plate on each locker, engraved with a different justice's name in an antique font. The other seven justices were already there. Several had slipped on their plain black robes and now stood around the star emblazoned in the maroon carpet. Killian and Sarah greeted them quietly. Justice Kolmann opened her locker and removed her pressed robe. It was hard to be certain if she was in real emotional trouble, but he didn't think so. Sarah's expression was steady and sure as she fluffed her lengthy jabot, zipped up her robe. Yes, she was okay. She had that stalwart ability to bracket her personal problems and remain fierce at work. Neither the press nor the spectators in the Court Chamber would detect anything amiss.

The others chatted, but Killian didn't feel like joining their conversation. Feeling somber now, as he slipped on his robe, Killian thought of Jerusalem's destroyed Temple, King Solomon's proud work, with its chambers inside chambers, and the Holy of Holies at its core, accessible only to the highest priest once a year, on the day of atonement, under strenuous circumstances. The Bible described bowls of blood—goat's and bull's—to be sprinkled eight times in eight directions, the scattering of glowing coals and incense, all that Old Testament savagery. Sometimes, when Killian was plagued with a heavy mood, the Robing Room reminded him of that inner Holy of Holies, and made him feel like an ancient Judaic priest.

"So, Rodney,"—Justice Katsakis was speaking—"are you going to read your concurrence from the bench?"

Everyone turned to hear Rodney's answer. Crazy or not, Justice Sykes's concurrence in *Al-Tounsi* was the most significant work of his career, and would certainly remain so well after his retirement. But Rodney, dressed in his robe, standing quietly on the carpet, just shook his head *no*.

"Why not? If I'd written something that bold, I'd sing it out, loud and clear."

"The idea speaks best for itself on the printed page." Rodney spoke curtly, which immediately stopped Talos's interrogation.

Bernhard Davidson broke the awkward silence. "Come on, hands." He was whispering to his fingers, while sitting in the Oxford chair, the room's only piece of furniture. That chair had been brought into the small room because Davidson was too old to stand for too long. Bernhard struggled to steady his shaking hands and zip up his robe. "Comply, comply . . ."

"Do you need any help?" asked Justice Arroyo, who was standing beside him.

"Yes, please." Bernhard reclined with a defeated sigh, and let Manny zip up the robe for him. "My fingers today are just not my own." Bernhard's voice cracked and rose, and he shook his head in disappointment. He glanced at the others. "I'm not even sure these legs of mine are willing to get me into Court!"

"We'll help you if you need it."

Joanna's offer made Killian hang his head. Elyse was the one who had always taken responsibility for aiding Bernhard whenever they were all together as a group. Joanna Bryce and Manny Arroyo seemed poor substitutes. It was good that Justice Van Cleve's unnecessarily political, legislative, and liberal vote was gone, but how he missed the presence of that fine woman. Maybe it was Jonathan's impending death, or Sarah's mood, but now he felt humbled and diminished by the still-fresh shock of Elyse's sudden passing.

"In the spirit of *Al-Tounsi*," continued Davidson, "my legs are my captors and I'm their enemy combatant. My body is a Subic Bay all its own, and I find myself at this advanced age unable to issue a writ of habeas corpus to get these damn legs to release me."

Several justices laughed at Davidson's bad joke. He pulled himself out of his chair, and grabbed his resting cane. "Well, look at that. I'm not dead yet!"

"Time." Charles Eberly tapped his watch.

The justices gathered themselves on the carpet's laurel emblem, Davidson refusing help from Joanna or Manny, and they shook hands with each other, one by one. After their 36 handshakes, the nine justices exited from the Robing Room through the long crimson curtains, entering the back of the Court Chamber.

"Oyez! Oyez! Oyez!" The Court Marshal cried, as the justices ascended the mahogany bench before the packed room. Many of these guests had waited outside on First Street since early that morning. It was always a challenge to get seats to the Court in the last week of June, at the end of the term, when the big cases were announced. This was when justices would read portions of their opinions or dissents from the bench for added emphasis. *Al-Tounsi v. Shaw* was such an important case that some people had camped out overnight for seats.

Eberly began proceedings, and the first of the day's three cases was announced. Samuel Sykes was working in the press section, and Killian absorbed whatever information about him that he could garner from his peripheral vision. Young Sykes took notes, whispered something to Lyle Dennison, and scribbled in his little book.

Every morning for days now Killian's heart palpitated as he picked up *The Washington Post* from the 7-Eleven near his house and scoured its pages for any articles under Samuel Sykes's by-line, any mention of his name. So far, there was nothing. But it wasn't even guaranteed that Samuel would pen his scandalous story for the *Post*, since he could probably get paid far more for a full exposé as a freelancer for *Washingtonian* or *Vanity Fair*. Lord knows *Vanity Fair* had proven itself willing to dive into Supreme Court gossip. With its liberal leanings, that magazine would no doubt be thrilled to publish a vicious article catching the dreaded Justice Quinn with his pants down, and spinning a couple thousand words on the hypocrisy of his rulings. Every day since his conversation with Katherine, Killian had been tempted to call or email her, asking if she had spoken to Samuel yet and, if so, what she had told him. But Katherine would tell him what she wanted and when. The only respectable thing to do was suffer and wait.

The scribbling and murmuring increased in the Court Chamber as Justice Rosen announced the Court's ruling in *Al-Tounsi v. Shaw*, and then read, in a subdued voice, a small fragment of his plurality opinion. As Gideon spoke, Killian extracted his dissent from his folder. Gideon read as if he was embarrassed by his own work. *I would be, too*, thought Killian, but certainly not for the same reason.

When Justice Rosen finished, Killian tapped his pages on the bench, announced his dissent, and began to read. He spoke slowly at first, and lowered the register of his voice—Gloria had once told him that a deep voice added gravitas to what you are saying. He read steadily, with determination and intensity, without caring if anybody was paying attention, and as he did so, he swelled with anger and passion. "Today's ruling is a travesty for the nation." His veins pulsed, and his cheeks were hot. "I am one hundred percent certain that this Court and the American people will eventually rue this day, and lament the folly of our reckless decision."

When Killian's clerks returned from lunch they told him that Justice Sykes's chambers was already being flooded with calls, that all the newspapers and networks were talking about his astonishing concurrence in *Al-Tounsi*, and only skimming the results of the ruling itself. That was not surprising. But it was hard to imagine how staid old Rodney Sykes was handling that onslaught. He might be cracking, all alone in his office. Killian marched down the hall toward Rodney's chambers, his second impromptu visit to Sykes in a month.

Rodney's wild-eyed and overwhelmed secretaries tried to bar Killian from even announcing his presence—*Justice Sykes doesn't want to see or speak with anyone this morning*, they said—but then they came to their senses. A fellow justice stopping by wasn't the same as other people. A colleague's visit should at least be reported, and then Rodney could decide for himself if he wanted a visitor. Rodney told them he was delighted to see Killian. Please would they mind sending him in right away?

In chambers, Justice Sykes was leaning tranquilly against his desk, holding a baby. Killian, blinking hard, must have looked astonished, because Rodney laughed gleefully and bounced the baby in his arms.

"Well, that is not something I expected to see."

"Come in, Justice Quinn!" Rodney was beaming. "Come meet my grandson!"

One of those portable cribs, like the one Killian's daughter sometimes brought to his house for dinner, had been erected in the middle of Rodney's Italian rug, and there were bright-colored stacking toys strewn across the floor, a couple of fuzzy blankets, and a plush green rabbit with big round eyes and buck teeth that looked like it was on drugs. A whitish stain of baby vomit streaked across Rodney's lapel.

"This is Reuben. Named in honor of Rebecca."

Killian stuck out his pinkie and let the boy's tiny hand clasp his five fingers around it. "Well, isn't he a beauty."

"Daycare emergency. So I offered."

"Today?"

"Why not? I don't have any more writing to do. It's not like I'm going to invite the press in here to interview me."

Baby Reuben released a high-pitched wail of indeterminate meaning and smiled at Killian. Well, maybe it was a smile. It might be gas.

Rodney dandled his grandson: Arroyo's kid. "Amazing." Killian shook his head. "None of my kids'll let me come within ten feet of their spawn until they hit the age of two, let alone babysit. I think they've consulted each other, decided the policy as a group. I don't know what the heck they think I'm going to do—crush 'em, or step on 'em, or mistake them for the pot roast and stick them in the oven."

"Oh, it's hardly better for me." Rodney's whole body awkwardly nodded along with the cooing child. "I annoy my daughter to no end. You should see her face when she drops Reuben off, rolling her eyes at my every word, and obviously she can't wait to get away. Her instructions are endless. The overparenting of this generation. I can never do anything right. Apparently I do not administer a bottle correctly, or a nap. And it seems that one needs a higher degree from a prestigious university in order to change a diaper. My dear daughter treats me as if I were a blubbering idiot, all of which I tolerate with a shocking degree of happiness and joy, because, well, one, she's speaking to me—"

"Amen," laughed Killian.

"—and two, I've been given the extraordinary opportunity of seeing this little man, this boy, this gem, yet again." Rodney kissed the kid's forehead.

"Cassandra must trust you a little. The ones that don't, don't leave their kids."

"I think she does, yes." Rodney's pride was evident. "I really do."

They took seats on the couch, and passed the baby back and forth, as they talked about their kids and grandkids. It wasn't until the end of the conversation, after the baby had fallen asleep in Rodney's arms, and Killian sensed it was time to go, did he think of addressing *Al-Tounsi*. Obviously, Rodney was unfazed by all the hubbub going on outside his private chambers. He had taken the right approach to it, to batten down the hatches, to play with his grandson, and wait for the storm to pass.

"Why did you do it, Rodney?" Killian asked him, suddenly.

Justice Sykes looked up from his sleeping grandson. "Do what?"

"Write such an inflammatory concurrence. It's so radically different from anything you've written before, and such a risk on so many levels. It goes so far. Frankly, Rodney, it's not like you."

Rodney took a moment to consider his answer. "A confluence of streams, Killian. I can tell you this: as I was writing my opinion, I found myself thinking, time and again, about a cat I had, Rebecca's cat, who died last year. Stone was his name. I was shaken by his death. Well, I was upset for an hour or two, but not much after that, and not since, and the truth is I never liked that damn cat much anyway. I don't think I treated him very well. I never petted him. I forgot to feed him sometimes after Rebecca's death, and certainly didn't clean up after him properly. But I was with Stone when he died. As he stopped breathing I thought, *I did not want you. I did not like you. But you were my responsibility, and I failed you.* You see, I did not *have* to like that cat. He was bequeathed to me by the circumstance of my wife's death. He had no one but me; therefore, I had no choice but to care for him. And if I refused to do so, as I did too often, I still could not deny the fact of that refusal. I was aware that his memory would someday haunt me. And he has haunted me. I thought about Stone an absurd amount this term, and eventually I decided: if the well-being of any pet or person is again my responsibility, whether I like it or not, whether I want that burden or not, I will not let him down. I won't do it. I made a decision to never make the same mistake. And as much as I hoped to keep that resolution quiet, to limit it to my private life, I found that I had no choice but to consider it carefully when I read Majid Al-Tounsi's petition. I thought of that lost and unseen man sitting in his cell in Subic Bay, and I had no choice." Rodney smiled. "Crazy, yes?"

Killian shrugged. "No crazier than anything else."

"Well, I am not entirely sure if I'm ready for the consequences of what I've unleashed."

"Nah. You are."

Killian returned to his chambers. In the larger room, one of his clerks was fixed to the news reports on TV—all about *Al-Tounsi—*

but two other clerks were watching snippets from a recent Democratic presidential debate on a laptop. He hovered behind them, listening to the speeches given by the last two candidates left in the race. One was a second-term senator from a northern state, and also the former First Lady of the United States. The other candidate, a freshman senator from another northern state, was a skinny black man. Either way, the country would have itself a *first* with this nomination, and Heaven knows Americans loved their *firsts*. These two dueling northern senators of limited electoral experience debated their marginally contrary approaches to how they would revitalize payments for health care services, all the while bickering and interrupting each other.

"They're saying the exact same thing!" cried Killian.

"Uh-huh," said a like-minded clerk, "and all of it's bunk."

Blasted Democrats: may they wear each other out. Their debate didn't really matter anyway, as the skinny black senator had already won the party's nomination with all his silver-tongued rhetoric. *There is no black America, there is no white America, there is only the United States of America.* He had a real talent for slicing the emotional jugular, that one, like Williams Jennings Bryan reincarnated, except unlike Bryan, this guy was going to win the presidency. The election cycle of 2008 wanted a smooth-talking northern Democrat to steal the whole shebang: no doubt about it. The prospect of a bona fide liberal, Democratic presidency, launched in a mere six months, made Killian's shoulders sag.

He lingered before the screen. It seemed inevitable now that all his recent good fortune and happiness would come crashing down. He could hold Samuel Sykes at bay for only so long, or if not him, another inquisitive reporter, and then Killian would be forced to take the position he had advocated in Katherine's office all those months ago. He would have to forgo his *Miranda* rights, refuse to weasel out of wrongdoing and exalt in his own guilt. His career would take a big hit. And soon after that Bernhard Davidson would retire, and then Kolmann and Katsakis, and with this new President in office appointing justices of a liberal persuasion to the bench, Quinn's precious status as the go-to majority justice of the United States Supreme Court was sure to be short-lived. Yes, this present term was his peak, and in particular the *Wallace* decision, announced tomorrow. Tomorrow was the day Killian Quinn's power would crest, and thus would begin his slow, inevitable descent. He closed his eyes.

"Ah, hell," he told his clerks. "Wake me when it's over."

THE
CONCURRING
OPINION
OF JUSTICE
RODNEY SYKES

SUPREME COURT OF THE UNITED STATES

No. 07-1172

MAJID AL-TOUNSI, ET AL., PETITIONERS V. MARK LEWIS SHAW, PRESIDENT OF THE UNITED STATES

ON WRITS OF CERTIORARI TO
THE UNITED STATES COURT OF APPEALS
FOR THE DISTRICT OF COLUMBIA CIRCUIT

[June 25, 2008]

JUSTICE SYKES, concurring in part.

I do not join the plurality's full opinion today, except for majority sections V (A, B and C) and VI (A and B), holding that the mandated procedures of the Detainee Treatment Act (DTA) and Military Commissions Act (MCA) do not meet the threshold for an adequate habeas substitute, and remanding the case to the United States Court of Appeals for the District of Columbia Circuit as instructed. Nei-

ther do I join JUSTICE QUINN's full dissent, except
for majority sections II (A and B). I concur with the
plurality's holding that petitioners are granted the
privilege of habeas corpus, although I do so on separate grounds.

In what is now a prelude to this case, we held
in *Bayat v. Shaw*, 542 U.S. 481 (2004), that statutory habeas jurisdiction extends to foreign nationals detained by the United States in Subic Bay
for the purpose of "determining the validity of the
executive's indefinite imprisonment," *id.*, at 491.
Bayat turned on questions of statutory jurisdiction
that have since been rendered moot by subsequent
legislation, see Military Commissions Act of 2006
(MCA), 28 U.S.C.A § 2241(e) (Supp. 2007), and thus
do not apply. Therefore JUSTICE QUINN is correct in highlighting the dramatic scope and novelty
of today's holding. See *post*, at 1. Here, for the first
time in our history, constitutional habeas jurisdiction is granted to aliens imprisoned by the military
in regions outside national sovereignty. Nothing in
the Constitution, founding-era precedents, or subsequent common law indicates that an alien prisoner
held abroad under any comparable standard would
have received the writ. *Id.*, at 17. Thus, without the
introduction of a novel doctrine or standard, court
intervention is outrageous and well beyond our
jurisdiction.

I

I have joined an odd pairing of two majority
opinions, sections V (A, B, and C) and VI (A and
B) of JUSTICE ROSEN's, and section II (A and B)
of JUSTICE QUINN's, which taken together serve
as a necessary prelude to my concurrence, holding

for petitioners. The Court, with JUSTICE QUINN, finds no conflict between the MCA and the Suspension Clause. *Ante*, at 7. Aliens abroad do not hold rights under the Constitution, and therefore the MCA does not run afoul of separation of powers principles. The relevant statute, MCA § 7, 28 U.S.C.A. § 2241(e) (Supp. 2007), remains intact: Congress may lawfully prohibit habeas jurisdiction for the detainees in Subic Bay.

In addition, the Court, with JUSTICE QUINN, holds that all "functional" tests for an extraterritorial reach of the writ, which JUSTICE ROSEN draws from precedents, are incorrect. See *post*, at 34, and *ante*, at 17. De jure sovereignty remains the only relevant factor in determining a purely jurisdictional question. I do not need to repeat JUSTICE QUINN's lengthy, careful analysis of the Insular Cases, *Reid v. Covert*, 351 U.S. 487 (1956) and our holding precedent, *Johnson v. Eisentrager,* 339 U.S. 763 (1950), except to emphasize how this string of cases, and *Eisentrager* in particular, underscores the bright-line test for a jurisdictional issue: sovereignty of an applicable territory. JUSTICE ROSEN claims sovereignty is "an easily misused and unnecessarily vague word," *ante*, at 26, quoting 2 Avigdor's Condensed Foreign Relations Law of the United States, Vol. 3, § 869, p. 54 (1992). It is a definition that intends to destabilize the term, positing an open-ended and highly partisan notion of sovereignty, strategically selected from a misleading document, and allowing the introduction of functional tests derived from precedent, *ante*, at 29. But by no means is sovereignty that mysterious or hard to grasp. Sovereignty is "the exercise of dominion or power," see *Webster's New International Dictionary*

2406 (2nd Ed. 1934) ("sovereignty", definition 3). If sovereignty cannot be understood in the dictionary's plain language, *supra*, we have problems far more tangled than those arising in Subic Bay, and our docket will soon be opened to countless unresolvable and unnecessary questions. We should know from our past experience with problematic terms, such as *obscenity, Roth v. United States*, 354 U.S. 476 (1957); *Jacobellis v. Ohio,* 378 U.S. 184 (1964), *inter alia*, that we should think twice before disturbing our already stable definitions.

We need not debate the nuances of de facto sovereignty here. Both opinions and dissents agree that Subic Bay is not formally part of the sovereign United States; it remains under the ownership of the Philippines. De jure sovereignty is not an active question, and we should not make it so. It is worth re-emphasizing that our precedent *Eisentrager* did not grant habeas to foreign soldiers detained in Landsburg Prison for the express reason that the prison lay outside de jure sovereignty of the United States. "At no relevant time were [they] within any territory over which the United States is sovereign, and the scenes of their offense, their capture, their trial and their punishment were all beyond the territorial jurisdiction of any court of the United States." 339 U.S. at 778. The rule here could not be more clear or definitive. No applicable "functional" tests can *ever* apply constitutional rights to extraterritorial foreign nationals, because formal sovereignty excludes them by definition. Sovereignty means precisely what it says. So must *Eisentrager*'s holding.

II

Constitutional habeas jurisdiction is strictly disallowed for petitioners by the MCA, *supra*. Any functional considerations of the writ, or any practical applications, do not overcome a jurisdictional prohibition. The plurality's specious opinion to grant is therefore a covert subversion of established law, although it is bold indeed to witness how that blatant action is denied. The law, here, is not as malleable as clay; one cannot mold it to this side or that with a little deft massage. It remains as solid as a brick. That rigidity, however, presents us with a serious conundrum: the law is also wrong.

There are exceedingly rare cases when the overt subversion of established law is warranted. Such cases arise only under the most extreme circumstances, similar in physics to when conditions of relativity render Newtonian laws moot. It should go without saying that when a sworn justice willfully subverts the law, it is a grave and serious matter. Any decision to do so must be interrogated with strictest scrutiny and frank skepticism. The plurality, in contrast, has hidden their radical subversion within the common law itself, by sneaking "functional tests" and "practical considerations" into cases, *supra*, notwithstanding our precedents to the contrary. This is dangerous reasoning, and does nothing to establish guidelines for subsequent cases, as to when and where an overt subversion of established law might be warranted. We are left thinking, with JUSTICE QUINN, that the plurality's holding is based solely on the preferences and whims of unelected federal justices. *Post*, at 17.

The conditions that justify a subversion of established law must be extreme, and rely in part on gut feelings—a discomfort or queasiness that is perhaps impossible to express with pinpoint accuracy. Nonetheless, those conditions must be quantified. They can be done so as a function of two independent variables: first, the acute vulnerability of petitioners (or respondents, in some cases); and second, the exclusivity of the judge's ability to respond to that vulnerability. With these variables in mind, a good faith doctrine of subversion can indeed be established: when petitioners or respondents cross the tipping point into a perpetual state of acute vulnerability—occurring when (a) they are rendered subject in entirety to laws or holdings that severely restrict life or liberty, *and* (b) when *every* available state or federal court has denied jurisdiction, and therefore cannot apply the appropriate level of judicial review to those laws or holdings—*and, in addition*, when the judge in question is singled out by his or her exclusive ability, *both as a representative of the law and as an individual*, to respond to that severe restriction, then the judge *must* hear the plea of the vulnerable party, and subvert established law, in the slightest manner possible, to alleviate the conditions of the severe restriction. In short, the human response ability of adjudicators is a necessary precondition to the law's validity. Without the essential ingredient of human responsiveness, i.e., the naked openness of a judge willing to take personal responsibility for his or her holding, the law that he or she adjudicates has no legitimacy.

A doctrine of subversion is as radical as it sounds, and therefore it must only be applied under the most extreme circumstances, when the rule of law has failed to deliver its promise of justice. It should go without saying that any past, present or future access to due process would be enough to prevent a petitioner, or respondent, from slipping into a state of acute vulnerability. If there is ever any reasonable and honest means of avoiding the doctrine, it *must* be avoided. Misused, the doctrine of subversion could be one of the greatest threats to the rule of law. There can be no exceptions to the exception. Therefore, we must strictly examine the facts of *Al-Tounsi* to determine if this case falls within that doctrine's rigorous confines.

A

There are two parts to our present examination. First, we must establish with strict scrutiny whether or not petitioners remain in a perpetual state of acute vulnerability.

Regardless of any crimes that they may or may not have committed, petitioners have been held by the U.S. military in Subic Bay without charge for six years, and will continue to be held without foreseeable end, and without any meaningful recourse to challenge their detentions. The government argues that the DTA-MCA mandated CSRT procedures offer a meaningful recourse, but the Court's plurality opinion, which I have joined for majority sections V (A, B, and C), *ante*, at 42–64, offers a lengthy and convincing analysis of how those procedures are deficient. Although said procedures are not legally required to act as an adequate substitute for habeas, their deficiencies are nonetheless astonishing and severe. They offer no reasonable mechanism for any inappropriately held detainee to challenge his detention, let alone earn his release, *ante*, at 45, 47, 48–50, 53, 55. Multiple *amici* agree. See Brief for Former Federal Judges *as Amici Curiæ*; Brief for Retired Military Officers *as Amici Curiæ*; Brief for American Bar Association *as Amici Curiæ*; Brief for

American Civil Liberties and Public Justice *as Amici
Curiæ*; Brief for United Nations High Commissioner
for Human Rights *as Amici Curiæ*; Brief for Professors of Constitutional Law and Federal Jurisdiction
as Amici Curiæ, inter alia. As petitioners are barred
by statute from every state and federal court, and
thus do not have *any* habeas jurisdiction, they continue to be served only by the grossly inadequate
DTA-MCA mandated procedures. They have, under
closest examination, entered into a perpetual state
of acute vulnerability: trapped and confined for an
indeterminate period without charges laid against
them.

This did not have to be so. Had the detainees been
treated as prisoners of war under the Geneva Conventions, or had they been served by court-martials,
conducted under the strict guidelines of the Uniform
Code of Military Justice, we would have had ample
doubts about their having entered into a perpetual
state of acute vulnerability. Had Congress or the
executive established by statute or fiat adequate
military commissions with flexible recourse, again
the petitioners' perpetual state of acute vulnerability would be denied. See *ante*, at 57–59. Had they
wished, the political branches could have arrived at
any number of reasonable alternatives that would
have avoided the creation of a legal black hole. It
would have been better had they done so.

B

Thus we come to the second part of our present
examination. To invoke the doctrine of subversion,
we must establish whether or not the judge or judges
hearing the petitioner's plea have been *singled out,
as representative(s) of the law and as individual(s),*

to respond to the severe restriction. This determination depends in large part on the exhaustion of appeals for habeas questions. The case has reached this Court of Appeals after the establishment of the MCA, which has prohibited all levels of federal courts from hearing the detainees' pleas, except for the DTA review process in the Court of Appeals, see DTA § 1005(e). That process merely allows that particular court to determine

"(i) whether the status determinations of the [CSRT] . . . were consistent with the standards and procedures specified by the Secretary of Defense . . . and (ii) to the extent the Constitution and laws of the United States are applicable, whether the use of such standards and procedures to make the determination is consistent with the Constitution and laws of the United States." § 1005(e)(2)(c), 199 stat. 2742.

As the Court of Appeal is prohibited from addressing any other questions pertaining to petitioners' detentions, *ante* 47, the DTA review process cannot be considered an alternative to this Court's consideration of habeas jurisdiction. Thus today's case is the final foreseeable opportunity for petitioners to access a review procedure pertaining to their detentions. We are the court of last resort, and are therefore singled out, as representatives of the law, for our ability to address the legal question.

It is obvious that if petitioners were U.S. citizens or foreign nationals held within our territorial sovereignty, we would have an array of legal arguments at our disposal, including infringement of the fundamental right to habeas or substitute, as protected by the Due Process Clause of the Fourteenth Amend-

ment. We might legally invalidate MCA § 7, 28
U.S.C.A § 2241(e) (Supp. 2007), and thus allow the
Court of Appeals to undertake meaningful review.
But as petitioners have no recourse whatsoever to
fundamental rights under the Constitution, our
hands are tied. We have no legal doctrine to support
us, no rule of law underpinning a holding to grant
habeas jurisdiction. We have been strictly prohibited from acting in our capacity as representatives
of the law. Thus, in addition to our capacity as such
representatives, we have been isolated as the only
individuals left to hear the petitioners' pleas. Our
situation fulfills the second criterion for subverting
established law: the judge(s) on this Court have been
singled out both as *representatives of the law* and as
individuals by our exclusive ability to respond to the
perpetual, acute vulnerability of petitioners. If we
do not respond, here and now, no one will.

So it is both as a Justice of the United States
Supreme Court and as an individual citizen that I,
Rodney Sykes, observe the severe and unwarranted
restrictions laid upon petitioners, and say: *this is not
just*. As representatives of the law, we can claim that
our duties and the limitations of our power prevent
us from acting on several grounds. Two reasonable
arguments with such claims are forwarded by dissents. See *post*. However, those legal restrictions
cannot prevent us, as conscious, humane citizens,
from understanding that the responsibility for petitioners' acute vulnerability nonetheless remains
with *us*, the *individuals* chosen by law to hear their
plea.

C

JUSTICE QUINN argues that granting writs of habeas corpus to the petitioners is not only illegal, but also an onerous burden on our nation's liberty, by severely endangering us in a time of war, and exposing classified information to public scrutiny. See *post*, at 25. These are legitimate concerns that must be weighed seriously when determining whether or not to act as individuals under the doctrine of subversion. Nonetheless, in majority sections which I have joined, the Court outlines the manifold protections and limitations that the Court of Appeals and the executive must institute to prevent any unnecessary or damaging exposure of sensitive information. No risk need ensue from hearing petitioners' habeas appeals in federal court, and we can safely determine that JUSTICE QUINN's security concerns are unfounded. JUSTICE QUINN has also argued that unelected judges are not qualified to second-guess clear determinations made by political branches. See *post*, at 21. Although we are indeed much less qualified, neither Congress nor the executive has properly balanced their solemn responsibility to national security with their equal responsibility to uphold the human (if not constitutional) rights of those in their care, and therefore the responsibility for the petitioners has awkwardly fallen to us, the branch least qualified to balance petitioners' needs with those of national safety. This is an unfortunate and painful fact. But our limited qualifications do not present an overwhelming barrier to our greater responsibility to act under the present circumstance.

III

"Must the citizen ever for a moment, or in the least degree, resign his conscience to the legislator? Why has every man a conscience, then? I think that we should be men first, and subjects afterward. It is not desirable to cultivate a respect for the law, so much as for the right . . . If injustice . . . is of such a nature that it requires you to be the agent of injustice to another, then, I say, break the law. Let your life be a counter friction to stop the machine. What I have to do is to see, at any rate, that I do not lend myself to the wrong which I condemn."

—Henry David Thoreau,
Civil Disobedience, 1849

There have been rare instances in U.S. history when the subversion of established law has been deemed appropriate and even celebrated by the public at large, not least of which was the revolution from England that established our nation in 1776. The series of non-violent Civil Rights protests led by Dr. Martin Luther King, originating in Montgomery, Alabama, in 1955, and then spreading throughout the southern United States in subsequent years, was another such instance. By and large, the American people have collectively decided that Dr. King's subversion of established law was warranted, given the grossly unjust circumstances afflicting African-Americans at that time, and have gone so far as to create a national holiday in honor of Dr. King and his work. The principled, morally justified subversion of law is an American tradition at least as old as our nation itself, and was articulated most eloquently by Henry David Thoreau in the above quotation, which served as a source of inspiration for Dr. King.

Although today's action is far less monumental than the preceding examples, it is executed in the same spirit. After strictly examining the facts of *Al-Tounsi v. Shaw,* and my own position within that case, I have determined that our predicament falls within the exceedingly rare and rigorous confines required to invoke the doctrine of subversion. Therefore I invoke it, and grant habeas jurisdiction to petitioners, concurring with the plurality.

Our decision today is deeply unfortunate. There is nothing more taboo for a sworn justice than to willfully subvert established law. Unfortunately, I see no other choice. The law in this case is clear and constitutionally valid, but opposed to justice. I have too much respect for the integrity of our legal process and for the larger probity of our legal code to massage or manipulate any single law to accommodate my desires, and so I will not do it, even when the gravest need presents itself, as it does here. If I do not invoke the doctrine of subversion, I am entirely unable to reconcile my sworn, twin obligations to "faithfully and impartially discharge and perform all the duties incumbent upon me as a Justice under the Constitution and laws of the United States" *and* to "administer justice *without respect to persons.*" See 28 U.S.C. § 453, oath of federal justices and judges, italics mine. I took that oath with pride and commitment, and I continue to uphold it today. The other branches of government have not fulfilled their sworn responsibilities. That does not mean I must ignore mine.

ACKNOWLEDGMENTS

I'm grateful for the help of many people as I researched and wrote this book: Richard Abel, Justice Rosalie Abella, Chris Abraham, Alan Ackerman, Jill Bernstein, Brianna Caryll, Shantona Chaudhury, Brian Current, Jonathan Farber, Andrew Ferguson, Dan Garodnick, Kim Hawkins, Shayana Kadidal, Pasha Malla, Les Nicholson, Craig Offman, Paul Pape, Ryan Peck, Auran Piatigosky, Joram and Lona Piatigorsky, Sven Poysa, Allen Pusey, Jonathan Rosenstein, Hanna Rosin, Justice Marshall Rothstein, Zoe Segal-Reichlin, Larry Shepley, Simon Stern, Kristen Thomson, Tonje Vetleseter, Martha Magor Webb, Diana Winters, and a large number of other anonymous sources.

I am heavily indebted to a huge number of books and articles, most notably by Jill Abramson, Scott Armstrong, Robert Barnes, Emily Bazelon, Joan Biskupic, Erwin Chemerinsky, Felix S. Cohen, David Cole, Lyle Denniston, Ronald Dworkin, Noah Feldman, Robert A. Ferguson, Karen J. Greenberg, Linda Greenhouse, Stephanie Guitton, Henry Hansmann, Peter Charles Hoffer, Williamjames Hull Hoffer, N. E. H. Hull, Peter Irons, Kenneth Jost, George Kannar, Duncan Kennedy, Reinier Kraakman, Anthony Lewis, Dahlia Lithwick, Adam Liptak, Jonathan Mahler, Desmond Manderson, Jane Mayer, Richard Posner, Roscoe Pound, Jeffery Rosen, Michael J. Sandel, Mohamedou

Ould Slahi, Ronald P. Sokol, Seth Stern, Cass Sunstein, Jill Bolte Taylor, Jeffrey Toobin, Nina Totenberg, Laurence Tribe, Melvin I. Urofsky, Jeremy Waldron, Artemus Ward, David Weiden, Stephen Wermiel, James Boyd White, Bob Woodward, and Andy Worthington. I relied on the briefs, opinions, dissents and transcripts from *Rasul v. Bush* (2004), *Hamdan v. Rumsfeld* (2006), and especially *Boumediene v. Bush* (2008) to fashion my fictional string of "Subic Bay" cases, ending with *Al-Tounsi v. Shaw*. Thank you to all the lawyers, judges, and organizations that worked on those cases.

In addition to the hundreds of opinions by Supreme Court justices, past and present, that I studied, I am particularly thankful for the justices' popular books and autobiographies, particularly those written by Justices Stephen Breyer, Benjamin Cardozo, Sandra Day O'Connor, William Rehnquist, Antonin Scalia, John Paul Stevens, and Clarence Thomas. Two lines in this novel (on pages 58 and 121) are adapted from writings by Justices John Paul Stevens (in *Boumediene v. Bush*) and Antonin Scalia (in *Grutter v. Bollinger*).

I am deeply grateful that the publisher of Ankerwycke, Jon Malysiak, championed this novel, offering tireless support and excellent editorial assistance. Thank you, also, to Elmarie Jara, Jill Nuppenau, and everyone at Ankerwycke.

I could never have written *Al-Tounsi* without the extraordinary help, wisdom and friendship of three people.

David Sandomierski guided my entire legal education. With great generosity, he offered me detailed and clear explanations, extensive reading recommendations, a tour of the Canadian Supreme Court (including introductions to several Canadian Justices), teaching opportunities, and hours of patient conversation. David's profound insight into the history, function, and use of law was essential.

Bethany Gibson offered me multiple careful, astute readings of this novel. Her honesty, curiosity, and discerning judgment were crucial to my writing process from the early partial (and abandoned) drafts to the penultimate version.

Ava Roth was a vital and astute judge of character—quite literally. Through years of conversation, she gave invaluable and subtle insight into the characters, plot, and themes, often as they were taking form. I took Ava's brilliant ideas and recommendations throughout the process. Her help was indispensable; the novel would not exist without her guidance.

I love you Ava, Sivan, Dalia, Reuben. Thank you for your love and support as I ventured down this rabbit hole.